I0841069

A UNIOVERSE™ ANTHOLOGY

STORIES OF THE
RECONVERGENCE

EDITED BY

ANGIE HODAPP
AND JOSHUA VIOLA

A UNIOVERSE ANTHOLOGY
STORIES OF THE RECONVERGENCE

Edited by Angie Hodapp and Joshua Viola
Creative direction by Joshua Viola

Narrative consultation by Andy Baker, Brent Friedman, and Wyeth Ridgway

Developmental edits by Mario Acevedo, Angie Hodapp, and Joshua Viola

Fiction copyedits by Marshall Jones, Bret Smith, and Jeanni Smith

Poetry copyedits by Carina Bissett, Marshall Jones, Bret Smith, and Jeanni Smith

Cover illustrations by Aaron Lovett and Stuart Jennett

Cover layout by Mira Sestan and Joshua Viola

Interior illustrations by Stuart Jennett

Map by Colton Hoerner and Stuart Jennett

Timeline graphic by Colton Hoerner and Stuart Jennett

Art direction by Ken Hall and Joshua Viola

Typesets and formatting by Alec Ferrell

A Random Games/Hex Publishers Book

Published & Distributed by Random Games/Hex Publishers
PO BOX 298 Erie, CO 80516

www.Unioverse.com   www.Random.Games   www.HexPublishers.com

Joshua Viola, Publisher

e-Book ISBN: 979-8-9880827-5-0
Color Paperback ISBN: 979-8-9880827-4-3
B&W Paperback ISBN: 979-8-9862194-0-0
Color Case Laminate Hardcover ISBN: 979-8-9880827-6-7
B&W Case Laminate Hardcover ISBN: 979-8-9880827-7-4
Color Dust Jacket Hardcover ISBN: 979-8-9880827-8-1
B&W Dust Jacket Hardcover ISBN: 979-8-9880827-3-6

First Edition: August 2023

10 9 8 7 6 5 4 3 2 1

Printed in the U.S.A.

TABLE OF CONTENTS

TABLE OF CONTENTS

FOREWORD

Tony Harman

YEARS AGO, I was asked during a panel discussion about my proudest moment in the game industry to date. I'd made dozens of games by that point, so it wasn't an easy question. Like trying to pick your favorite child, you know? Then I flashed back to a moment that's always stuck with me.

My wife, Amy, and I used to shop for our children at Toys "R" Us back in the '90s, and I would always wander to the videogame section. One time, I stumbled onto a scene every parent is familiar with: a child between the age of 8 and 10 pitching a fit at his very angry and embarrassed mother. She was doing all the right things, telling him his behavior wasn't acceptable. The kid just went on kicking and screaming. I tried not to react and turned my back to walk away when I heard, "Mom, I will *die* if you don't buy me *Donkey Kong Country!*"

I couldn't hide my ear-to-ear grin any more than I could help the reactionary fist pump or accidentally saying out loud, "Yeah!"

When you're in the videogame industry, sometimes your best moments are seeing the public reactions to the finished product. Seeing that excitement, the awe, the need to start playing the latest release. I'm thinking about that kid right now because I'm involved with a new game franchise, and this book is a part of it. I think the concept is powerful enough to make you say, "I'll die if I don't get to play this."

Videogames keep you young. I don't believe anyone's too old to game, and the market offers something for everyone. From simulation and sports games to puzzles, shooters, and real-time strategy, there's a game for every interest. I got caught up in the possibilities of gaming when I was in my twenties, boldly going into the headquarters of Nintendo of America in Redmond, Washington, and announcing I was there to stay. I'd come armed with a business degree and fifteen years of experience playing videogames. Nintendo *needed* me, and I was there to patiently explain why.

My strategy worked and Nintendo gave me a shot that changed my life. I buckled down and learned the business of gaming and project development, eventually running Nintendo's development and acquisition department for just shy of a decade. I had some incredible opportunities and even more incredible mentors and partners. I got to develop *Killer Instinct* with Rare. Shigeru Miyamoto—the genius behind *Mario*, *The Legend of Zelda*, and *Star Fox*—entrusted me with his creation, *Donkey Kong*, and gave me his blessing to make *Donkey Kong Country*. Learning from such a maestro led to opportunities to head up independent studios and partner with brilliant designers like David Jones, whose 1991 hit *Lemmings* went on to sell 20 million units. Not long after that, David and I developed the team that created the original *Grand Theft Auto*. Then we co-founded Realtime Worlds and developed *Crackdown* and *All Points Bulletin*, GTA's MMO successor.

It's been a wild, gratifying ride. Game progression and evolution is astonishing. I don't just mean the quality of the graphics and the sophistication of gameplay. Narratives have never been more immersive, and characterization has never been more important. Gaming offers whole alternate universes now, lived, open-ended experiences designed to engage and expand the creativity of the player. I'm so proud to be a part of it by continuing to shepherd the imagination and brilliance of the newest generation of designers who grew up playing the games I helped make possible.

Except they want to make something even *better*.

I recognize something familiar about these people. They've got the same desire I had at their age. They've got ideas and passion, and they're going to do something with them. Pretty much no one today could follow my literal example of walking into a corporate lobby and asking for a job. Most people don't live anywhere near a videogame studio, and let's just say building security has a lot more *presence* these days.

So, getting a break in the gaming industry isn't quite the same now as it was then, but the metaphor of finding your way into the building remains pretty apt. Huge media conglomerates don't lack for capability in terms of technology, but they tend to wall themselves off from the incredible pool of talented storytellers, artists, and programmers who can't get discovered and, consequently, can't get a shot.

That's always bugged me, and it's something I've been trying to address. That's one reason why in 2021, I partnered with Wyeth Ridgway, president of Leviathan Games, to found Random Games. Wyeth and I are both old hands in the industry. Wyeth has over a hundred games to his credit, and we're talking major licenses like *Lord of the Rings*, *South Park*, *Pirates of the Caribbean*, and *The Terminator*. We decided we'd use our combined experience to champion a project that excites me like no other, a game franchise designed to maximize the creative opportunities of artists from many mediums to make a story that never fails to delight our audience.

Having a vision is only part of the formula. You need funding, a great team, and a bit of luck to get a project from inception to completion. But one important lesson that Wyeth and I have learned is that life's too short to deal with drama, so we wanted a team that could work together without the turmoil that kills productivity. This was a special passion project for us, and we pulled in the best talent we could from the decades of experience both of us have in the industry. We also wanted to give emerging writers and artists their big break by creating a fresh concept that will definitely have your inner child screaming, "I will die if I don't play this!"

There's a new Big Bang coming, and from the explosion, we give you the *Unioverse*: a massive, game-first franchise whose story has a team of more than twenty-five world-class authors and writers, some of whom are getting their first opportunity to develop gaming storylines and characters. Random Games selected its team based on pure talent, and their vision encapsulates music, short stories, novels, comics, TV, and film. There are future stars in this Unioverse as well as established pros who've written for impressive entertainment properties like *Star Wars*, *Dune*, *The Walking Dead*, and *Call of Duty*.

Now, many of those titles are multi-media events. The *Unioverse* is a new vision for all the iterations of its storytelling. The basic idea is to build a world-class "community-owned" franchise that allows independent developers to make games for the Unioverse. Royalty free. Interested developers can access all of our code, art, stories, animations, etc.—literally millions of dollars of assets to start their project. Again, royalty free. Independent developers would get laughed at if they walked up to Disney and asked to make a *Star Wars* game. Our vision lets those talented developers use our assets, have fun with them, commercialize them, and help us build a following for themselves along with the *Unioverse*. It's a revolutionary new way to create and play. To date, we have 140,000 registered *Unioverse* users eager to get started.

The *Unioverse* is an immense sandbox, and the anthology you're holding in your hands is just a taste of how expansive and creative that sandbox is.

That's because we have a solid team. Our narrative director is Brent Friedman, writer for *Star Wars: The Clone Wars*, *Halo*, and *Call of Duty*, assisted by writer Andy Baker (*House of the Dead*). Joshua Viola—who worked with Wyeth on numerous games in the past—is on the story team and is our creative director for novelization and comics, along with his co-editor for this anthology, Angie Hodapp (best known for her work at the Nelson Literary Agency, who is responsible for projects like *Bird Box*). Together, Joshua and Angie are developing several narrative *Unioverse* experiences, such as comics, with Hex Publishers, an award-winning publishing house of genre fiction that's been putting out daring, high-concept anthologies for the better part of a decade. Hex's art department has a reputation, too. Their dynamic covers are the result of Aaron Lovett, whose work has been spotlighted in *Spectrum 22* and *24*, was an inspiration for AMC's *Fear the Walking Dead*, and who did conceptual art for the global bestselling game, *Monster Train*. And then there's the music. We've got the soundscapes of Klayton, the multifaceted producer behind Celldweller. His music has appeared in games like *Killer Instinct Season 3*, *Dead Rising 3*, and *Assassin's Creed*.

But let's get back to the stories. The tales collected here are meant to give you a hint of what the *Unioverse* is all about. You're on the verge of entering a galaxy-spanning sci-fi saga.

Centuries ago, an astronaut on humanity's first manned expedition to Mars uncovers an ancient transportation technology that once connected worlds all over the universe by instantly sending one's consciousness across the stars. His boldness and curiosity reactivate this long-dormant network, and planets whose names and cultures were lost to time begin to reconnect—leading to great and often perilous adventures. Some of those adventures are in the pages that follow, written by some of today's best literary talents, such as Linda D. Addison (*Black Panther*, *Predator*), Kevin J. Anderson (*Dune*, *Star Wars*), Stephen Graham Jones (*Earthdivers*, *The Only Good Indians*), Tim Waggoner (*Halloween Kills*, *Resident Evil*), and Dayton Ward (*Planet of the Apes*, *Star Trek*). We've also got gifted new voices, such as Shirley Jackson Award Finalist Sean Eads, Maxwell I. Gold, Jamal Hodge, and Jezzy Wolfe. The result is a fantastic collection of stories you'll want to read again and again as you wait for the first game to drop.

The *Unioverse* is unique because it's built on a terrific foundational premise that lets the story team expand the narrative opportunities organically, creating options and possibilities no one could have planned. As a result, there's a genuine energy in these stories (and poetry) that demonstrates the open-ended adventures in store for readers and gamers alike. We're following in the tradition of classic science fiction exploration and wonder like *2001: A Space Odyssey*, as well as more recent, grittier offerings like *The Expanse*. But we aren't letting one genre define us. The *Unioverse* also explores fantasy, horror, and almost any sub-genre you can think of. Like I said earlier about videogames, the same rings true for the Unioverse—there's something here for everyone.

The various genres also elevate the aesthetic—and this project is a visual feast, equal to the imaginations of the story team. We're talking world concepts unlike anything you've ever seen before, architecture and cityscapes that will start to occupy your dreams. This is all courtesy of the Random Games art team, led by Ken Hall and Stuart Jennett (*Star Citizen*). As you turn the pages that follow, try to keep your jaw from hitting the floor, because Stu's beautiful imagery introducing each tale is guaranteed to astound. Beyond this book, we have the artistic contributions of Tyler Kirkham (DC, Marvel), Aaron Lovett (*Inkbound, Monster Train*), Ben Matsuya (*Jupiter Jet, LOOM*), and AJ Nazzaro (*Hearthstone, Overwatch*) in our forthcoming comic books (written by Joshua and Angie). All of our designs are developed with incredible attention paid to the most minute detail. Our AAA 3D playable characters by Swame Art not only look unique and awesome, but they have powerful backstories as well. Maybe you'll try an adventure as Reyu, the legendary Ja'din warrior of the fabled Origin 5 species that claims genetic sequences from conquered foes to integrate with his own DNA. Or Krishah, an orphaned human raised by thieves to become one of the most feared assassins in the cosmos. Perhaps you'll try Tor Gret, the idealistic heir to his planet's throne who discovers his family's genocidal past and becomes a vigilante officer. Or maybe you'll explore life through the eyes of Vella Janx, a four-armed cybernetic human-oid who sometimes lends a hand (or three) as a bounty hunter, smuggler, and mercenary.

Excited yet? Then I suggest you start reading the stories in this collection. These adventures are just a taste of what the *Unioverse* has to offer.

A NOTE FROM THE EDITORS

WITNESSING THE BIRTH OF ANYTHING is a special feeling. Children, animals, even stars (thanks to infrared telescopes). Being present for the birth of an *idea* is special too. Right now, you're in the front row for the start of an exciting franchise and new paradigm in gaming. You're witnessing the beginning of an open-ended story called the *Unioverse*, a new videogame series with a narrative mythology that spans more than a million years.

The founding lore of the *Unioverse* is both complex and elegantly simple, mysterious enough to prime anyone's imagination for a grand adventure that encompasses all genres. *Coming together* is the core theme of the *Unioverse*, and like all great themes, it carries contradictions—joy and despair, desire and resistance, opportunity and curtailment. The mythology provides texture to the gaming experience as players are invited to set out on their own adventures across countless worlds. The stories in this book do the same. They explore the rich storytelling possibilities of the *Unioverse*, giving you a glimpse into the types of worlds and situations you may encounter across all media our franchise has to offer. It also introduces key figures like Nova Orion and Olen Gray, important members of The Merge government.

There's also a comic book series, written by the two of us and set between various events in this book. The comics delve into the backgrounds of the game's first five heroes—Reyu, Krishah, Tor Gret, Annill, and Vella Janx—as well as their nemesis, Silas Kyruk. When you read these comics, you'll learn that "hero" has a broader meaning in the *Unioverse* than in other franchises.

Yes, you're here for the start of something new and unique, a storyverse that can't be confined to a single genre, work, or medium. The *Unioverse* converges all avenues of storytelling in a way that's truly refreshing.

Welcome to the adventure.

Welcome to the *Unioverse*.

Joshua Viola and Angie Hodapp, Editors

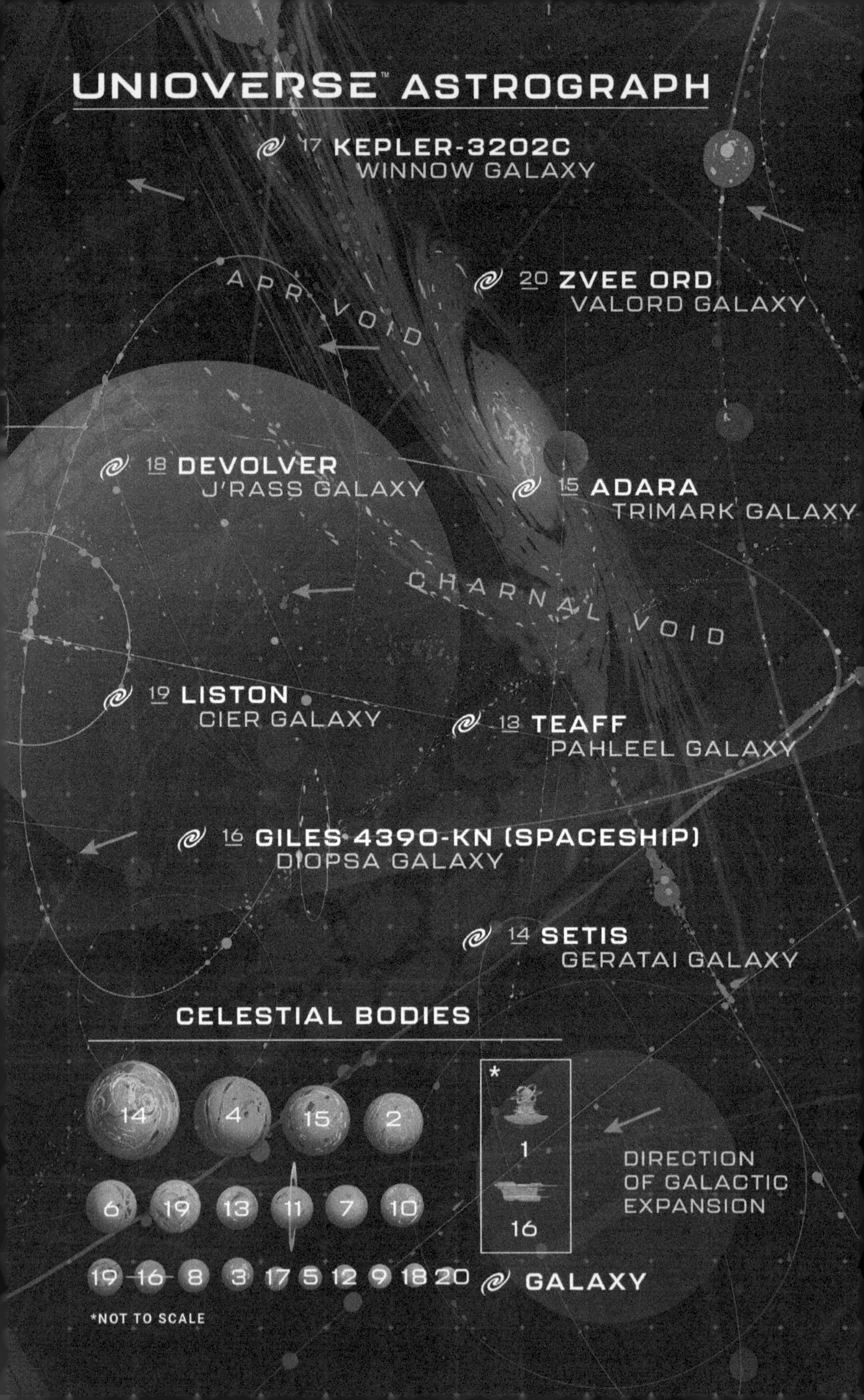
UNIOVERSE™ ASTROGRAPH
17 KEPLER-3202C
WINNOW GALAXY
APR VOID
20 ZVEE ORD
VALORD GALAXY
18 DEVOLVER
J'RASS GALAXY
15 ADARA
TRIMARK GALAXY
CHARNAL VOID
19 LISTON
CIER GALAXY
13 TEAFF
PAHLEEL GALAXY
16 GILES 4390-KN (SPACESHIP)
DIOPSA GALAXY
14 SETIS
GERATAI GALAXY
CELESTIAL BODIES
14
4
15
2
6
19
13
11
7
10
19
16
8
3
17
5
12
9
18
20
*
1
16
DIRECTION OF GALACTIC EXPANSION
GALAXY
*NOT TO SCALE

8 CYGNUS-2H
ONRAGO GALAXY

10 GLYMERIA
TELARHIAL GALAXY

KRIM VOID

6 LLUXIV
XINNIX GALAXY

4 BRIR
BRISH GALAXY

3 KAPEHU
EHL GALAXY

1 HELIOS NEXUS (THE HUB)
NIDIS GALAXY

CHARNAL VOID

2 VANETTA 4
KARHEEL GALAXY

9 MARS
MILKY WAY GALAXY

5 NOVUS-337
BURNELLI GALAXY

7 AMDURAHH
NERTOMAAL GALAXY

11 CYLARUS
ROSARI GALAXY

RHHAL VOID

12 NAIDU
MAHZARON GALAXY

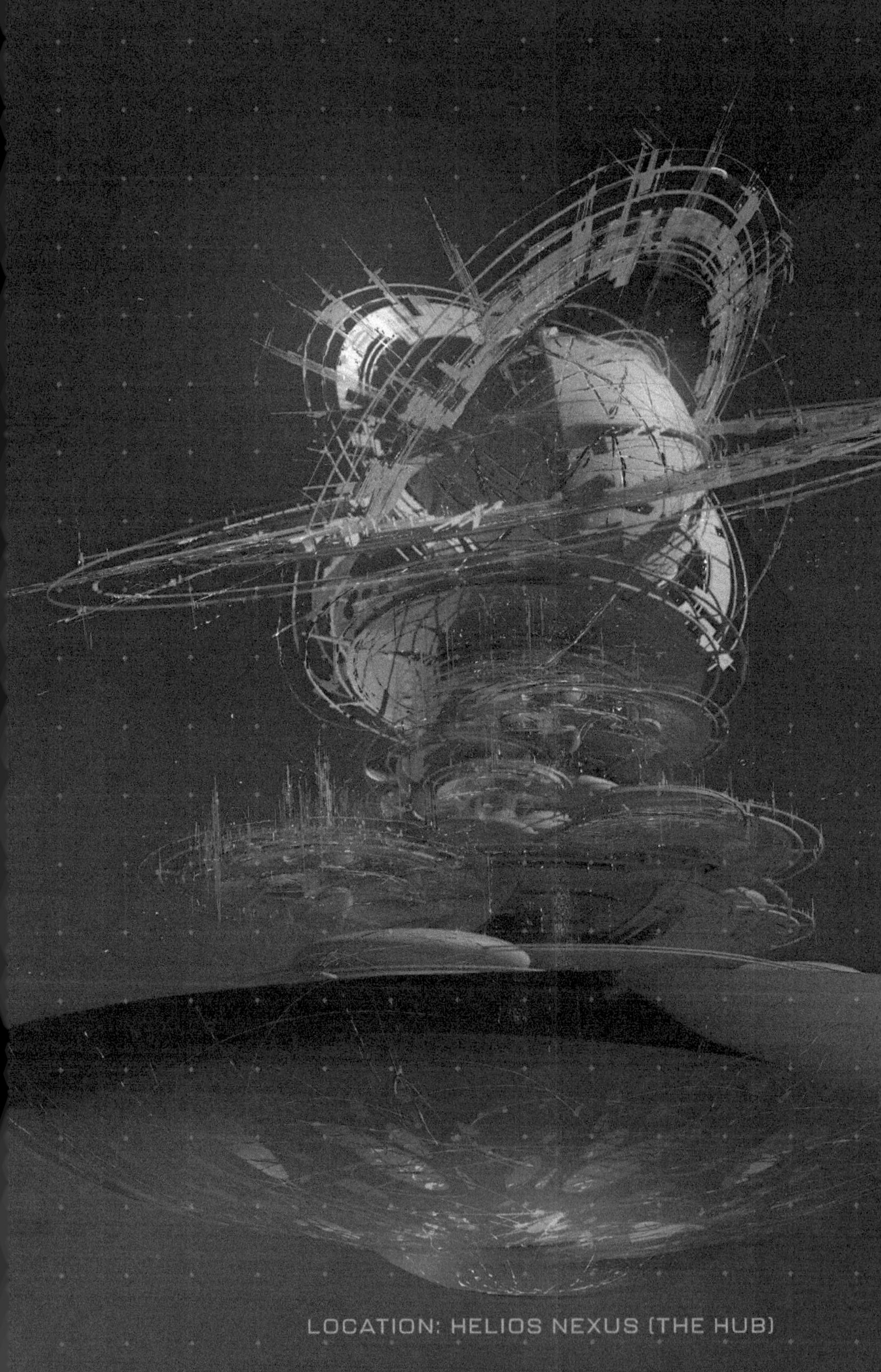
LOCATION: HELIOS NEXUS (THE HUB)

UNIOVERSE™ TIMELINE

Time measured in Earth years from 1,000,000 BC - 2145 AD.
Time measured in Hub helicas from 0 HD to 493 HD
(1 Hub helica = 1.4 Earth years)

1,000,000+ BC - THE CREATORS

The Creators build the Masson Zero (Mass-O) and The Hub to send out Progenitor Ships to locate and connect life throughout the Unioverse.

1,000,000 - 300,000 BC - THE FIRST CYCLE

This period refers to all post-Creator civilizations using the Mass-O to converge at The Hub. In this cycle, five original species (Origin 5) discovered and used the Mass-O for millennia, discovering dozens of new worlds, before suddenly disappearing without a trace.

300,000 BC - THE GREAT FRACTURE

Something cataclysmic happened and the Creator Tech locked Hub access to all Discovery Lander locations discovered in The First Cycle. All the Origin 5 tech and structures built at The Hub were abandoned overnight, as though everyone simply disappeared. All Hub worlds were locked for millennia until humans found and repaired a crashed Progenitor Ship on Mars (see below) and then managed to unlock access to The Hub. Once at The Hub, humans were able to unlock additional locations.

40,000 BC - SOLAR FLARE EVENT

A massive solar flare causes a Progenitor Ship to crash into Mars; A Discovery Lander never gets to Earth.

2044 AD - MISSION TO MARS

First manned mission to Mars.

2089 AD - MARS COLONY

Permanent Mars colony established.

2130 AD - MARS SURVEY

Mars planetary exploration begins.

2142 AD – PROGENITOR SHIP DISCOVERY

Progenitor Ship discovered on Mars; excavation starts.

2145 AD/0 HD – MALCOLM ORION REACTIVATES THE MASS-O

Malcolm Orion uses the Mars transpod and jumps to The Hub, reactivating the Mass-O—now known as the year 0 Helios Discovery (HD).

0 HD – START OF THE SECOND CYCLE

Malcolm Orion discovers Reyu in a transpod from The First Cycle. Reyu is awakened, and he declares Malcolm Orion as the Herald of The Second Cycle.

173 HD – THE MERGE IS FORMED

A governing body on The Nexus (called Helios Mergence aka The Merge), is established. The Merge is a multi-species coalition focused on the integration of new species at The Nexus to resolve disputes and guide the growth of the intergalactic community.

233 HD – OLEN GRAY APPOINTED LEADER OF THE MERGE SECURITY COUNCIL

After witnessing a brutal civil war on his home planet of Calak shortly after the world was accepted into The Merge, Olen Gray is appointed Leader of The Merge's Security Council at 20 helicas old. His focus is to bring stability to new worlds who are accepted into the coalition. He has served for the last 260 helicas.

470 HD – DEGEN VIRUS

The DeGen virus is discovered on Kepler-3202c; lone survivor infects the Mass-O with the virus when jumping to escape.

485 HD – THE RISE OF SILAS KYRUK

Silas Kyruk uses a new technology based on Cylarian hivemind biology to tap into the CZ waves of Reyu, Krishah, Tor Gret, Annill, and Vella Janx. This allows him to manipulate the bodies of those infected with the DeGen virus. He hopes to use the infected as a weapon to shut down the Mass-O.

493 HD – PRESENT DAY

IN TRANSLATION

Carina Bissett

Blessed be The Creators
who seeded the cosmos,
the discovery of hope
in each branching connection
heavy with the harvest,
beacons of becoming.

Fear not the ascension, acolyte,
for you are pure of heart,
form anointed, spirit
tethered to our intentions,
the ways watched, guarded
by the Sacred Three.

Fear not the dragon,
for you exist beyond Time
clenched between iron teeth,
your faith unshaken
by the armored tail wound
around invisible roots.

Fear not the splintering,
for you have been chosen
to don Death's antlered crown,
the frisson of neutron stars
spinning—filaments binding
your life with ours.

Blessed be the Servitors
guarding Discovery,
the path of enlightenment
laid out for those brave enough
to open their eyes, intention bound
to the unification of the Wyrd.

Seek out the winged one
roosting in the aether,
those talons—curved to crush galaxies—
clutching the golden bough,
that prismatic parallel path
leading to the cosmic records.

Seek dark matter flowing
around Orion's gate,
but be wary of the gallows,
the tree mouth gaping wide,
eager to consume centuries,
scions, and sybils alike.

Seek solace in your sacrifice,
the price that must be paid,
your true name swallowed
for greater good and glory,
the key to locked doors
now yours for the taking.

Blessed be the Enlightened One
who dares to reach beyond
the stars to pluck the fruit
bittersweet on the tongue, untied,
language unfurling, unobscured
in The Creators' gift of translation.

EXCERPT FROM LEADER OLEN GRAY'S OPENING REMARKS TO THE MERGE AMBASSADOR ACADEMY GRADUATING CLASS OF 493 HD

WELCOME TO THE ADVENTURE. The Masson Zero offers countless worlds across the galaxy, with something to offer every taste. Ahead of you lies the wonder of meeting new lifeforms and learning their cultures. There will be political intrigues where the stakes always threaten to escalate out of control, but that's where you come in, Ambassadors. You, the universe's revered diplomats.

Let us review how we got here. Millions of helicas ago, a mystery species known only as The Creators designed a transportation system called the Masson Zero or Mass-0, a quantum device that extracts consciousness from the body, shoots it instantaneously through an intergalactic network and downloads it into an organic replica on another world. The Mass-0 is a massive artificial structure (similar to a moon) that is adjacent to a space station called The Hub. The Mass-0 dispatches the Progenitor Ships, galactic nomads designed to identify suitable worlds and seed them with a single Discovery Lander containing transpods that will connect that planet to the Mass-0 network.

No one knows what happened to The Creators, but the Mass-0 continued to work long after their departure, connecting worlds otherwise doomed to permanent isolation. We call this long time period The First Cycle, and it was dominated by five species, the Origin 5, who used the Mass-0 for hundreds of thousands of helicas, exploring each new world identified by the Progenitor Ships.

And then, some 216,000 helicas ago, they too disappeared.

Even now, the fate of the Origin 5 remains a mystery. There is evidence of a cataclysm, a catastrophe so great that the Mass-O shut itself down, denying all access to The Hub. The Hub itself shows signs of panicked abandonment. Contemporary forensic historians and archaeologists call this dark period The Great Fracture, a time of galactic isolation and despair that might have continued to this day-if not for the boldness of Malcolm Orion.

Before we get to Orion's hour of glory, though, we must take a moment to dwell on the horrible consequences of The Great Fracture. Imagine the Mass-O dormant and cold. Meanwhile, across the void, numerous species contemplate the inexplicable loss and the loneliness weighing upon them like a new gravity. The generations that remembered the glory days of The First Cycle gave way to those who knew of it only as an inherited memory-an icy bequeathal! As the centuries and millennia passed, memory became rumor, rumor became legend, and legend became myth. Bitter isolation took hold, and the worlds forgot each other's existence. The Creator Tech left behind on those many planets, otherwise invincible to time, fell into neglect, and in many cases their very locations were marked as places of superstition and taboo.

All was lost.

Until Malcolm Orion turned the tide.

I direct your attention now to the start of The Second Cycle. According to our best reconstruction, a Progenitor Ship discovered Earth around 40,000 BC in old Terran time and was on course to add it to the Mass-O network when a solar flare disrupted its navigation system. The ship crashed on Mars and remained buried there. Meanwhile, on Earth, civilization continued its precarious advancement—so rapid in summary view, so slow to live through. In 2044 AD, humanity made its first manned mission to Mars. Forty-Five human years later, a permanent colony was established and terraforming commenced. By 2130 AD, full planetary exploration had begun.

It took many helicas to uncover the broken husk of the Discovery Lander and explore its interior. At long last, one of the transpods inside could be powered on. It was clearly designed for someone to climb inside—but to what purpose? Discovering that required a person of exceptional bravery and inquisitiveness. But who would dare subject themselves to so many unknowns?

The universe has a way of pairing the right person for the right moment, and so it was with Malcolm Orion and the Martian transpod. Volunteering, he entered the transpod—and it activated. The first piece of Mass-O technology to operate in over 216,000 helicas. The transpod launched Orion's consciousness through the slumbering network, bringing him to Helios Nexus, integrating him into a replica body in a Creator Tech transpod. Orion found himself in an environment rediscovering itself. Lights were coming on everywhere, Servitors were powering up, the mighty strum of the reawakened Mass-O sent its powerful chord across the galaxy, and the Creator Tech on all of those lonesome worlds sparked with new life in an instant.

Reconvergence!

A new era, and with it a new timeline. 2145AD became 0 Helios Discovery. So many civilizations like to restart their calendars around events of great magnitude, and what could be greater than the resumption of the Mass-O? But after so many helicas of isolation, reconvergence brought with it great danger and distrust, paranoia, even outright hostility. From these early and sometimes tragic difficulties came the multi-species coalition government of Helios Mergence, colloquially known as The Merge. To ease more worlds back into reconvergence, The Merge developed its Ambassadors to go forth in the spirit of Malcolm Orion, braving dangers and wild challenges while representing The Merge before new races.

This is what awaits you now. The rewards are great—but so are the risks. Right now, your minds dream of the stories you'll create. Yes, all of you yearn to add yourselves to the ranks of those whose names are known across the universe, whose exploits even now shape The Merge. Who among you wouldn't like to be the next Annill, famed bodyguard on The Hub whose humble demeanor seems so at odds with her military skill and strength, and who will stop at nothing to free her homeworld from the locust-like DeGen?

Or is it the great and mysterious Reyu you seek to emulate? Reyu, whose mind and body were trapped in a transpod during The Great Fracture, and who Malcolm Orion freed? Reyu of the Ja'din, one of the fabled Origin 5 species, whose predatory instincts are only just held at bay by his stoicism and introspection?

Or could it be Vella Janx that occupies your thoughts, that ruthless and amoral cybernetic being whose only code is survival at any cost? Vella Janx the smuggler and assassin, Vella Janx the great escape artist, Vella Janx of the Null Agent Network, the most notorious mercenary organization in the entire universe?

Maybe some of you would style yourselves after Tor Gret, the exiled crown prince of Urdak, made idealistic and cynical in equal portions by wild twists of fate. I know him well, personally recruiting him into The Keepers, The Hub's non-military security force. He is an effective marshal, and you will no doubt encounter him—but be warned. He has no problem with violence, and despite his position, he has no love for The Merge or its agents.

And last, I think it might be Krishah who haunts the nightmares of you and your peers. Krishah the orphaned human who has traveled the galaxies acquiring fighting techniques from the natives of countless worlds, Krishah the mercenary, Krishah the walking encyclopedia of intergalactic combat, Krishah the Ambassador-slayer and The Merge's most wanted fugitive. Yes, she is alluring. Yes, she must be found. But seek and bring her to justice at your peril.

I could go further, but I can see your growing impatience. The names I've mentioned have only stirred your desire for action. Remember, their stories are already well under way. Yours is just beginning. But as earnest, eager young Ambassadors, there can be no doubt all your stories are bound to converge.

MARS YOU SAY?

Jane Yolen

I spit on your Mars
a mere transit stop,
turnpickle,
not turnpike,
a subset of Nex,
too old to be remembered,
too young to be considered
anything other than a time larder
where ideas remain,
stasis maintained
and the last ranked rovers
run out their days
searching for Malcolm Orion
to entice The Merge.

THE BRAVE TRAVELER

Andy Baker and Brent Friedman

Abridged Anthology Version by
Mario Acevedo, Angie Hodapp, and Joshua Viola

MARS, 0 HD

AS THE SHUTTLE TOUCHED DOWN, Malcolm Orion looked up. Up through the shuttle's window, up through Mars's dusky night sky, up at the twin points of light that, 196 million kilometers away, were Earth and her moon.

This, he realized, might be the last time he saw them.

He closed his eyes and thought of his wife.

"Touchdown," said Command Pilot Conrad. "You okay, Orion?"

Malcolm nodded.

"Bullshit," said Conrad. "You're thinking about Rayla and the kids."

"Never stopped." Malcolm busied himself unbuckling his harness. "I'll be thinking about them until I take my last breath."

Conrad put a hand on Malcolm's shoulder. For a moment, as the two men looked at each other, the unprecedented enormity of Malcolm's mission sat heavy on both their shoulders.

"Takes a strong person to marry into the corps, and Rayla's the strongest of them all."

"You got that right, Sir."

Conrad cleared his throat. "Listen, Orion. Whatever happens—to you, to us, to our used-up planet—I want you to hear something. Win or lose, everyone knows you were always the best man for this job. Got that?"

Malcolm clenched his teeth, a tightness forming at the center of his chest. Win or lose… He didn't intend to lose. He was a goddamn Navy SEAL turned astronaut. He'd pulled through far too many missions where failure wasn't an option.

But this mission...this mission was different. Failure wasn't only an option—it was a near certainty. And on this mission, failure meant death.

"Thank you, Sir. I'll do my best to make you proud."

"No use making me proud." Conrad started flipping switches and punching buttons, running the shuttle's power-down procedures. "Make Rayla and the kids proud."

Malcolm thought again of his wife, her dark eyes shining with tears, her smile strong and true as he looked back at her for what would likely be the last time. "I already have, Sir."

Half a million civilians lived on Mars, but their settlements were nowhere near the polar ice cap where the alien ship had crashed some 40,000 years ago. They didn't even know it was here—no one did until the survey team discovered it a few years ago. The few global leaders who knew about Project Celeste had decided the public wasn't ready to learn that humans weren't alone in the universe.

A good decision, Malcolm thought as he followed Commander Conrad off the shuttle. Gazing at the ship for the first time with his own eyes, he could hardly comprehend what he was seeing. Not even his top-level access to all the related intelligence could have prepared him for this.

For one thing, the ship's size was staggering: more than sixty-four kilometers long. A metropolis. A mountain range. For another, its tubular shape was more organic than mechanical. What engineer would think to create a ship like this? No one could say. The design seemed unnecessarily complex, more form than function. Massive overlapping lobes shingled what was presumably the bow, while narrower petal shapes trailed from the stern.

More intriguing than the monolith's exterior was what the survey team found inside. There were no signs of life; this had never been a colony ship. Instead, it carried smaller spacecraft and a myriad of semi-organic machines.

A warship? That was the next theory.

The science and engineering corps eventually figured out how to power up the ship's mechanicals, but only after eighteen months of global debate back on Earth—and the assurance from the survey team that the ship held no weapons—was the green light given to flip the switch.

Once they did, they powered up something they all knew would alter the course of human history.

ン

Malcolm followed Conrad toward Celeste Base, their gait made slow and heavy by their suits and Mars's gravity. Once they approached the command center, Space Force General Alvarez—head of Project Celeste, and the man who had selected Malcolm for this mission—emerged to greet them.

"Welcome to Mars, Commander Orion."

"Glad to finally be here, Sir."

"You ready to take your first look inside?"

"Lead the way."

Conrad gave a quick salute, then ducked into the command center, leaving Malcolm to follow Alvarez toward the entrance to the ship.

Inside, Malcolm gasped. Once again, the endless photos, vids, and schematics he'd poured over back on Earth had failed to prepare him for the experience of being here in the flesh. The cavernous interior was undeniably organic and indisputably alien.

"Incredible, isn't it?" Alvarez pointed up at a series of long, translucent, rib-like tubes, each over a kilometer in diameter and each carrying a spacecraft. "Those are the gestation chambers. We think the big ship was growing smaller ones."

"Gives new meaning to the term *mothership*," Malcolm said.

Alvarez chuckled. "That's a good one. Look at this." He led Malcolm toward a craft that had fallen from its tube. They walked alongside it for some time until they arrived at the entrance.

Malcolm ducked inside, where several droids lay in pieces on the floor. There was nothing human or even humanoid about them—they were some three meters tall, their exteriors a complicated series of tentacular cables and whiplike structures, and their exposed wiring impossibly complex—but Malcolm felt a stab of pity. Tens of thousands of years they'd lain here, looking as though they could power up at any moment. It was clear they had been built to ambulate, to perform work. But what work?

"We call them sentinels because we don't really know what they were built to do," Alvarez said. "Mechanical and Science worked together to dissect a couple of them, as you can see."

"And?"

"And nothing. These things are tens of thousands of years old, and the tech is still so far beyond anything humans have ever seen that none of us really knows what we're looking at. This way."

Alvarez started down the corridor, disappearing deeper into the mothership. Malcolm stepped out of the smaller, though still decidedly massive craft, but he stopped to glance one last time at the dissected sentinels.

What were you built for? he thought. Immediately, he realized that thinking at the sentinels was a strange thing to do. And yet it felt...right. It felt as if they, or whatever beings had created them, were listening. As if they understood his thoughts. *There's a lot we don't know about you,* Malcolm continued, *but we're trying to learn.*

I have come here to learn.

A ten-minute walk brought Malcolm and Alvarez out of the gestational cavern and into a second, smaller chamber. On the floor at the center were four illuminated ovals.

"Are these the pods?" Malcolm asked.

"They are. Watch."

Slowly, the oval closest to Malcolm began to shimmer and shift. A substance Malcolm could only describe as iridescent oil and cerulean light pushed up out of the floor. He tensed, but Alvarez put out an assuring hand.

"They do this whenever someone comes in here. Keep watching."

The substance rose higher and stretched itself out into a glowing shape resembling a seed pod, a gently pulsing cocoon exactly the right size and shape for an adult human. Then it stilled.

In an instant, Malcolm understood: It was waiting for him. Something—the pod, the ship, the beings that built all this?—was reaching out to his consciousness. Searching. Exploring. Connecting.

Malcolm stepped toward the pod, one hand out before him. In the pod's shimmery surface, he saw his own face reflected, saw his own eyes shining with the pod's blue light.

"What's happening, Commander?" Alvarez spoke softly. "What do you feel?"

"It's...it's inviting me to take a journey."

Alvarez grinned. "I knew you were the right man for the job."

Malcolm lowered his hand. The impulse to press himself into the pod, to let the pod reshape itself around him, was almost as strong as his impulse to breathe. Yet he forced himself to step back.

"What do you mean?" he asked Alvarez.

"Not everyone feels the connection as strongly as you did just now. Some don't feel it at all. But I saw it in your eyes. The world might think I chose you for this mission, Commander Orion, but trust me: It was the ship who chose you."

⋔

The mission was scheduled to commence the following morning. First, Malcolm was required to eat, rest, and submit to a final battery of physical examinations and psychological testing.

Yes, he understood no one had ever climbed into one of those blue pods.

Yes, he understood no one knew what would happen to him when he did.

Yes, he understood pain, disfigurement, insanity, and death were all possible.

Yes, he understood he could end up a castaway someplace from which he could never return.

And yes, his affairs were settled, and he had told his family he loved them.

When the hour came, Malcolm suited up. His helmet, now locked in place, amplified the rasp of each inhale, each exhale, filling his ears with the sound of his own fear. Sweat trickled down the back of his neck, the sides of his ribs. He'd told the mission psychologists what they wanted to hear; he'd said what humanity, back on a depleted, dying Earth and desperate for a new frontier, needed him to say. But he was only human, and as he approached one of the illuminated ovals in the chamber floor, flanked by General Alvarez, Command Pilot Conrad, and the rest of the Project Celeste team, he resigned himself to his fate. *Fate.* He recalled the words President Fuller had spoken to him: "The fate of humanity may very well rest on your shoulders, Commander Orion. Please come back."

The fate of humanity? He looked at the people who'd accompanied him into this alien chamber. Could they sense his misgivings? Or did they only see Commander Malcolm Orion, caught up in the monumental significance of the moment?

Camera drones floated above him. One hovered close to his helmet, and he did his best to give the people back home a resolute smile, a mask of stoic determination. But his mind was reeling, flipping through the hours of psychological training he'd undergone in preparation for this moment. Every imaginable scenario Malcolm might experience after he stepped into the pod, the Celeste team rendered in intensely realistic XR imagery and loaded into the VR training module. Sometimes the fictional beings on the other side were friendly, and he practiced rehearsed diplomacy. More often, they were hostile.

It was time.

The shimmering blue substance rose from the pool in the floor and, just as it had yesterday, formed a human-sized pod. Malcolm stepped closer, once again sensing that the energy inside it was reaching out to him, inviting him to connect. To trust.

Mind and body, he began to relax. Each breath became full and deep, and the throb of his pulse against his temples slowed to a steady, calming rhythm.

Stepping closer still, Malcolm watched the pod's translucent membrane separate, revealing at its core a single seat. Part of him remembered he was supposed to turn around now and address the team, look directly into the drone's lens and deliver a memorable one-liner that would go down in history alongside Armstrong's "one small step." What was he supposed to say? He'd rehearsed it so many times, but he couldn't recall now, and he couldn't bring himself to believe it mattered.

All that was left to do was accept the invitation.

Without a word, he eased himself into the seat and relaxed. For a moment, as the pod closed seamlessly around him, his mind went blank. Then the lights inside the pod pulsed and flickered. Tendrils of light-matter snaked around his arms and legs, holding his body still. Bioluminescent cables emerged from somewhere behind him and latched onto his helmet.

The pod became one with his mind; his mind became one with the pod.

The presence entered his consciousness again, searching. And then... inquiring.

It wanted to know his intentions, the depth of his desire to make this leap into the unknown.

Malcolm hesitated. His hands, bound to the armrests, clenched into fists. The pod, seeming to register this as fear and doubt, also hesitated.

Malcolm exhaled slowly, searching his own mind, moving inward toward what mattered most: his family. His intention was simple: to save them, and to save the entire human race before the dying Earth could no longer sustain life. He intended to do this. For them. For all mankind.

His intention now clear, his vision flooded with pure, bright light.

Then Malcolm Orion was gone.

A vortex of colored light.

A technicolor kaleidoscope.

A swirling array of constellations.

A gleaming white filament that stretched out before him.

He was traveling at a speed he could not comprehend through a twisting, translucent tunnel, beyond which there was an infinity of other tunnels. All intertwined. All connected. Together, they formed a vast matrix of cerulean light.

Malcolm had no body with which to feel, no eyes with which to see. Yet his consciousness still existed, and with it, he sensed.

Sensed an orange planet. Gnarled trees that scraped the sky. Birds that flew through clouds of ash. Fish that swam through seas of flame. Beings. Two arms, two legs, long and lean.

And then...

Rain on a jungle canopy. The screeching song of an alien creature. A saltwater breeze and sun-blasted sand. The heavy air of a gathering storm.

All around him in that ocean of blue light were innumerable planets, all teeming with sentient life. Everywhere—life! Humans had never been alone. What hubris to think otherwise!

But then...

The images began to shift. *Time* began to shift.

Malcolm saw himself as an old man, an ancient traveler in the same ethereal void, looking back at him and remembering this past even as he himself was remembering his own future.

Next, Malcolm's middle-aged self, worried, troubled.

Finally, Malcolm's current self. His near-future self, bruised and battered and fleeing from danger.

Malcolm sucked air into corporeal lungs and opened his eyes.

He was in a pod, but not the same pod. In a chamber, but not the same chamber. He peered out through the translucent membrane and saw not four glowing blue pools in the floor, but rows upon rows of them. Was it possible the pods were portals, and that they allowed people to jump from one pod to another? This seemed the obvious explanation. They were transportation pods, then. *Transpods.*

Then Malcolm saw something else. Standing over him, balanced on its mechanical tendrils and tentacles, was a sentinel.

Malcolm's heart—he had a heart again!—began to race. He blinked sweat out of his eyes and stared up at the thing. Back on Mars, the dissected remains of these strange bio-machines had elicited pity. But now, cocooned in a transpod underneath a sentinel that seemed poised for action sent a spike of adrenaline through Malcolm's chest. The tentacles were all attached to a sphere that hovered some twelve feet overhead. Embedded in the sphere's surface were smaller orbs. Eyes, Malcolm thought. Eyes that, for now, were dark.

No sooner had he set his intention to exit the transpod than the membrane split open to allow it. Carefully, quietly, he climbed out and stood.

Reality seemed to skip, to stutter, to lurch and lag. He was unsteady, like his bones and muscles and skin were puzzling how to fit themselves together.

It wasn't painful so much as...nauseating. For a few disturbing minutes, his synapses fired in haphazard circles: when he tried to move his left hand, his left foot moved instead.

Eventually, he regained control. Yet he couldn't shake the feeling that he was not fully himself. His envirosuit and his gun, still at his hip, felt familiar. But everything else was off.

Different transpod. Different chamber. *Different body.*

He turned and stared at his reflection in the transpod's surface. Staring back at him was the same face he saw in his bathroom mirror every morning. Yet he knew that these cells, these tissues, were facsimiles of those he'd left back on Mars.

He was a clone.

Frantically, he began to conjure memories of Rayla and the kids. In rapid succession, he replayed their lives together, testing his ability to recall the joy of their wedding day. The deeply fierce love he felt at the birth of their two children. The bone-deep exhaustion he felt night after night while he paced the floor with a colicky Perdita in his arms so that Rayla could sleep. The agonizing distress he endured when Bean fell out of the tree in their yard and required surgery to set his broken ankle and wrist. Birthdays. Holidays. Trips to the beach.

It was all there. All of it. He allowed himself to breathe again. Different body, same consciousness. This relieved him beyond measure. But did this mean his original body was still in its transpod back on Mars? Would Alvarez and the rest of the team assume he had just climbed into that transpod and died? Gods, he hoped not. If he was right about the transpods and how they worked, then he wanted to be able to jump back into his original body.

He looked again at his reflection. Then again, what did having an original body matter if each transpod you jumped into could create a perfect replica of your physical self?

Glancing up at the still-dark sentinel, he stepped quietly away from the transpod.

That's when the sentinel woke up. In the near darkness of the chamber, the multiple eye-orbs glowed blue.

Malcolm froze, staring up at the body-orb, and once again held his breath. Slowly, he inched a hand toward his pistol. Pulled it from its holster. Flicked the safety.

At the sound of the click, the thing's body-orb swiveled atop its tentacles. It zeroed in on Malcolm's gun, and in the air between them appeared a holographic blueprint of the weapon's architecture.

Malcolm forced himself to stand his ground. Was this some sort of analytics droid? Did it even know what a firearm was?

Suddenly, the hologram began to flash red.

Shit. Malcolm didn't need help interpreting what was apparently the universal signal for danger. Before he could decide whether to shoot, surrender, or run, one of the sentinel's tendril-like cables lashed out and wrapped around his forearm.

Malcolm fired. He didn't intend to, but he'd tensed, and with the shot still ringing in his ears, he cursed himself. He'd been here—wherever *here* was—five minutes, and already he'd committed an act of war. The bullet had traveled straight toward the center of the body-orb...

...but then pinged off an invisible energy shield and clattered to the floor.

Malcolm stared. Still caught in the sentinel's grasp, he dropped his gun. The sound of it hitting the floor was almost more startling than the shot. *Friend. Sorry. Peace. Explorer. Husband. Father.* He thought at the sentinel the way he had thought at the others back on Mars, willing it, or whatever had created it, to understand. Willing it to show mercy.

The sentinel didn't let go, but it stilled, and its many eye-orbs now seemed to look at him more closely. Malcolm's breaths came hard and fast. *I came in good faith*, he thought. *I accepted your invitation.*

A second tendril snaked through the air—not toward him, but toward his gun. As Malcolm watched, the tendril altered its shape like quicksilver. Its tip now a wickedly sharp stiletto, the tendril shot out and pierced the weapon. The gun shattered into several pieces that skittered across the floor.

Malcolm squeezed his eyes shut. He was next. The machine was showing him what it could do. Intimidating him. Communicating its intent. Malcolm drew a final breath. "I'm sorry," he whispered. To his family. To General Alvarez. To every human left on Earth. "I wasn't the man for this mission after all."

Nothing happened.

Instead, the tendril around his arm withdrew, and the other—now returned to its original shape—handed him the largest piece of his broken, useless gun. Then the sentinel turned and glided away from him down the endless row of transpods.

Malcolm watched it go. Inside his helmet, sweat trailed down his face and neck. He fought to regain his composure as he stared down at the useless scrap in his hands. He was defenseless.

You're not defenseless.

Rayla's voice echoed in his mind. He was imagining it the way he always did when he was away from her. The way he always did when he was on a mission and feared he would never see her again.

You were a goddamn SEAL, Malcolm Orion. Don't you forget that.

Malcolm smiled. "Hooyah."

Then he turned his back on the retreating sentinel, on the transpod he now knew would send him back to Mars in an instant if he wanted it to, and jogged down the tunnel toward the chamber's exit.

The air outside was not breathable.

Malcolm checked the readings on the small datapad on his wrist. The ambient temperature was hospitable, at least, but the ratio of nitrogen to oxygen and the trace amounts of methane and ammonia meant his helmet had to stay on.

He looked around. A dark mist loomed over a desolate, gray landscape of colossal alien structures. Some still stood, but many had been reduced to ruin—and not just by time. Something had happened here. Something cataclysmic.

Of the edifices that still stood, some were tall and tiered, resembling Meso-American temples. Others were reminiscent of Norse construction with wattle walls and thatched roofs. There were even nomadic tents that reminded Malcolm of Mongolian structures. Beyond that, another architectural style employed canopies of wood that sat on brutalist foundations, their sharp overhangs knifing the sky, while still others had rounded obsidian walls, their lower levels made of stone and buttressed by circular blades; narrow slits punctuated the accompanying towers. Past that, Malcolm saw a vast lake. Numerous round structures broke the rippled surface, forming hints of a much greater assembly hidden within those depths.

Multiple distinct types of buildings. All abandoned. All damaged by...what? War? Did they kill each other off? Or did they suffer some other devastation?

For nearly an hour, Malcolm walked among the ruins, memorizing what he saw and keeping an eye on his datapad in case it suddenly detected life. So far, nothing. Clearly, sentient beings once thrived here. How many eons ago? Where were they now?

As he approached a stone-and-alloy skybridge, he realized he felt drawn to it. Some presence—the same presence he sensed back on Mars when he saw the dissected sentinels—was here with him. Guiding him. It wanted him to cross the bridge.

Wary, Malcolm peered through the gloom toward the other side. Several blue lights floated in the distance. Only when the mist thinned did he see that the lights were large cerulean crystals being carried by sentinels.

Not sentinels, thought Malcolm; they did more than merely watch and defend. They also worked in service, though to what or whom, he didn't know.

He began to think of them as service droids. *Servitors.*

Perhaps they served the presence in Malcolm's mind, still urging him across the bridge. Drawing a breath, he obeyed.

The bridge was at least fifty meters long, and as he made his way across, he realized the dark mist had continued to lift. All around him, more and more blue lights blinked into existence. More Servitors carrying more crystals. A low hum and steady whir dissipated the eerie silence, reminding Malcolm of machines coming to life, electronics booting up.

Halfway across the bridge, his datapad pinged. He looked down at his wrist. The icon next to *air quality* had turned from red to green. Stunned, Malcolm tapped the command to run a manual test. Again, the icon glowed green. Tentatively, he lifted his visor slightly and took a sip of air. It was fresh and cool and, most importantly, not toxic. Grinning, he flipped his visor all the way up, filled his lungs, and looked around. This entire place, this space station, if that's truly what it had once been, was waking up. In the span of an hour, the presence—he knew it was the presence, but he didn't know how he knew—had scrubbed the atmosphere to replicate that of Earth.

It had made the air breathable. Just for him.

How? Humans' best terraforming equipment would take decades to make a station this size habitable. With Earth slowly dying and Mars still generations away from being fully terraformed, perhaps this station could be the haven humanity needed. While the station couldn't possibly sustain billions of humans all at once—or could it?—it could certainly buy them time and help them avoid extinction. It could serve as a temporary stopgap. But then again, the post-cataclysm ruins were a stark reminder that this station, miraculous as it was, had a violent history.

By the time Malcolm reached the far side of the bridge, the mist had disappeared. The sky, still the deep, dusty blue of twilight, revealed itself—a celestial dome teeming with stars that surrounded a large, glowing moon.

Ahead of him stood a distinctive building shaped like a parabola, illuminated by the same blue light as the Servitors' crystals and decorated with elaborate carvings in its translucent surfaces. Its architecture was unlike that of any of the other structures Malcolm had seen, leading him to believe that this must have been a place where all who lived here were welcome. A place that existed outside, or perhaps above, sectarian beliefs or practices.

As he approached the front of the building, it opened for him. Again, he felt the presence urging him to enter.

The logical part of Malcolm's brain told him he was foolish to so blindly and willingly trust this non-voice in his head, this thing he had termed *the presence*. But his intuition told him otherwise; his intuition told him the presence wanted to help him accomplish his mission.

Maybe establishing contact with the presence was his mission.

He walked inside.

The space was shaped like a cylinder, open and airy. He followed the lights on the floor to the center of the room.

Above him, the roof unfurled. He looked up and gasped. The stars seemed to press down on him, the result of some invisible lens, some optical effect. Myriad constellations spiraled across the sky, while beams of light shone from the floor. A hologram appeared, aligning itself with the stars above.

An interstellar map! *An Astrograph.* Malcolm felt he was being invited to choose a destination. But how could he choose, with what seemed like infinite choices, infinite possibilities?

He visualized Mars, the crashed ship, and the transpod.

The hologram dipped and spun through space, reminding Malcolm of the images and sensations he'd just encountered on his first jump. Soon, it slowed, and Malcolm saw that it was approaching the Milky Way. The image zoomed ahead, found Earth's solar system, hovered above Mars, and gently descended to its surface.

Malcolm held his breath. Home—only a jump away. What would everyone think of his discovery? This nexus, this hub of an intergalactic transportation network that could provide humankind access to millions of new habitable worlds?

The Hub. Yes. The space station now had a name. And this structure that housed the Astrograph would be the *Lighthouse.*

Before he exited the Lighthouse, Malcolm looked back at the hologram of Mars. It was so tempting to jump back now, to tell everyone that he was okay, that humanity was going to survive. But the presence was beckoning him again, and he knew that there was more it wanted to show him.

Outside, Malcolm saw that the Servitors had been busy: The Hub was now fully illuminated. Fully functional.

Fully...*awake.*

Malcolm peered up at the blue light that ribboned the moon. He looked closer. The moon was not a moon at all. It was a machine, a manufactured satellite set into The Hub's orbit. Or did he have that backwards? Perhaps The

Hub was the satellite, and the machine was the body around which he was orbiting. Another question laid out before him. Another mystery he would have to solve.

He crossed back over the bridge and turned toward an area of the ruined city he had not yet explored. All the while, he breathed slowly and deeply, focusing on keeping his mind open to the presence. Where did it want him to go? What did it want him to see? To know? To understand?

Soon, he found himself near a mostly tumbled-down building. Into its fractured walls were carved scenes of brutal violence. He ran his fingers over the grooved lines, many of which depicted a singular figure—a monstrous warrior with snakelike hair who wielded twin blades and cut down his enemies with decisive savagery. Was the artwork intended to venerate this warrior or to warn others of his coming?

Intrigued, Malcolm moved broken rocks and other debris away from another panel of the tableau, but what he revealed was a shimmering blue crack in the building's outer wall. He knelt to bring his eye to the crack, and what he saw inside made his heart hammer against his ribs.

It was a transpod. Nearly twice the size of the transpods Malcolm had used to jump, it flickered as if it were short-circuiting, struggling to operate. Inside, blurred by the translucent membrane, lay a humanoid shape. A shape at least three meters tall. Hair like snakes. Twin blades at its sides.

Malcolm's datapad pinged. *Life detected.*

Malcolm sat back on his heels, adrenaline pulsing through his blood. For the first time since he arrived here, he doubted the presence. Why did it guide him here? Did it want him to fight this warrior? Defeat it? For whose benefit? Whatever threats or conflicts The Hub's inhabitants faced before the whole place was reduced to rubble, Malcolm had no way of knowing. And Malcolm always made it his business to know who he was fighting, and what he was fighting for. He was a soldier, yes, but he was also a thinker. That's why he was the top contender for this mission: They needed someone who could reason as well as he could swing his fists, someone who would question orders when orders required questioning.

But then the presence seemed to calm him. He felt his pulse slow. This was not a fight. It was a parley.

Still cautious, Malcolm skirted the building and located the entrance. Inside, the transpod's glow flickered as if it were out of sync either with the life inside it or with whatever forces governed its function. Malcolm approached, his eyes drawn to the data display on the side of the transpod. He couldn't read the writing, didn't even know if the symbols represented letters or numbers, but he understood the pictograph. An incomplete outline of the warrior, undeniably the same warrior depicted in the stone carvings outside, was pulsing red.

The clone wasn't done forming.

But it was close.

Now was the time to run. Malcolm considered it. He was sure he understood how to use intent to activate a transpod, and the jump back to Mars would be almost instantaneous. If he went now, the warrior would never know he was here. But as Malcolm watched the red outline on the display grow closer and closer to complete, he couldn't shake the feeling that he needed to be here. The warrior had something to teach him.

At last, the walls of the transpod dropped away. Malcolm drew back into the shadows, crouching instinctively into a defensive stance. The transpod opened, and the alien warrior, clad in blood-red armor, twin blades held high, leapt to his feet. He was immediately ready to attack or defend, but then he halted, chest heaving, masked face sweeping the room. He stumbled and lowered his blades.

Malcolm watched, remembering those first moments of unsteadiness and disorientation he felt when he first stepped out of the transpod. He waited, careful not to speak or move, not to startle the warrior in any way that might provoke aggression.

The alien, bent down, continued to breathe and recover. The heavy ropes of his hair hung to either side of his face.

Malcolm thought he was still hidden, undetected, in the shadows. But then the alien spoke to him.

"HIZZ N'AKI CHUN."

Somehow—Malcolm could only assume the presence was translating—he understood.

"*You will approach.*"

Malcolm forced himself to stand tall and step forward.

"Who are you?" The alien's voice was deep, guttural, clear. He lifted his face, revealing two glowing eyes.

Eyes on the blades still clutched in the alien's lowered fists, Malcolm held his hands up in what he hoped was a universal gesture for *I mean no harm.* "My name is Malcolm Orion."

"Do you know of my people, the Ja'din?"

"I know nothing. I only just arrived. The whole place is abandoned. In ruins. I think you and I are the only two here."

The alien sheathed his blades, yet even standing there empty-handed, he looked as though he could break any opponent in two. "Show me."

Malcolm nodded, and though he didn't like the idea of turning his back on this formidable warrior, he turned and led him out into the open air.

Outside, the alien scanned the broken landscape, taking in every detail of the ruined city that had crumbled down around where he now stood.

"What happened here?" Malcolm asked.

"I don't know. My memories from the time before are...gone. You are the first traveler to come here in eons. To a Ja'din, this means you are important—or will become so. Your arrival reawakened the station, finally allowing me to emerge from my pod."

Malcolm stared. "You've been trapped in that pod for eons?"

"Time is not the same there. I was gone many lifetimes. Long enough for all the Ja'din to leave. Or to die."

"But you were aware of time passing?"

"I was aware of many things."

Malcolm shook his head, unable to comprehend the mental anguish that must have accompanied such an unimaginable length of time spent alone and trapped. "How did you survive? How did you stay sane?"

"Ja'din endure. Heal. Our bodies and minds can withstand much." The alien's gaze seemed to rest on the Lighthouse. He began to walk toward it, but he paused when he saw the images carved into the broken wall.

"Is that you?" Malcolm asked.

"Yes. They called me Reyu the Reaper." His voice was pained, and Malcolm understood that the alien didn't care for the epithet. He was a killer, but he was more than that. Or believed himself to be.

"Your name is Reyu?"

The alien nodded, then set out again for the Lighthouse. His strides were quick and sure; he was in full control of his cloned body now, and Malcolm was forced to jog to keep up.

"Did the Ja'din build The Hub?"

"No. We are not The Creators. When my people arrived, The Creators were gone."

The Creators. A shiver snaked down Malcolm's spine. "Who are The Creators?"

"Nobody knows. They are beyond knowing."

"Okay, well...what about the Servitors carrying the blue crystals?"

"Servitors!" The alien came as close as Malcolm imagined he could to chuckling. "Well named, Malcolm Orion. Yes, the droids serve The Creators—or, rather, all that The Creators have made. Your arrival awakened them, too, and now they must power up the station—*The Hub*, as you call it. The crystals are Protens. Energy."

Malcolm's mind spun. *Creators. Servitors. Protens. The Hub.* Everything lying dormant and in ruins for ages, waiting for...him? That didn't make sense. He was nobody, a speck of dust in what he now understood to be a universe so vast it defied comprehension.

As they neared the Lighthouse, Malcolm felt the air shift, like the onset of a lightning storm.

Reyu looked up at the mechanical moon. "Watch."

Malcolm obeyed. The moon pulsed with blue light. Rings rose from its surface and started spinning, discharging waves of energy and peals of thunder. The rings stopped spinning and dropped back into the sphere. Apertures opened all over the moon's surface, hundreds of them, thousands, and from them, long, cylindrical shapes emerged.

"That is the Cradle of Creation. From time beyond memory, it has birthed the Mothers who bear the Children who collect the gems to form the necklace worn by the Infinite."

Malcolm stared up in awe as the motherships headed off in all directions. "One of those ships crash landed on Mars thousands of years ago. That's how my people found the transpods, and how I got here." He remembered the gestation chamber inside. "Am I right that they spawn smaller ships?"

"When the Mothers detect sentient life on a planet as they pass by, they eject a Child. The Child *lands* on the planet and invites its inhabitants to *discover* the Infinite. Is that not what I just said?"

Malcolm ignored the annoyance in the alien's tone. *Progenitor Ships. Discovery Landers.* He looked at the Cradle of Creation. Something that powerful didn't exist solely to manufacture spaceships; he suspected it lay at the heart of the intergalactic transportation system that had brought him here. Given what he knew about quantum physics—and the theoretical transmission of a consciousness through space—he surmised that the Cradle was itself a massive Hadron collider. Meson particles must be involved. Yet the tech was ancient, as were those who created it. In his mind, Malcolm changed the *e* to an *a* and added a second *s*. To that he added *Zero* because that miraculous sphere was ground zero for all Creator Tech.

Masson Zero.

Inside the Lighthouse, Reyu stood beneath the Astrograph. Yet for the Ja'din, the holographic database remained inert.

"I don't remember," Reyu growled. "Not the name of my homeworld. Not the details necessary to bring up the map. Nothing. Without my memories, I cannot jump home. I do not even know if my home still exists."

Malcolm pitied Reyu, but he resisted the urge to reach out a comforting hand. Somehow, he knew the gesture would be neither understood nor well received. "What *do* you remember?"

"I was the first of the Ja'din to arrive here, before the other four species joined us. My people believed that this place had been built for us. Back then, I could communicate with The Creators. But now, that connection has been severed." Reyu's voice grew fervent; it seemed that as he spoke, some of his memories returned. "It was foretold by the Circle of Five, wise representatives of the species who lived here, that the end was approaching. They felt it within the jumpspace, a darkness and a foreboding. A war would come, the union would dissolve, and The Great Fracture would begin. One of us would remain to rebuild, they said, but he who remained would not rule The Second Cycle. That was an honor reserved for another." Then, Reyu the Reaper dropped to one knee before Malcolm Orion. "I pledge my blood and body to the one who has started The Second Cycle. A title once mine is now yours. Malcolm Orion, you are The Fel'Akrin—the Herald."

Malcolm felt the weight of the moment, the deep reverence and respect Reyu had bestowed on him. Yet once again, he felt inconsequential, no larger than a speck of dust. Rule The Second Cycle? What did that mean? This was a mistake.

"Reyu, I'm just a human looking for a new home for my people. Our world is depleted. Dying. I came here hoping to find that home but fully expecting to die."

Reyu rose slowly and looked down at him. "You would have sacrificed yourself for your people?"

"Yes. And for my family." Once again, Malcolm recalled Rayla's smile and the feeling of his children cradled in his arms. "I still will, if that's what it takes to save them. But I'd prefer to live and find humanity a new home."

Reyu seemed to consider this. "I seek a home forgotten. You seek a home unknown."

Malcolm nodded.

"Then let me help you. Let this be my redemption, Malcolm Orion. I failed as the Herald. The Voice of The Creator told me that everything they built was meant for Convergence—the bringing together of all life. Instead, it is possible my people brought about the Fracture. I must atone."

Malcolm stepped into the center of the Astrograph, and the Astrograph, in response to his intent, his curiosity, his commitment, exploded in a panoply of light and stars. Of infinite possibility. In his mind, the presence assured him: Reawakening the Masson Zero—reconnecting sentient life across the universe—was not just Malcolm's mission. It would forever be his purpose.

"Let us help each other, Reyu," said Malcolm. "We will find our homes. And we will find the others who once thrived here. If they came together once, they can do so again. Let that be the goal of The Second Cycle: Reconvergence."

Malcolm Orion and Reyu climbed into two side-by-side transpods. Would they jump alone or together? Would they find themselves at the same place, at the same time?

The only way to know was to jump.

And so Malcolm and Reyu—the Heralds of The First and Second Cycles—jumped together. Two brave travelers. Both seeking homes, one old, one new, among the stars.

BLOOD AND BEGINNINGS

Jeanne C. Stein, Mario Acevedo, Angie Hodapp, and Joshua Viola

KEPLER-3202C, 470 HD

CASSIAN SLAMMED THE STEEL DOOR to the lab and engaged the deadbolt.

Allayus beat her fists against the other side. "Let me in! Damn you, Cassian, let me in!"

Cassian stumbled back from the door. She glanced at the video monitor, the image an overhead shot of Allayus outside frantically clawing the steel.

"Goddamn you, let me in!"

"I can't. I can't." She backed into the lab table. Several jars fell to the floor, shattered, and filled the room with the odor of Tru-Solv 7.

On the other side of the door, Allayus's pleas became screams.

This can't be. The thought echoed in Cassian's mind, threatening to swallow her. She was trapped here, in a lab equipped with advanced Merge Tech, none of which was any use against...whatever the hell was out there. All Cassian could do was barricade herself here and pray her message for help had been received.

She covered her ears to smother Allayus's screams. Allayus was her best friend, but Cassian had no choice but to lock her out and condemn her to die in the clutches of those...*things*.

She heard the grinding of metal behind her and spun to face the door to the supply bay. The exterior gate to the bay was being wrenched from its hinges. The ceiling lights flickered and dimmed.

Panicked, Cassian searched for a flashlight. The overheads flickered again. She settled for the gas torch.

Her attention swung between Allayus on the video monitor and the supply bay door. Something huge crashed into the bay, thumping, moaning, groaning, tearing shelves and equipment to pieces. The door shook, shook again, then fractured.

The horror in Cassian's mind yawned open, her scientific brain unable to comprehend what she saw.

A grotesque amalgam of body parts—arms, legs, torsos, heads—jammed itself through the doorway. It was covered in pustules and pierced with glowing green crystals. On the mass of flesh, bulging eyes on distorted faces swiveled obscenely in her direction. Bile dribbled from hideous mouths twisted in rapacious hunger.

The lights clicked off, and darkness engulfed the lab.

Cassian fumbled for the torch's ignite switch. A flame shot from the torch, illuminating the misshapen monster and its horde of repulsive, glistening eyes.

Then the pool of Tru-Solv 7 on the floor burst into flames. One after another, the jars on the table exploded, spraying shards of glass and burning solvent. Arms flailing, Cassian collapsed, her clothes on fire, her hair aflame. As she burned alive, she screamed for salvation that would never come.

Nerida's transpod hatch opened with a hiss of escaping gasses.

Her body felt heavy, but her mind was clear. Her recovery time had been brief and her jump sickness mild since she'd jumped into a skin identical to her human birth form. The other members of her team were still gelling inside their transpods. It had been decided they would all jump into humanoid skins, which were quite different from their natural physiques, so they would need more time to acclimate. When they awakened, they would be groggy and disoriented. Still, taking humanoid forms was a good decision; it would help them determine what this planet, Kepler-3202c, would do to bodies similar to those from Soto.

Within the next orbital cycle, an asteroid belt in Soto's planetary system would intersect the planet's path and pulverize it. The Merge offered to help relocate the inhabitants, but large segments of the population decided not to jump, preferring to keep their birth bodies due to deeply held religious beliefs. A fleet of deep-space arks would transport them from Soto to Kepler-3202c, a voyage that would take nine helicas.

Nerida welcomed the time alone. She wanted to see the lab the last crew had set up outside the Lander. Her mission was not only to determine if this planet was suitable for an immediate population relocation from Soto, but to investigate why the original team went dark.

Nerida made her way to the foyer outside the transpod chamber for any clues Alpha Team may have left. The lights hummed and flickered above her as she emerged into the atrium to find a panorama of carnage. Machinery lay scattered and broken across the deck. Large gashes spiraled from the ceiling down the walls to the floor where they ended in streaks of dried blood. The remains of Servitors—*Servitors!*—were strewn about in piles of lacerated and smashed pieces.

What the drek?

The transpod data—details regarding Alpha Team's jumps, then yesterday's arrival of her own team's security detachment—revealed nothing unusual.

Next, she brought up the communications log. Some documentation of signal interference from the planet's two suns, but other than that, nothing strange.

According to Turmeric Corporate, Alpha Team began relaying reports shortly after they set up. Everything was going smoothly. Then, moments after Lab Chief and Lead Scientist Cassian Vall sent her last report, all communications abruptly ended. However, yesterday's status updates from the newly arrived security detachment had gone through.

It would be at least an hour until her team emerged from their pods, so Nerida decided to check in with the security detachment. The Merge required representatives of their Armed Force's Harbinger Team to be onsite for all planet evals. The suns' interference prevented her from using her MindLink to contact them, but the device could guide her to their encampment.

She walked down a long corridor that lay in shambles to an Assembler that was churning away, manufacturing replacement parts for the damage that had been done to the Lander. She continued past the Proten farm—a large, cavernous room filled with the blue crystalline growths that functioned as the universe's most robust power source. Typically, these farms were guarded by protective energy barriers that only allowed Servitors to enter, but this one was down. Something had clearly disabled it. Violently. But what could have done such a thing, and how? Creator Tech was impervious to all known threats.

First the destroyed Servitors, and now the Proten farm. What happened here, Alpha Team?

Nerida swallowed hard as she turned up one of the Lander's many exit tunnels and emerged on the surface.

At the threshold, she gasped. She wasn't expecting such a beautiful landscape. Whenever she prepared to visit a new planet, she focused on charts and data, not aesthetics. But Kepler-3202c was picturesque. The terrain was a patchwork of gently rolling hills and meadows covered in green moss and yellow grass. Two suns tracked along the silver sky, casting overlapping shadows across the undulating landscape. Clouds thick with rain drifted over the distant horizon. She saw no animals in the fields, no birds in the air. Surveillance had indicated no sentient creatures of any kind. Strange in such a hospitable environment.

Captain Nurmi and his soldiers had set up their bivouac just outside the tunnel entrance. Six personnel huts meant twelve soldiers. She noted a command post, two hexagonal supply cabins, and four perimeter bots. A small surveillance drone circled above. Protens were piled in a crate. The soldiers must have gathered them from the farm inside the Lander before she and her team arrived.

On the other side of the bivouac lay a blackened mass of twisted metal and construction textile—the remains of Alpha Team's lab and encampment.

Dread prickled the back of Nerida's neck. Turmeric shared nothing about what happened to Cassian's team, though it must've been bad. Really bad.

Captain Nurmi and four of his soldiers huddled near the debris. They wore combat kit, and each carried a Proten-powered plasma rifle as well as a generic battery-powered laser pistol.

Nurmi greeted Nerida and described what was left of Alpha Team's camp. The lab, admin office, supply bay, and living quarters had been constructed as one unit—and had burned as one unit.

Nerida examined the ruins. "Data logs indicate heavy rain before we arrived. Evidence of whatever happened probably washed away."

"Not all evidence." The captain's tone was dispassionate. "We're looking at a chemical explosion. And we found remains. Human."

Nerida winced. "How many?"

"Two," said a soldier. He pointed toward where the lab had been. "Over there."

Nerida peered at the scorched debris, but from where she stood, she saw nothing resembling bodies. She took a deep breath to steady herself. "There were eight in Alpha Team. Four lab crew and four soldiers. That means six are missing. Any ideas where they went?"

"Nothing yet," said the captain. "But there's something else you should see." He led Nerida to the other side of the destroyed lab. What was left of a door had been torn from a steel frame, its substantial hinges twisted like cheap aluminum. "This was the exterior gate to the supply bay. What's troubling is that the door was forced to the inside. When the lab exploded—"

"The door should've blown outward," Nerida said.

Nurmi nodded.

"How?"

"That's up to your team to figure out."

Nerida bristled. "We were sent to complete a habitability study for the population of Soto."

"And whatever happened here is part of that study." Nurmi pointed toward the bodies. "Any objections to leaving them there for now? I think it's more pressing for us to secure the bivouac before..."

He didn't have to finish. Nerida already knew what he meant: *Before something bad happens to us.*

"No objections," she said.

Venni, a biochemist, was the first of Nerida's team to exit her transpod. Minutes later, geologists Rotha and EEtu, a husband-and-wife team, emerged.

Venni stretched for a long moment and examined her new humanoid body, dressed in standard Synthtex coveralls, with curiosity. "Never been in a skin like this before."

"The first time I jumped into a humanoid skin," EEtu said, "it took a while to get used to walking on two legs. Take it easy today."

"Listen up," Nerida said. "Remember to pay attention to any unusual sensations. Log any reactions your skin might experience in this environment. Everything is data, and no detail is too small. It's up to us whether to greenlight the relocation of an entire population to this planet. Let's make the right call."

"You got it, Boss," Rotha said.

Nerida led them out of the Lander to the bivouac.

"Drekking hell," said Venni. Her eyes were fixed on the burnt-out husk of Alpha Team's lab. "What happened?"

"Chemical explosion," Nerida said. "Two confirmed casualties. Six still missing."

"Rax," Venni cursed. "What about all the damage to the Lander?"

"We're still trying to piece everything together," Nerida said.

"Nerida!" Captain Nurmi strode toward them from the direction of the soldiers' quarters. "Turmeric wants an autopsy done on those remains."

EEtu folded her arms. "This is a habitability study, and I'm a geologist. I don't do forensics."

"You'll assist," Nerida said, injecting due authority into her tone. "Section 5R of your contract: 'Perform other duties as necessary to complete the assignment.'"

EEtu scowled but remained silent.

Nerida turned toward Nurmi. "Tell Turmeric my team will report on the autopsies as soon as they're completed."

Nurmi nodded.

Nerida glanced at the remains of the lab and suppressed a shudder. Two souls lost in a chemical explosion. What did Turmeric expect the autopsies to reveal?

Rotha gazed back at the Lander. A lone Servitor crawled industriously over the massive structure, its mechanical tentacles carrying equipment needed to repair the damage that had been done inside the Lander.

"What are you thinking, Rotha?" Nerida asked.

"That it's too bad we can't communicate with the Servitor. It had to have seen what happened."

"We don't even exist to Servitors," Nurmi said. "Unless we piss them off by messing with Creator Tech."

"What about that surveillance drone?" Rotha said. "Have you done a sweep beyond the immediate area?"

"Solar flare interference from the twin suns prevents MindLink or drone communications past a hundred meters. If we want to see what's out there"—Nurmi gestured out past the bivouac—"we have to go on foot."

The greater sun had set, and the lesser hung just above the horizon. Nerida sat outside her team's newly assembled lab. Ash and soot smeared her coveralls, her boots, the mask she had worn for the last six hours while she and her team recovered the bodies from the rubble and sifted for clues as to what caused the explosion. Tru-Solv 7, as it turned out—highly flammable and foul-smelling but, luckily, nontoxic.

She pulled the mask away from her nose and mouth and drew a deep breath of fresh, evening air, staring out at the long shadows that crept over the distant hills.

Venni stepped out of the lab and sat beside her. She, too, pulled her mask down and sighed. "Are those what I think they are?"

Nerida looked down at the two small devices she was turning over in her soot-blackened gloves. She nodded. "The biometrics tags EEtu extracted from the bodies."

"Did you scan them?"

Nerida nodded again.

"Who were they?"

"Cassian Vall, the Alpha Team's Lab Chief." A hard lump formed in Nerida's throat. She had served under Cassian on the Elnonus expedition. The two hadn't seen eye to eye on a lot of things, but Cassian was fearless when it came to making hard decisions, and Nerida respected that. Knowing Cassian had died here put a face on the tragedy and brought a stab of remorse. She cleared her throat. "The other was Allayus Tir, a Gananian botanist. I never worked with her, but she was highly respected."

Venni lifted her hand to pat Nerida's knee but seemed to think better of it and instead crossed her arms. "Rotha made an interesting observation. No Protens in the debris. There should have been quite a few powering their equipment."

"Could be they set up a satellite lab somewhere afield. Maybe they moved their Protens out to power that." She bit her lip. "What about the back door to the lab? What do you think could have breached it?"

"Some kind of vehicle? A cargo bot? An animal we haven't yet discovered?" Venni shrugged.

"The autopsies...any pathologies? Anything unusual?"

"No. Burns, smoke inhalation, blunt-force trauma. All expected. One was cut up pretty bad, though. Lots of glass embedded in her skin. All those shattered jars of Tru-Solv 7."

Nerida froze. "One was hit by glass, but not the other?"

"EEtu figured out where the lab's main door was. Cassian and Allayus died on opposite sides of it. Almost like..." Venni trailed off.

"Almost like one had locked the other out," Nerida finished.

The two women looked at each other for a long moment, their expressions grim.

"Okay," Nerida said, clearing her throat again. "I've got a report to write. Bag the bodies. We'll bury them in the morning."

Nerida had just fallen asleep when she heard shouting. She bolted from her cot, yanked on clean coveralls, and sprinted out into the night.

Captain Nurmi's soldiers stood at the edge of the clearing, rifles drawn and trained on the trees beyond the reach of the bivouac's lights.

Nerida rushed to Nurmi's side. "What is it?" she whispered.

"Not sure."

A security bot hovered close, sweeping a spotlight across the darkness. Nothing. Then, caught in the sudden glare some fifty meters away, a humanoid figure staggered out of the darkness.

"Halt!" Captain Nurmi shouted. "Identify yourself!"

The figure shambled closer.

"Halt or we'll shoot!"

Nerida shoved past the captain. "Are you crazy? That could be one of the missing members of Alpha Team." She peered out at the figure, still making slow, steady progress toward them. Still not responding. Her heart thudded against her ribs. She shouted, "We're with Turmeric! What's your name? Do you know what happened here?"

The figure—in the spotlight's glare, it looked male—faltered, then stopped. He wore the same gray coveralls she and the other scientists wore, but his were tattered, one sleeve torn clean off. His head swung slowly side to side, as if he were sniffing the air.

The way he moved sent a chill down Nerida's spine. It looked unnatural. Animalistic. But was he predator, or was he prey?

"Drekking hell," Nurmi muttered. "That guy's not right. We need to take him out."

"Wait," Nerida hissed.

After a moment, the man in the field rolled his shoulders back and lifted his chin. "Leave." His voice was low, guttural. "Leave this planet and never come back."

Nerida took a step forward. "We can help—"

"Go!" Pointing at the Lander, he yelled, "Go now!" Then he turned and lurched back into the darkness beyond the trees.

"Captain!" yelled one of the soldiers, his rifle still at the ready. "Orders?"

"Eyes sharp," Nurmi yelled. "I don't think he's coming back, but whatever he was warning us about might. Tonight, we hold the perimeter. Tomorrow, we search."

"What's going on?"

Nerida spun around, her pulse racing. Rotha stood behind her, and behind him stood EEtu and Venni. All eyes were on her.

Nurmi glanced at Nerida and shook his head as if to say it was up to her to explain.

Nerida sighed and turned back to Rotha. "I think it was one of the scientists from Alpha Team.”

“He told us to go,” Rotha said. “We need to contact Turmeric right now and tell them to get us the hell out of here.”

“That’s not your call.”

“So we wait around until our camp gets blown up too?” EEtu’s voice shook.

“That’s not going to happen.”

“Turmeric can’t stop us from jumping, Nerida.”

“No, but I can.” Nurmi eyed Nerida. “Just say the word, Lab Chief.”

Nerida nodded, and Nurmi commanded a soldier to stand guard at the transpods.

“What the hell, Nerida?” EEtu said.

“Listen,” Nerida said. “We all knew when we signed onto this mission that it might be dangerous. But we have a job to do, and we’re getting paid good credits to do it. That means we stay and figure out what’s going on.”

Rotha’s eyes narrowed. “Alpha Team’s security detail was four. Ours is twelve. You were expecting trouble.”

“That was Turmeric’s call, not mine.” It was the truth, but it still felt like a lie. As the Lab Chief, Nerida always had more intel on this mission than the others, but she wasn’t sure now was the time to show her hand.

“And we’ve got enough firepower to repel a battalion of Star Saber mercenaries,” Nurmi added.

Nerida cringed. The captain meant to be reassuring, but the implication was one her team wouldn’t miss: the greater the firepower, the greater the possible threat.

“Get some sleep,” she said before her team raised further objections. “Tomorrow, we search for survivors.”

The twin suns were high in the sky when Nerida and the two soldiers Nurmi had ordered to join her returned to camp. Their exploration of their assigned search area to the east had turned up nothing. Not so much as a footprint in the soil or broken blade of grass.

Throughout the morning, the temperature had climbed to thirty Celsius—hot but not unbearable. Sweat prickled Nerida’s hairline and dampened the skin beneath her coveralls. Her stomach rumbled with hunger.

At the center of camp, most were already seated at the low tables, hunched over MREs. Nerida hoisted her field pack to the ground and did a quick count. Two missing. One soldier and...

"Where's Venni?"

Rotha and EEtu looked up from the table where they sat. EEtu gave an exaggerated shrug. "Maybe she's dead already. Like all of us are going to be soon if we don't jump off this planet."

Rotha placed a hand on his wife's arm, and EEtu bowed her head, her cheeks flushed with anger.

Nerida drew a slow breath. She wasn't military, and neither were the other scientists on this mission; they owed her none of the unflinching respect Nurmi's soldiers owed him. But as Lab Chief, she had an obligation to keep interpersonal discord from interfering with their work. Cassian would have known what to say in this moment. But Nerida had no idea.

Luckily, she didn't have to say anything.

"There she is," Nurmi said.

Nerida looked west toward where the captain was pointing. Venni and the soldier she had partnered with had just appeared over a low hill and were sprinting toward the camp. Venni's eyes were wide, and her hair, usually pulled back into a tight knot appropriate for lab work, flew wild around her face.

Nerida cursed the suns for rendering their MindLinks useless this time of day and joined the others already running toward Venni. When they reached her, she fell to her knees in the grass, gasping for breath.

"We found something, Sir," the soldier told Nurmi. His skin was in decidedly better shape than Venni's. Matching her pace had probably felt less strenuous than a daily physical training run, and Nerida was grateful he had stuck with her colleague. Her *friend*.

Venni sucked in a giant breath and looked up at Nerida. "We found the man from last night."

His body lay in a shallow depression, half hidden in the tall grass a kilometer to the west. Nurmi and the three soldiers he'd brought hung back, but Nerida and Venni stepped carefully toward the dead man. He had been reduced to skin and bone, his face eerily skeletal. Where the sleeve had been torn from his coveralls, the veins and muscle fibers of his arm lay like cords and string beneath desiccated flesh.

"This can't be who we saw last night," Nerida said, though she knew that it was. "Decomp doesn't work that fast."

"It's him," Nurmi said.

They all stared at the body in silence for a long, uneasy moment.

Then Venni said, "Samples?"

Nerida nodded.

Venni took a sampling kit from her pack and activated the bio scanner. "Human. There's a biometrics tag in his arm, but it's damaged. Unreadable. Time of death approximately"—she glanced at Nerida and Nurmi, brow furrowed, then looked back at the scanner—"thirteen days."

Thirteen days. Not possible. And yet... Nerida's head swam. They had seen him alive last night, but something had accelerated the rate of decomposition. Certainly not the climate; the planet's temperature and humidity weren't conducive to breaking a body down that fast. Which left one obvious possibility: microbes. Potentially very dangerous ones.

"Stop!" Nerida shouted.

Venni jerked back from the body and stared at her. The swab she swept inside the man's mouth was pinched between her fingers.

"Suit up," Nerida told her. "Full protection. The rest of you"—she gestured at Nurmi and his men—"back off. Ten meters at least."

"Biohazard?" Nurmi asked, already backing away from the depression.

"Probably not," Nerida lied, "but let's be smart." She pulled her PPE kit out of her pack and tore open the sterile wrap.

"Something's happening!" One of the soldiers gestured with his rifle toward the body.

Nerida whirled. She saw Venni first, saw her scrambling backwards up out of the depression. Saw the whites of Venni's eyes as she, too, stared at the man in horror.

Then she saw the body.

It was...moving. Collapsing in on itself. Withering to dust with a sound like dry leaves. In seconds, all that was left was a Synthtex shroud and two shriveled eyes sunken in a grinning, yellowed skull.

"Drekking hell," said Captain Nurmi.

Nerida turned to him. "We leave. All of us. Now."

Nurmi circled his hand in the air and barked an order. The soldiers seemed all too happy to move out, but Nurmi hung back, standing protectively over Nerida as she zipped her pack and hoisted it onto her shoulder.

"We've got to get off this planet," she said.

"Agreed," Nurmi said. "I'll contact Turmeric as soon as we get back to camp and request mission abort."

Nerida nodded. She turned back toward the depression, toward where she thought Venni was gathering up her pack, but Venni was gone.

"Where did she go?" Nurmi growled.

A dark panic began to rise in Nerida's chest. She fought it down as, for the second time that day, she scanned the distance for her missing friend.

"There!" Nerida began to run.

"Wait! She's going the wrong direction!" Nurmi shouted.

But Nerida was already closing the distance, sprinting across the field, calling Venni's name.

Venni didn't respond. But she had slowed considerably, and her path was now cutting an uneven zigzag through the high grass.

Nerida caught up to Venni, grabbed her elbow, and spun her around. "Where are you going?"

Venni's skin was flushed, her breathing jagged. At the sight of her blank expression, Nerida released her and staggered back.

"Where are you going?" she asked again. This time her voice was a choked whisper.

"Home," Venni said.

"Yes, that's right. We're all going home." Nerida's tone was that of an adult speaking to a child. "When we get back to camp, Captain Nurmi is going to contact Turmeric and request—"

"Nerida?" Venni's eyes darted around as though she had suddenly gone blind.

"I'm right here, Venni." Nerida backed away, a hard lump forming in the back of her throat.

"Nerida, I don't feel well."

Nerida stared through the window into the lab's isolation chamber. The high, flatline monotone from Venni's biometrics monitor signaled the worst. Nerida tapped the pad on the wall to switch it off, but the tone still rang in her ears, a phantom sound she thought might never stop.

Venni was dead.

Three hours was all it took. Three hours since Venni touched that corpse. Three hours to become a corpse herself.

Nerida looked at her friend's colorless face, at the half-closed eyes staring at the chamber's ceiling. Running a hand across her forehead, Nerida wondered for the thousandth time why she wasn't symptomatic. Would she be? Venni's infection had been nearly instantaneous—which might be because Venni had touched the corpse. It was possible that by the time Nerida caught up to her in that field and touched her arm, Venni's pathogenic load wasn't high enough to infect her.

Or maybe Nerida was thinking about this all wrong. Making connections that didn't exist. Her own biometrics were still clean, but that didn't mean some microbe still too insignificant for the scanner to detect wasn't incubating in her blood and tissues.

In *all* their blood and tissues.

Then again, maybe Venni had had some biological or genetic vulnerability, an immunodeficiency that made her susceptible to accelerated disease progression. Maybe the rest of them would be safe.

Nerida wanted to believe that, but she couldn't. There was something darker happening on this planet.

EEtu emerged from the lab across the hall. For a moment, she stood at the window beside Nerida, both gazing at Venni in somber silence. Then EEtu said, "Turmeric denied Captain Nurmi's request to abort the mission."

"How'd he take it?"

"He didn't seem happy, but he's a soldier. He has his orders, and he's obviously enforcing them. He made that clear to the troops guarding the transpods: *Nobody leaves.*"

Nerida was too numb to respond. She'd expected that. The corporation they worked for, they *risked their lives for*, was holding their heads underwater. Turmeric knew something it wasn't telling them. Whatever it was, Nerida hoped she'd survive long enough to figure it out. That was the only way she'd be allowed to jump home.

"I'll take care of the paperwork," EEtu said. "Get some sleep."

"Tell me when you're done. I'll file the report with Turmeric and..." Nerida swallowed. "And notify Venni's next of kin."

⋒

"Nerida!"

Rotha's voice pulled Nerida from an uneasy sleep. She lifted her head from her pillow, not entirely certain she hadn't dreamed it.

"Nerida! Venni's alive!"

"What?" Adrenaline spiked her blood. She swung her legs over the side of her cot and reached for her coveralls. Two thoughts ricocheted in her mind: *Rotha is having a psychotic break and this whole frapping planet is worse than a nightmare.*

She bolted from her quarters and, in the starlit darkness, saw Rotha, EEtu, and Captain Nurmi running toward the lab. As she sprinted to catch up, she saw the two soldiers who had been assigned to night-watch outside the door.

One gave a tactical hand signal, pointing toward the Lander. "She broke out of the isolation chamber, Sir. Crashed right through the glass and went that way. Gave Jones here quite a scare."

The other soldier was doubled over, hands on his knees, breathing hard. He looked like he'd seen a ghost. Or worse.

Nerida peered through the lab door. Shattered glass littered the hallway outside the isolation chamber. Her pulse pounded in her ears. This was no prank, no psychotic break. In less than a day, she'd seen one body turn to dust in mere seconds and evidence that another had risen from the dead.

She glanced around at the others and realized all eyes were on her. Even the captain's.

"What the drek is going on here, Lab Chief?" Nurmi growled.

Nerida inhaled deeply, exhaled slowly. Then she spoke. "Here's what I think. That man we saw in the field last night had already died once when he came to warn us. Hours after that, he fully decomposed. That could be the state Venni's in now. Something kills the body, or rather takes it into a deep, deathlike stasis, and then temporarily reanimates it."

"Like what?" asked Rotha.

At the same time, Nurmi said, "Why?"

"A parasite, a fungus, a virus? Could be anything. Could be an organism we've not yet encountered or classified. Generally, a pathogen's motivation is proliferation."

"So, like, it wants to infect us?" Jones's voice waivered. "It makes zombies to wander around and get us sick?"

"That's one guess," Nerida said. She resisted the urge to rest a comforting hand on the soldier's shoulder. For the first time, she realized how young he was—probably fresh out of training when he signed on with Turmeric. "But think about it. If the pathogen wanted her to infect us, then Venni wouldn't have moved away from us and into the Lander. Right?"

Jones seemed to think about this for a moment. He nodded.

"Okay. So." Nerida looked at the others, all still waiting for her to tell them what to do. "We suit up. Hazard gear as a top-level precaution. Then we go see what this thing wants."

☒

They found Venni two levels down, deep inside the belly of the Lander. She stood facing the mouth of a tunnel, a black silhouette haloed by a shimmering blue glow.

"The Proten farm," Captain Nurmi said, his voice crackling through Nerida's helmet comm.

Nerida spread her arms wide. The others obediently halted.

"Why there?" EEtu whispered.

"Maybe she's attracted to the Protens' light," Nurmi said.

"Or their energy," Rotha said.

Nerida suppressed a shiver. She suspected Rotha was correct. But the implication that whatever was controlling Venni's body had taken an interest in their energy source was concerning, and without the farm's protective barrier in place, the Servitor would be on high alert.

Venni began to walk farther into the tunnel. Her steps were an uneven lurch and stagger, as though she were just learning to walk. Nerida signaled the others to follow quietly and maintain their current distance.

Venni led them into the main chamber. It was illuminated by the cerulean glow of Proten crystals, sharper than glass and growing inward from every surface. The effect was that Venni had entered an enormous geode.

The chamber was as beautiful as it was deadly.

The Servitor emerged from a second passage and halted, monitoring them. Passively standing by. Waiting.

"Drekking hell," Jones whispered.

"Be calm," Nerida said. "It won't do anything unless it thinks we're a threat to the Tech. And we're not a threat to the Tech. We're just observing. Okay?"

Jones gave a quick nod, and Nerida heard his jagged breathing slow.

Suddenly, a loud, metallic groan echoed down the corridor, the walls shuddering in its wake. The Servitor turned in the noise's direction, its optic scanner shifting from blue to red in an instant. A moment later, it crawled down the corridor and disappeared to investigate.

"What the hell was that?" Jones said.

"Not sure I want to know," Rotha said.

"Something outside?" EEtu asked.

"Let's get Venni and get the drek back to the others," Nerida said.

Without warning, Venni threw herself at the Protens, falling to all fours as though she were dying of thirst and the crystals were water.

"Venni! No!" EEtu dashed toward her.

"Stop!" Nerida shouted.

"She's hurting herself!" EEtu, who had forgotten that Venni was no longer Venni, tried desperately to pull her friend back to her feet.

Now Nurmi was shouting at EEtu to get back. So was Rotha. But Nerida could barely hear them. She could only stare at the blood oozing from the fresh cuts in Venni's hands and knees.

Blood that was still fresh and red.

Blood that meant Venni's heart was still beating.

Nerida's own blood ran cold. Had she been wrong to think Venni wasn't alive anymore? Wrong to think of her as some mindless host to an unknown pathogen—a zombie, as Jones had put it?

Panic seized her. The shouts of the others grew loud again as she forced herself to focus. "Quiet!" she barked.

To her surprise, the chamber fell silent. And to her horror, even Venni's vacant eyes turned toward her.

"Venni," Nerida pleaded, "if you're still with us, if you're still in there, please..." She trailed off. Please what?

EEtu backed away, her thick-soled boots teetering on sharp crystals with every step. She seemed to have recovered her senses, remembering that Venni was no longer *Venni*. She was different now. An unknown entity. A thing to be handled with caution.

Then Venni, too, stood. In a moment that seemed to freeze in Nerida's brain, Venni turned to face her. With a hollow expression, she stared at Nerida. Then a skeletal grin split her face. Holding her arms out wide, Venni fell backward.

She lay on the ground, smiling into an imaginary sky. Her limbs twitched. A Proten shard jutted from the center of her chest, and her blood, so much blood, pumped out to the slowing beat of her dying heart.

"What the drek?"

"Why did she do that?"

"Holy hell!"

Exclamations of shock mixed with screams echoed in Nerida's ears. She wasn't sure which had come from her. She wasn't even sure what she had just witnessed. Her brain refused to make sense of it. The man in the field had retained enough presence of mind to warn them. Had Venni retained enough of her own sense to understand that she was infected? That she was a danger to them? Had she killed herself to save the team?

Before Nerida could untangle her thoughts, yet another horror unfolded.

Venni sat up.

She looked down at the Proten shard in her chest and pulled it out. Tearing open the neckline of her coveralls, she revealed the wound, a jagged, bloody hole to the right of her sternum.

Dumbstruck, Nerida watched as Venni's skin pulled itself over the wound.

In seconds, the skin fused itself into a scar. Seconds after that, the scar, too, was gone.

Venni looked up, her eyes clear. "What happened?"

EEtu let out a choked sob. "Are you...are you...?"

Venni shrugged. "I'm fine."

"You were dead," Rotha said. "Twice."

She stared at him as though he'd spoken another language.

"What do you remember?" Nerida asked. She was desperate to believe this was her friend, fully restored. But the scientist in her was skeptical. First, she had witnessed impossibly fast decomposition. Then, what appeared to be resurrection. Now, impossibly fast regeneration. Could this be yet another phase or a different manifestation of the infection? Gods. What if the pathogen was intelligent? What if it was learning?

Venni furrowed her brow. "I remember the body in the field. I examined him. And then you and I were walking through the grass, and...and now here I am. How did I get here? Why am I covered in blood?"

"Let's get out of here," Nurmi said.

"That would be great," said Venni. "I need a change of clothes."

EEtu studied Venni's biometrics. "Normal."

"And the rest of us?" Nerida asked. She, EEtu, Rotha, and Captain Nurmi stood outside the newly assembled isolation pod. Having the Assembler make a new, smaller pod was easier than repairing the chamber Venni had smashed her way out of. Venni had agreed to be quarantined inside it, though she seemed simultaneously annoyed and agreeable. Exactly like she would have been before any of this had happened.

"We're all normal," EEtu replied.

"We can't deny that exposing Venni's blood to Protens seems to have reversed the effects of her infection," Rotha said.

"You two are geologists," Nerida said. "Is there any precedent for something like this?"

Rotha rubbed his forehead. "Back on Ancient Earth, some humans believed crystals had healing powers and could aid in their spiritual journeys, but they were laughed at. There was no science behind their claims."

"Nothing more recent? Nothing to do with Protens?"

Rotha shook his head.

Venni knocked on the inside of the pod's glass.

Nerida tapped the control pad beside the door to activate the intercom. "You doing okay in there?"

Venni rolled her eyes. "I told you, I'm fine. I've been in here five hours already. My biometrics are clear. I've recited today's date and all your names, species, and home worlds. You want me to tell you the story of how Malcolm Orion turned the Mass-O back on, too, to prove I'm fine? When are you going to let me out?"

The other three scientists exchanged glances, and Nerida said, "Can you hang on a little longer?"

Venni turned away and threw up her hands in exaggerated exasperation. The gesture was so characteristically Venni that despite her skepticism, Nerida smiled. Maybe Venni really had returned to normal. Maybe everything really was going to be okay.

Then Venni began to quake. It started with her arms and legs, like she had just climbed out of a pool and was shaking water from her body. But when she turned to face them, Nerida knew her friend would never leave the isolation pod alive.

"Venni," she whispered. She pressed her hands against the glass as EEtu and Rotha backed away.

Blood spurted from Venni's terrified eyes, from her nose and ears. She opened her mouth, and blood geysered forth, splattering the glass that separated them and spilling down her chin onto the front of her gray coveralls. Convulsing, she collapsed onto the floor. Her skin became leathery, dark, shrinking in toward her skeleton. Then it flaked away from her bones.

"Venni!" Nerida screamed. This rapid decomp was similar to what happened to the man in the field. No, not similar. Nerida stared at the pile of bones and red-stained cloth where Venni had just lain, and then at the pool of blood spreading out beneath it. There had been no blood with the man in the field. None at all. But Venni's blood was...gods, there was so much of it. It was as if her body could no longer contain it. As if it broke out of her, popping her body like a blister.

As Nerida watched, Venni's blood began to move. Red rivulets snaked out in all directions, like vines crawling up a trellis. Like fingers feeling their way across the floor, up the walls, across the ceiling.

Venni's blood was searching. Searching for a way out.

At last, Nerida backed away from the glass. "Nurmi!" she screamed. "Burn it down! Burn this drekking pod to the ground!"

ᚹ

"You can't expect us to stay here," Nerida said.

Loran Ekamoniki, Turmeric's Mission Chief and, as such, Nerida's boss, tapped a pen against his chin.

Nerida started in disbelief at his smug expression on her screen. "Did you not read my report? There's a pathogen here, one we're ages away from understanding. Blacklist Kepler-3202c immediately. Find another location for the people of Soto. They cannot come here. Do you understand me? No one can."

The pen-tapping stopped. "Biometrics?"

Nerida bit her lip to keep from screaming. "The rest of us are clear, Sir. But that means nothing. This infection acts fast. Within minutes. And as you read in my report, the pathogen's exposure to Protens caused it to mutate. I swear, it looked like Venni's blood was *sentient*. Most pathogens find some way to proliferate—air, water, body fluids. But this one isn't just blood-borne. I think it uses blood as a vehicle to actively seek out new hosts."

Loran set his pen on his desk and steepled his fingers. "Shelter in place and continue to monitor biometrics."

"What? Sir! If you don't authorize our return, we'll all die."

"We need more data on this pathogen, Nerida. Turmeric will not be responsible for starting a pandemic. We've given the captain orders to keep the team in place."

"Let us jump back to Helios Nexus. We can quarantine there."

"Not going to happen."

Nerida slumped back in her chair. Loran was right. Even if she could somehow convince Nurmi to let them go, that would be reckless. Until they had a complete understanding of this thing—not only the symptoms it caused, but also preventions and treatments—leaving Kepler-3202c was irresponsible. She studied Loran's face. There was still something he wasn't telling her.

"Alpha Team warned you about this, didn't they?" she said.

Loran's expression was blank.

"You sent us into a trap," Nerida pressed. "Why? What about Soto?"

"We've already made other arrangements. Their ark-ships have been rerouted to Verba-345k."

Nerida's hand clenched into fists. "So the Soto mission was a ruse. This was never a habitability study, was it?"

A muscle in Loran's jaw twitched.

"Then why did you send us here?" Nerida pressed.

"That's classified."

"Be honest with me, Chief. Are we ever coming home?"

He seemed to weigh his options: keep silent, lie, or do as she asked and tell the truth. After a moment, he shifted in his seat. "We hope to bring you home, Nerida. Keep me apprised."

His avatar dissolved, and Nerida was left in the dark. Left to wonder if she'd imagined the slight emphasis he'd placed on the word *you*.

Rotha was the next to become infected.

The three scientists, in full hazard suits, had been bio-bagging the charred debris of Venni's isolation pod while sifting for any organic material they could put under a microscope—messy, methodical work—when EEtu sat back on her heels.

"Where's Rotha?" she said.

Nerida glanced around. Not far off, Nurmi spoke with several of his soldiers. Another group of soldiers squatted on low camp stools, cleaning their pistols. Two more patrolled the camp's perimeter, cradling the plasma rifles slung over their shoulders.

"I don't see him," Nerida replied.

Jones ran toward them, then stopped at the caution tape strung up around the debris. He waved his arms at EEtu.

"Your husband! He just wandered into the Lander! I asked where he was going, but he walked past me like I wasn't even there. His eyes looked...bad."

Nerida stood, commanding her limbs to function despite the leaden dread in her chest. "It's happening again."

"No!" EEtu said. "Rotha's okay. He was just here. He's fine. He's fine."

"I hope you're right," Nerida said, though she knew that Rotha wasn't fine.

How had he gotten infected? He was wearing a hazard suit, same as them. Unless...drek. Could this pathogen permeate the suits' material? Only a couple hours ago, two soldiers swept flamethrowers over Venni's isolation pod. Nerida recalled how the snaking tendrils of Venni's blood had popped and sizzled, turning into a fine red mist. A fine red mist that rose with the smoke and ash and dissipated into the air.

No. *No, no, no.* Nerida was the one who'd commanded that the pod be incinerated. Had she turned a blood-borne pathogen into an airborne one?

Just then, the two soldiers on patrol swung their rifles toward the tree line.

"What the glap is *that*?" one of them shouted.

"A drekking *monster*!" yelled the other. "Captain Nurmi! All hands *now*!"

The soldiers fired, their plasma rifles slamming a succession of percussive bursts through the air.

EEtu screamed. Nerida cursed. She couldn't see what the soldiers were shooting at, and she didn't want to. "Jones!" she shouted. "With us!"

"Yes, Ma'am!"

The three of them sprinted into the Lander.

What the hell was going on? What monster were the soldiers shooting at? Nerida fought the urge to press her hands to her ears, even as the sound of gunfire faded behind them. She ran harder, faster, legs and lungs burning as she wound through the Lander's passageways, then down toward the Proten farm. When they rounded the last corner, they skidded to a halt.

Rotha stood at the opening to the chamber, facing away. He had stripped off his hazard suit and peeled his coveralls down to his waist. He was backlit by the Protens' crystalline blue glow, and before him, blocking his way, was the Servitor.

The Servitor towered over him, its thin, whiplike tentacles plucking at the air as though it were tasting Rotha's intent. To Nerida, the Servitor's intent was clear: It had decided their visits to the Proten farm were suspicious. It had decided it would deny them entry. It had decided this standoff was the last peaceful warning anyone who tried to enter the chamber would get.

"Rotha!" EEtu screamed. "Back away. The Servitor thinks you're a threat!"

It was as if EEtu hadn't spoken at all. Instead of heeding his wife's warning, Rotha crouched like a predator preparing to leap.

"No, Rotha!" Nerida shouted.

Slowly, Rotha turned to look over his shoulder. His eyes were wide and wild, red-rimmed and hungry. So hungry. He peeled his lips away from his teeth and growled as he swung his head back toward the Servitor.

Then he lunged toward the Protens, weaving between the twisted mass of the Servitor's thicker tentacles as its thinner ones whipped the air around him. Just before the Servitor clamped one cabled appendage around his ankle, Rotha clawed at the blue crystals that grew like teeth around the edge of the chamber's doorway.

Then Rotha's jaw opened wide, and, ferociously, he bit the crystals.

The Servitor swung Rotha high into the air. For a moment, it held him there, suspended, dangling. A high-pitched whine came from his throat as blood and broken teeth fell from his mouth. Then the Servitor slammed him to the ground.

EEtu screamed and tried to run to her husband's aid, but Nerida held her back. Rotha groaned and tried to push himself up, but his body and mind were too broken. He rolled onto his side, coughing blood. And then...

Rotha's bare chest and arms began to bubble and blister. Fist-sized pustules rose on every centimeter of exposed skin, turning a phosphorescent green before breaking open. Glowing sludge that smelled like rancid meat oozed from every wound. And from every wound, a shard of green crystal jutted forth.

EEtu struggled against Nerida's grip, crying her husband's name.

Nerida shook EEtu's shoulders. "There's nothing we can do for him. Let's go!"

But go where? There was nowhere to go. Except...

"Transpods!" Nerida shouted. "Now!"

Nerida didn't care that Loran had denied them access to jump, or that Nurmi's soldiers might still try to enforce that order. They were leaving. The transpods, like the Servitors, operated on intent. Right now, Nerida's only intent, pandemic risk be damned, was to get the hell off this planet. She grabbed EEtu's arm and turned back the way they had come. Over her shoulder, she shouted, "Jones! Come on!"

But Jones was kneeling on the ground, clawing the Proten out of his pulse rifle. Nerida watched, horrified, as he bit down on the blue crystal. Broke his teeth on it. Stared at it as though it were a puzzle to be solved. Tore open the front of his uniform and plunged it into his chest.

His flesh, now beginning to roil with putrid pustules, now sprouting green crystalline shards, parted easily. Then it closed around the Proten like a hungry mouth.

Nerida backed away, arms outstretched to keep EEtu behind her. But EEtu was watching also, as Jones crawled to Rotha and fell like a starving animal on the green crystals sprouting from his skin.

"He's eating Rotha!" EEtu's voice was a high-pitched shriek. "Eating him alive!"

Nerida froze. The horror ebbed away from her brain, leaving a numb fascination. The pathogen, she realized, had gotten a taste of Protens. Protens made it stronger, and it wanted to be stronger still. It would never stop wanting to be stronger. Its desire to proliferate was so great that it had taught itself how to synthesize Proten-like crystals from the bodies of its infected. *What we have here on Kepler-3202c is a self-perpetuating organism that can, in essence, become its own food source*, she thought, already composing her report to Turmeric.

Suddenly, Jones's body began to...*melt*. So did Rotha's. In seconds, the two bodies fused together into one nightmarish mass of limbs, torn cloth, hair, eyes, glowing green pus, and broken teeth.

It stood.

Nerida's brain snapped back to the present. "Transpods," she said, her voice hoarse.

The two women sprinted back through the Lander's passageways, back toward Level I. But just before the final turn toward the transpod bay, they were forced to halt.

Blocking their way was another abomination that defied comprehension. Another fused conglomeration of meat and bone, this one at least four meters tall.

A monster.

Nerida's eyes juddered across the thing's blistered, pulsing skin, slicked by infectious pus and pierced from the inside by glowing green crystals. Here and there, misshapen in the obscene mass of flesh, were faces she recognized and faces she didn't.

Captain Nurmi.

His soldiers.

The missing members of Alpha Team.

Nerida didn't bother counting. They were all here. All part of this gruesome leviathan that wanted only to feed, to grow, to add more parts to its sickening whole.

The monster advanced, at times slithering, at times propelling itself with legs and arms.

A wet wheezing sound came from behind Nerida. She lunged to the side, pulling EEtu with her. They flattened themselves against the passageway, both fighting to hold their breath as Rotha-Jones limped toward the monster—a wounded child approaching its mother for comfort. The two creatures reached for one another, their many mouths opening and closing. Searching. Hungering. Then the larger thing absorbed the smaller.

Nerida's eyes darted toward the tunnel to the transpod bay. They had to get past the monster before it noticed them. Before it came for them.

The monster began to shift as though it were reorganizing itself, making room for Rotha-Jones. From inside came the clack of bones, the pop of joints, the rubbery snap of tendons and ligaments, the soft sucking sounds of mingling fluids.

"Let's go," whispered Nerida. She ran around the undulating thing, certain EEtu was right behind her. But when she reached the tunnel, she paused to look back.

EEtu stared hungry-eyed at the thing. The thing's many eyes, equally hungry, stared back.

Nerida bit back a scream. Chest heaving, she watched Eetu peel off her hazard suit, watched as the first green pustules broke out on her face and arms. Watched as Eetu embraced the monster, her teeth closing around a green, protruding shard.

It was over. Nerida was the lone survivor. Why wasn't she sick yet? Why did she feel nothing but terror and revulsion and the will to live?

Now wasn't the time for questions. Now was the time to escape. To survive. She turned and sprinted toward the transpods. Jumping away was her only hope, but she wasn't certain she could. One had to have a clear mind to initiate a jump, and Nerida's thinking had never been more frenzied.

A wet, sucking sound echoed through the tunnel behind her. *Drek.* It had followed her rather than descending toward the Proten farm. Sweat blurring her vision, she ran full speed to a transpod and launched herself into it.

It closed around her, a protective shell that would cocoon her until she jumped away...if she *could* jump away. She stared through the transpod's semitransparent membrane. The monster hadn't emerged into the bay yet, but the Servitor had. It scuttled out of the shadows, its whip-tentacles wafting gracefully through the air like seaweed. It watched and waited.

Hope bloomed in Nerida's chest. Maybe she wasn't what the monster was after. Maybe it sensed the Servitor's Protens. Maybe if the two entities battled, the Servitor would win.

Or at least buy her some time.

She inhaled, exhaled, closed her eyes, and forced herself to focus. Then she projected her intention to the transpod.

JUMP DENIED.

She gritted her teeth. Her heart beat faster—the opposite of what she needed to happen.

And then...she felt a sudden, strange pull to stay.

Her thoughts grew slow and muddled. She fought to calm herself. No. She wasn't sick. She wasn't! She closed her eyes again and pictured Micaro, the first planet she had ever jumped to, on a vacation with her family.

JUMP DENIED.

Drekking hell. It wasn't working.

Suddenly, her MindLink flickered to life. Loran Ekamoniki's face materialized before her.

"Nerida! I'm so pleased to see you've survived. How many of you are left?"

"I'm the last," she gasped.

"Tell me what you saw," he said, his voice calm. "Tell me what the DeGen pathogen did to the others."

"DeGen? What the hell does that mean?"

"Degenerative affliction."

"You've already named it?"

"The others, Nerida?"

"Monster," she managed to choke out. She was sweating now, yet her skin felt clammy and cold. Her body tingled as though it were covered in ants. "The most terrifying thing I've ever seen. They're all one giant monster. A monster that eats Protens."

Loran smiled. "That's promising. You've done well, Nerida. Very well."

"What are you talking about?" Her tongue felt twice its regular size.

"You're special, Nerida. A carrier. We had a vague idea from Team Alpha that we were dealing with something unprecedented on Kepler-3202c, but they all went dark before we found out exactly what. We needed you there to observe how this pathogen evolved. Specifically, what it would do to non-carriers."

"I don't understand."

"We've long known from your very first pre-mission medical exam that your blood is teeming with natural universal antibodies. You're impervious to most if not all infections. When you're exposed to viruses and bacteria, you carry them in your body for a short time, but then your immune system successfully fights them off."

Nerida looked down at her hand. It was shaking. A small, green, crystalline boil blossomed across her knuckles, but as she watched, it faded, leaving the skin once again unblemished. She stared. The others were covered head to toe in these boils almost instantly. But Nerida's body was fighting them off. Healing before her eyes.

"What happens now?" she asked.

"Now you jump home to Nexus City."

"And cause a pandemic? You said—"

"We've taken precautions. We need to move fast, though, before your body destroys what's left of the live pathogen in your blood."

Realization dawned in Nerida's fevered mind. "You want this pathogen. You think you can control it. Cultivate it. Use it as a weapon. Let me assure you, Loran, you can't. No one can! This disease is absolutely beyond anyone's ability to—"

Through the transpod's membrane, Nerida saw the monster emerge from the tunnel. Saw the Servitor take up a defensive stance.

"Jump," Loran told her. "Do it now!"

Nerida buried her face in her hands. She should abort the jump. Step out of the transpod and let the monster end her. She had just been told she carried in her blood what was potentially the most dangerous biological weapon any sentient being could possibly imagine and that Turmeric Corporation, her employer, intended to harness it for use against living beings.

Instantaneous genocide available to the highest bidder.

Abort the jump. That's what she should do.

But all around her, the transpod began to hum. The gentle vibrations calmed her body and mind. She felt sleepy.

"Think of your family, Nerida. Your home. Think of your work. You're a very important scientist. You have so many good things left to do for Turmeric. For the universe."

She thought of those things. She tried not to. She knew what Loran was doing, and she'd never tried harder at anything in her life than not thinking about home.

"Now jump," said Loran.

The transpod's low hum and soft, pulsing lights were now accompanied by flowing blue images. Herself. Space. Stars. Galaxies. She lost herself in the sensation of floating. Her molecules disassembled, the energy of her atoms converting into code. The map of her DNA spiraling around a Proten-hungry pathogen projected instantly into the Masson Zero.

REUNION ON DEVOLVER

Wyeth Ridgway

THE FJC PETERSON, 482 HD

WHOOSH.

The sound nudged Vella Janx awake. He blinked and let his vision come into focus. Beside his sleep capsule stood 9bot, his droid, waiting.

Still in a sleep-fog, Janx sat up, and mumbled, "How long?"

9bot swiveled its saucer-like head to its master. "Three months, sixteen days, four hours."

Janx swung his legs from the capsule and levered himself upright. *That's time in my life I'll never get back.*

The aroma of hot tea brightened his mood. 9bot offered a mug, a curl of steam bringing the pleasant fragrance.

Janx took the mug and cupped it in his lower left hand, the one missing two fingers, then in both of his lower hands to absorb the fresh brew's warmth. "Thanks." He added a nod of appreciation to acknowledge 9bot's helicas of faithful service.

"Just doing my job, boss." The droid wiggled the two feather-like antennae along the back rim of its head.

Janx planted both feet on the floor. Through the carpet he felt the low hum of the starship, the muted drone signaling the engines were in orbit-idle, meaning the FJC Peterson had arrived at their destination. Still a bit groggy, he shuffled to the porthole of the well-appointed executive stateroom, a luxury he treated himself to, and gazed upon the huge, bright planet below them. Sipping the tea, he let thoughts coalesce.

9bot must have read his concern and reaffirmed what Janx already knew.

"Devolver. In the Prolo-14 system. With only one significant city, also named Devolver. Total population, approximately thirty-three thousand. 74 percent Human, 16 percent Mirith, 10 percent other—"

The reason for Janx's visit to this neglected, faraway planet sharpened into one detail: *Sinfed Reyu.*

The name caused self-doubt to wriggle down Janx's spine.

Self-doubt? Or was it fear?

As a sixth generation Halloran cybernetic, Janx had been bioengineered to be a relentless killer. Ruthless. Fearless. He had also been developed with a conscience, that with experience, would hone his tradecraft and efficiency. Make him a better hitman, ironically. However, with every assignment and every close call, he became more appreciative of his mortality and that for all his skill, survival was ultimately a roll-of-the-dice against the law of averages.

Janx clenched his jaw and tamped down his misgivings. To strike down prey with lethal fury was his calling, his only reason for being.

Time to get ready for work. He handed the mug back to 9bot and proceeded to the center of the stateroom. Still in hypersleep garments, he began his routine of calisthenics, spreading his legs into a combat stance, then wind-milling his four arms to the left and right. He set his hands on the floor to balance himself in a head stand, then began a sequence of one-arm push-ups, deftly swapping arms until his shoulders felt the burn.

Throughout the exercise, his mind kept circling back to Reyu.

He's hiding on Devolver, the Taylean agent admitted after a beat-down to get him talking.

Impossible! Janx had killed Reyu eight helicas ago and collected a substantial bounty for the hit. Whacking Reyu had been no easy feat because of his alien DNA—the ancient Ja'din warrior had survived countless battles and ambushes. Revered by some, loathed by others, he had nevertheless been hailed as one of the greatest warriors across the cosmos—emphasis on *had*.

Vanquishing The Merge's most capable enforcer had been the crowning achievement in Janx's career and elevated him to elite status among the brotherhood of assassins in the Null Agent Network.

Then came the hushed rumors, announcing that Reyu was indeed alive. If word of this reached the Null Agent Network, their message to Janx would be swift and concise: *We want our credits back.*

This would put Janx in the humiliating position of not only paying back what he had already spent, but watching his reputation plummet in the Network.

He couldn't let that happen.

He balanced on his four arms, then sprung backwards onto his feet. He stood a moment, chest heaving, thinking.

As he followed Reyu's trail across the galaxy, to hide his identity, Janx jumped from anonymous skin to anonymous skin and assumed aliases along the way. He'd learned that Reyu was using Cepp-D, no doubt to cope with lingering psychological fallout from what Janx had done to him. This pleased Janx, but regardless of the pleasure he reveled in knowing he reduced the universe's greatest warrior to a reclusive junkie, Reyu was still alive. But now that he had Reyu cornered on Devolver, Janx opted for his own skin, compromising surprise for the dexterity and speed of his original body. Regardless of how withdrawn Reyu had become on this planet, Janx would need every millisecond of reaction time to keep the odds in his favor.

9bot arranged Janx's garments on a nearby table. Janx got dressed and ruffled the cloak of armored cloth around his shoulders to drape his upper arms. He pulled the cloak's hood over his headdress and arranged his breathing tendrils to fall alongside his throat and over the front of his chest.

9bot led him to the cargo bay. The threshold between the executive suite quarters and the common area was marked by a line of rust and chipped paint. Frayed cables had been spliced together with adhesives. Ceiling panels hung crooked. The floor grates were likewise mismatched.

When Janx continued through the cargo bodega, he winced at the sour odor, heavy with the smell of perspiration and squalor wafting from the dozens of shipping containers crammed together, repurposed as berths and teeming with passengers traveling in steerage. He adjusted the filter dial on his faceplate. "Should've warned me about the stink."

"What stink?" The droid shook its antennae. "Oh, that. Didn't think it would bother you."

Janx waved away his concern. At the far end of the bodega, they proceeded down a ramp to the docking bay. Looking somewhat pristine compared to the dilapidated starship, a sleek and beetle-like Tugurt-class dropship rested on the aft docking platform.

9bot pointed to a very tall woman in a blue officer's uniform. "The deckmaster."

She was giving orders to the crew as they in turn herded passengers toward the dropship. When Janx approached the deckmaster, she read the scanner in her hand and acknowledged him with a tight smile. "My apologies, Sir, but we have no executive modules for your comfort. If you wish to make this drop, the only accommodations we have are in third-class."

"Fine," Janx replied. He and 9bot joined the ragged line filing into the dropship. Once onboard, the passengers jostled against one another as they searched for open seats, so preoccupied that they were oblivious to the warrior among them.

The air grew sharp and ripe. Janx again adjusted his mask filter. *Don't these people bathe?*

Luggage was jammed haphazardly into the overhead bins and a suitcase tumbled free. A hefty man wearing arm and leg augments backed out of the way and into Janx. "Hey, watch it!"

He did a double-take at the cybernetic's armored ensemble, then sheepishly whipped back around and busied himself with returning the suitcase to the overhead bin.

9bot wiggled its antennae. "This way, boss." It led Janx to the back of the compartment and gestured toward a row of empty seats, then to a ceiling ventilation duct. "Besides the extra leg room, the air is fresher."

A tarp behind the seats separated the passenger compartment from the cargo hold. Janx lifted an edge of the tarp and peeked at what was being transported. Stacks of crates and shipping containers were lashed to the deck, arranged around a large and expensive-looking military shipping pod. Various labels and black and yellow cautionary symbols decorated the pod's drab exterior.

He raised the tarp a bit more for 9bot to see. "Whaddaya think, Niner?"

The droid's optic scanner surveyed the pod. "According to the manifest, it's a Tier 3 Military Spec MatGen. Capable of printing various weapons in moments."

"Various weapons?"

"Both legal and contraband."

One drawback to flying commercial was that they screened for weapons and for now, Janx had only his wits and prowess to defend himself. He rubbed the fingertips of one hand. *Who the hell on Devolver has the credits and connections for this sort of thing?*

He turned his attention to the droid. Part of the reason Janx kept 9bot as a companion was its ability to circumvent sanctioned protocols, by law hardwired into all servant robots. "Do you think you can...?"

"Sorry," the droid answered, "not this level of Merge military-spec hardware."

Janx smoothed the tarp back into place. "Well, when we touch down, we'll need to find something."

Loudspeakers squawked a message to prepare for departure. Janx sank into one of the adjacent seats and buckled in. 9bot extended hooks from its back and fastened them to brackets on the nearby bulkhead.

Somewhere amongst the passengers, an infant human started crying.

Janx shook his head in disbelief. *Who brings a baby to a hellhole like Devolver?*

Janx swung his plasma blade at Reyu, landing two blows in rapid succession.

Reyu moved with feline grace, using the armor plates on his arms to block the attacks. Smoke rose from his damaged wrist guards. In the same motion, Reyu seized Janx and heaved, throwing his much smaller opponent several meters. Janx bounced off the wall.

Reyu pounced and landed on top of Janx. His massive hand engulfed Janx's faceplate with a SMASH! Janx's head pounded against the floor.

Stars blurred Janx's vision, then cleared to reveal Reyu standing over him. A corona of electrical sparks alerted Janx that his helmet had been torn off. Then a sudden burn in his nostrils, his mouth, now his lungs warned Janx that the planet's poisoned air poured into him.

He panicked. I've got thirty seconds, *he thought.*

DEVOLVER

Janx watched a video monitor and followed the descent of the dropship on final approach to the shuttle port. A swampy landscape extended to a murky horizon. There was little to recommend Devolver other than vast deposits of fossil fuels deep underground. Decades of terraforming to make the planet inhabitable—though just barely—had brought about unintended consequences like acid rain and mutations among the indigenous life forms.

The dropship's landing struts extended with a squeal and clunked into place. The ship swung into a gentle glide, then hovered before settling into place with another squeal from the landing gear. Loudspeakers repeated directions as the passengers gathered their belongings and hustled for the exit.

Janx let the crowd thin before stepping out, 9bot at his heels. Reaching the bottom of the boarding ramp, Janx took in the forlorn surroundings. From a leaden sky, rain drizzled across the oily sheen puddled on the tarmac. The outpost of Devolver spread beyond the perimeter of the shuttle port though it was difficult to get a sense of the settlement as a blanket of fog swallowed everything beyond a hundred meters.

Why would Reyu come to this glaphole?

"This way, boss," announced 9bot as it ambled for one of the streets.

Tumbledown buildings emerged from the mist, leaning against one another like misshapen, waterlogged carboard boxes. Janx adjusted his mask filter. Other than the stink of rotting vegetation, the ambiance reminded him of other rim worlds he had the misfortune of visiting.

9bot slowed and pointed to a rusted sign, *Cescar's Pawn Shop*, jutting above a narrow doorway. They entered and found the place filled with miscellaneous electronics, tools, and parts. Behind a counter also buried under random junk, a skinny human woman sat on a tall stool and was occupied dismantling a small device with her mechanical arm augments. An optical enhancer hid her face. The tech seemed somewhat out of date, not surprising, being so far from a Hub planet without a Discovery Lander.

"Cescar?" Janx asked.

The woman shook her head and answered, "Eva."

"Lugar," Janx replied, lying about his true identity. Vella Janx was probably not a name known this far from The Hub, but he had a lot of enemies, and if things went south on Devolver, better to disappear in the confusion. He added, "I need tools."

Putting down what she was working on, Eva's arm augments retracted and tucked themselves underneath her human arms. She rotated her stool to look at him, her eyes distorted by the lenses of the optical enhancer. Only now did she seem to notice Janx was Halloran, and his four real arms oddly mirrored her human form with its two extra android arms. "What do you have in mind?"

From a port in his chest, 9bot projected a hologram between her and Janx.

Eva lifted the optical enhancer to better study the hologram. She appeared about thirty, but an old thirty, like a shoe that had been left too long outside, especially in this soggy climate.

The hologram was a spreadsheet with the logo of the Guild at one upper corner and a listing of available balances. The Guild was a shadowy organization that spanned many star systems, serving as a counterpoint to the bureaucracy of The Merge, for the Guild existed to break the rules. If you needed contraband and had the credits, or the other way around, the Guild could help make the connections. They were not a criminal enterprise as much as an anything-goes, no questions asked marketplace for goods and services. Over the course of his career, Janx had become a loyal and frequent client.

Eva seemed impressed enough by the large balance in the account that she said, "Come with me."

The hologram blinked off.

She slid from her perch and walked in a quick gait, her augmented arms set against her sides like folded wings that gave the appearance she was half-human, half-avian.

She led them down a hallway, the floor beneath them spongy with rot. Janx wiped the slimy film collecting on his visor. They passed a series of doors, opened to reveal rooms littered with heaps of clothing, piles of bottles and jars, tangles of rusted tubing, gutted appliances, all covered in greasy filth.

At one door, Eva pivoted to slide through a gap in a thick plastic tarp. Janx and 9bot followed. The room was airy and brightly lit. And besides looking clean, it smelled clean.

In glass counters situated on either side of the room, several intriguing pieces of black-market tech were on display. Against the back wall sat a MatGen, one of the newer models. It was a long cabinet about one meter tall and three meters wide with a conveyor belt that fed onto an adjacent table.

9bot approached the MatGen, presented the Guild spreadsheet hologram, and established a laser communication bridge to download files. Lights on the MatGen flickered, a mechanism in the cabinet hummed, and after a moment, a Darian Revolver appeared on the conveyor belt to clatter onto the table. Next, a Fission Repulser Grenade, followed by an assortment of different tools and weapons. As each item scrolled from the MatGen, its price was deducted from Janx's Guild account. *Darian Revolver: 1,200 ADU... Fission Repulser Grenade, 625 ADU...*

Janx tallied the items and their costs. He looked back at the door. "No security?"

Eva snorted derisively. "There's no law around here. The civil guard is a joke. If it wasn't for the bribes we pay them, the lazy bastards would starve. Besides—" She motioned to the ceiling.

Janx looked upwards to an inconspicuous metal plate. He flipped his helmet's vision setting and detected the outline of a self-targeting drone, then counted a half-dozen more arranged above them.

"Anyone makes trouble," she said, "ka-blewie."

"Right," Janx replied in admiration. He picked a replicated shooka off the table. It was an uncommon weapon–initially just a handle the size of his forearm, but upon being powered up, it expanded into a short spear topped with a long energy blade. It made a crackling sound as he moved it around, for the blade was alive and seeking blood. He shut it off and ran his thumb along the grip. A fifty-millimeter-long gouge had been replicated into it. Most people made perfect copies of their goods, but this gouge was a reminder against being overconfident, as it had cost him two fingers and very nearly his life. He tucked the weapon into his belt and collected the rest of the items.

"Too bad the MatGen can't replicate Cepp-D," he said offhandedly.

"How much do you need?"

"Large quantities," Janx replied. "Something only your supplier could provide."

Eva stared at him, considering.

Janx eyed 9bot, who picked up on something unspoken, then recited in his voltaic voice, "That information would be billed as miscellaneous services, 5,000 ADU."

Eva raised an eyebrow before she caught herself, and her opaque expression returned. In a bland tone, she offered, "Go downtown to the *Massaria*, it's a nightclub owned by Mirith thugs. They control the shuttle ports. Nothing interesting gets planet-side without their OK."

"Nothing interesting?" Janx asked. "Would that include me?"

Eva shrugged.

"Got it," he said and turned to leave.

Drekking Miriths, just great.

Sinfed Reyu loomed over Janx's sprawled form and his helmet emitted a synthetic voice, "Go home."

Through a smear of black and white stars, Janx looked up at his adversary. Mouth and nose stinging from the caustic air, he groped for a button on his wrist and pressed hard. An electric crackle erupted from underneath him, followed by a globe of white light bursting from a device on his back.

Too late, Reyu retreated a step.

The white globe enveloped both opponents, swelling to a diameter of thirty meters, then dissipating like smoke. The platform became eerily silent.

Reyu remained still, as if paralyzed.

He's blinded, *Janx thought.* I've got fifteen seconds. *He jumped to his feet and tried not to breathe.*

∩I

Vella Janx walked into the Massaria, the largest nightclub in the middle of a row of dive bars and juke joints. It was hours since they had landed, and Devolver was still dull gray, foggy and raining, making Janx wonder if daylight ever came to this planet.

"Welcome patron," purred a comely bot by the door, a simple greeter or a "companion"—Janx couldn't tell. He ignored it and continued towards the bar. When 9bot entered behind him, the greeter bot called to Janx, "Sir, your bot needs to wait outsiiidddeee—" and went suddenly dormant.

9bot retracted one arm, having zapped the greeter with a disabling pulse. 9bot shoved the motionless greeter to the side and took its position by the door. "I got your back, boss."

The club was as Janx expected. Loud and drunken rabble clustered around tables and at the bar, guzzling booze and gambling. Music boomed from a backroom, lights pulsing in rhythm to the tune. The ambiance reminded him of the hedonistic bacchanal on a nebula vacation ship. From one corner, an attractive woman tracked his entry.

Janx elbowed a space against the bar.

"What's your drink?" the barkeep asked, squinting through an optical piece over one eye, his only visible enhancement. Nothing special about the man, clearly a lowborn, maybe even born here.

"I'd like to talk to the owner," Janx said.

The barkeep's eye piece lowered to the pistol on Janx' hip. The barkeep paused as if mulling the Halloran's intentions. He nodded and disappeared through a door behind the bar. Another server caught Janx's attention, asking if he needed a drink, and was waved away.

"You look like you can handle yourself." It was the woman who'd been watching him. She edged closer. "You aren't from around here," she said in a slow and sultry voice. "I'm Nonoquin, but you can call me Nono."

Even in the fleeting light, Janx could tell she had dolled herself up. Likely pimped out by the establishment, but he wasn't sure. There was a sickly, off-putting hue to her skin that only Janx's helmet display picked up, probably from the prolonged use of an enhancement drug.

"Nono, you should take the night off," he said.

"Oh come on." She ran her fingers along one of his arms. "You're just the sort I've been waiting for. You might not have picked up on it yet, but this town is on the brink. One little nudge and…" She pushed an empty glass across the bar, making it tip into a sink full of ice. Pivoting to wedge herself between Janx and the bar, she rose on tiptoes to better display her substantial cleavage.

The barkeep reappeared, accompanied by an oversized goon wearing an alloy flex-metal shirt and clasping a shockrod in one meaty hand.

"Hebbet here will take you downstairs," the barkeep said.

Slyly, Janx reached into his tunic and palmed something.

"The gun," Hebbet growled.

Simultaneously, Janx made a show of leaning past Nono to lay his pistol on the bar. *Thunk.* "Make sure I get this back." With his other hand, he stuck the object from his tunic under the bar. The barkeep and Hebbet remained distracted by the pistol. Nono scooted aside, pouting at being ignored.

Hebbet turned on his heels and headed back to the door. The barkeep lifted a partition in the bar's countertop for Janx to pass through.

The goon led him through a maze of passages, then down stairs to a large security door. Judging by the din of music, Janx concluded they were directly below a stage. Hebbet mouthed something, which Janx couldn't make out through the noise. He gestured for Janx to stand against the wall and when he did, a beam of green light scanned him. The beam flashed red and lingered where it detected weapons on Janx's person. Hebbet pointed to a small empty locker on a shelf of similar lockers. Taking the hint, Janx stashed his shooka and other items as requested.

The goon pressed a code into his wrist compad. The security door opened. Hebbet motioned with his thumb for Janx to proceed on his own.

Janx walked in and passed through a noise-cancelling field. The music also played here, but was muted. The humid air turned dry and warm. He was in a medium-sized room, sketchy-looking patrons scattered about. On the far side sat three Miriths in front of an array of vidscreens broadcasting a hover-bike race. Their huge forms spilled out from their chairs. Ropes of gold chain hung over the tops of high-end armor, the display of wealth advertising them as the owners of the establishment.

Everyone else in the room appeared to be human. At the door behind Janx, a guard wearing battle-scarred armor and a helmet cradled a rifle. Another man lounged on a couch along one wall. He wore no armor but a rifle lay on a low table within easy reach.

As Janx panned the room, the display in his visor pulled up detailed information on everyone. Five were felons with rap sheets in multiple systems. The guy on the couch was wanted for sabotaging a space station.

One of the Miriths turned away from the vidscreens and motioned for Janx to approach. "Vella Janx."

"You're a long way from home," said another Mirith. "Are you hunting or hiding?"

"I'm on vacation," Janx replied dryly.

The third Mirith smirked. "Yeah, right. Devolver is everyone's favorite holiday spot."

Janx's helmet display alerted him that the guard from the door had eased behind him. To the left, the guy on the couch was sitting up, attentive.

"Then enjoy our hospitality," the Mirith said and jokingly offered his drink to Janx.

To the Mirith's surprise, Janx took it. Then the first Mirith hollered as the race began, and everyone in the room turned to watch.

The roar of engines blasted from the monitors. The Miriths took turns yelling encouragement and profanities at the screens.

"I'm looking for some Cepp-D," Janx shouted to compete with the din.

The Miriths acted as if they ignored him and traded secretive hand signals.

A deep, dull THUMP reverberated from the distance and made Janx's chest rumble.

Right on time, Janx thought, picturing the repulse grenade he placed under the bar.

Before anyone else could react to the explosion upstairs, Janx threw his drink at the wall of electronics behind the vidscreens. The devices sparked and flickered, and the room went black.

His four arms were in fluid motion all at once. He pulled the pistol from the holster of the guard behind him and shot him in the neck. With two of his other hands, he initiated his favorite weapon upgrade, and balls of plasma swirled above him. He swung his arms and the plasma balls flung across the room, hitting two of the Mirith bosses, dissolving their forms. The guy on the couch fumbled for his weapon, and a shot from the rifle clipped him in the head. In less than a second, the room was silent and dark.

"What's going on?" exclaimed the remaining Mirith. His associate's body slumped from the chair to land with a dull thud.

With his helmet's starlight vision, Janx studied the Mirith. "Tell me about Cepp-D."

The Mirith winced. "We can't get it here." He struggled to keep his voice steady. "Look, Vella..."

"But you did have it," Janx pressed.

The Mirith wrung his hands and shifted uncomfortably. His comrades lay sprawled about on the floor, some bleeding out, others charred and smoking from the plasma attack. "Yeah, maybe. Yeah, ok... Once, a while back. The client paid a fortune."

"Who?" Janx leaned closer.

"I don't know... some nutjob settler. Lives by himself on an island." The Mirith accessed a map on his compad and its dim glow lit his face. "Here." He showed the location.

"Anything else?"

"Yeah. A few months later we sent some muscle to rob him. Figured he must have a big stash since he had paid so much for the drugs."

"And?"

The Mirith cleared his throat. "They didn't come back."

"And you left it at that?" Janx asked.

The Mirith nodded, then looked at the door as it opened.

9bot stood on the threshold, haloed by the bright light from the hallway behind the droid. In one of the bot's hands hung the limp form of Hebbet. "Your grenade was quite effective, boss. The place has cleared out." 9bot dropped the goon.

Janx started for the door.

"What about him?" 9bot gestured to the remaining Mirith.

Wanted: Dead or Alive.

Janx pivoted and shot the boss in the chest, sending him toppling from the chair. Tossing the pistol aside, Janx said to 9bot, "Collect the bounties. Then find us a ride to the shuttle port. I'll take it from here."

Janx strode out the door, confident of his next steps.

Sinfed Reyu, I know where you are.

I've only got seconds! Janx charged at Reyu and thrust with all his strength. Reyu was more than a head taller, with a giant, muscled and armored mass double that of Janx's leaner form. Nevertheless, blinded and confused by the bright globe of light, Reyu stumbled backwards against the platform's railing. Reyu grabbed his helmet and snatched it off, revealing his skull-like appearance and blinking in the glare from the twin-setting suns.

Janx wrenched a steel beam from the platform and swung it, smacking Reyu across his chest. The Ja'din warrior sprawled over the railing. Janx hit him again and Reyu flipped backwards, somersaulting, a blur of arms and legs, falling. Falling. Falling.

It was over. The legendary Reyu the Reaper had been defeated. But Janx had no time to celebrate. Five seconds!

The noxious atmosphere seeped into his lungs. Slowly, his vision started to fade and shrink. He crumpled to his knees, dizzy, nauseous, wondering if killing Reyu had been at the cost of his own life.

He felt Death's cold hand at his throat.

A shadow crossed his face. In the dim light of his receding consciousness, he made out the outline of 9bot coming to his rescue.

The skiff put-putted away from the dock.

"Can't we go any faster, old man?" Janx turned to the geriatric geezer at the controls.

"If we do, the noise from the engine will attract a grock," the old man gestured toward the opaque waters.

Janx had no idea what a grock was, or if the old man was senile and talking nonsense, but ignored the comment and turned back around.

Earlier, Janx had ventured through Devolver to inquire about the location the Mirith had shared. A few bribes later, he'd been referred to the pier where he found this old man. The wizened coot navigated the vast marshlands west of the city, delivering supplies to the settlers inhabiting islands scattered about the murky and fetid waters.

A transport barge plowed close and rocked their skiff with its wake.

The old man pointed to drilling rigs in the far-off, hazy horizon. Though appearing tiny at this distance, Janx realized the platforms were gigantic.

"The boat's carrying the next work shift," the old man explained. "What they suck from the ground is what props up the economy. Those yellow clouds surrounding each rig are poisonous by-products of the extraction process." He spit over the side. "Anything for credits, right?"

They continued in silence, gliding over brackish waters dark as oil.

"You're Vella Janx," the old man said without prompting, his creaking voice loud after such a long quiet.

No point in denying it. "Yes."

"Your reputation resonates even here," said the man, "in this toilet bowl of a planet."

Janx didn't reply.

The old man continued. "Heard you *chose* to fight in the Palladium. The only combatant to ever do so."

The Palladium was a combat arena in the Certi system. The crowned prince of Certi-Four dispatched scouts all around the system to abduct the most skilled fighters they could find. Once in captivity, the proposition was simple: Fight and win your freedom, or die trying. Since there was only one winner from dozens of participants, the odds of surviving were not good.

"You'd have to be crazy to do that," said Janx.

Several moments of silence followed as the old man lazily steered around rotted stumps jutting from the marsh waters. Then, showing a gap-toothed smile, he said, "And you won."

"Don't believe everything you hear."

The old man kept silent, as did Janx.

What the hell was Reyu doing out here?

From the mist emerged enormous clumps of vegetation. Janx noticed that the water had cleared, and that the vegetation extended deep, past his ability to comprehend the depth.

Something splashed next to the boat, and Janx leaned over to see a tentacled arm emerge from the water. The old man hollered an alarm.

Another tentacle seized Janx's wrist. The appendage was many centimeters thick, with one eye at the end and a mouth beneath it, and a second mouth beneath that. Rows of serrated teeth glistened in its maw. The repulsive creature looked like an Earth snake and leech had mated. From all sides, more tentacles erupted from the swamp.

Janx drew a pistol and fired into the water. Yet another tentacled arm circled his ankle, and he was yanked off balance. His pistol flew from his hand and across the deck. Using his two lower hands and his feet, he braced himself on the railing as the thick tentacles tried to drag him over the side.

Another shot rang out. It was the old man firing Janx's pistol. The bullet severed one of the tentacles wrapped around Janx.

Now free to move, Janx pulled a small globe from his belt and activated it. When the globe blinked with blue light, he let it roll from his fingers and plop into the turgid waters.

"No!" the old man hollered. "The noise will attract—"

An ear-splitting blast heaved the boat, and water cascaded upward. A dismembered tentacle flopped between the two of them, its mouth snapping at the air. The old man flung it overboard and returned to the ship's controls. He rammed the throttle forward, and the skiff accelerated to a high speed.

Janx steadied himself on the railing. In the water behind them, the bloody mass of the creature thrashing in pain became smaller and smaller as they sped away.

Janx was about to relax when another, even larger mass broke the surface of the water. It was a gargantuan hump, a good fifteen meters wide, and covered in vegetation and slime. The side of its round shape opened, revealing a toothless cavern of a mouth. The monster closed upon the wounded, tentacled creature and engulfed it all in one chomp, then sank, fading into the depths and vanished.

"Grock," said the old man and handed Janx his pistol.

Fog enveloped the waters behind them, and Janx wondered if he had imagined the entire ghastly scene.

The old man soon slowed the boat, and they traveled for another half hour in silence. From his belt, Janx withdrew a double-bladed knife and started twirling it through his fingers. A nervous habit, but it helped him focus.

A horizontal line materialized ahead and, moment by moment, took the form of a shore.

"Is that it?" Janx asked, hoping that after so much time underway and surviving the encounters with the water creatures, they were at last at the destination.

The old man throttled back as they neared a small, wooden dock, coated in slime and moss like everything else. A path from the dock disappeared into the undergrowth beyond. "Who's this guy you're so eager to meet? Some relative of yours?"

"Let's just say that he and I have unfinished business."

"How did you find him?"

"He's got a rare addiction," Janx answered. When the skiff bumped against the dock, he hopped from the boat and looked about. "You sure he's here?"

"For sure," replied the old man who caught an upright post on the dock with his bony hand. For some reason, he added, *"Oua'chi quso rohal d'ena."*

Janx didn't know the language. He scanned the area through the various optics in his helmet. A moment later, the translation of what the old man had said, scrolled across his visor: *The best battle is the one you didn't fight.*

Janx shrugged off the local proverb. He started up the path. *Reyu, let's finish this.* Over his shoulder, Janx said to the old man, "Be back for me in a few hours."

After Vella Janx disappeared in the undergrowth, from his pocket the old man pulled out a vintage pipe, packed it with the contents of a small pouch, lit the pipe, and began puffing as he motored from the dock.

The trail led to a hut tucked into the dense thicket. Janx scanned the structure and the adjacent brush with the thermal-enhanced vision of his helmet. No evidence of heat trails, confirming his hunch that the hut would be empty. Reyu was too clever to be caught napping.

Janx entered the small dwelling, surveying the spartan accommodations. A cot. A table with only one chair. A shelf above a counter with assorted containers of food. The one-burner stove was at ambient temperature.

Had Reyu taken a vow of poverty? Or was he injured, so traumatized by his encounter with Janx that this was as good as he could get?

Reyu isn't here. What next? Set an ambush and wait? Prepare a trap?

Curious, Janx inspected the items on the table. A cup. A plate. A datapad. When he touched it, the screen flashed on. Janx scrolled the contents. Reyu was apparently researching something. Pharmacological reports caught Janx's eye, which seemed an odd interest for a hardened warrior like Reyu. The Cepp-D?

Janx looked about, puzzled. Propped on the shelf was a snapshot of the old man sitting on a crate outside the hut. So far, no clues that Reyu had ever been here. What if this wasn't Reyu's abode, but the old man's?

Gasses rushed out from the transpod as its hatch opened, and Sinfed Reyu stepped from the chamber. He flexed the muscles of his hulking frame, standing over two meters tall. The jump back to Helios Nexus was one he'd done hundreds of times. Ordinarily, the trip wouldn't have been noteworthy, but leaving that old man's skin and reorienting to his own had been more jarring than he anticipated.

I loathe jumping.

But he felt full of vigor... his body wanted to run and jump and climb. The heartbeats from his two massive hearts rang in his ears, like warring drummers. *Boom-boom, boom-boom.* Six helicas in an aged human body on Devolver, living in the marshes and running errands for the locals was not exactly a retirement. Considering how things turned out, he'd happily have stayed there longer if he had to.

When Vella Janx picked up his trail, everything changed. It meant the Guild would soon be after him. He imagined Janx searching that decrepit hut, wondering what to make of it.

Reyu smirked. He hadn't survived these decades as a Merge operative by being anyone's fool. As for Janx? The cyborg was smart enough to track him down on Devolver by following his Cepp-D trail, something Reyu had been using to combat cognitive issues relating to his extraordinary lifespan. But how long would Janx remain marooned in that swamp, surrounded by grocks?

Long enough for Reyu to set another trap if needed. Provided that stubborn Janx survived the hostile surprises waiting for him all over Devolver.

Reyu took stock of where he was, a small room in a military facility. It was utilitarian and plain, unlike the luxury transpods the highborn used. Green lights blinked on the wall med scanner. The only exit was on the opposite wall, a large door reinforced with metal bars. He accessed the MindLink on his wrist to open the door, but an error message hovered over the display: *Please see the station director.*

The med scanner beeped and turned off. With a *Chunk!* the door opened and The Hub's reprocessed air flooded into the room. Reyu took a deep breath. Nothing was quite like the aroma of station air; it smelled like home.

Exiting the room, he ran into a young military tech, a corporal.

"Excuse me, Sir," the soldier backed away from Reyu's imposing form, "we weren't expecting you. When your skin was pulled from storage, it caused a bit of a stir."

Reyu walked past the soldier to a bank of windows overlooking The Hub. Transports of all sorts zipped back and forth over the vast city. In the distance, starships cruised placidly outside the military zone.

"Are you okay, Sir?" the corporal asked.

"No need to 'Sir' me, I'm not in the military."

The corporal nodded and cleared his throat. "But I'm confused about something, Sir."

Reyu turned and looked at him. "What's that?"

"You're supposed to be dead." The soldier held up a compad. It blinked: *Sinfed Reyu—Deceased.*

Reyu said, "So I am."

TOWARDS ZERO HOUR

Maxwell I. Gold

When the transpod clamped shut, the darkness peeled away; my synapses
bent and bowed, thrusting my consciousness between worlds where the wide,
quantum pathways created by the Masson Zero opened:

> Mind and matter,
>> a break in continuity,
>>> towards Zero Hour.

In an instant, I inhabited a temporary *skin*, its pale body on some new world
where light and status began to dim. Once my labors were done, the Mass-O
pressed heavy on my neurons, leaving that husk in the dust:

> Mind and matter,
>> the next jump,
>>> towards Zero Hour.

New sickness, brain fog heavy in the mind of a lanky, alien body that would
push me closer towards convergence, gods, take me away from these primitive
jungle planets—the awful creatures of cerulean flesh and unimaginable
hunger—*click, tick, flash*:

> My mind didn't matter,
>> but the next jump,
>>> towards Zero Hour.

I'll never be like *them*, pure ones without a care. The unbroken line of Malcolm
Orion, how lucky they were, their celebrated ancestry granting them prized

skins, never stepping into the sticky residue of someone else's broken nightmares or twisted fates:

> How many I've left behind,
> the parts of myself,
> towards Zero Hour.

> Two hundred,
> Three hundred,
> the jumps incalculable,
> towards Zero Hour.

Gods, the fog got worse each time, murky and sometimes bloody in each new
body—*skin*. Identities were also different, especially with the excess residue.
Nightmares were frequent, the Other Dreams like cobwebs in my crackled
neurons:

> Tired, tissued matter,
> ready for the jump,
> towards Zero Hour.

Nothing made sense anymore, the lights grew darker on the edge, then
brighter, again and again, a break in continuity, a crack in myself, the mirror
that once was:

> The light before,
> the next jump,
> towards Zero Hour.

> Four hundred,
> Five hundred,
> the final call approached,
> *my* Zero Hour.

Nothing had to make sense when the stars changed, and the perceptions,
commitments, and sentience were no longer my own. The phantoms of
ageless, imperceptive space:

> Before The Fracture,
> my last jump,
> towards Zero Hour.

Faster and faster I went, away from the burning, beautiful core whose lights danced in fluid veracity while the Ghosted Ones continued their masquerade with replicated consciousness, the perceptions that were never their own—wishing, dreaming, hoping to reach The Creators, the Origins of a misplaced, broken existence.

Worshipped in fragmented mythologies that shaped our twisted reality, only to present us with a misunderstood future which carried us farther:

> Mind and matter,
>   flying deeper,
>   towards Zero Hour.

THE AMBASSADOR

Sean Eads and Joshua Viola

HELIOS NEXUS, 492 HD

THE GALAXY SQUEEZED INTO A ROOM.

Ambassador Nova Orion never forgot that description of the Astrograph—The Hub's constantly evolving map vault on Helios Nexus—given to her by Leader Olen Gray some twenty helicas ago. She was only ten at the time, and she thought she was seeing the whole universe.

"No," Leader Gray said, smiling, "the Astrograph *can* display the universe in its entirety, but this is just one galaxy. That's good enough for most people, but most people aren't you."

Leader Gray hadn't seemed so old to her then, in part because the bald, blue-skinned Deruian stood only a few centimeters taller than her. They were like two classmates adventuring together through a void populated by nebulae and star clusters and cometary clouds circling around them. Planets glowed as faint dots, like fireflies held in suspended animation in the vast, deep darkness, so lonesome in their far-flung isolation.

But not alone.

Connected always.

Merged.

Today, Olen Gray looked every bit of his two hundred and eighty helicas, but urgency had him moving with the speed of a much younger man.

"Come," he said. "I need to show you something in the Archives."

Nova kept pace as they exited the Astrograph and made their way down a long corridor to the database repository The Merge assembled containing planetary information regarding politics, sanctions, and other matters of importance. They entered the dark chamber and Leader Gray stepped up to a podium in front of a large holo screen. The database blinked to life. Leader Gray cleared his throat and stroked his thick white beard with one hand as he used the other to sweep through a series of stereoscopic planets.

"Cancer now riddles The Merge," he said in an icy tone. "How is it that every sentient race in the cosmos can fall prey to religious fervor? Your ancestor would be so disappointed with what the True Souls have done to his legacy. Twisting it like they have to spread their message."

Nova chuckled, earning one of Olen Gray's disapproving *ahems*, the kind that made even squabbling Merge Security Council members go quiet.

"I'm sorry," she said. "It's just so difficult for me to imagine Malcolm Orion as some galactic messiah."

"He fits too many messianic archetypes on too many worlds," Gray continued. "Even when he doesn't, legends and lies hew the rough edges and make him fit. You underrate the man who brought The Merge into existence?"

Nova rolled her eyes.

I don't, Olen, she thought.

And how could she? Malcolm Orion who, five hundred helicas ago, made the first jump through the Masson Zero—the Mass-O—in three centum millennia, reigniting a bright path of light to all those scattered planets. Malcolm Orion, the man who brought about the Age of Reconvergence.

Malcolm Orion, her grandfather twenty generations removed. History's great galactic ghost, the Herald of The Second Cycle.

"Never ignore who Malcolm was, Nova. Who *you* are," Olen Gray said.

She'd heard it all so many times before. Here in this very room. She was a child when Olen Gray first lectured her on the importance of her heritage.

"*All of this*," Olen Gray had said, pointing to the holographic display of galaxies and planets on the screen, "*is part of your special inheritance. It would be impossible to calculate how many persons have transited through the Masson Zero in the hundreds of helicas since your ancestor dared to make the impossible journey, the jump into the abyss. When I was about your age, I used to imagine being Malcolm Orion—the Brave Traveler—on that Martian colony, interacting with the first known transpod that might have been built just as humanity's forebears were leaving the water for land. To do that—to have the strength and the will, the fearlessness to do what he did and find himself here on Helios Nexus, whose long-dormant technology began to awaken in his presence. An end to The Great Fracture—the isolation of all worlds when the Masson Zero ceased to function and all connection between sentient races was lost for so many millennia. The beginning of what would become The Merge. We are all now brave travelers and have each inherited different parts of that legacy, but never forget you're the direct inheritor of its entirety, the last living descendent of the man who made it all possible. I have to think you're bound for even greater glories, Nova!"*

She could almost hear those words echoing off the walls as if he'd been speaking them now, and if she didn't change the subject, he'd be sure to start reciting them once again.

Nova cleared her throat. "So, what's the mission? Where am I going?"

Olen moved his hand faster, scrolling through solar systems, traversing thousands of helicas of interstellar travel with the flick of his wrist. Merge worlds were always recognizable as shimmering green dots, but now many of them blinked red, a warning designation from the Security Council.

"I'm sure you can guess, Nova," Olen Gray said.

"The Sol system," she said. "Any cult based on Malcolm Orion has to involve Mars."

"Wise reasoning. The cancer's origins remain unknown, but its stronghold is Mars. Like metal filings drawn to a magnet, the extremist acolytes have gathered there in great numbers recently."

Mars now glittered before Nova the size of a thumbnail.

"We estimate a quarter of the Martian population is at least sympathetic to the True Souls' claims now."

"Already? This is a new extremist faction, is it not? How is that possible?"

"Assignments have kept you away from The Hub for a long time, Nova."

"If these True Souls extremists are *that* popular, how is it I never heard of them until I was summoned back?"

"Simple logic should answer that question for you." Gray's tone made her flinch. Was it so obvious? Did he feel he needed to lead her to the answer like a child?

Her career as a Merge Ambassador had been centered around departure. She thought of all her journeys through the Masson Zero, subjecting her mind to quantum bursts of quarks that sent her consciousness across the galactic network to a skin awaiting her in a transpod on a planet thousands of light-years away. She did these things out of a desire for discovery, a thirst for galactic unity. Yet despite her best intentions, her role often kept her in the dark beyond the mission at hand.

"Because I've been on new Merge worlds," she said.

"Quite so. Such planets have too many travel restrictions on them, and they still know little of The Merge's history. But if you look at the older worlds, the core worlds, you'll find their adherents. I suspect they've infiltrated our own bureaucracy."

Nova winced, and Gray nodded.

"I don't say they follow because they *believe* it," he said. "There are administrators and politicians who seek power no Proten can provide. Fanaticism is a crop sown from many seeds, and those who cultivate it will always be threats to The Merge. Deceptions abound, Ambassador, as if birthed like stars from a nebula. Three days ago, True Soul cultists infiltrated Jump Point Alpha and stole highly classified materials."

"What kind of materials?"

"The Malcolm Orion kind. The kind that could elevate their goals and threaten ours."

Gray removed a small datapad from his pocket and handed it to Nova. Her eyes went wide with shock and disbelief.

"Is this true?"

Gray offered Nova a subdued nod. "I'm afraid so."

"Have you put a team in place to keep this from leaking?"

"I gave the team a direct order to stand down."

Nova raised her eyebrows. "Why?"

"We're too late, Nova. The truth has already been revealed. We cannot keep this a secret any longer."

"Since when did the Director of The Merge's Security Council stop caring about security? The danger's obvious, yet you've done nothing."

"Nothing?" Leader Gray seemed affronted. "I've summoned you here, haven't I? The situation calls for our best ambassador."

"And what am I supposed to do?"

"The True Souls may know the reality of the situation now, and they will surely be spinning their own versions of that truth, but we need to keep the physical materials they stole out of public circulation."

"How are you expecting me to do that? Ask them nicely to give them back?"

"Find out what they want. Let them know The Merge is willing to hear their concerns, but only if they're willing to cooperate. Urge them to cooperate, Nova. You're Malcolm Orion's last direct descendant. That should give you an edge."

"And if that doesn't work?"

"If that fails, then do what you must. You'll have protection, of course. I've assigned a Martian Administrator to be on hand to receive you."

"Anyone I know?"

"Doubtful. Administrator Ducane came to us recently, but he has proven his loyalty to The Merge. I'll send additional details to you shortly."

Nova nodded. "No time to waste then," she said, handing back the datapad and turning to leave.

Leader Gray called to her in his softest voice. Nova pivoted and hunched down in front of him.

"I know you have limited jumps left, Nova," he said, cupping her hands in his palms. "You must know that I'm only asking you to do this because the circumstances are so dire."

She put her hands over his and smiled. "I know, but don't worry. I may be Malcolm Orion's only living descendant, but I'm *not* him. Zero Hour won't take this Orion down."

Zero Hour.

Nova tried to put the words out of her mind. Despite what Nova had told Gray, she didn't actually believe it. Succumbing to the same fate as her ancestor was always in the back of her mind.

Zero Hour.

She tried to put the words out of her head and glanced at the four great spires of The Merge Citadel in the distance, then moved down a ramp into a restricted zone toward her private jump chamber. She stepped onto an automated anti-grav walkway that connected to the westernmost spire.

Wind struck her face. She knew it was absurd since she was accustomed to Mass-O travel, venturing thousands of light-years in an instant, but she always considered the autowalk a little too fast, as if she were being flung toward The Merge's awesome halls of power. However, in the silence and uncertainty of the present, she wished it were swifter.

The autowalk was private, reserved to carry Merge representatives and dignitaries between government facilities. The four spires extended over three thousand meters into the sky of Helios Nexus, their height marked with a thousand more automated corridors connecting them to the upper sections of Nex City. The elite, the wealthy, and the established bought their way up to lofty heights, walking among the clouds in luxurious skins with far greater sensitivity than their original flesh, purchasing customizations from Assemblers to indulge every peculiar appetite or dream. Meanwhile, the Strivers—poor, desperate immigrants, refugees, and seekers from across the thousands of worlds connected by the Masson Zero—eked out their days in the squalid lower rings, a subterranean existence locked inside skins of the most basic type, stripped of all cultural identity and expression, indistinguishable except for their consciousness and their particular reason for trusting the Masson Zero to cast them across the stars.

Nova at last arrived at her jump chamber and approached her transpod. The large pod tilted into a vertical position to allow her easy access. Ambassador-class transpods were luxurious by most standards, spacious enough to not feel at all claustrophobic in those few moments between the pod hatch closing and the first storm of quarks blasting a consciousness clear of its mind.

The launch cycle started, and the typical holographic interface appeared before her, but Nova was startled by what she saw. All transpods scanned the minds of their occupants, measuring them in a million data points: physical, chemical, and some might say metaphysical. Transpods seemed to sample the *will* of its occupant, and the cycle would shut down if it detected reluctance or fear. The interface was meant to be a summary reflection of the jumper's mind. It was never the same for each jumper, and seldom the same for each jump.

This time, Malcolm Orion's face hovered in front of Nova.

What the hell? She thought. *What am I seeing? This can't be the transpod UX.*

She'd first seen Malcolm's face either in a history book or a family archive before she was old enough to comprehend his importance. He was a handsome man, with rich ebony skin, gentle brown eyes, and close-cropped curly hair graying at the temples that framed his strong jawline. Everyone said Nova had his nose and mouth.

Malcolm Orion, the Brave Traveler, the grand adventurer whose courageous jump reactivated the ancient, dormant Creator Tech and sparked a new light following the long darkness of an unknown apocalypse now called The Great Fracture.

Malcolm Orion, first in so many things.

Including Zero Hour.

Nova couldn't escape it, no matter how much she tried to convince herself she wasn't even close to Zero Hour.

Little by little, every transit through the Mass-O deteriorated your consciousness. This was well known—*now*. Some experienced no symptoms until around jump four hundred, when mental problems such as voices and hallucinations akin to schizophrenia became obvious. Others experienced this sooner—a fluke of individual biology. Some noticed no symptoms at all. But no one was immune. Everyone who made enough trips through the Mass-O would eventually have so little native consciousness left that a transpod would detect no presence at all. Your mind would go blank.

Zero Hour.

Historians who studied Malcolm Orion's journals believed he reached Zero Hour around jump five hundred, but analysts found a pattern of strange behavior beginning around jump four hundred. Since the deleterious effects of frequent jumping were not then understood, his contemporaries thought he was suffering from standard mental illness. His fame and admiration were too great for anyone to deny him. Until one day, sitting in his trans-pod, Malcolm Orion's consciousness was sent to a waiting skin–but it never arrived. Most summed it up to Zero Hour, but the True Souls believed it was something else: that his mind had been liberated. That his many experiences in the Mass-O gave him a deeper understanding and empathy for life in the universe, and on his last jump, he joined the collective.

Nova didn't believe any of that, nor did she have time to think about such myths and legends right now. Her own concerns about Zero Hour had to be mastered first, otherwise the transpod might refuse cooperation.

I'm at jump four hundred sixteen, she told herself. *At the rate I'm going, I'll be failing Merge psych tests on my next mission.*

Malcolm Orion's face began to waver, and Nova worried she might have even fewer jumps ahead of her than he had at this point in his jump history.

Zero Hour is just around the corner, waiting for me, she thought.

Nova looked Malcolm's fading image dead in the eyes.

Then I make every jump count. Duty is what matters. Every mission is more critical than ever.

The face became bright, almost solid.

A moment later, a burst of blue quarks blasted her consciousness away, sending her millions of light-years across the cosmos in an instant. But within that short span of time, everything seemed to slow, and she perceived herself as floating through the Astrograph, gliding and twirling between stars. Then she felt like some marble shooting through pathways of greased tubes—a frictionless, brakeless existence. As the acceleration increased, she flattened, shrinking into an atom of a single grain of sand on an infinite beach.

Uoy-nraw-tsum-I gnimoc-regnad

Niaga-neppah-nac-erofeb-deneppah-tahw erutcarf-taerg-eht—

A scream seemed to reach her from the middle of the Mass-O itself, a quark cry, and then—

MARS

Nova opened her eyes as a warm transpod in the Martian embassy finished integrating her consciousness into her new body. She breathed and willed her fingers to curl, her toes to wriggle. Every flex showed obedience. Integration was complete.

The hatch lifted and Nova squeezed her eyes shut, driving the strange fragment of sound from her consciousness. The voice was something heard in the particlized transit between worlds, the quantum pathway created by the Masson Zero.

What was that? What happened? How could I have heard–

"Ambassador Orion?"

"Yes," she said, working hard to keep her tone neutral.

Slowly, she left the pod, concentrating on her new skin—a copy of her body from when she was twenty-eight helicas old. As with all skins waiting for her on other planets, this one was already fully dressed in official Ambassador garb, emblazoned with the vibrant red insignia of The Merge.

This skin seemed to sync with her consciousness faster than most and Nova found herself trying to drive away the unsettling implications of what just happened to her.

You can't hear voices in transit. It's something jumpers approaching Zero Hour would claim in their delusions.

I'm not near Zero Hour.

Only four hundred sixteen jumps.

Four hundred seventeen.

Reconers hovered overhead, the small, spherical drones scanning and analyzing her vitals. She fought for composure, realizing several Merge personnel were staring at her. One was outfitted in a sleeveless, bright red tunic. He was humanoid in appearance, but lacked any visible hair—not even an eyelash—and his skin was sulfurous yellow. She recognized him from the mission details Leader Gray sent to her MindLink before her jump, but Nova couldn't pin down where he hailed from.

"Administrator Ducane," she said, offering a slight bow. "The Merge Security Council brings you greetings and assurances."

"It's an honor to have you here, Ambassador Orion. These are my subordinates–Corazed, Fulbrand, Kel-Mon-Dur, and Pullman. We'll give you an updated briefing."

Nova nodded and took in the crew.

Corazed, a burly Ogantuan, offered a slight grunt as he chewed on an old Earth-style cigar. Nova assumed he was the latest recruit since Ogantu was the most recent planet being considered to join The Merge.

Fulbrand was a middle-aged human male. He stood to the side, smoothing the fabric of his uniform and adjusting an emblem on his lapel—a bronze spiral of triangles with a sea-green patina. The symbol of the Cylarians.

Odd that a Martian human would be sympathetic to the Cylarians enough to wear their symbol, Nova thought.

Kel-Mon-Dur gave Nova a slight nod. Like Olen Gray, he was a blue-skinned Durian, but far younger than the leader of The Merge. From what Nova could tell, there wasn't a single strand of white in his beard. And while he was the shortest of the bunch standing before her, he'd still tower over Leader Gray if they were in the same room, as his legs were affixed to robotic extensions.

And then there was Pullman, the Ordovian. Nova was very familiar with the people of Ordovi, having served with Representative Zittel on The Hub for many helicas. The cephalopodic creatures occupied water-filled domes mounted atop bulky 2.5-meter tall mechanical frames. Their iridescent-blue tentacles emitted nerve impulses to control their robotic avatars.

Nova couldn't be sure, but as members of The Merge, she assumed each of them were occupying skins of their respective homeworlds.

"What's the status of my weapons?" Nova asked.

The officials exchanged looks. Corazed pointed to the Assembler. All Creator transpods had one nearby, a sleek metallic matter-printing machine characterized by glowing slots of different sizes. The hum and heat coming off the Assembler told Nova it was wrapping up a job. Two slots opened at once, each cavity revealing an identical item.

Ducane gestured to Pullman, who retrieved the objects and held out a platter like some colossal alien butler. Nova saw two black flame-bladed Varstal daggers there.

As soon as her fingers wrapped around their hafts, a crackling yellow energy erupted from each blade and orbs of light encased each hand. Pullman backed away.

"I've never seen anything like them," he said.

"You'll never feel anything like them either," Nova replied.

She'd trained and earned expertise in a vast array of weaponry since her adolescence, but Varstal blades were her favorites. Even the inert daggers could cut most substances. When activated, the knives drew energy from a rare ore inserted into the handles, which the daggers channeled into small but impregnable shields against any projectile weapon. With a well-practiced flick of her wrists, she could summon the energy to the tips of the daggers and launch devastating bolts at opponents, almost as if she were throwing the actual blades.

Ducane gave a hurried summary of the situation, though it contained little Nova didn't already know–until the end.

"A special strike team is assembled in case you fail to convince the True Souls to give up the material they stole."

"What are the strike team's orders?"

"Extermination."

"These cultists may be dangerous in their delusions, but they're not vermin, Ducane."

"The order comes from Leader Gray himself."

She had no trouble imagining a broader directive. *Do what you must*, she recalled Gray saying before she jumped here. She thought of all those planets in the Archives shaded in red. How many more *special strike teams* had The Merge's Security Council authorized?

The *cancer*, as Olen Gray called it, was going to be removed one way or another.

The magnitude of the consequences settled over her as she strapped the daggers into place on her hips.

"I'm going this alone. I'll call if I need backup."

An arrow blinked on Nova's MindLink holo display, guiding her down a shimmering stream through a stand of trees. The grass was thick underfoot and the shadowy cover of foliage made it hard to believe that only a few centuries ago—before the terraforming project was completed—this place was nothing more than a vast field of red dirt and rock stretching from crimson horizon to crimson horizon. Nothing but the desolate desert of Mars.

Nova reached the peak of a hill and looked back to where she'd hiked from: Jump Point Alpha—the site of the Creator transpod Malcolm Orion used for humanity's first jump that brought the universe back together. Areo, the capital of Mars, stared back at her. The vast, bustling city was built atop the gigantic Discovery Lander housing Orion's legendary transpod. Nova turned and put a hand over her eyes, scanning the horizon, angling her head in the direction of her destination.

Well, she told herself. *That's different.*

An ancient-looking temple sat on the outskirts of the city. The structure sparkled in the sunlight, its eerie glow enticing Nova to advance. A short trek later, she approached the glistening building and noticed architectural samplings from several Merge worlds. Spires from Cerattos, columns from Dyridon, and a narrative frieze typical of Halvarii. When she was close enough, the temple's radiance was easy to explain. The True Souls had gone out of their way to construct a very detailed holographic projection to support their delusions. But the elements at play gave Nova pause. The Merge was no stranger to terrorist groups and fringe cults after five centuries, but they were always separatists.

This architecture suggested something else. She examined the frieze. It showed a man on his back, surrounded by mourners. As the scene progressed from right to left in the Halvarii style, the man—Malcolm Orion—stood tall, holding a radiant ball of light that had been given to him by the Herald of The First Cycle: the legendary Ja'din warrior, Reyu the Reaper. The mourners in the frieze were now on their knees in prayer.

Better live up to the family name and step into the unknown, she thought and moved through the holographic entrance of the temple.

"Hello?" she said. Nova saw no one but realized there could be any number of people concealed in the holography. She immediately regretted not jumping into a skin customized with enhanced sensory perception. Her Martian skin was for more ceremonial purposes, like wreath laying rituals at Malcolm Orion's memorial site.

The temple's hologram was even more impressive inside and must have taken hundreds of projectors working in unison to perfect the detail. The illusion was designed with one designated forward path, and Nova followed it until she arrived at a room both breathtaking and provocative. The walls were decorated with elaborate frescos showing Progenitor Ships with sinister eyes moving toward worlds like monsters stalking black seas. Nova blinked, taking it all in before she even realized there was another element at play, at the very center of the room but almost merged into the busy background scenery.

Malcolm Orion's body rested in a transparent casket, like a deceased dignitary lying in state. Nova, never one to take easy offense, found herself so repulsed she couldn't even appreciate the holographer's skill in the re-creation. The face she saw was as clear and detailed as the image she saw in her transpod.

A wave of disorientation hit her, followed by–

Niaga-neppah-nac-erofeb-deneppah

The gibberish was like a comet blazing through her thoughts and she swayed. Was she under attack? Was this some unknown psionic weapon?

Was it Zero Hour?

No. Can't be Zero Hour.

She clutched her head, desperate to drive the noise from her mind. Her efforts only made it spike, until the disorientation was so great, she pitched forward, straight atop Malcolm Orion's casket. She braced herself to fall through the hologram and hit the floor—

—but the casket was solid.

Perhaps the shock was enough to rid her of the voice. As Nova pushed herself up, dozens of figures stepped through the holographic walls. The skins she saw represented many Merge worlds, but the man they stood behind occupied a human skin. Something about him seemed off. He stood about 1.9 meters tall, with striking blue eyes and dark hair. In the center of his forehead was a small, green node that glimmered ever so slightly.

"Sorry to interrupt the family reunion," he said. "I am Titus Restorius, High Priest of the True Souls."

Family reunion? Nova thought, looking back at the container. That couldn't be *the* body of Malcolm Orion. That wasn't possible.

Another jolt of gibberish shrieked through her mind. She could swear it came from the corpse, and it stopped as soon as she looked away.

"Something wrong, Ambassador?" Titus said.

Nova straightened her back and assumed the welcoming but authoritative stance she'd repeated time and again on her various missions as a diplomat. She cleared her throat. "The Merge—"

"Right to business. I like that, Ambassador, but unfortunately The Merge doesn't recognize us, so I don't know what you're doing here."

"They're willing to hear you, Titus. That's why I'm here. To negotiate the return of the materials you stole and find a peaceful solution to all of this."

"The only solution the True Souls will ever accept is the immediate abdication of The Merge."

"You know that isn't possible."

"Then I suppose we don't have much left to discuss, Ambassador. The Merge will just have to learn the *hard way* to accept the existence of the True Souls."

"If you're implying terrorism, Titus, you know The Merge will never tolerate it. If that's your plan, you might as well forget the intergalactic community ever recognizing your authority."

"They'll recognize us once we've proven the truth."

"What truth?"

"That Malcolm Orion's soul still exists, awaiting the time of return to destroy this false and corrupt unity you call The Merge that plagues the universe."

Nova chortled. "Is that really what the True Souls hope to peddle? There's nothing left of Malcolm Orion. You know how Creator Tech works. His body atomized when his consciousness was first transported to The Hub five hundred helicas ago. And his original skin—his Ori—was destroyed not long after. He even indicated in his journals that every skin he ever used was to be accounted for and destroyed. There's no trace of him."

Titus smiled. *"Another* Merge falsehood. The Merge has withheld much about Malcolm Orion for centuries, but we recently discovered the truth."

Even more acolytes came into view. Nova gave them a sweeping look and took a rapid census. About fifty of them. She looked back at the body.

"We retrieved the original imprint of Malcolm Orion from his very first jump," Titus said.

"I'm well aware of the material you stole. That's why I'm here, to negotiate the return of his DNA. But you've already..." She paused and acknowledged the body under the glass once more. "...cloned him..."

Titus chuckled.

"Why? What do you want?" Nova said.

"We seek rebirth, Ambassador. Reunion. Restoration."

"And a bit of revanchism? Revenge? Retaliation–against The Merge?"

Titus touched his chest, looked back at his followers, and offered a hearty laugh. "We mean no one harm except those who find the truth dangerous. Leader Gray perverted Malcolm Orion's original plans for The Merge. We are on a mission to restore our Herald's true intentions." Some of those behind him celebrated the statement. "I really must thank you for coming, Ambassador. We have great plans for you."

Titus made a slight motion with his right hand, just a quick touch of the node on his forehead.

A signal.

One of the cultists approached. Nova slowly moved her hands to her waist, reaching for the daggers holstered there, but stopped. She was an ambassador. She had to talk them down. Violence was a last resort.

"Stay put," she said. "Don't take another step."

The approaching cultist stopped and looked back at Titus.

"I'm here to negotiate, Titus. Not fight," Nova said. "Tell your man to stand down."

Titus laughed, and then nodded to his follower. "Restrain her."

The cultist charged, but a terrible searing noise echoing off the walls startled him. Nova's Varstal blades crackled with yellow energy and she gave two warning slashes. Titus's followers were not cowed and more sprang after her. Nova ducked away from the closest lunging figure, pivoted, and amputated the attacker's right leg with one cleaving stroke. Two more lunged and she lopped off their feet before sending six bolts of energy into an advancing wall of acolytes through three efficient flicks of her wrists.

"Who's next?" she said.

Titus touched the node again and his followers backed away. Nova stood in place, daggers ready, her challenging stare just as sharp. This was still a staggering mismatch, and if they just swarmed her all at once, it wouldn't matter how quick she was with the blades. She glanced to her left and right. The holography kept her from knowing how much space she really had.

"I'd rather inflict no more harm here, especially over religion. Believe what you wish. The Merge has always guaranteed the sanctity of its member worlds' cultural practices."

A new but familiar voice said, "That's a lie."

Nova pivoted as new figures emerged from her left. It was Administrator Ducane and his four subordinates, who were armed with plasma rifles.

Well, Olen, you were wrong about Ducane.

Titus touched his node again, and the remaining True Souls backed away, disappearing into the walls.

"Administrator," she said, forcing a smile. "This must be that promised strike team here to help me."

"Drop the daggers," Ducane said.

"Why would I do that?"

"Because the firepower we have is too much for even you to deflect. We'll blow your arms and legs off. And, I must admit, I do have the desire to inflict that level of pain on you."

"*Why?*"

"To avenge a violated Grenajad."

Nova flinched. "I–"

"The sudden blush confirms your guilt," Ducane said, then ordered his men to form a close ring around her. Their plasma rifles hummed in readiness, none pointed at the same spot on her body.

"You're Grenaj?"

"You say that as if it has meaning."

"Of course it does."

"Not after the Progenitor Ship cast The Merge's shadow over my world. I was a child when the Discovery Lander came to establish the first transpod. When the Servitors emerged and scouted our planet. Such chaos and confusion. What were these machines? What did they want? There were mass suicides–my older brother among them. Then a glow from within the transpod. The body of an emissary forming inside. And who should that emissary turn out to be?"

"It was my first assignment," Nova said.

Did she hear or imagine a tremble in her voice? Ducane took a small step into the circle.

"My father was Jan Grandjeur."

"I remember him," Nova said.

"*What* do you remember?"

"He ranked high in the government and opposed Grenajad being welcomed into the intergalactic community."

"He wasn't alone in that sentiment," Ducane said.

"No, but he didn't represent the majority. Worlds don't join The Merge unless there is a peaceful consensus among their inhabitants. Your father was in the minority."

Ducane came closer. Nova's grip on the daggers tightened. She felt the menace of the plasma rifles pointed at her, cold barrels brimming with lava heat.

"A minority," Ducane continued, "that you helped defeat. You and a small faction of frapping usurpers pushed Grenajad to join The Merge by spinning a fanciful tale of us taking our rightful, proud place in the galaxy. You promised wonders beyond compare. You told us of Malcolm Orion and how your people were transformed and uplifted by his daring. Your inspiring speeches made everyone I knew want to be Grenajad's version of him. Still there were doubts, pushback. But you saw all dissent crushed."

Nova took another sly look through her peripheral vision. Corazed, Fulbrand, Kel-Mon-Dur, and Pullman were getting worked up by his talk.

"The political division wasn't as great as you claim. I only wanted to help."

"You wanted a trophy. My world was your first Merge assignment, and you were determined to show success. You used Malcolm Orion to accomplish that. You said The Merge valued us so much, had so much faith in us, saw so much potential, that it sent his last ancestor to greet us."

Nova bowed her head, focusing on Ducane's feet and the distance between her and him.

"After that," Ducane continued, "all dissent crumbled, and our values went with them. The Grenajad of my youth is unrecognizable today. We keep so few traditions, and religions from other worlds take precedence over our own! All because of *you*."

Ducane lunged, shrieking, and Nova turned in one fluid motion to throw the dagger in her left hand at the gunman behind her, the blade catching Kel-Mon-Dur clean in the throat. Nova had already swiveled back to kick Ducane's leg and used her free arm to get him in a headlock.

"Fire! Fire!" he shrieked.

She tightened her hold until his voice became a strangled gargle and gave Ducane's remaining subordinates a defiant gaze.

"Act with care, gentlemen," she said, holding the remaining dagger ahead of her.

"You can't block all of us," Pullman said.

"Plasma rifles aren't discriminating weapons at this range. Fire and you'll vaporize both of us. You might even vaporize yourselves."

Doubt showed in their expressions and Nova seized upon it.

"There's no skin, no armor that could survive the heat at this proximity. But it won't matter to me. My consciousness won't be bothered at all."

"Good luck making it to a transpod," Fulbrand said, tightening his aim.

"The Merge has a jump method for Ambassador-class skins. It's called *bailing*. A single thought command throws my mind out of this skin, shunts it to the nearest transpod and then back to The Hub."

"You're bluffing," Pullman said. "The Merge has failed at every attempt to create bailing tech. We'd have heard otherwise."

Rax. Frustration shrouded Nova's face.

Corazed laughed. "Everything that comes out of your mouth is a lie, Ambassador." He pushed the nozzle of his rifle closer to Nova, his finger hugging the trigger.

"Let's just all calm down and—"

Nova cried out as the voice in her head returned louder than ever. She dropped the dagger and lost her grip on Ducane. Someone hit her in the face with the butt of a rifle. She collapsed, rolled onto her back, and stared up in pain and defeat.

She made a blind grope for the dagger only to have someone step on her wrist and bear down.

"Hearing voices, Ambassador?"

Nova thrashed. "How...who..."

She saw Titus appear beside Ducane. His right hand was touching the green node in his forehead.

The voice in her head became splitting. She writhed, reduced to pleading as a scream built inside her skull.

Must be a weapon. Can't be Zero Hour. Nowhere near enough jumps. What's happening what's happening—

Her vision blurred. She felt herself hoisted up and carried. When she could see clearly again, Nova found herself in another room strapped to a table with Ducane standing to her right. A low, steady sound came from her left, where she saw the remaining True Souls gathered before Titus like a choir and its director. The noise came from them—a collective subvocal hum rather than a chant. It was almost pleasant compared to the now muted voice.

"What did you do to me?"

Ducane looked down at her. "Titus and his minions over there are Cylari-ans–another proud people whose lives were ruined by your ancestor."

Nova closed her eyes for a moment. She knew there was something off about Titus. His human skin was just a disguise. "Malcolm Orion isn't to blame for what happened to the Cylarians."

"No? When he made his first jump, he restarted the entire Mass-O and ushered in an era of galactic doom."

"He brought light after The Great Fracture–"

Ducane bared his teeth and bent toward Nova's face. "What The Merge calls The Great Fracture, other planets call freedom. No world suffered more from Malcolm Orion's hubris than Cylarus. The telepathic people there were unified in one brilliant consciousness. The Mass-O's reactivation shattered that unity–"

"I don't need a history lesson, Ducane."

"The education I'm going to give you goes far beyond history, *Ambassador*."

Titus came to the table.

"The modified auricular is ready," he said, holding out what appeared to be another green node, almost identical to his own. Nova squinted. Up close, she could see the truth. It was some sort of alien augment.

"A Cylarian patriot created this device," Ducane said, taking up the node. "The augment reduces the Mass-O's interference with the cortical zeta waves that make telepathy possible if they're strong enough. Once perfected, Cylar-ians wearing the auricular will have their telepathic unity restored to them—like that lot over there."

Nova looked at the small cluster in the choir Ducane pointed to. "Then I'm glad. The Merge has been working from the beginning to solve the Cylarians' plight."

"And they've produced nothing. The Merge is better at propaganda than science. I realized that a long time ago, just as I realized strength had to be matched with strength. The Merge traffics in mythology, and a more power-ful myth will destroy it. Malcolm Orion is about to return from the dead, his vacant body occupied by yours truly. And he will decry The Merge and every-thing it's done *in his name*."

"That's your plan, Ducane? To treat his body like some skin? Why do you think anyone would believe you?"

"Every messiah needs a prophet, Ambassador. Who better than his only living descendent? The Merge worlds will believe *you*, just as my people bought all of your lies."

"No amount of mind control could get me to do that."

"It won't be mind control. It will be Titus occupying your skin."

Nova laughed. "You haven't thought out your plan very well, Ducane. Unless you assume a galaxy given over to blind credence. There'll be a demand for proof."

"Yes," he said. "An active scan of your own CZ waves."

His casual, even dismissive tone confused Nova. CZ waves, the so-called fifth brain wave, weren't even discoverable in humans unless they made a trip through the Mass-O. Even five hundred helicas later, their exact nature was mysterious, but everyone agreed CZ wave patterns were unique to the individual and impossible to forge. Before The Merge created True Names, recording CZ wave patterns was a key component of one's official identification.

Ducane held up the node. "During the auricular's development, an unintended ability was discovered. Once attached to someone, it begins to record and then imitate the wearer's CZ wave. Like this."

Nova squirmed and bucked against her restraints as Ducane brought the device closer. She bit at his hand, making him draw back.

"Tame her, Titus."

Titus touched his own device, and the voice exploded through her mind again, clearer than ever before.

Danger coming.

I must warn you.

The Great Fracture.

What happened before can happen again.

Nova screamed in agony, unable to concentrate on anything else. Her vision went dark from pain. She felt Ducane's hands but couldn't fight back. A moment later there was a snug heaviness against her forehead.

"The auricular is attached," Ducane said. "Titus, begin monitoring its signal. The human adaptation should work just as fast as the original. Once the recording is secured, Ambassador, I'm afraid we'll need to wipe your mind and get your skin emptied out so Titus can occupy it when the time comes for Nova Orion to become the apostle of her ancestor's return."

Nova, I am here.

I have been here since your first jump.

I must warn you.

The voice's clarity jolted her. She recognized it from so many historical recordings. Deep, resolute, trustworthy. Commanding.

Nova looked at Titus, certain he must be projecting his thoughts into her, just as he'd filled her mind with debilitating gibberish. Titus was facing her but staring down at holographic controls. He went rigid. A second later, their gazes locked. His mouth opened but he made no sound.

Part of me exists in you, in everyone. Part of you exists in everyone. The Masson Zero expels and gathers, separates and merges. I must warn you.

"Warn?" she said, whispering.

Ducane looked down at her. "Imperious to the last. As if you're in a position to warn me of anything. How are the readings, Titus? Can we be done with her yet?"

Comminuted, spiral, transverse.

"Oblique, impacted," Titus said, his voice distant. He blinked, shaking his head. "I hear it too. I hear *him.*"

"What are you talking about?"

Titus's hands began to shake. Nova saw him gaping at the hologram. He stepped back.

"The auricular is detecting the presence of two different CZ waves," he said. "Nova and...Malcolm Orion."

Conchoidal, hackly.

"Earthly," Titus said, swaying. Ducane came around the table as Nova watched and listened to the voice continuing.

Greenstick, segmental, avulsion. I must warn you.

"It's true, Ducane. Malcolm Orion has returned. He's here. He's *her.*"

Ducane shook him. "What's this? Are you falling for your own religious claptrap? Are you becoming a slave to our own mythologizing?"

"Ducane, I tell you–"

Planar, ductile, brittle. I must warn you.

"–I hear him talking–his voice–in her head–"

Ducane scowled and turned to Nova. "There must be something wrong with the auricular. A minor setback."

He tore the device away, and Nova and Titus shrieked in unison as the voice ceased.

"Snap out of it, Titus!"

Ducane spoke into a comm on his wrist and called for his subordinates. Corazed, Fulbrand and Pullman arrived in moments. Pullman and Fulbrand had claimed the Varstal blades for themselves, while Corazed still carried a plasma rifle.

"Titus may be turning on us. Detain him."

They moved to obey. Titus, however, had other ideas. He touched his node, and the subordinates sank to their knees in ruin, dropping their weapons to press their hands to their heads in agony. Ducane must have realized his own vulnerability because he lunged to pick up the gun and shoot. A fiery rope of plasma struck Titus's right leg, rendering it a burning pulp before Titus hit the floor. He shrieked and flailed his arms.

All the remaining acolytes quit humming and raced toward Ducane, who managed two more shots before they overwhelmed him. The reek of burning flesh sickened Nova as she worked against her bonds. They were too tight. She saw no way of freeing herself, until—

Titus clutched the end of the table and dragged himself onto his remaining leg. He had taken up one of the daggers and the blade cut through the restraints with a simple swipe. Nova leapt off the table and took the dagger from him. The acolytes continued their frenzied attack on Ducane, tearing him to pieces with their bare hands.

"How dare you attack the High Priest!"

"Blasphemer!"

"Embrace the wrath of Malcolm Orion!"

Nova looked past the chaos and observed various tunnels at the edges of the room, but she couldn't tell which were real and which were projections.

She aimed the dagger's tip at Titus. "How do I get out of here?"

He groaned and winced, pointing to one of the tunnels with one hand as he grasped his injury with the other.

"Come on," she said, taking him up over her right shoulder as they shuffled into the passageway.

They moved through the dark corridor until they returned to the chamber holding Malcolm Orion's clone.

Nova regarded the copy of her ancestor behind the glass for a moment.

She frowned. "What was that voice, Titus?"

He looked at the clone, working to focus on something other than the pain in his leg. His groans turned to words. "M-Malcolm Orion's."

"It *wasn't* you? You weren't double-crossing Ducane?"

"I-I thought it was all a fabrication, but there were two CZ waves. Yours and—"

"Titus, that's not possible."

Sounds of the cultists came from the tunnel. Nova activated the dagger, electric energy dancing on the blade's edge.

"Where is the auricular?" she said.

"I can't detect it. It must have been destroyed."

"I *need* it. I have to understand what I heard. Do you have the schematics?"

"No, I'm not the inventor."

"Then who is?"

Titus winced again, then offered the thinnest of smiles. "He will reveal himself when the time is right."

Nova sighed with frustration. The sounds in the tunnel grew closer.

She raised her arm and brought it down hard, slashing open the casket holding Malcolm's clone, the dagger slicing through the glass like water. The blade's energy charred the interior in an instant. Fire erupted from within and smoke filled the chamber. The cultists who emerged from the tunnel worked frantically to fight the growing blaze as Nova and Titus limped to their escape.

Once outside, Nova left Titus behind and made her way toward Jump Point Alpha. When she reached the hilltop she had scouted earlier, she glanced back one last time at the temple whose holographic walls were now hidden behind flames.

Mission accomplished, she thought.

For the first time in her life, Nova had trouble jumping. Her mind was too focused on the voice and the implications of it. Zero Hour. Madness.

Or something else?

Come on, she told herself. *I'm ready. I must get back. I want to get back.*

What if—somehow—there really was a second consciousness occupying her skin? What if that's why the transpod refused the jump? If so, how would she ever leave Mars?

Nova closed her eyes.

Jump four hundred eighteen. I must make jump four hundred eighteen. I've never desired anything more in my life.

The transpod was quiet a moment longer. Then the familiar hum of the launch cycle started.

Nova breathed out a long sigh and tried to make her mind blank.

The transpod's schematics appeared in her eyes and Malcolm Orion's face came into focus in front of her once again.

Despite herself, she reached out a hand to touch it. Her fingers passed through his forehead. She felt like she was reaching into his mind.

The way he had reached into hers?

The face began to waiver. The transpod verged on shutting down. Nova squeezed her eyes shut and threw all of her will into the jump.

The quark storm began.

Her consciousness was jettisoned. As before, she seemed to see herself in The Merge Astrograph, moving between stars and planets, crossing thousands upon thousands of light-years in a series of chutes and junctions.

When she opened her eyes, Nova found herself back at The Hub. Olen Gray was there to meet her and took the almost unprecedented step of reviewing the details of her mission without another member of the Security Council present. Nova wondered if any of them even knew about her assignment.

When she finished, the little old man sat back and looked thoughtful.

"A most elaborate deception," he said.

"Indeed. So, what's next?" Nova asked.

"As far as the True Souls go, we have a new weapon."

"We do?"

"Quite," Olen Gray said. "You. Titus will spread the word that Malcolm Orion lives inside you. When it comes to the True Souls, your words will have more weight than ever."

"You want me to impersonate Malcolm Orion?"

"I want you to continue your excellent work of promoting The Merge and its interests. You need say nothing regarding your ancestor. Their own belief will fill that gap."

Nova shook her head. "Fine."

"You're understandably tired, Ambassador. Get some rest. We'll finish this another time."

She stood up, happy to accept the offer. But she had one parting question.

"The words I reported–did they have any meaning for you?"

"But of course," Leader Gray said.

"Well?"

"They're types of fractures. Biological, geological, metallurgical."

I must warn you.

For a moment, she wasn't sure if she was remembering what the voice said or if the voice had just spoken. She thanked Leader Gray and hurried away, her thoughts on present fissures and greater cracks to come.

THE
SACRIFICE

Andy Baker

CYLARUS, 493 HD

Sinfed Reyu seized his opponent by the neck and leaned over him, growling, "Give up." Reyu knew he had to kill this assailant, but his Ja'din warrior code obligated him to first offer mercy to an enemy vanquished in close combat.

The Ascended assassin, True North, winced in pain. "Never."

The defiant answer didn't surprise Reyu. Without hesitation, he smashed the thick vambrace on his forearm hard against the assassin's brow, cracking the skull. Reyu let the fanatic slump to the ground, dead, and then scanned his surroundings: an abandoned area in Kellex Prime, a confusion of towers and skybridges, a maze of light and shadow.

A voice brought Reyu to this place, one that whispered to him in his dreams.

The answers you seek, Reaper, start on Kellex Prime.

Answers to what fueled his restlessness. Answers to the mysteries of what lurked deep inside the Ja'din warrior.

But to find those answers, he had to keep his focus on the here and now.

Ascended assassins always attacked in teams. True North, as leader, was proscribed to meet the targeted enemy eye-to-eye. A fair enough tactic against an opponent caught unaware or easily intimidated. But suicidal folly against Reyu.

The second member of the team, the backup known as The Right, would attack from a distance, like a sniper. Reyu's gaze skipped across the towers that overlooked his position, first latching onto the most likely place for a sharpshooter. Too obvious. His eyes swiveled to windows behind a balcony. Still too obvious. He decided on a perch to his left, one draped in shadow.

Pulling his spear from his back sheath, he swung it into position and fired. The energy bolt zapped the perch, revealing a figure jerking upright in the explosion of electric light, screaming, then tumbling to the ground hundreds of meters below.

The air trembled, tripping Reyu's nerves. To the left, on an adjoining skybridge, The Inverse—the third assassin—skulked into view and aimed a Proten-powered rifle. But he had underestimated the Ja'din's reflexes. Before the Inverse could draw a bead, Reyu whipped his arm at the assassin, flinging a spinning blade from inside his glove. The blurred curve of razor-sharp metal cleaved into The Inverse's chest, emerged out his back in a spray of blood, then whirled like a boomerang to return to Reyu's hand.

Reyu considered how easily he had dispatched his enemy and gloated, *Ascended assassins. Three, always three.*

He reflected back to why he was here. The voice. Its enigmatic message.

Follow The Ascended to The Compass. Request Direction.

Then an electrified bolo whipped around his ankles, binding them in a clutch of agonizing pain. Another bolo seized his knees, making them buckle, and as he crumpled to the ground, another bolo pinned his forearms to his waist, with a fourth cinching his elbows tight against his ribcage. The bolos were tentacles of paralyzing torture. Bound and helpless, Reyu rolled onto his back to glimpse this second group of attackers.

From a skybridge downwind, Krishah, tall, lithe, and shrouded in a hooded cloak, approached. Eight helicas ago, they had crossed paths and even helped each other escape death from Silas Kyruk, who had nearly killed them and a handful of others—Annill, Tor Gret, and Vella Janx—with a viral monstrosity known as the DeGen. But in this underworld of crime and treachery, loyalties could flip in an instant.

"You know us too well, Reyu," Krishah said and gave him the barest hint of a smile. "Were you only expecting three of us?" She motioned to her companions, and another pair of Ascended assassins emerged from the nearby shadows.

Reyu felt the energy of the bolos ebb, bringing welcome relief. Stealthily, he worked his arms and legs to get slack. He lifted his head to regard his attackers. "Two teams of three. Your tactics have changed."

"You're special, so we made adjustments," Krishah said and then called to the young assassin approaching Reyu. "Norlin, make sure he's secure."

Norlin towered over the Ja'din and sneered. "Reyu the Reaper. I was expecting better."

In an instant, Reyu drew his knees to his chest and kicked, sending Norlin reeling backwards against the railing, where he flipped and fell, arms flailing, to his death.

Krishah ordered the other assassin forward, "Saden, get those bolos recharged!"

Saden, an intense, wiry man with a meandering scar from chin to scalp, rushed to Krishah's side with a controller in his hand.

Even as he manipulated the controller and renewed bolts of energy tightened around Reyu, the Ja'din warrior struggled to his feet, grimacing to withstand the pain. Through clenched teeth, he managed, "I request Direction from The Compass."

Krishah stiffened in disbelief. "What did you say?"

Reyu gasped, then added, "You heard me."

"You?" Krishah pulled the hood from her head to reveal eyes wide in astonishment. "An audience with The Compass?"

"To seek clemency."

Krishah traded looks of surprise with Saden, then turned back to Reyu. "How did you know to ask? Direction is for the devout. You are anything but."

"Like you said, I know you well."

Ambient light glimmered in Saden's cold and ruthless eyes. "We must kill him."

Krishah shook her head. "We cannot. Not now that's he's asked for Direction."

Saden tightened his grip on the controller. "We'd be legends, Krishah! Ending the Reaper. Think of it!"

"I said no, Saden."

"He killed Norlin! Plus, The True North, The Right, and The Inverse!"

"For the last time, *no*. We are Ascended and bound by Compass law."

With an angry grunt, Saden mashed a button on the controller. Four loops of blue light arced around Reyu, crackling like fire, knocking him down for good.

As the troop transport rocked from side to side, Reyu tugged at the heavy chains anchoring him to the floor.

Krishah sat across from him on a bench and noted his struggle. "Kallinium alloy," she said. "No way you're breaking free."

Reyu locked eyes with her. "After everything I told you about The Ascended, you're still a—"

"A what?" She quirked an eyebrow.

"A believer?"

Saden sat beside Krishah and was inspecting one of Reyu's swords. "What's he talking about?"

"Lies. Nothing."

Saden ran a thumb along the sword's blade. "So, which is it? Lies? Or nothing?"

"Nothing."

"Doesn't sound like nothing."

"Let it go, Saden."

"Fine." He eased the sword into its scabbard, then glanced at Reyu. "How are we going to get him to jump?"

"He asked for Direction. For him to get it, he has to jump."

Saden stared at their prisoner. "Rumor has it, the notorious Reaper is afraid to jump." The Ascended assassin laughed. "What's the matter, jumpspace gives you the jitters?"

"I've heard the same," Krishah said. "But he either overcomes that fear or he dies here. His choice."

Saden leaned toward Reyu, "Why do you want to stand before The Compass?" then smiled wryly. "So you can kill him?"

Reyu kept his voice flat as he answered. "I want to meet the man who wants me dead."

Krishah grinned. "A worthy request. Everyone should have a chance to witness greatness at least once in his life." She turned to Saden. "What do you think?"

Saden narrowed his eyes at Reyu. "First Cycle relic. Worse than Inner Ring trash." He pursed his lips. "Sure, have him experience the judgement of Azzik and then know the regret of wasting his life outside the light. After that, he dies. Like the antique he is."

Reyu ignored the insult. After all, things were going according to plan.

Saden was wrong about Reyu. The Ja'din warrior wasn't afraid of jumping or jumpspace. The fact was, he longed to return to jumpspace. His memories were there, everything and everyone he had ever been were contained in The Flow. During The Great Fracture, he had spent 300,000 helicas in jumpspace, isolated, but never alone.

What prompted every cell in his body to resist getting into the transpod now was not that he might get trapped in jumpspace, but that he *wouldn't*. Leaving the astral sanctuary and returning to the physical world, with all its complications and loss, filled him with anxiety and reacquainted him with an emotion he never felt in any other context: fear.

But what choice did he have? To keep cycling through the transpod, repeating the despair and release, until the day that he at last and forever merged with The Flow?

For Reyu, every trip through the Mass-O network was an encounter with madness. He had heard others talk of their jumps, and what they described—tunnels of light through a vast azure ocean—was nothing like his own. Yes, it was blue, but it was a roiling midnight sea, and the tunnels around him wove in every direction, complex patterns of unknown origin and destination, a fraying tapestry of destiny, with threads pulling apart under the weight of age and decay.

Reyu assumed this had to do with the number of lives he had lived. Ja'din were self-spawning, and the essence of their identities endured even as their biological bodies did not. As a result, for Reyu, The Flow was a mausoleum of memories, the preserved moments of countless lives. Each permutation of his existence endured here, intersecting the tunnels of those he had known before and would know in the lives to come.

And then there were the 300,000 helicas he had spent as part of this place when he was trapped in his transpod. All of who he was, over the millennia, became part of The Flow, merging with the many, where every voice sang as one. When Malcolm Orion had at last freed him from the transpod and Reyu returned to his body, his mind, his consciousness—his soul—had been ripped from this place, an excruciating liberation, one he had welcomed yet had never quite recovered from. One does not exit the eternal lightly.

In truth, only part of Reyu had returned to the world. Most of him remained here in The Flow. It was a fragmented existence, but he had grown accustomed to not feeling whole. The day of unity would come. Because every time he jumped, parts of him were restored.

Reyu had learned how to accommodate the chaos. To surrender to what he could not control. To let The Flow give back the part of him that would serve the circumstances. Somehow it always knew what he needed, even if he didn't.

Reyu trusted that someday he would return here and never leave. While jumping did not affect his mind as it did others—the consciousness of a Ja'din was different—he sensed that he would eventually hit Zero Hour and longed for that perfection. Until then, he would welcome back the pieces of the puzzle that was his existence, hoping to have enough to understand who he was, where he was from, and what was his purpose.

While in the bliss of jumpspace, he calmed his mind and opened it to receive The Flow. A single image came to him: an ancient tome, with a rune on the cover. The symbol looked like a mountain—no, it was a sand dune. Though Reyu had walked through deserts on scores of far-flung planets, never had he struggled with arid heat or frosted, desiccated nights. He imagined flipping through the mysterious book and though he didn't know the language, it felt familiar. Could this book, this relic, lead him to the cradle of his people?

A thought sprouted in Reyu's mind, *that book is at The Ascended temple, where I will find answers. I must find it. Maybe the book is the real compass, the one that can point the way home.*

ZARTA

A dozen Ascended acolytes were waiting around his transpod to seize him after he had gelled, all of them afraid. His fearsome appearance did nothing to allay their unease. Whenever he returned to his body after a jump, he roiled with murderous anger but had learned how to tamp down that rage.

He let them strap him to a grav-lifting rover which was then loaded into a cargo wagon. Strangely, Krishah and Saden were his only guards.

"Where are we going?" he asked.

"To the Temple Transcendent," replied Saden.

"Where is that?"

Krishah answered, "Kapehu, a moon orbiting Zarta, the planet we just jumped to."

Saden winced. "We're not supposed to tell a non-believer where it is."

Krishah rolled her eyes. "It's not like he's ever going to leave."

"True," Saden admitted begrudgingly. "He'll meet the same fate as all who serve The Merge." Saden turned to Reyu. "The Age of The Ascended is upon us, heretic."

"You believe lies."

Krishah furrowed her brow. "It is you who follows the way of liars!"

Saden lowered his voice. "We have proof that The Creators favor us." He tipped his head toward Krishah. "Should we show him the Veil?"

"Why not?"

"Veil?" Reyu asked.

"Prepare yourself," said Krishah. "It's...a bit overwhelming." She hit a button on the bulkhead behind her. The ceiling faded, then became transparent as glass.

A blazing light cut through the blackness of space, a meteor streaking past them. Then another. And another. Then so many that the sky became cross-hatched with slashes of light.

"The Veil of The Creators," explained Krishah. "It protects Kapehu from prying eyes."

"One hit," added Saden, "and even a Star Cruiser would be vaporized."

Reyu considered what he was watching. The meteors were not only numerous, but random, unpredictable. "Shields can't stop them," he said. "Then how are we passing through?"

"There's a pattern," answered Krishah.

Reyu couldn't imagine finding a path through such destructive chaos. "Impossible."

Saden replied, "You keep underestimating us—"

"It took time," Krishah interrupted. "Many minds and a lot of math."

"And prayer," said Saden, then added reverently as if reciting a familiar proverb, "Devotion invites inspiration."

"Of course, Saden." Krishah nodded. "Prayer, too."

"Why show me this?" asked Reyu.

"I want you to understand that no one is going to save you, Reaper." Krishah put an edge to her voice. "Once you're on Kapehu, you're never going to leave."

"Only we know the sacred pattern of the Veil," said Saden. "All trespassers are doomed."

Reyu looked up at the impenetrable web of meteors. What did this so-called Veil of The Creators hide? The Temple Transcendent? Why such effort? It must have taken ages to create an algorithm that could predict the pattern of passing through.

A thousand lifetimes, Reaper.

Reyu cocked his head. That whisper. What did it want from him?

Reyu, still bound in chains, was shackled to a large ceremonial dais in the center of a cavernous room. A vast collection of relics surrounded the dais: statues, suits of armor, weapons, and artwork. On one table, his armor, spear, and swords were laid out in some sort of exhibit. Reyu's attention turned to the huge array of books, shelves upon shelves, until he noted one glass case that was noteworthy because it was empty.

Yes, it held the book you seek.

There was that voice again, sounding closer and a bit clearer. It belonged to someone old beyond measure, who had witnessed the dawn of time. An image flashed in Reyu's mind: the tome with the rune on the cover. Whoever or whatever this being was, it knew what he wanted.

Reyu was alone in the room with Krishah and Saden. They were kneeling on the floor, shockspears beside them, facing the empty glass case, eyes closed, chanting quietly. The words bounced back and forth between the two of them:

"On the blank pages of the void, The Creators wrote the universe," Krishah said.

"The Creators wrote the worlds and the pathways between them," Saden replied.

"The Creators' words were divine."

"And only to The Ascended did The Creators give their divine words meaning."

"For they are divine and were written by The Creators."

"I serve The Ascended."

"I serve The Ascended."

The prayer ended, they remained in silence, meditating.

Reyu interrupted. "You serve liars."

Saden lifted his head and glowered. "Silence!"

"The Creators will condemn you."

"I said silence!" Saden grabbed his shockspear and rose to his feet.

"The many will reject you." Reyu raised his voice. "The Flow will not welcome you. You will spend eternity alone and forsaken."

Saden rushed forward, hurtled onto the dais, and jammed his shockspear into Reyu's chest. Chain lightning arced and sizzled around the Ja'din's trembling body. Smoke and the odor of burning flesh filled the space and still Saden kept the shockspear firmly pressed against Reyu until Krishah said, "Our prayers are not to be interrupted, Reaper."

Saden withdrew the shockspear and admired his handiwork.

Reyu clenched his teeth and let the pain ebb. He glared at Saden. "You will regret that."

"Not in this life, infidel." Saden readied the shockspear for another blow.

"Saden, enough." Krishah turned from the dais. "It is time for judgment. The Compass will point the way."

KAPEHU

Kapehu was an airless, lifeless moon, pockmarked with craters. Within a great desolate plain stood the Temple Transcendent, placed in the middle of a circular complex of buildings laid out to form a large compass. Above, a dense shower of meteors—the Veil—lit up the black sky. An occasional meteor smashed or ricocheted off the energy dome protecting the complex.

At the bottom of the temple, Reyu waited, restrained in magnetic shackles, and surrounded by a phalanx of armed guards. Thousands of Ascended acolytes flanked the esplanade leading up to the temple, the multitude shouting, cheering, jeering.

On command, Krishah and Saden prodded Reyu forward while the phalanx marched alongside. They passed eight elevated plinths, each occupied with a prisoner chained to anchor points. The eight prisoners were from different alien species and each wore a shroud of silken fabric. The shrouds bore the symbol of The Ascended, a golden circle with eight sinuous lines reaching across a field of white.

Despite their imprisonment and threat of doom, the prisoners were in the throes of a joyful, religious rapture.

"The Creators wrote the universe!" one cried.

"I serve The Ascended!" shouted another, sobbing in ecstasy.

At the top of the steps waited a tall, gaunt figure in purple robes trimmed in gold. A golden mask—a frozen visage equal parts intimidation and inspiration—obscured his face. He wore an enormous, hexagonal headdress emblazoned with The Ascended symbol that announced him as The Compass.

The armed guards fell away until only Krishah and Saden remained beside Reyu. They forced him onto the altar dais in front of The Compass, secured his chains, and stepped away.

The Compass regarded Reyu with an accusing gaze. "How many of my children have you killed, Reaper? Was causing The Great Fracture not enough? And yet you have the audacity to ask The Compass to point out your path to redemption?"

Reyu raised his chin to show that he had plenty of fight in him. "I do."

"There is no redemption for you, Reaper." The Compass's voice boomed across the temple. "You are lost, irretrievably so. Death is your only deliverance."

"It is not my death that is approaching."

The Compass looked at Reyu with amused pity. "I may die, Reaper, but not by your hand."

"I did not say that I would hold the blade."

The Compass hesitated ever so briefly, surprised, unnerved. Recovering quickly, he pressed on, "You have caused us much grief, Sinfed Reyu. But no longer. You once loomed large in our fears and plans, but now you are small, insignificant, no more than a crumb."

As he spoke, the gathered masses murmured angrily.

The Compass raised his arms. All fell quiet.

Then when he spoke again, his voice thundered across the entire complex. "Children of The Creators, the Reaper is ours, thanks to two of our sworn protectors. Saden, from the Sect of the Sanguine, and Krishah, our Guide, whose path has journeyed through failure to find glory. They Ascend ever higher, doing what so many others have failed to do. We thank them."

The crowd chanted their names.

The Compass continued, "This creature you see before you is an abomination. A demon. Evil incarnate! The Creators saw fit to end The First Cycle and begin anew. He is all that remains of those who had the sacred duty to protect the pathways, and yet they did not! His very existence is an affront to the divine. To destroy him, the last of the Origin Five, is to erase all memory of that forsaken past and to usher in the Age of The Ascended!"

A roar erupted from the crowd, a raising echo of unbridled passion:

AGE OF THE ASCENDED! AGE OF THE ASCENDED! AGE OF THE ASCENDED!

"I ask you," The Compass pivoted from side to side, "is he guilty?"

YES! YES! YES! YES! YES!

"He is guilty in the eyes of all!" The Compass shouted. "We now awaken the Ancient One, who will pass sentence upon him!"

Below, a hooded figure appeared by each of the eight prisoners on the plinths and tore open the fronts of their shrouds. The hooded figures then raised Varstal daggers and paused. The prisoners waited, their faces flushed in devotion and anticipation. Meanwhile the crowd watched, chanting, screaming, louder and louder, until they reached a deafening crescendo.

ANCIENT ONE! ANCIENT ONE! ANCIENT ONE!

The Compass nodded and the hooded figures struck in a round of choreographed murder. They plunged their daggers into the naked chests of the condemned and twisted. Gouts of blood spurted and soaked into the shrouds. A series of ritualized cuts followed: across the neck and down the arms. Blood flowed in rivulets, collecting in designs carved into the stone that when filled with blood, a pattern became apparent: it was the symbol of The Ascended, those eight arms growing out from the center.

The Compass shouted a call and response: "Sacrifice makes us sacred!"

The crowd answered:

SACRED!

"We offer you these souls!"

SOULS!

"Awaken so that the lost can seek solace!"

SOLACE!

The hooded figures reached into the plinths and yanked on recessed levers. Below each of the sacrificed victims, the slabs of stone gaped open on unseen hinges. The bodies slid loose from their chains, fell into the voids, and disappeared.

You will come to me, Reaper.

The voice again. Stronger now, louder. Whatever it was, it was down in that darkness, feeding. Demanding. Malevolent.

You will come. I have seen it. We have much to discuss.

The Compass lifted his arms to the sky. The crowd did the same. They all looked up, expectant.

"Beloved Creators," exclaimed The Compass, "you who gave us this sanctuary and the Ancient One who dwells within, if the Reaper is guilty, show us a sign. Reveal your wrath. Heaven fire!"

BOOOOOM!

A large meteor struck the dome, detonating with a blinding light.

"The Creators illuminate us!" said The Compass.

THE CREATORS ILLUMINATE US!

The Compass reached into his robe and withdrew a ceremonial dagger. "You are guilty, Reaper. Make peace with your past. It is time for you to Ascend." He lifted the knife, then froze in shock.

Reyu's mag-cuffs clattered by his feet. He had broken free of his restraints and straightened, rising to his full height.

Cowering, The Compass staggered backwards.

Reyu seized Saden by the throat and lifted him off the ground. "Fool, when you attacked me with your shockspear, the current disabled my mag-cuffs." He threw Saden aside like a ragdoll.

Krishah swung her shockspear, but Reyu snatched it from her.

Guards charged as a mob to join the fight but held position when The Compass waved them off. "No! Let the Guide prove her worth yet again."

Reyu eyed Krishah cautiously when she reached into her robe and pulled out twin daggers aglow with Proten energy. He took a fighting stance. The two of them circled each other, searching for an opening.

"Kill him," rasped Saden from where he had fallen.

"No, that pleasure belongs to The Compass." Krishah sliced her daggers through the air. "But I can put him to sleep."

Sleep? Reyu noted vials in the dagger hilts, filled with a glowing yellow fluid. A sedative?

Krishah lunged, whirled, and jumped. Sensing an opening, she threw her daggers. Reyu spun the shockspear, impaling one dagger on the staff and expertly redirecting the other at Saden. Reyu pulled the dagger from the shockspear. Saden tried to get up then slumped to the floor, unconscious.

Dropping the shockspear, Reyu cupped the dagger in his hand and maneuvered around Krishah. The two warriors feigned and parried, then in a flurry of thrusts, swipes, punches, and kicks, fought to a stalemate. They faced each other, breathing hard, chests heaving.

"Had enough, Reaper?" taunted Krishah.

"No." He lifted his dagger. Blood dripped from the tip. "But you have."

Krishah brought a hand to the blood trickling from a nick on her right cheek. "Rax," she cursed, becoming wobbly.

Reyu watched her collapse.

Come to me.

That voice again.

You've made it this far.

Reyu felt pulled by it, like it possessed the ability to compel, a psychic ability not unfamiliar to the Ja'din. He was hesitant to heed the call. His mind was not so easily bent to the will of another. That changed when an image was pushed to the forefront of his mind: the tome.

Complete your journey. Now.

Whatever the voice was, he could not resist it. With The Compass watching, Reyu crouched and groped for the recessed lever on the dais. He grasped its handle and pulled. As with the eight Ascended slaughtered earlier, the dais split in the center and the two halves swung downwards. Cool air burst from the dark void, bringing the rumble of forced wind.

Voices shouted, *STOP HIM!*

Before anyone had a chance, Reyu leapt down into the pitch-black unknown.

⋒

Reyu had assimilated Pyrillian night vision when he was a child, part of a rite of passage for the Ja'din, but navigating the gloomy, underground labyrinth was no easy task. He could tell he was going ever deeper into the moon's surface. But where he was going, Reyu was unsure.

The subterranean maze was populated by swarms of spider-like creatures:

a round body, eight legs, but with four mouths lined with rows of fangs. Eyes all over their bodies glittered in the meager light. The smallest of these creatures was the size of his hand, the largest had a thorax at least two meters across, with legs twice that length. They scurried about him, ignoring him as long as he headed into the depths. At one point, he followed a path that led him back up, but a horde of larger creatures blocked the way. The message was clear: keep heading down.

Bioluminescent algae appeared on the walls, indicating a route to follow. Before long, he spied a brighter glow up ahead. Then, after several more turns, the tunnel opened into a massive central chamber.

Reyu stepped into the space, which was filled with an otherworldly glow. Eight circular openings ringed the room's ceiling. He suspected that these tunnels connected the chamber to the sacrificial plinths in the temple.

He gagged on the fetid odor coming from a nearby heap of corpses, undoubtedly the recently sacrificed Ascended. Dozens of spider creatures picked at their bodies.

A massive rock formation dominated the middle of the expansive chamber. Reyu's augmented vision picked out microtremors. Something was off about this pile of stones.

At last you are here.

The voice seemed to have been projected from the largest of those rocks. As Reyu studied the biggest stone, he realized it wasn't a boulder at all, but a colossal spider creature. It shifted, then lifted its immense bulk on its eight legs and turned a craggy aspect crowded with eyes to face him.

Showing no fear, Reyu stood his ground. The creature had summoned him for a reason and so the Ja'din reached out with his mind.

What are you?

I am Azzik, the always and ever was.

The creature's reply carried the weight of centuries, an ancient being likely as old as the first stars in this galaxy.

Did you know The Creators?

Azzik remained quiet, its countless eyes judging.

Reyu had come here for a reason, so he asked.

The tome, where is it?

It is not here, yet you will have it. So long as you pay the price.

Price?

Assimilation.

Somehow, Azzik knew that the Ja'din were assimilators, able to absorb and integrate the DNA of other species into their own. The genetic code of twenty-seven different sentient beings existed within Reyu, altering his body and providing numerous useful adaptations, the reason for his continued survival despite the odds.

You want me to assimilate you?

Yes.

Why?

To see the stars.

Azzik's longing was palpable, filled with deep desire and a profound sadness.

You can't jump?

No.

The reply was heavy with frustration and pain.

Could you, once?

Yes.

Reyu contemplated the creature's response and realized why this chamber lay beneath the temple. Was Azzik the god of The Ascended?

It is you that The Ascended worship?

Azzik nodded.

Have them help.

It is not my body that holds me here.

What, then?

The many burdens the one.

I do not understand.

My mind is encumbered. Entangled with my people.

Then I cannot help you.

You can.

I cannot assimilate a soul.

Are you so sure? I am different. As are you.

You ask too much.

And yet I ask.

The image of the tome returned to Reyu's mind, only now he could see more than he was shown in the jumpspace. An austere room... a slab of rough-hewn stone covered in runes serving as a table... and someone standing behind it, turning the pages of the tome: The Compass.

In return, I offer answers you seek.

At last, the promise to end Reyu's wandering? Was this worth assimilating the essence of Azzik, if such a thing was even possible? Reyu pondered the question until finally:

No. I do not trust you.

Azzik shifted again.

You deny me?

Yes.

Then you must die.

A swarm of creatures, large and small, thronged over Reyu. He had no choice but to cut a path through them. Without his swords and armor, his fists would have to do. Despite their overwhelming numbers, the advantage was his as existence in this twilight underworld had made these things soft, and their bodies tore apart in splats of viscera.

Azzik himself made no move to attack Reyu, remaining still, simply observing the slaughter.

Another wave of creatures surged into the chamber. Reyu called upon one of his assimilated skills, an instinct that allowed him to retrace his steps. He lunged toward that corridor, smashing a path through the creatures.

We will both get what we seek, Reaper.

No.

With an army of the creatures at his heels, Reyu saw light shining from above. The dais! He leapt up, grabbed the edge, and for the instant that he dangled there, he expected the creatures to cluster around his ankles and haul him down.

Looking past his legs to an ocean of mouth, fangs, and eyes, he saw that the teeming mass had halted. Why didn't they follow him? Could they not survive on the surface?

Breathing a sigh of relief, he hoisted himself onto the dais and received one final message from Azzik:

Your pride will be your undoing—and my salvation.

The temple was empty and Reyu knew where he had to go. The image that had been projected into his mind—the room with the table, The Compass, and the tome.

As he climbed the stairs leading to the room, Reyu could sense movement up ahead. He shifted to a different set of ocular lenses, and the air vibrations coalesced into the shape of a human. He took a tentative step into the hallway...when a blade pressed to his neck, one that glowed with the pulsing energy of Protens.

Krishah hissed like a snake. "I could kill you where you stand, Reaper."

"But you will not, Guide of The Ascended."

Krishah lowered her dagger and stepped back. "Don't call me that."

"Why not?"

"One who does not believe cannot guide."

Reyu nodded. Few were as devious as Krishah, and he was glad she was on his side.

"So our plan?"

"Has worked to perfection. The Compass is in the room down at the end of the hall."

"Alone?"

"The Compass has everyone looking for you. Even his personal guard."

This puzzled Reyu. "That is strange."

"They're scouring the spaceport. The Compass assumes that if you escaped the tunnels then you'd commandeer a ship and fly off."

"Not yet."

"Did you find what you were seeking?"

"No. It is with him."

Krishah opened her cloak to reveal Reyu's swords. "You'll need these."

"Let's finish this."

As Reyu sheathed his swords, Saden appeared and brought his shockspear to the ready. He glared at Krishah. "Traitor! Now I realize everything. Capturing the Reaper was too easy unless you two were colluding."

"The Compass is the traitor, Saden. He is the enemy. We were orphaned because of him!"

"Lies!" Saden waved the shockspear. "Lies!"

"It is fact," said Reyu.

Saden pivoted to face the Ja'din. "Enough! You may have corrupted Krishah, but it won't work with me! I serve The Ascended!"

Reyu drew his swords and danced around Saden, keeping him occupied. Krishah brandished a dagger and rushed forward. Saden tried to parry their attack but going against two of the best warriors in the known universe left him pinned to the wall in seconds, Reyu's short sword through one shoulder and Krishah's dagger impaled in his left.

"This won't end here," Saden whispered as he weakened.

"It will," answered Krishah, gesturing at the vial of poison in her dagger. "Bindari extract."

Saden rallied a bit. "Bindari?"

"It will be a peaceful passing."

The fear of death seeped into his eyes, panic rising as his end drew near, and he turned to Reyu. "You told me that I am not welcome in The Flow and because of that I will spend eternity alone. Is that true? Am I condemned to be alone in The Flow?"

"No." Reyu cupped Saden's face. "Your voice will join the many."

Saden's eyes became filled with a sudden clarity, as if he glimpsed the light of wisdom that lay just beyond the edge of mortal existence. The next moment, his eyes clouded and he was gone.

Reyu held Saden against the wall as he pulled his sword free and then delicately lay the dead man on the ground.

Krishah regarded the Ja'din as if seeing him for the first time. "You are never what I expect, Reaper."

Reyu ignored her words. "The Compass. It's time."

Reyu found The Compass standing behind the rune-covered stone table exactly as he'd seen in Azzik's vision. The Compass was silhouetted by a large window that framed the night sky and the sweep of meteors. His face was bare, his aspect reptilian, with deep-set, red eyes peering from garish swirls of tribal Givnali markings. He watched calmly, unconcerned, as Reyu and Krishah advanced. His gold mask lay on the table, beside which rested a thick, leather-bound book.

He drummed the book with a finger. "This is what you seek, is it not, Reaper?"

"It is."

"Do you not wonder how I know?"

"It does not matter."

"Ah, but it does! Azzik sent me a vision," exclaimed The Compass. "Of this book. Of you both. I understand why the heretic is here now. He wishes to know his past." He swiveled his gaze to Krishah. "What puzzles me is why you have helped him?"

"The same reason."

"Your past?"

"My parents."

"You know the pledge you made, my Guide. You have no family but us. You were not born until you Ascended."

"You had them killed."

The Compass closed his eyes momentarily as if to understand her reluctance in letting go of a trivial past. "Child," he replied with feigned empathy, "they were already dead. Addicts. Criminals. Burdens to The Merge. Their release was a blessing."

"How many have you murdered to swell your ranks of assassins?" Krishah's voice quaked with quiet rage.

"My poor, confused child. We saved you. Gave you purpose. In time, you will see."

"That will never happen." Krishah pulled two vials from inside her cloak. The fluid was a deep, radiant purple. "The Age of The Ascended is over." She dispassionately inserted them into the hilts of her daggers.

"You think that my death will have any meaning?" asked The Compass, his voice steady. "I am a willing sacrifice. A means to an end."

"You? A sacrifice!" shouted Krishah. "You brought the Reaper here to be a sacrifice. You sacrificed my parents, my childhood. Everywhere I look—sacrifice! Death! And what has all this loss gained? Nothing!"

"It has brought us to this moment. This conversation. And what is about to happen."

"This is our moment," affirmed Reyu. "We are in control."

The Compass was about to reply when Krishah said, "All that is about to happen, Compass, is that you will die, and we will leave."

Reyu expected The Compass, like all tyrants, to shrink from justice like the cornered rat he was. But he stood firm and emboldened with a conceit that he had one more trick up his sleeve. Reyu traded perplexed looks with Krishah; this was not unfolding as either of them had planned.

"Have you learned nothing, child, from all of your journeys through the sacred pathways? From all of the bodies that have been a temporary sanctuary for your soul? The Ascended, like The Creators, understood that these mortal vessels are imperfect, but our minds can be pure, if we let them."

The Compass looked at Reyu and continued, "As I told you, Reaper, I may die, but not by your hand." He turned toward the window to stare into the relentless shower of meteors. "The C-compass points n-n-n-orth, its d-d-days of d-d-direction d-d-d-one. Another C-c-c-compass c-c-c-comes." The Compass began to quiver as if overcome with palsy.

Krishah gripped Reyu's wrist. "What is happening?"

Reyu tensed in alarm, unsure of what he was seeing and suspicious of what The Compass could do next.

"I Ascend! I Ascend! I Asc—" Tiny cracks spider-webbed across The Compass's skull.

Reyu unsheathed a sword as Krishah readied her daggers. They retreated several steps, too astonished to speak.

The cracks on The Compass's skull widened until the top of his head burst open, revealing a quivering brain punctuated by finger-sized holes. A small spider creature like those from the underground tunnels appeared in one of the holes.

Suddenly, the creature launched itself at Reyu, who stepped aside and swatted with his sword. But the creature evaded every blow and landed on Reyu's arm to cling tight.

Krishah quickly sheathed one of her daggers and raised her open hand to smash the creature but was too late. It sank sharp fangs into Reyu's arm, easily penetrating his zopelyn armor.

The venom paralyzed the Ja'din warrior, dimming his senses, and sped through his body. Reyu imagined the poisonous liquid doing its work, polluting his blood, soaking into his two hearts, dissolving into his essence, blending with his genetic code, splicing into the quintuple helix. Assimilating.

Ja'din warrior, your pride was your undoing—and my salvation!

The voice again, louder now. But inside of him. Part of him.

No! Assimilation is a choice!

Not this time. You will carry me from Kapehu. You seek your people, and I seek mine. We will search the stars together.

The outside world coalesced around Reyu. He heard another voice.

"Are you okay?" Krishah asked.

Reyu blinked and studied his arm where the creature had bitten him. What remained was a smudge of dust with no sign of puncture marks. Reyu sloughed away the remains. "I do not know."

"We need to leave."

Reyu didn't move, not certain what part of him was still him.

"Now!" Krishah insisted.

He nodded to acknowledge her demand, reached for the tome, then hesitated when the voice returned.

It has no answers for you, Reaper. But I do. I will share them—in time. So long as you go where I ask, when I ask.

An image appeared in Reyu's mind: a tall dune of shimmering green sand in the middle of a vast desert, shaped like the symbol on the tome's cover. The perspective pulled back, revealing the edge of an oasis and a tall wooden building with jagged angles and a flared roof. A Ja'din temple, Reyu realized, just as the image disappeared.

A hint of your homeworld.

Krishah pulled at his arm. "The Compass has a ship on the roof. Let's go."

Reyu left the book on the table and followed. With every step, a feeling of impending liberation—though of Azzik and not his own—poured through

Reyu.

I will not burden you forever, Sinfed Reyu, Fel'Akrin and Chalak'Nor of the Ja'din. You carry me to freedom. I will be grateful.

Reyu was surprised to discover that he believed every word.

Ƨ

The Compass's ship cruised the Veil of The Creators, easily threading through the tight weave of meteors. From his seat in the observation station, Reyu looked back at Kapehu and asked:

Are The Ascended finished?

No, another of my kind will take my place. It will guide the next Compass, and he will point the way. The Ascended will endure.

"A shame," Reyu whispered.

Krishah was sitting beside him and asked, "What was that?"

"Nothing."

"You're acting strangely distracted," she replied. "Should I be worried?"

"No."

Krishah studied Reyu, then shook her head. "I don't believe you, but your problems are yours alone, Reaper. As for me, I'm done with this place and The Ascended. When we get to the transpods, we go our separate ways."

"For now."

She answered firmly, "For always."

Always? The word prompted Azzik—the always and ever was—to give Reyu a glimpse of his endless existence. The universe bloomed in Reyu's mind: galaxies forming, colliding, fading...a trillion stars shining, dying...countless planets forming, spinning, and crumbling to dust. All witnessed from Azzik's confinement on Kapehu.

In return, Reyu shared images of his millennia merged with The Flow, to convey that he, too, knew what it meant to be trapped outside of time. Azzik responded with one final image: a single grain of green sand atop a towering dune. Reyu understood that grain of sand was him.

The vision faded.

Reyu looked at Krishah and smiled. "Always is a very long time."

THOSE THAT WEAR SKIN

Jamal Hodge

Does one need to justify disgust?
Explain revulsion?
Forgive what crawls beneath the skin?
All things within, indwelt deep as soul,
are not of the same kind and quality.

Since the Progenitor Ships arrived
to root unwanted, in the stars of our ancestors,
Those That Wear Skin have come,
gallivanting on false legs,
from the gleaming husk of a cancerous
Discovery Lander.

Adorned in our flesh,
they hum a second song,
imitating each buzz,
each dance of wing,
to a mockery of us
while remaining *them*.

Those That Wear Skin
wear war. Too well.
Proten arms of heated plasma,
light spears penetrate the hardest carapace.
They call us 'natives.'
They name us: *Apis linnaeus superior.*
We name them: *Invader, False Soul, Skin Wearer.*

You will know them from their lie of friendship,
the eyes appearing right,
but feeling wrong.

You will know them
from their MindLink holographic systems,
the train of Servitors slaving away
on their Progenitor Hives,
far beyond the reach of our wings.

The indwelt ones,
singing the wrong songs.
You will know them,
and you will look away...

THE MONK

Warren Hammond

NAIDU, 493 HD

MADHYA COUGHS, and so do I. Again.

I lift the pickaxe and strike a stubborn root. It splinters and I breathe in the scent of sweet turnip used to flavor several of the spirits we craft in the distillery.

A deep breath makes my lungs sting. My eyes and throat are getting scratchier. The air has begun to yellow. Begun to turn toxic. In another ten or twelve hours, it won't be breathable, and we will confine ourselves to the monastery inside the biodomes for another four helicas. Such is the quadrennial pattern of life on Naidu.

I knew what I'd signed up for. So did Madhya. So did everybody who made the decision to abandon their old life and make the jump to Naidu in order to adopt the Way. We came to live a simpler existence, one of labors and study. We volunteered for this arduous existence inside the claustrophobic domes packed with chapels, oratories, and dormitories.

But this was the Gift Season, a single month that arrives every four helicas to clear the poisonous air and offer a meager bounty of prickly fruits and root vegetables. A single month filled with nightly festivities and daily forays to the outside world of sharp sunlight, jagged rock, and razor-edged cacti.

Most importantly, the Gift Season gives us the opportunity to feel unfiltered sunlight on our faces and arms. To reconnect with our more natural selves. Our human selves.

This is why I came.

I swing the pickaxe again and drive it straight through the root's center. I tug at the vegetable, careful to avoid the spines, but the plant stays tethered to the earth.

"Let me use the sawblade," says Madhya.

"No," I say to my wife of several helicas. "I can do it."

"The only thing more stubborn than a zuvet plant…" She doesn't need to say the punchline.

Smirking, I lift the pickaxe, and she helps by pulling the plant's root taut. I take a hack followed by three more before the root breaks free and Madhya falls backward to land harmlessly on the hardscrabble, or so I think. A yelp escapes her lips and for a second, I think she's joking, but then I see the spines lodged in her forearm.

"I told you, Rennok," she says through tight lips.

"Should've used the sawblade," I mumble. "Yes, you were right." I'm already pulling tweezers from the first aid kit. When I turn to her, I bow my head as is our way. "I'm so sorry."

One by one, I pull the spikes out, and droplets of blood ooze from her heavily tattooed skin. She angles her arm into the sunlight, and I duck low to see where the sun glints off the finer spines. It's not the first time a zuvet plant has gotten the better of us. The better of me.

I work the tweezers until I think I've gotten them all. Madhya passes her fingers lightly down the length of her arm and sucks in a breath when she brushes over one I must've missed.

"Gods," I say.

"It's okay," she says. "I'll live." I've heard those exact words once before. Except he wasn't okay, and he didn't live. I realize, this is the first time I've thought of my previous life in several days, and I'm glad of it.

It was a shameful life that I came here to escape helicas ago. No, it was more than shameful. It was unforgiveable.

The memories never go away. As much as I'd like to erase them, they continue to lurk in my subconscious. Most of the time, they stay hidden behind my monk's regimen of daily routines: chores and repairs; prayers and studies; ablutions and meditations.

But then at the slightest provocation, a memory will burst into my mind in full color detail. Triggered by something as simple as a turn of phrase or a trick of the light. And this is one of those times. Smoke stings my eyes. He tells me he'll live and gives me a confused look when I take his hand. That's when he realizes he might be hurt worse than he thought. That's when he sees that the bottom half of his body is an obliterated mess of charred flesh.

That's when he gets scared.

Just like I've been taught, I don't try to stop the memory. I let it roll forward until the life of Private Cheung comes to its close. Much as it hurts, I allow the memory to churn up a familiar stew of foul emotion in my gut.

"Want to talk about it?" asks Madhya. She knows my faraway looks all too well. She always offers to listen. I always decline. She knows nothing of my life as Jaxon Sutton. No one here does.

It's forbidden to ask about the past, though some choose to volunteer. I've had many opportunities to share. I never have. Don't think I ever will. The shame of who I am is too great.

Who I *was*, I have to remind myself. I made my break with life as Sutton the instant I arrived here a fresh pilgrim, my consciousness emerging from the transpod wearing this new skin that wasn't my own.

The first words the abbot spoke to me were, "Devote yourself to the Way, and you'll find the peace you seek."

That was the greatest gift I'd ever received. A lifeline for a soul lost in an ocean of self-loathing. I certainly didn't deserve such grace, but I remained thankful just the same.

"Are you okay?" asks Madhya.

I nod and lift her arm toward the sun to search for the last offending zuvet spine. Finally, I spot the little bugger and tweeze it free. I dig into the first aid kit for antiseptic spray. The rumble of a groundroller approaches, and I look up to see the abbot drop down from the cab. She's in her work tunic smeared with dust and dirt just like my own. The gold piercings running through her biceps reflect the sun, and the tattoos on top of her shaved head are dewy with sweat.

"Got bit, did you?" She winks at Madhya before starting to collect our harvest. "When you're all bandaged up, join me in the 'roller. I'll give you a ride."

"But the night festival isn't for six hours," I say.

"Yes, but a new pilgrim just came through the transpod, and he's from Bolstek. Your homeworld."

The abbot is the first to greet the recently arrived pilgrim. She gently guides him into the grasping-forearms handshake that is our custom.

Madhya mentions the injury to her forearm and offers a hug instead.

Me, I don't know what to do. What to say.

I know him. Or at least I know this skin he's chosen for himself to inhabit.

Every nerve tells me to run. But there's nowhere to run to. The domes cover less space than a small university. Outside the domes, noxious gasses and swirling storms will soon swallow the planet. I place a hand on a stone column. It feels cool and solid. Calming.

Covering for my speechlessness, the abbot makes the introduction. "This is Rennok who came here from Bolstek just like you did."

The pilgrim is looking at me, his familiar eyes bearing down. My heart is hammering at my ribs. He knows who I am.

"Bolstekian?" asks the pilgrim. "Are you the only one?"

I stay frozen, unable to move my lips. Madhya's eyes pinch in puzzlement, as if to say, 'Where did your tongue go?'

"There are a few others," says the abbot, "but Brother Rennok has been one of our most devoted. He will conduct your preliminary intake, then he and Madhya will be your guides for the evening. You must get a good night's sleep, and then we can start the formal vetting process early in the morning."

The abbot steps away, leaving me and Madhya alone with the pilgrim. "Come," she says to him, "let's escort you to the study. Rennok's interview will be just a getting-to-know-you kind of exercise. Nothing at all to be nervous about."

She takes my hand and leads me forward. The deliberate squeeze of her fingers tells me her words are really meant for me. She thinks I'm nervous.

Terrified is more like it.

The skin he's chosen to jump into is instantly recognizable to any Bolstekian. The most infamous war criminal of the so-called Xu'Xa Rebellion. The Star Sabers' most vicious henchman. He is the Butcher of Bolstek. The slaughterer of innocents.

He is Sutton.

He is me.

I find comfort in the scents of recently polished wood and aging paper. The north chapel's upstairs study has always been one of my favorite locations in the monastery. I look at the mustached man seated across the table from me inhaling a cigstick just like I used to, smoke curling from his nostrils like a dragon. The hard-earned scars on his neck and arms remind me of secret operations and war. His well-muscled bulk is coiled tight, ready to spring into action when the call of duty sounds. Knowing how much work, how much training, how much bloody hand-to-hand combat went into sculpting that body almost makes me proud of my service.

Except it was all a lie, and that knowledge sticks in my throat like a burr off the zuvet plant. I'd shed so much blood of my own and so much more of my enemies. I'd watched the life drain from so many under my charge like the young Private Cheung. All of it for nothing more than greed cloaked in the flag of patriotism.

I clear my throat. "Why did you come here?"

"To find my purpose," he says, turning off the cigstick and tucking it into his pocket. "I've been seeking for a long time."

"Seeking what?"

He shrugs and turns up his hands, leaving me to wonder what the gesture is meant to say.

"Please." I point at the microphone hovering over the table. "Speak your thoughts out loud so your words can be transcribed. The abbots will review the transcript."

He nods and speaks into the mic. "If I knew what I was looking for I would've found it by now. I just know I'm looking for something. Many seem to find what they're looking for here on Naidu, so maybe I will too."

Something in his tone, or maybe his posture tells me those lines are rehearsed. A simple platitude to get beyond this little formality to whatever it is that really brought him here.

"The vetting process requires more honesty and introspection than that," I say. "Tell that to the abbots tomorrow and they'll send you straight back into the transpod."

His jaw moves ever so slightly. I imagine he's grinding his teeth as he decides how much to divulge. "I'm seeking finality," he says.

"I don't know what that means?" I cough into my hand.

He cocks an eyebrow, the way a schoolteacher does upon catching a student in a lie. I find the expression doubly disconcerting. First, because I fear I've somehow given myself away, and he knows who I am. Second, because I don't think I've ever moved my eyebrow that way, and it seems uncanny and disconcerting to see my birth face do something so unlike me.

He smiles. "Why do you keep coughing and clearing your throat? Are you scared of something?"

"I spent a lot of time outdoors today. The air is getting bad."

If I had any doubt he came here to find me, it's quickly evaporating. Already, he's trying to flip the interviewer/interviewee relationship. He knows I'm from Bolstek, but he was also told by the abbot that I'm not the only Bolstekian. He can't be certain I'm Sutton, and I let that piece of deduction buoy my confidence.

"Don't change the subject," I say. "You said you came here seeking finality. Tell me what that means."

"It means I want to know how the story ends."

"What story?"

"Do you like books and holovids?"

I nod my head.

"Do you enjoy happy endings, or do you prefer a tragedy?"

"I don't see how this is relevant."

"I want to find out which type of story I'm living," he says. "The one where the hero defeats the villain, or the one where the hero blindly causes his own undoing."

"You don't plan to join the monastery at all, do you?"

"Why would you say that?"

I cross my arms and stare. Do you really need me to say it?

He stares back. Evidently, I *do* have to say it.

"You are unfocused and unable to answer my questions without creating distractions and diversions. You didn't come as a pilgrim. You came here for something else."

He eyes me for several seconds, clearly trying to gauge my motivations. Am I the one he's looking for? Or am I just a monk who is trying to get his intake interview back on track?

He leans toward the microphone and accidentally bumps it with his chin like he's still getting used to his new skin. He waits for the microphone to glide back into position. "Absolutely, I want to join the monastery. Tell me, does it hurt?"

"Does what hurt?"

"The scarification."

I look at my arms, at the numerous scars burned into my flesh forming symbols and glyphs from the texts we study. "Not anymore, but when the burns are fresh, yes, it hurts quite a lot. But you're no stranger to scars."

He looks at his arms, where deep scars twist like gnarled branches.

"You recognize me, don't you?" he says. "You know this skin I've jumped into."

"I do. Any Bolstekian would. The trials dominated the news. Of all the skins you could've chosen to have made for yourself, why would you choose that one? Aren't you afraid of how people will react?"

"To a war hero? Who wouldn't want to be treated with such reverence?"

"Sutton was not a war hero. He was a war criminal."

"That's not what the tribunal determined. They said he was wrongly accused of murdering hundreds. The hospital he destroyed was sheltering spies and revolutionaries. Sutton had no choice but to raze it to the ground."

He watches me, studies my face. I can feel my cheeks turning hot, can feel the tightening of my facial scarifications. I keep my head level and hope the tattoos fully hide my flushed reaction.

"I don't just want to see how my story ends," he says. "I want to know the ending of his story, too. Was Sutton a hero or a villain?"

⊐

I tell Madhya and the pilgrim I need to run a quick errand. "I'll catch up shortly."

They continue toward the festivities at the gates, and I pull the earpiece I lifted from the abbot's office from my robe's pocket and sync it to my MindLink. I insert the earpiece in my ear and raise my cowl to keep it from showing as I step into the cloister, thankfully finding it empty of monks.

The voice-only call goes through, and I hear Talori's hello for the first time since I entered the transpod and came to Naidu. "You were supposed to destroy it," I say.

"Who is this?" she asks.

"You promised you would destroy my skin."

"I need more than that. Who's speaking?"

"You know who it is."

"You don't sound the same."

"I'm in a different skin. You promised to destroy my birth skin, but you sold it, didn't you?"

After a long pause, she says, "How did you know?"

"Because somebody had a bio-identical one made here before jumping into it."

"I didn't tell him where you went. We served together in the Vipers. You know I wouldn't do that."

I want to scream. "You sold him my skin."

"You're a celebrity of sorts. He told me he was a collector."

"Who is he?"

"His name is Kas D'bonak. I'm so sorry. I didn't think there was any harm in it, you have to believe me."

"Listen to me, Talori. You're going to research that name, and you're going to get back to me as soon as you can to tell me everything you can about him."

"Then we're square?"

How dare she even ask after betraying my confidence? She told me she'd destroy my old skin. She swore up and down that I had nothing to worry about. Nobody would ever see Sutton again. And now this *collector* of skins comes along, as if that's a real thing, and she jumps at the chance to make a few credits by selling him my skin, the literal embodiment of my previous life of disgrace.

My blood is ready to boil, but I turn to the courtyard, try to find peace in its simplicity like I have so many times before. I fill my lungs and tune into the trickle of the fountain. I seek centeredness in the balance of flowers and ferns, some of which I planted myself.

"Sutton, tell me we'll be square," asks Talori again. "I'm really sorry." Her voice cracks.

The anger has dissipated. "Get me the information I need, and then we're square."

I pass through the dome gates to the outside. The festival is in full swing. Many monks drink from tall steins full of ale, and others sip from squat tumblers of aged liquor. The band cranks out an upbeat tune that keeps the dancers bouncing.

My robes flap as I step in front of a large bank of air fans that pump filtered air from the domes across the fairgrounds. Even so, the air smells of sulfur and grows murky with a yellow haze that will force us all inside in just an hour or two.

I search for Madhya and the pilgrim named Kas. I find them at a long table in the ale hut. They sit across from each other, and I notice Kas has the ear of his neighbor, Solkor, one of the small handful of monks from Bolstek. I drop a hand on Kas's shoulder, "Come, let's chat." I have to shout to be heard over the music and drunken din.

He glances at Solkor. "But we were just having a nice conversation."

The sour expression on Solkor's face says their talk was anything but friendly. I squeeze down on Kas's shoulder. "Let's go."

"But—"

"He's not the one you're looking for," I say. "I am."

His eyebrows twist in a very un-me way. I can't tell if he's happy to have his search completed or if he's disappointed that he didn't get to identify me himself.

Kas stands, his hip catching the table as he does. The table tips upward and slaps back down causing drinks to slosh though none spill over. I think he might've drank too much, but when he faces me, I don't see any perceptible wobble to his posture.

A hand grasps my wrist. It's Solkor, and he guides me down so he can speak in my ear. "Be careful. I recognize him from back home. He's the war criminal. Sutton."

"I know who he is, friend. I'll be fine."

I step away and let Kas trail behind me. Madhya, too. I move well past the crowd of revelers to stop at the very edge of the grounds where the fog is thick, and I struggle to breathe without coughing. We stand about a meter apart, yet it's hard to see him as my eyes begin to water, and the fairground lights barely penetrate the haze. I see Kas holds a machete that seemingly came from nowhere, and I realize how out of practice I am. In my earlier life, I never would've turned my back on him without checking under the table.

Madhya sees the machete now, too. "What's going on?" she says.

"Do you know who you married, Madhya?"

"We're forbidden to ask about the past."

"He's Sutton, the Butcher of Bolstek."

She doesn't respond with shock or denial. Although I'm certain she's never known my previous identity until now, on some level, she's always known it was something ghastly and dreadful. Why else would she have to calm me after I startle at a loud noise? Why else would she have to spend so many nights holding me after night terrors?

"No," she says after a cough. "His name is Rennok. He and I are both monks devoted to the Way."

"He is Sutton. He destroyed a hospital, murdered everyone inside it."

"That was a different person," she says. "If you've come for vengeance, you're loops too late. Sutton doesn't exist. None of our previous lives do once we've gained the right to put on these robes. Rennok is the man who stands before you, a man of hard work and kindness. A man of deep studies and a valued member of this community."

My heart can't help but swell at having earned such devotion from one as smart and caring as Madhya. But I also know her words won't make a difference to Kas. He believes I'm a scourge, the murderer of his family. Talori called a short time ago to tell me Kas is from Xu'Xa. His entire family died in that hospital, his mother having just given birth to a baby sister. Kas, age fourteen at the time, spent days buried in the rubble before being rescued.

"I know who you are," I tell him. "I understand why you came so far to find me."

"You do?" He brandishes the machete. The steel is tarnished and chipped, likely stolen from one of our work sheds. I take little solace knowing the machete's edge is dulled by use in the field.

"Do you know what it's like to bury your family?" says Kas. "Do you know what it's like to have your legs crushed under a collapsed maternity ward? To be trapped for days on end fighting for breath against the weight of fallen stone on your chest?"

I want to tell him it wasn't my fault. I was following orders. But as incontrovertible as that fact is, I also know that following orders doesn't absolve me of the horrific crimes that happened that day. In the end, I was the one who snuck through the city gates with a missile launcher on my back. It was me who hid in a drainage ditch until nightfall. I was the one who retrieved the missiles smuggled into the city inside crates of fruit. And finally, it was me who blasted the building almost a dozen times, each time attacking the building's main supports until the entire hospital came down under its own weight.

I bow my head as is our way. "I'm so sorry."

"Kneel." He rubs his eyes and coughs. "Accept the death sentence that The Merge's sham of a show trial should've levied."

Madhya is crying now, and I ache to comfort her.

"I will not kneel," I say, my head still bowed. The air is becoming more difficult to breathe, and I have to cough before I continue. "I beg your forgiveness."

"You little coward." He spits on the ground. "You hid behind your orders and then your lawyers and then all the lies presented at the trial. Testimonies from royal trash like Tor Gret. And if getting absolved of your crimes wasn't insult enough, you skulk away to hide behind this reformed monk act. Do you know how disgusted I am to be wearing your skin? To be walking around as if I'm you?"

"Then why did you jump into that skin?" asks Madhya.

"To draw the murdering bastard out. Now kneel and accept the punishment you deserve so I can get out of this nauseating bag of flesh."

Tears run down my cheeks. Stinging fumes might've started the flow, but I know I'd be crying just the same. "I won't kneel," I say. "I have a life here. Unlike my last life, this is one worth preserving. I'll fight for it if I have to. So please, I beg you to go back home. You told me you wanted to know how your story ends, but it doesn't have to end today."

"Oh, yes it does," he says. "Don't you see? I should've died that day. Finding you, bringing you to justice is the only reason I've lived this long."

"You're a survivor against incredible odds," I say. "Take that victory with you back to your home. Let that be the end of this chapter and start a new one."

He coughs and shakes his head. "One of us must be the hero, and the other must be the villain. As history proves again and again, whoever out-survives the other gets to tell the story. Those who gave you your orders have redefined your crimes as a hero's deeds while the innocent victims who died that day have been recast as spies and saboteurs. Killing them isn't enough? You have to murder their character, too?"

He charges me, and I duck under the swing of the machete. I yell at Madhya to get to safety only to notice that she's already departed, likely to seek help.

I pull a small knife normally used to cut stems from my pocket. It's not intended to be a weapon, but a blade is a blade if I can get close enough to use it. He lunges forward, and I dodge to the left, too slow. The machete catches my shoulder, and I feel its bite. My entire arm goes instantly numb, and the knife falls from my fingers.

The machete comes at me again, and I tumble away from the arcing blade. I hope my training will kick in, but a lot of time has passed since then. That doesn't mean I've turned soft. Many of my labors require a physicality that keeps me trim and fit, but this skin doesn't have the size or power of his, and as evidenced by the blood seeping from my shoulder, the lack of recent training has made me slow. I'm no longer used to the speed and quickness of combat. Yet I manage to tumble out of reach of his next strike.

He is laboring for breath. As am I. The rapidly diminishing availability of oxygen is certain to make this battle a short one. He chops at my head, and I dodge to the side. He sweeps toward my midsection, and I jump back only to trip over a rock. I'm back on my feet just in time to dodge another attack.

My right hand is working again now, and I know I have to strike soon or let him overwhelm me. He swings, and instead of retreating, I duck the machete and drive my foot into what I remember to be a balky knee. I don't hear the crunch I'm hoping to, but it does manage to stop him for a moment. I don't go in for a follow-up blow, instead I retreat to snatch my knife from the ground. He's charging again, and it comes to me to me in a flash just exactly how I can end this.

I remember how he bumped the mic with his chin and how he almost dumped everybody's drink getting up from the table. He's not used to his skin.

I leave him an opening, and the machete digs painfully into my ribs. I grab his wrist with my left hand and pull him toward me. His center of gravity is easy to manipulate, and at least for a second, he's tipping forward. His right foot juts ahead to reestablish his balance, but it's too late. He's let me get too close and the knife in my hand is sunk hilt-deep into the center of his chest.

He collapses almost instantly, and I'm already fetching a wheelbarrow that sits nearby. Madhya and others arrive, and I beseech them to help me load him into the wheelbarrow. If we can get to the transpod quickly, he can jump out of this body. A second after his body slides into the wheelbarrow's bed, I push off as fast as I can run.

I falter as I shove the wheelbarrow through the biodome gate. Madhya takes my place, and I have to hurry to keep pace. Clean air is a relief for my lungs, but breathing is still painful, likely due to a broken rib or two.

We pass the Lander, and as I'd arranged, the abbot waits by the transpod with a med kit. Her eyes go wide at our approach. "Rejuve!" I shout. "Now."

She readies the syringe.

I tell Madhya to dump Kas through the hatch into the transpod. "Are you sure?" she says. "He might come for you again."

"If he does, it's not like I won't deserve it. But let's give him this chance to find another path. His story doesn't have to end in tragedy."

She does as I ask, and the abbot jumps in after to plunge the needle into his sternum. She leaves it sticking from his chest, right next to the knife's hilt.

Kas's eyes open, and I lean down close to make sure he hears me. "You're dying. Soon. You have to jump."

His eyes swim left and right before landing on me again. I repeat myself, and I see recognition in his eyes. He understands what I've told him.

I close the hatch, and my knees go weak. Madhya steadies me.

The abbot studies the display. I slump to the floor as Madhya begins to tend to my wounds. Though I know he can't hear me with the hatch closed, I tell him, "Please jump. Please."

"That's it!" shouts the abbot. "He jumped."

I lower my head and speak to Kas's departed consciousness. "Be well, my friend."

As is our way.

VANETTA
4

Mario Acevedo

HELIOS NEXUS, 493 HD

WHEN SANTIAGO CHACÓN saw the young woman, he was certain his search was over. They were on a crowded sidewalk in the toney shopping district of New Paris, within the Middle Circle of Nexus City. Overcome with joy, he reached for the woman to clutch her shoulders. "Carlita!"

She recoiled from him, expression brimming with fear. The telemetry bubble from her MindLink flashed aqua to orange. Her two companions jumped back, equally startled.

Santiago realized his mistake. This woman was Carlita, but not his daughter. He let go and retreated. "I'm so sorry. Your...uh...I mean her, DNA trace led me here and..."

The woman sloughed her arms as if he had left her with a bad smell. "Creep."

As he became aware of what Carlita had done, his mood collapsed into despair. She had sold her skin to finance a jump through the Mass-O. But why? That was obvious. To get away. From her past. From him.

He met this other Carlita's glare, her eyes devoid of empathy. It was like he trailed after a ghost, a memory rather than a living person.

A Servitor emerged from the gathering crowd, its crown of antennae weaving back and forth to sense the air. Although Servitors only concerned themselves with safeguarding Creator Tech, the untimely appearance of the device made Santiago suspicious.

He regarded this Carlita and raised his hands. "Sorry, my mistake."

The woman exchanged looks with her friends, then sneered at Santiago. "No problem."

The Servitor continued past them, oblivious to the drama.

Santiago backed away, slipping into the crowd, walking faster, faster, until he reached the shuttlepod station for a ride back to the Inner Circle. Troublesome thoughts churned through his mind. To have seen his daughter, only to discover that a stranger occupied her body, left him sweaty and nauseous. This wasn't the first time he'd chased someone hopping from skin to skin to evade him, but it was the first time it was someone he cared for.

Traveling over the bridge linking the Middle and Inner Circles, he couldn't help but look from his window seat to the Mass-O below. Carlita had disappeared, dropping like a stone through that gigantic globe, a vast mosaic of gray upon gray, its distant horizon illuminated by the penumbra of the Triad Star system on the reverse side.

Through the MindLink, the Merge Tech communication device, it should be a straight-forward process to find anyone, especially for an experienced investigator like himself. But Santiago was retired, and his search was off-the-books since she hadn't broken any laws. Not recently, that is.

The issue was that Merge Tech saw the cosmos through a lens that sorted and organized everything according to a precise template. However, a common trait of all people, all sentient beings regardless of species, was to bend the rules, hop outside that template. Society needed flexibility, exceptions. Too much regimentation and control led to a rigid, ossified structure incapable of innovation or dealing with chaos. For the universe was itself constantly seeking equilibrium between order and entropy and to that end, people constantly exploited gaps in the system.

Since his daughter made a jump away from Helios Nexus, she had to have passed through The Hub's Jump Central. And jump where? When? Like most urban centers throughout Helios Nexus, tech surveillance in the Inner Circle was in a constant state of repair—make it disrepair—so backtracking her DNA trace and crosschecking it with MindLink ping points and time stamps proved to weave little more than a threadbare record of her whereabouts. Though Santiago's last assignments had been behind a desk, he had no problem recalling fugitive apprehension procedures. Well aware of her checkered past, he searched the usual hangouts—dive bars, flophouses, crib joints—and followed the leads to a jobs scalper, whose address was in a squalid neighborhood deep within the bowels of Striver Town, home to lowlifes, outcasts, and the down-and-out.

"I'm looking for this woman." A hologram shimmered inside the aura of Santiago's MindLink to show the images of Carlita scrolling through the jobs scalper's mind. The scalper was a slender blonde with features that looked a little off—loose mouth around teeth that didn't seem quite human, long skirt that dragged past her ankles like she was hiding her feet, and eyes about ready to pop out of their sockets—which told Santiago that she was wearing a cut-rate synth-skin. Never mind where she was originally from, just as long as she pointed him in the right direction.

The woman's eyes changed focus, the irises momentarily thinning into slits before widening back to circles. "Carlita Chacón?"

His heart jumped with rekindled hope. "That's right." He lay a gold ducat on the table between them. "Anything else?"

The woman picked up the coin, enjoying its heft, then dropped it into a vest pocket. "Carlita was here." That loose mouth caused the scalper to slur. "She jumped."

"That much I figured. Where to?"

The woman pointed to the floor, indicating the Mass-O. "Vanetta 4. They need workers for an archeological dig. Reclamation engineers. Health physicists."

Santiago took in the grimy and dilapidated surroundings. "Not many of those here."

"But there are those willing to go to Vanetta 4. You know, do the shit work. Get away. Get lost."

Sounded like Carlita. "How can I get to Vanetta 4?"

"Depends. As a tourist or as a worker?"

Worker obviously, since on his pension he couldn't afford passage as a tourist. He thought-zapped his work profile to the scalper. As she perused his résumé in her MindLink, he mulled over what had brought him here. When he left the service, he thought he was done searching for people on the lam. Hoping for tranquil golden years, back together with Carlita, the two of them making amends for decades of neglect and abandonment. But he hadn't figured his daughter would take off without explanation.

Hell, he didn't blame her for running away. When he was her age, he'd done the same thing, signing a six-helica contract in the Helios Nexus space army, a hitch that stretched into a career. There were brief interludes of "normal" life. Marriage. The arrival of Carlita and all the hopes a new life brings. Then the divorce. A bitter estrangement from his relatives, those moochers. Being on his own but not caring because he had a uniform and a title, emphasis on "had." Lapsing into PTSD.

Carlita was his touchstone to an idyllic existence and if he could reunite with her, then the pieces of his disjointed life would click together into a coherent whole.

The scalper regained his attention when she said, "Mars Station. You're a long way from home."

"So are you."

She let the comment slide and said, "Ex-military."

"Infantry and security."

"Fugitive recovery."

"Yeah, that too."

"But no experience in reclamation or salvage." She gave him a once-over. "For a big guy like you who knows how to use force, there's work. However, the queue for applicants is long." The pause in her voice told Santiago she was getting at something.

He stared at her.

She said, "I can bump you to the front of the line..."

"If?"

"If you're willing to moonlight."

"Doing what?"

She placed one hand on the desk and opened her fist. Nestled in her palm rested a thin silver capsule. "The gig requires that you take this." She pulled the capsule apart to reveal a hypodermic needle attached to an ampule filled with an amber liquid. "Hex-42. Helps cope with Jump Sickness."

Meaning, travel through the Mass-O, where minds risked being demateri-alized, scrambled, and reconstructed on the jumps back-and-forth.

The risk was C-RA, Consciousness ReAlignment—your thoughts, emo-tions, memory, personality—melding the pieces of your mind back to their original whole. But not quite. One jump, one dozen, and you were more or less okay with temporary jump-lag. After two hundred jumps, meaning regu-lar roundtrips through the Mass-O, C-RA would start degrading. The effects were cumulative and after four hundred, five hundred—it depended on the person—your mind reached Zero Hour and that left you a catatonic schizo.

"If Hex-42 is such a hot-shit cure for Jump Sickness, why haven't I heard of it before?"

"It's not available by prescription."

"Did Carlita take it?"

"What do you think?"

"What's the catch?"

"Actually, two catches," the scalper replied. "Catch number one, my commission. That ducat you gave me isn't going to cut it. And two, unless you're sitting on a big bag of credits, I'll be fronting the cost of your jump."

"You have that cash?" He made an obvious sweep of her shabby office.

"My investors do. Not to worry."

Figured that this dump was a front. "What are we talking about?"

"Twenty-five percent of what you earn for the next two loops. And life insurance naming me as the principal beneficiary should the worst happen."

Santiago recalled the shock at seeing a stranger wearing his daughter's body, which explained how Carlita paid for her jump. He'd do the same. "What about I give you full rights to my skin?"

The scalper cocked her head, those weird eyes elongating a bit as she gave him another once-over. "It is a nice skin. Sure you won't miss it?"

Fair question. Psychologically, giving up your skin was like a full-body amputation. The rich had the credits to keep their skins on "ice" when they jumped. Proles like him didn't have that luxury. Why had Carlita shed her skin for keeps if she was doing the hokey pokey through The Hub? And why the need for so many jumps?

"I have a feeling my trip is gonna be one-way." His eyes swiveled to the Hex-42. "Is that really necessary?"

"You wanna go?" She gestured with the syringe. "Take this now and I'll schedule you ASAP for tomorrow's pre-jump orientation."

He stared at the tiny vial, asking, *Had it come to this?* At this juncture in his life, he'd thought it would be a smooth ride with regrets behind him. But Carlita, like too many times before, had vanished and all his misgivings came tumbling back.

Santiago took the vial and weighed it in his hand.

VANETTA 4

Numbers. Santiago sensed numbers. And letters. Then a new name. GH235T. Followed by form. When he became aware of himself, he felt as though he was made of liquid flesh poured into a new body. He perceived filling the extremities of this new envelope until he became solid, his mind congealing as it aligned itself with the mechanics of his new body. The skin's residual memory—physical exertion and violence—bled into his mind. Excellent, this skin was a blank with experience and not a fresh clone.

His blood warmed. Muted beeps matched the cadence of his pulse. A soft light teased his eyes open. Dim illumination surrounded him, outlining devices and accouterments. Through the blurry wall of the transpod he perceived the smeared outline of a Servitor, this one squat with a dome-like head.

Santiago willed his eyes fully open. His mind bloomed, everything within and about snapping into sharp focus with a clarity that lashed through him. The last of his jump brain-fog evaporated. His gaze ranged past the transpod to the rest of the jump center and fixed upon the Servitor, whose head was covered with lenses that caught the ambient light like a multi-faceted diamond.

From behind the Servitor stepped a technician wearing white overalls. In pre-jump orientation, he had been briefed on what to expect on Vanetta 4. The local "skin" type was "humanoid"—symmetrical bipedal morphology. MindLink comprehension—seamless. He compared the tech's body, a female, to his own. Large bulging eyes above the corners of a wide, lipless mouth. Skin mottled pink and gray, spots of green. Tendrils of dense, curly hair—frogs with dreadlocks. He inhaled the aroma of moist swamp air. Feeling breath puff from his neck, he touched his throat and discovered ridges of gills.

He levered his arms to pry himself from the gooey restraints of the sensor-harness. The pod tilted forward and the cushions beneath Santiago heaved slightly, like a tongue working him from a mouth. He slid through the transpod's membrane and onto his feet, pausing a moment to regain his equilibrium. The goo sloughed from him and collected about his ankles where it caught the floor's soft blue glow. He stood considerably taller than the tech. Her body was thick boned, as was his, but lacked his large, ropey muscles.

She regarded his nakedness with blasé indifference. "Welcome to Vanetta Nexus, GH235T." A smile of sorts. "My name is AN991Z. Call me Anzee. Your arrival concierge." Her voice was soft and feminine and easily understood.

When Santiago clenched and unclenched his webbed hands—massive, powerful—Anzee said, "You requested a job with security."

He nodded. So far, so good.

Anzee tapped a console. Santiago recognized her actions; she was activating his skin's MindLink implant. Anzee then ushered him down a corridor. They entered a cavernous atrium beneath a domed ceiling where stars floated in the velvet void. For a moment, Santiago thought he was looking into deep space until realizing it was an enormous video screen.

On the ceiling, a circle of neon green highlighted an object. The circle and the object within grew in size, magnifying into a jumbled mass of ruin. Scale was difficult to comprehend until the view zoomed in on a blip crawling across the nimbus of debris. A Bercu Class Space Cruiser, gigantic but a speck compared to the colossal wreckage behind it.

"Vanetta Major Artifact Omega, MA-Ω for short. A Discovery Lander," she said, referring to the wreckage. "And the most significant find of Pre-Fracture Creator Tech since the derelict Progenitor Ship was uncovered on Mars five hundred loops ago."

Santiago was taken aback by the far-flung scattering of destruction. "What happened to the Lander?"

"A failure in the ship's zero-point drive caused its main Proten drum to implode. That's a guess, of course." Anzee smirked. "In a way, it's comforting to learn that The Creators, our gods, weren't perfect."

As he finished processing into Vanetta 4, Santiago wandered about, all the while panning for clues about Carlita. The environment wasn't much different from that on the other side of The Hub, though wetter, greener—moss was a common decorative motif. People were segregated into three strata. At the top, representatives from The Merge Alliance and the Vanetta 4 Municipal High Council. Then mid-level bureaucrats and their counterparts in business plus physicians and scientists. Occupying the bottom, worker cogs like Santiago.

He left Vanetta 4 on a commuter ferry to arrive at Van-03h, itself a city of two million, and the logistical support complex recovering artifacts from MA-Ω.

After reporting to his new bosses, Santiago went through the familiar routine—assigned to a unit and barracks, issued uniforms and equipment, immersed in virtual training. The work consisted mainly of stroking clients' egos, making them feel special enough to be worthy of armed protection, cakewalks compared to when he hunted felons for a living. At those assignments, Santiago, despite his imposing size, might as well have been invisible, his eyes masked behind security shades, his black clothes blending into the furnishings.

Tonight he was on duty at a soiree on the balcony of a luxury high-rise with a view of MA-Ω, an iridescent smear of colors and shapes stretching across the sky.

As a waitress poured wine, one of the hosts, clad in a sheath of sapphire cloth, gushed to her bejeweled audience, "Much better than standard Assembler fare. Who knew the ancients were such oenophiles?"

Santiago upped the gain on his scanner to eavesdrop. For their part, the guests had enabled the presentation function of their MindLinks so when telemetry auras touched, the introduction would radiate with a crystalline chime.

<TU312L. Tulee. Magistrate of Revenue, Security Council, Merge Alliance.>

<RR878Y. Roree. Chief Financial Officer, Adinerado Services, Vanetta Nexus.>

Santiago cataloged the names, a Who's Who of the upper crust and their privileged lackeys.

Security work proved to be monotonous, his attention drifting from his guests, to acknowledging alerts on his MindLink, and speculating about Carlita. He had considered searching for her True Name but found he lacked the authorization to make such an inquiry.

Why had she fled here? If she'd gotten in a bind, were things so torn between them that she couldn't ask for help? Was she running toward opportunity or running from him and all that he represented? Broken promises. Frustrated intentions. Honey-coated lies. *I meant well.*

What kind of trouble was she in? Again?

What about the Hex-42? He'd been told it was necessary to prevent Jump Sickness and a requirement for moonlighting work, certainly something under-the-table. So far though, no one had approached him. Plus, illicit drugs were typically addictive, and as of yet, he hadn't felt an itch for a fresh dose. The Hex-42 had led to nothing. But just because he didn't perceive something didn't mean it wasn't there.

⚓

Santiago and another security guard, KC991M, a fellow muscle head who went by Kacey, boarded the shuttle barge traveling from Van-03h to Dig Site Delta. Other passengers included the flight crew, three archeological specialists, plus two Municipal officials. The route took them through the debris field that surrounded MA-Ω like an asteroid belt.

Negotiating the field was tricky. Debris was always shifting and impossible to map. Undiscovered Protens, though ancient, could release bursts of energy that played havoc with navigation and communication systems. To compound the dangers, bandits exploited the treacherous clutter of the field to ambush easy targets.

He and Kacey were to ward off any such attack and so carried sidearms, with plasma rifles and laser blasters stowed in ready lockers.

The more anxious leg of the journey was the return to Van-03h because that's when they'd be transporting artifacts and were most likely to be hijacked. *Why bother?* Santiago asked himself. Aside from their desirability as collectibles, what were these artifacts worth?

Santiago and Kacey's post was aft of the VIP cabin. Its only passengers were Tulee, the Magistrate from The Merge Security Council, who he remembered from an earlier assignment, and Marut, whose profile identified him as a newly appointed Vanetta ambassador.

Cargo safely onboard, they were twenty minutes outbound from the dig site when Santiago sensed something wrong with his MindLink. He checked a nearby systems status panel. It said his MindLink had been deactivated. As was Kacey's and those of Tulee and Marut. Moreover, Kacey seemed unconcerned, like this was expected. Santiago looked through the transparent blast door into the VIP compartment and observed Tulee and Marut.

Kacey read Santiago's surprise. "Shoulda told ya earlier. We have to suppress the MindLinks."

"Why wasn't this mentioned in the mission briefing?"

"Kinda unofficial." Kacey nodded toward the cargo hold behind them. "We've had instances of Merge Tech activating dormant Progenitor technology. Don't know why it happens but it does." He made a *ka-blowie* motion with his hands. "We wanna sail through the debris field, not be part of it."

Opening a small cabinet in the bulkhead, Kacey withdrew a pair of headsets, complete with boom mikes that attached to the wall by cable.

Santiago inspected the antique devices. "What's next? Tin cans and a string?"

Kacey chuckled. They took stations in the observation bays, he at starboard, Santiago at portside. An array of screens by the windows relayed sensor readouts from the cockpit. Santiago adjusted his tendrils around the headset. He plugged into the intercom box and did a commo test with the crew. This was definitely a screwy arrangement. Cruising through hostile space with a big target on their back and no way to call for back-up.

The return to Van-03h was a long, four-hour trip. Santiago kept alert by switching his attention between the screens, Carlita, and why shutting off the MindLink wasn't part of the mission checklist. Seems that a precaution to prevent the barge from blowing up was an important detail.

He noticed the VIP passengers were in lively conversation and wondered what animated them. Pressing a button on the intercom, he tuned in.

"—fifty thousand ducats, easy." It was the female, Tulee.

"For the artifact in container LK3?" asked the male passenger, Marut. "It's a husk of calcified polymer. A bit much for a curio."

"The value is what's embedded in it," the Magistrate replied. "Hopefully."

"Hopefully?"

"It's better to think of these digs not simply as recovering archeological treasures but more as prospecting. In this case, we're almost certain it's a fragment of a star chart."

"So?"

"A star chart not in The Hub's Astrograph. From other artifacts from Pre-Fracture times. A chart leading the way to Quantum 19."

"Don't the Servitors monitor reconstruction? Keep us from analyzing Creator Tech?"

"On this side of The Hub." The Magistrate looked around, implying vigilance yet unaware that Santiago was listening. He wondered about his deactivated MindLink implant. Now he knew why disabling the MindLink was unofficial policy. It wasn't as much to prevent the inadvertent triggering of a Progenitor device as it was about scheming workarounds to the safeguards protecting Creator Tech.

Was Kacey also eavesdropping? His relaxed posture and vacant stare out the observation windows signaled he wasn't worried about anything but the passing of time.

What about the flight crew? Santiago patched into the cockpit and listened to the pilot and copilot chatter and bitch about work. If they knew what the Magistrate and the Ambassador were discussing, they weren't letting on.

The MindLink was a crucial component of the barge's systems, and they were at this moment sailing through the debris field cut off from Van-03h. Should something happen, an accident, a robbery, who would know? Why take the risk?

In the next instant, he was overwhelmed by an *Aha!* so intense that he wondered if this was the Hex-42 kicking in. The awareness bloomed and he realized that the Magistrate, the Ambassador, the pilot and copilot, Kacey, technicians on both ends of the shuttle voyage, not to mention those processing the artifacts, were all players in an elaborate smuggling ring.

A voice brought him to the present. "What are we talking about?" Marut rubbed his fingertips together, the universal gesture for credits.

"Depends," Tulee answered. "Raw data files on this side, forty-thousand ducats and up. On the other side, at least one-hundred thousand. After download, a quarter of a million before decryption. After decryption, starting at a million. That's before analysis to verify what you have."

"Hold on. You said download. How are you getting the files through The Hub's Communication Screening?"

"Data mules. Carrying the files"—the Magistrate tapped her head—"in here."

"How is that possible? What about thought monitoring? Consciousness reconstruction?"

"Hex-42. It's marketed as a prophylactic measure against Jump Sickness. But its real utility is that it creates voids in the subconscious—"

The Ambassador considered this a moment. "The part unreadable by thought scanners."

"You know your tech." The Magistrate smiled. "Hex-42 allows the storage of a septillion bytes of data into a subject's memory. We can transfer every aspect of an artifact's composition at the Assembler's subatomic level into a person's subconscious. To The Hub's Communication Screener, all that is indistinguishable from the usual mess in one's subconscious."

Santiago connected the dots. Hex-42. Data mules. Carlita was a data mule.

What about Hex-42's effect on him? The only side-effect had been that rush of awareness. As for voids in his subconscious, Santiago shook his head, perhaps thinking he should hear it rattle. Instead, more questions crowded together, aligning in parallel, and he knew they all pointed toward Carlita.

A claxon screamed, jolting Santiago awake. The barracks ceiling lamps blared full-bright. The team chief, VV324H, glowered from a wall screen. "GH235T, get your ass up! Tactical situation in Reclamation Sector 91, Dig Site Tango. Level C Pacification. Rally at the deployment bay in fifteen."

Level C Pacification. Riot. Deadly force authorized.

Thirty minutes later, Santiago and the rest of the REACT team, Kacey included, were in the tactical intervention transporter whooshing at sub-light speed through the MA-Ω debris field, MindLinks at maximum gain. No worries about detonating any random Creator Tech. The team was strapped in their seats, swaddled in armor, helmets on.

VV324H narrated the mission brief, a copy of which scrolled through Santiago's mind.

```
<Another beef about safety violations. The usual. Salvage
techs not advised of dangerous working conditions. You
know how that goes, known exposure to Feem gas would've
triggered special hazard pay and it's no surprise that
our Merge bosses—those tightwad bastards—love to pinch
ducats.>
```

<Which reminds me,> Kacey interrupted. <We ain't getting any special pay either.>

With that comment, everyone in the team double-checked their masks and breathing collars for leaks.

The MindLink relayed telemetry from inside the Reclamation Site. Grainy images of bodies scurrying along the curved passageways, smoke glowing from the pale blue light emitted by the floors. A readout inside Santiago's visor listed the casualties so far. The dead: two security techs. A salvage crew supervisor. Seven others injured and awaiting evacuation. These rioters weren't kidding around.

The readout gave the distance to the docking port of the dig site, the numbers shrinking as Santiago's blood pressure ticked upward. *I retired to get away from this rax.* He grasped his shoulder straps and braced for the impact. *Crunch.*

Machinery whirred, followed by *Boom!* when the breaching petard blasted through the dock's barrier door.

<Get ready to un-ass this sled.>

Santiago and team unbuckled their harnesses, activated weapons, picked up their shields and stun batons, then queued into a tactical stack. Sting bombs deployed. *Pop! Pop! Pop!* The transporter's assault ramp smashed through the remains of the door and the team charged forward.

∩

The riot took an hour to quell. Ventilation fans blew gales to clear the air of smoke. The ozone stink from plasma rifles seeped through Santiago's breathing filter. The last of the fires had been doused—one forklift, an ambulance, several excavators, an entire field office, and a pile of reclaimed Lander artifacts reduced to slag. Boot tread marks crisscrossed pools of coagulated blood, inky blobs on the phosphorescent floor.

At this point, standard procedure was for the REACT team to stand down. But the reserve shift, who should've conducted the arrest processing and interrogation, were serving as bodyguards at a shindig on Van-03h.

Santiago sloughed off his gear and unzipped his overalls. A meaty funk wafted out. He regarded the four prisoners on the steel bench, wrists and ankles shackled and secured to iron chains. Blood trickled from their neck gills and lacerated flesh. They glowered at him, but he was used to this. *Poke the bear, get the claws.*

He tabulated an encyclopedia of criminal charges—arson, conspiracy to commit insurrection, willful destruction of Creator Tech, attempted murder, murder—followed by sentencing—fines, forfeiture of property, including your skin, left with nothing but your mind.

He waited for his MindLink to signal access to the True Name database. No point in starting with questions until having enough background intel to apply psychological pressure, tighten the screws, get them to rat on each other. Santiago hadn't leaned like this on suspects in a long while and the power brought a cruel but enjoyable smile.

Ping.

From left to right on the bench, a listing of True Names and known aliases. The first detainee, the female, True Name, Ke-Chi-Tac-Toi-Neh-Neh-De-Tac. The Vanetta 4 assigned name: KZ114A. And the previous residence, Helios Nexus... Santiago's pulse quickened.

Home residence, Mars...his pulse quickened more.

Birth name: Carlita Chacón.

The astonishment zinged through Santiago. He gasped and choked, neck gills fluttering uncontrollably. The prisoners grinned and whispered to one another.

Kacey stepped beside him. "You okay?"

Santiago cleared his gills. He shouldn't have been surprised. Rarely in his investigations did the evidence take him directly to the fugitive. Got him in the vicinity and then it was fate closing the gap, like opposing magnets smacking together. He made the effort to deepen his voice. "Do me a favor. I need to question this one alone." He pointed at Carlita.

Kacey cocked his head toward an empty storage bay. "That do?"

On command through Santiago's MindLink, the locks on Carlita's shackles clicked open and her chains rattled to the floor. He motioned to the storage bay. Standing, she rubbed her wrists, then limped in that direction.

Once in the bay, he ordered her to sit on a crate. She lowered herself in painful increments. Blood stained the fabric of her overalls. The back of one hand carried the scorch mark from a plasma rifle but her injuries weren't anything that a Healing Chamber couldn't handle.

"You know me?" she asked.

"Why do you ask?"

"That look in your eyes." The assertive way KZ114A said this, in Vanetta language, so different from Common, confirmed that she was Carlita. Completely alien body but still his daughter.

"What are you doing here?" he asked.

Her eyes crinkled. "Stupid question." Exactly how Carlita would respond.

Slowly, their history of toxic episodes came oozing back.

Santiago dragged a crate so he could sit in front of her and stare, his heart aching for relief, the need for closure, the need to close wounds and move on, together. While they were close enough to touch, he sensed a familiar chasm between them creeping ever wider. Maybe he'd been wrong about her and him.

Finally, he said, "It's me, Santiago Chacón."

No reaction.

"Your father."

Still no reaction.

"I've been looking for you."

"So you found me."

Questions welled inside, like a pot boiling. "Why did you run away?"

She grimaced. "Run away? What are you getting at?"

He gave his little speech of contrition, listing all the wrongs and the hurts, and his assurances to make things right. She listened the way she always had, stone-faced, inscrutable. His adopted skin didn't cry but the metaphorical tears he wrung might as well have been rain drops spattering on hot concrete.

She looked away, not embarrassed but unimpressed. They kept quiet, the minutes stretching, that chasm widening. Despite the drama, Santiago saw the two of them shrink into a tiny corner of the universe, two fools stuck in each other's orbit.

Carlita blinked and made a tiny nod as if seeing through him. "What did you expect? Did you ever stop to think that if I wanted to be with you, I would've stayed put?"

"I just thought that—"

"That what? That somehow you could stitch the helicas together? Mend the loss?"

The words cut deep.

"To tell the truth, I quit caring loops ago," she continued, twisting the blade. "You left Mom. She left me. You were gone doing whatever, being the government bounty hunter. There was hurt but no different than the drek everyone goes through in their lives."

He thought about what he'd overheard on the barge, the big conspiracy to smuggle Creator Tech secrets through The Hub. "Hex-42. You're a data mule." It pained him to say this. "Why?"

"Don't look disappointed. I've done worse. You know that. Once I arrived on Helios Nexus, I found myself in another jam. Big surprise, huh? It was bad and to wriggle free, I had to make a deal. Offer the most valuable thing that

I had."

"Which was?"

"You."

"Me?"

"Because of who you are."

"I don't follow."

"Santiago Chacón, Senior Investigator, Criminal Counterintelligence, the best on The Hub."

He was about to reply when <Proten radiation detected. Safety protocol in effect.> He felt his MindLink click off. Sensing movement behind him, he turned to see Kacey accompanying the Magistrate. A glance to his data wrist cuff showed that their MindLinks were likewise powered off.

The conspiracy he'd pieced together took solid form and the walls, the floor, the ceiling, seemed to close in, smothering him. Santiago couldn't breathe.

Tulee radiated an imperial majesty, of someone who always got her way. She stood beside Carlita and said, "GH235T—Santiago Chacón—tell me what you know." She placed a hand on Carlita's shoulder, implying that her well-being depended on his answer.

So he shared everything. Decipher the secrets of the Creator Tech antiquities. Use Hex-42 to smuggle Assembler code in the subconscious of data mules. Traffic that code in the hopes of a big payoff, the rediscovery of a forgotten mineral deposit or better yet, an understanding of Creator Tech to duplicate it.

"Very good," Tulee said. "Your reputation is quite deserved. It's quite the operation we have here. This is where you come in. We needed to test our arrangement, find the flaws, identify the holes before the Servitors could. The surest way was to summon the best investigator on The Hub, send him through the maze and see how long it would take him to ferret his way to us."

"With my daughter as bait?"

"We do what works."

"All this risk? For credits? You're already rich as hell."

"We're after a bigger treasure," Tulee replied, eyes sparkling. "Being from Mars …Earth…you are familiar with the Bible, the Christian Holy Scriptures?"

Santiago shook his head.

"The Garden of Eden?"

"Okay, that I've heard of."

"The Tree of Forbidden Fruit? Rather the Tree of Forbidden Knowledge? The Book of Genesis, Chapter Three, Verse Five?" The Magistrate closed her eyes and recited, "*...that in the day ye eat thereof, then your eyes shall be opened,* *and ye shall be as gods...*"

Gods. Creator Tech. Santiago let his mind swoop to take it all in. This was a cell of the Freeworld Movement! The conspiracy wasn't just about making credits but about toppling the Creator Tech structure. Insurgency. Rebellion.

"The question now," Tulee asked, "are you in?"

"Meaning, keep my mouth shut?"

"You've already taken the Hex-42. Join our enterprise and you'll be set for life."

"As a data mule?"

"For starters."

Santiago saw a glimmer of remorse in Carlita's face. The box he found himself inside opened a bit. He saw a way out. A double-cross of his own. How much would this conspiracy be worth to The Merge, guardians of Creator Tech? Work a deal for himself. Save Carlita. Desperation had pulled her into this. Despite her treachery, they were still family. She wasn't too far gone. A smile formed as he thought about bringing this rotten edifice down around them all, but he kept his expression plain. "Where do we go from here?"

Tulee motioned toward the exit. "Forward. Together."

He started for the door when an intense pain knocked him to the ground, like he'd been skewered through the back with red hot rebar. Pushing up from the floor, blood gushed from the exit wound in his chest. Rallying against the agony, he rolled onto his side to gaze at Carlita.

She pointed a service pistol at him. Kacey's holster was empty.

Tulee said, "Your daughter fulfilled the first part of our bargain by bringing you here. The second part of that bargain was to prove her commitment to our cause."

Carlita spoke, her voice hazy through the pain. "You asked for forgiveness. For what it's worth, yes, Father, I forgive you." She tightened her grip on the pistol. "Now you will forgive me." She fired again.

RUINS OF MEMORY

Kevin J. Anderson

493 HD

AS HE LAY BACK IN THE TRANSPOD waiting for his consciousness to be sent across the Galaxy to his desperate destination, Arky held the photo in his shaky hands and focused on the picture of his wife one last time.

The actual photo would not travel with him, nor would his body, but he burned Etta's beautiful face into memory...as he had done so many times before. But the details kept slipping, slipping, disappearing.

He could not let her be forgotten, could not let *himself* forget, but his mind was riddled with holes like Swiss cheese. Once he arrived on Lluxiv, he wouldn't have to worry about forgetting anymore. Etta would be preserved in his memory—his clean memory—like a fly in amber.

Beneath her sparkling brown eyes in the photo, her soft lips smiled at him. Yes, that was the perfect picture of her. Arky smiled back at the image.

Then the transpod activated, and he was gone.

Lluxiv was an abandoned world once home to a vanished alien race—like so many others in The Merge Archives. For a xeno-archaeologist, the archives were a treasure trove of empty planets just waiting to be explored (or at least cataloged), whenever someone got around to it and whenever funding was available. He could have chosen any world, but Lluxiv would serve his purposes as well as any.

Arky had never thought he would go on an expedition again. He'd walked away from it all after he'd lost Etta, after Aan-oo, but it was getting harder and harder to think every day, and this was his only solution. Taking the transpod through the Mass-O network, to whatever planet, would fix things. Arky would arrive at the other end in a fresh new skin created from the genetic record of his previous trip thirty-five helicas ago.

For weeks, he had scoured the Archives, overwhelmed by the countless choices of unexplored worlds. The terse listing for Lluxiv noted the planet's breathable atmosphere, temperate climate. Its vanished people were called only "Inhabitants."

But the intriguing crystalline growths in the exotic ruins that looked like transparent Protens caught his attention. Etta had always liked crystals—he still remembered that much about her. On their fourth anniversary, he'd given her a beautiful refractive shard. The pendant hadn't cost much, but she loved it. She would gaze into the shiny surface, turning it this way and that in the light, looking at each facet. The happy fascination on her face was clear as a bell. Therefore, Lluxiv was his choice.

But while the solution was simple, the approvals were not, and bureaucracy was a difficult battle. He had to make his case to the Academy approvals bureau.

He did his homework, wrote down notes, martialed his arguments. Before contacting the board, Arky took all of his meds and waited for them to reach full efficacy. His tremors were down, almost unnoticeable, and he could fake being normal, healthy. Then he gathered his courage and contacted Lucinda Bakira of the Academy administration.

Though he had known her predecessor well enough, this woman hadn't even been an undergrad at the time of Arky's last expedition. But she was now Head of the Exploration Division, and she was the one he needed to convince.

He wore his nicest jacket, sat in his neat office in his Earth apartment. On the comm screen, Bakira brightened. "Why, Dr. Arky Sehar, this is unexpected! I thought you'd retired." He was glad that she at least recognized his name.

The woman had wiry blue-black hair that stuck out in strange shapes, making him think of a topiary on her head. Her soft round face suggested that she spent little time on rugged field expeditions, but rather dealt with bureaucratic matters.

That was fine. He needed a bureaucratic release now.

"Retirement isn't all it's cracked up to be," Arky replied. "I'd like to go back out into the field. I've found a planet that deserves to be cataloged."

Lucinda raised her eyebrows. "Oh? What's it been, twenty loops?"

"Thirty-five." He watched her expression change as she considered his age, but he pressed on. "The planet is called Lluxiv. You can call it up in your database. The civilization there is long gone, but well preserved."

"Lots of planets in that category, Dr. Sehar," she said. "The Academy has to be selective. Why should we bother with this…Lluxiv?"

"I've got a hunch about it. From markings found on the ruins and the distinctive appearance of the architecture, I think this race could be related to the Hithree, who left intriguing dimensional mathematics behind on several worlds, which The Merge has adapted. The place could be profitable, and I'd like to follow up on it." A completely fabricated reason, he knew, but he doubted she would dig deeper. "Just a small, preliminary recon, no need for a big expedition."

"We'd never fund a big expedition." Like all bureaucrats, she was skilled at saying no. "And you have been out of the game for a long time. Maybe I should put it on the list for consideration by one of the other candidates who's been waiting longer."

"I hope my reputation is still worth something." His earnestness was obvious. Maybe too obvious. "Lluxiv needs to be explored, and I'm the one to do it, Dr. Bakira." He put on a brave face.

She frowned, then mumbled, "It's just *Ms.* Bakira. Still intending to finish that doctorate." It sounded like an excuse she had given many times before. On the screen, her eyes wandered as she called up the data on Lluxiv. "Looks like a good candidate. You really think this race might be a Hithree derivative? No one else has shown interest in the place before."

"It's subtle, but definitely possible." He hoped she didn't ask him to prove it. "Or you can send me somewhere else, but I'm happy to go solo. Save costs."

She sighed. "There are so many worlds it would take decades and an army of explorers just to do a brief survey of them all. But there's no funding."

He nodded, showing he understood her dilemma. "That's why we should choose candidates with a good chance of applicable discoveries. The Academy certainly benefited from my previous work."

She looked up again. "People remember you positively around here, Dr. Sehar, and yes, you made The Merge plenty of profit. The Academy has a display case with some of the artifacts scanned from Aan-oo." Her sepia eyes filled with real sincerity. "But … are you sure about this, sir? You retired for a reason—a very good reason. I know your story, even read your book back at the university. Didn't you vow you would never do xeno-archaeology again after … after, you know, what happened to your wife?"

"Yes, I know what happened to Etta." *I still remember that,* at least. He realized he sounded terse.

"Transpod travel is expensive, and many skilled researchers are, quite frankly, higher on the Academy's list. You've been out of the game a long time. Even with your impeccable credentials, it may take a while for the request to be approved."

But Arky didn't have "a while," not by any stretch.

"I understand your financial quandary." He played his last card, though he had intended to play it all along. "I did earn a fair amount of royalties from the Aan-oo discoveries, the pharmaceuticals, the alien music. I am willing to cover part of the cost with my own funds, but I need the Academy to cut through the red tape so I can leave quickly."

He would sell every possession, liquidate his accounts. What was he going to use the credits for anyway? Some days he even forgot how to hold a toothbrush.

He crossed his arms in front of the screen. "I've made up my mind, Ms. Bakira."

"A very generous offer, sir, and that should make the difference." Bakira continued scanning information on her screen. "Ah, here it is. Your earlier body map is still in the Mass-O database from your prior travel, so that makes it easier. When you emerge from the transpod on Lluxiv, you'll be in a forty-helica-old body." She smiled again. "I doubt you'll mind that."

"Not at all," Arky said. A clean slate for his consciousness, and that was the most important thing. Pristine brain tissue that wouldn't forget everything… "Please be sure to use the genetic map from my original outbound transit to Aan-oo, not the return body."

"We usually use the most recent one. It's only a few months' difference."

A few vital months. "It is important to me," he insisted. Very important. "And the cost is the same."

"Very well." Bakira shrugged. "I'll authorize the mission, provided you bear half the costs of transportation. We can't afford a team to go with you, though. This will be a solo field expedition."

Even though this was exactly what he wanted, the idea was still daunting—going to an uninhabited, unstudied world without any support other than what the Discovery Lander provided. But he was more frightened of losing his memories forever. "That's fine."

She ticked off the final points on her fingers. "Go see if you can find more Hithree mathematics, or anything else of value. Send the Academy regular updates. Let's hope Lluxiv is as fascinating and as profitable as your previous expedition was."

LLUXIV

Now, when he woke in the Lluxiv transpod, he braced himself for the nausea of jump sickness, which he remembered from the previous expedition, though it had been decades. Nevertheless, when he emerged inside a clone of his forty-helica-old body, even the physical sickness and mental confusion did not diminish his joy.

His head pounded like the worst hangover he'd had in college, but the thoughts were *there*, the memories clear in an uncorrupted brain. Alas, he would never know how many poignant experiences and conversations had been lost forever as his old mind deteriorated, but any memories that were just inaccessible due to ruined neural pathways were now there again.

He could print a new copy of Etta's photo if he wanted, but he didn't need it. He didn't need it! Now she was there in his mind, so bright and clear. He could picture her as if he had just seen her yesterday.

Arky was already smiling as he climbed out of the pod and set foot inside the ancient Lander. In wonder, he brushed his hands down his durable travel shirt and trousers—the same clothes he had worn when he'd arrived on Aan-oo as a younger man. It gave him a strange sense of déjà vu, and he glanced over his shoulder, as if Etta might emerge from the other pod, joining him as before.

But of course not.

Inside the Lander, Servitors moved about, monitoring the equipment. The quicksilver spiderlike robots remained unobtrusive, uninterested in him, but they weren't of interest to him either.

At the console, he programmed the Assembler to generate the archeological equipment he would need: exploration tools, recording apparatus, a translation database, even an old-school paper notepad and stylus. All the while, he recalled going through similar activities with Etta on Aan-oo, savoring details that had been blurred by time and his own disability.

Back then, she had programmed the food synthesizer with some of her favorite recipes from Earth, and he suddenly recalled their first meal on Aan-oo, a spicy vindaloo. His mouth watered now; he could almost taste it. He hadn't eaten vindaloo in helicas...

He already had what he had come here for. In fact, he could just sit back inside the Lander and reminisce, which he did for several hours, feeling the wet tears down his face. There was no hurry. He didn't have to explore this place immediately, but he would carry the memories along with him whatever he did. And Etta would have wanted to go out and have a look at Lluxiv, even sketch some of the things she found interesting.

Before long, he was ready. "All right, my dear. Let's see what this place has to offer."

He stepped outside, a new man on a new world, excited and alive again.

Ages ago, the Progenitors' Discovery Lander had settled near a complex of Inhabitant ruins, a hive-like city surrounded by a prairie of spiky grasses and flowering plants. He inhaled the odd air, caught an undertone of cinnamon and dust. Scarlet bird analogs flitted about.

He set out for the nearby city. The blue-white sun shone on the curves, arches, and pockmarked windows in the high structures. The tan, weathered architecture wasn't at all like the Hithree civilization, and he was glad Lucinda Bakira hadn't asked for too many justifications. Arky was sure he could find something worthwhile to earn his keep.

Most remarkable were the strange transparent growths that wound through the silent ruins—crystal vines, tubes of glass that branched out in all directions, like voracious weeds that had turned to silicon. Etta would have found them pretty. He didn't see any immediate purpose to the vines, could not tell if they were some kind of implanted infrastructure or wild crystalline accretions.

Arky walked among the outer structures, feeling the oppressive grandeur of infinite age. How long ago had this exotic race fallen? What had destroyed them? And what had they left behind? This titanic civilization was now simply vanished from memory, from history. Ruins and memories—just like him.

Etta had been so excited when they'd first arrived in the jungles on Aan-oo. And he felt just as much excitement to think of it now, the childlike smile on her face, the sparkle in her eyes. Yes, that was better than any xeno-archaeological treasure.

Occupying himself as he daydreamed, he spent the first day taking a general survey of the Inhabitant ruins, filing numerous images to send back to the Academy. He found no markings on the buildings, no writings or stelae or chiseled statues, and in his initial report he promised to continue his search for Hithree-inspired equations. He downplayed his excitement, so as not to intrigue other xeno-archaeologists, not that the Academy would send a second expedition here.

He would have the world to himself.

The intriguing crystalline growths were wild and random, like weeds, yet he suspected there was a pattern somewhere, one he simply couldn't see. Had the Inhabitants planted these glassy vines to adorn their structures, or were they natural growths, crystalline weeds that had taken over the long-forgotten ruins? Power conduits? Defensive systems?

He chipped away samples of the glassy nodules so that his analytical equipment could run tests. He took images, spectral analyses, thermal signatures, and brought everything back to his base camp at the Lander. He spent each evening documenting his work and planning the next day's activities.

And all the while, he basked in his rediscovered memories of Etta.

He worked his way deeper into the ruins. He was all alone, surrounded by history, though he still had learned little about the vanished race, certainly nothing that would excite The Merge. Before The Great Fracture, the Progenitors had begun their extensive search for inhabited worlds. When a Lander had finally stumbled upon Lluxiv thousands of helicas ago, was the planet already a tomb? Had these extinct Inhabitants just barely missed being saved?

He didn't understand the curvature of the doors, the prominent towers and stubby lumps, all infested with crystal vines. He found no squiggles and lines that denoted language, no artwork or detailed carvings. It seemed the Inhabitants had left no written or visual language, no record of themselves at all.

Looking at the towers, he inhaled the faintly cinnamon air and shook his head. Back on Aan-oo, he and Etta had been sounding boards for each other, bouncing ideas back and forth, the wilder the better.

Now, trying to imagine what the Inhabitants had been like, he mused aloud, "I wish I understood you."

Out of the corner of his eye, Arky caught a flicker of light, shades of color awakening within the crystal vines. The transparent stalks shimmered, and then they displayed images for him. He turned around amid the transparent stalks and saw ghostly holograms in the air, like whispers of the past struggling to be seen and heard again.

The crystal growths began to show him the Inhabitants at the height of their civilization! Locked inside the silicon matrix was a panoply of stories, like video recordings.

As he walked from vine to vine in wonder, each stalk displayed a new set of images. Arky stared at all the different stories as the Inhabitants flitted about. The creatures were like locusts with long wings and oval insectile heads, but they walked upright, with four arms and two legs.

The records showed Inhabitants building their cities, burrowing in the ground, flying in daredevil moves that were apparently mating dances. They participated in races across the sky or clashed in large groups—warfare, or perhaps just sporting events.

Next, the transparent vines began to hum, and then he heard actual music, atonal melodies created and recorded by the Inhabitants. He moved in awe, realizing that perhaps these glassy structures were how the aliens preserved their memories, keeping them intact, frozen in crystal. Just waiting for someone to remember them.

And Arky was here.

His pulse raced as he wandered through the structures, watching the light-show inside the vines, but he could not absorb so many recordings at once. It would take him months and months just to sample them.

As he experienced a sense of joy and discovery, how he wished Etta could be here with him, just as she had been on that glorious, and damnable, expedition to Aan-oo. His mind was clear now, not addled by the rapid degeneration. She had been such a perfect partner back in those perfect days...

As that thought occurred to him, Arky gasped as Etta's image danced like a ghost inside the alien crystal growths. Her face, her slender body, her quick yet agile movements. She was there, as clear as any memory!

He moved from stalk to stalk, and Etta was reflected back, drawn from his memories, treasured there along with the alien history. The crystal vines recorded it all.

Arky reached out with trembling fingers to touch her embedded image—and he received another burst of memories.

⚓

All his life, Arky had dreamed of doing fieldwork for the Academy. The Mass-O offered instantaneous transpod travel to so many worlds, vibrant cultural and business centers, members of The Merge. But he was more interested in the empty and untouched ones, the mysteries that were mere footnotes in a catalog.

Arky dreamed about the unexplored planets with once-grand civilizations that had fallen into the obscurity of time and history. What had happened to them? What went wrong? How many remarkable races had died out before the unification of the races, just missing what might have saved their people? A tragedy.

He wanted to see for himself.

Fascinated to fill in some of those blanks in the Archives, he got his certification in xeno-archaeology, and yet his expedition requests were declined seven times before he finally got approval to go to Aan-oo. But the Academy couldn't afford a research team to go with him, except for a possible research assistant.

When he was an undergrad, he had met Etta, a shy history major studying the background of The First Cycle and The Great Fracture. She was also an artist who loved to sketch the plants, flowers, bugs, and birds around them on Earth. They had fallen in love, stuck together. Although she wasn't specifically trained in xeno-archaeology, Arky pulled strings to get her named his research assistant, and the two of them were off to a pristine world that had once been home to a powerful race.

Aan-oo was a lush, jungle world covered with sluggish mosses and towering fern groves, flowers and seeds, and (inedible) fruits of all kinds and colors. The Assembler inside the Discovery Lander created anything they needed—tools, shelters, food, analytical devices.

He and Etta scanned the genetic profiles of native flowers and berries, uploading the data for possible Merge pharmaceutical uses. Despite the perfectly accurate and detailed images from their recording apparatus, Etta preferred to sketch the odd plants and fungi herself; she added her own flair, comparing herself to the intrepid historical naturalists Darwin and Audubon.

He and Etta slept in open tents; they made love in the fern groves. Whenever they didn't want to get soaked by the warm jungle rains, they could run back to the Lander and collate their notes, clean up, and sometimes make love again. Arky picked pretty bouquets and gave them to Etta. She drew sketches that featured him next to the alien flora. It had been a genuine honeymoon: Adam and Eve on an alien Eden. Aan-oo was idyllic, or so they'd both thought at the time.

The Aan aliens constructed ziggurat structures out of black rock quarried from jungle outcroppings. The identical buildings were spaced in geometric patterns like an extraterrestrial connect-the-dots, visible only when Arky dispatched drones to take images from high above.

Though the alien civilization had vanished millennia ago, the ruins were pristine, the edges still sharp. He and Etta cracked open chill vaults within the pyramids, where they found the cadavers, perfectly preserved Aan inhabitants. They were a race of salamander-like creatures, their dead spotted skin somehow still moist and covered with a protective slime. It took days for Etta to get up her nerve to sketch them in close detail, but eventually she did the lost race justice.

Inside other ziggurats they found libraries, and the two of them settled in to scan the material, running images and words through translation approximators and sending data back to the Academy Archives.

Etta discovered pinecone-shaped objects, which proved to be alien music players, and she and Arky spent weeks recording the lost music of Aan-oo.

Now, in a perfectly sharp memory, he could hear her humming along, trying to match the atonal melody with human vocal cords.

As the lead xeno-archaeologist, Arky narrated the reports dispatched to the Academy; naturally shy, Etta refused the attention, preferring just to be his assistant. After all, xeno-archaeology was *his* passion, although her sketches and paintings added something unique to each report.

When at last their allotted time was over and they had to say goodbye to their little slice of Eden, he and Etta returned home through The Hub. Rather than reusing their outbound clone map to create new skins, they had asked the Academy to pay for a fresh, up-to-date scan. Retaining every detail of their bodies after months working on the field expedition was considered a reward, a small pat on the back, and they wanted to retain even their slight biochemical changes, as their love had grown.

They were happy, even minor celebrities in their academic world. Merge pharma researchers found that the strange Aan flora contained a unique chemical structure that led to new drug families. The music from the pine-cone-shaped recorders became immensely popular across the inhabited worlds.

Although the Academy, and hence The Merge, retained the rights on all such discoveries, Arky earned a small fraction of royalties as lead researcher. That eventually became a significant source of income. He and Etta talked about the next expedition they would undertake.

He even wrote a book about their blissful expedition, playing up the mystery of Aan-oo, including her artwork. He gave Etta every speck of credit she deserved, but she had been shy since the first moment he'd met her, and he respected her wishes to stay out of the limelight.

Six months later, Etta's first symptoms manifested—initially as forgetfulness, then piercing headaches. Her thoughts became more and more disorganized. He spotted the differences right away, but doctors weren't able to diagnose the cause until the damage was so extreme they couldn't help but notice it.

In addition to all those wondrous memories, Aan-oo had also given Etta a brain parasite, an insidious alien retrovirus that encoded itself into her DNA like a worm wrapped around her neurons. It began to flourish not long after they were back home, at which point the plaques and nodules appeared, growing throughout her cerebrum like fern forests on the alien planet.

Etta had holes in her memory, holes in her mind. Whole sections of her past were eaten away until she couldn't remember the simplest things, couldn't remember her life...couldn't remember him. With astonishing rapidity, she couldn't even remember how to *live*.

Arky begged for medical help, called upon the Academy as well as those pharmaceutical companies that had benefited from his discoveries. But the news cycle had moved on, distracted by other incredible discoveries, other scandals, other political upheavals. Some news reports did mention Etta's plight, but she had never been the star of the expedition. A little-known "research assistant" did not fire the imaginations of The Merge, and the publicity generated nothing more than impotent "thoughts and prayers."

During that brief gray area when Etta understood what was happening to her and before she lost her capability to think, she worried that Arky was infected as well. He endured tests and scans, but the doctors found no sign of the parasite in him. Etta must have had the misfortune of catching the parasite from something in the air she breathed, the water she drank, from one of the odd fungi she sketched, maybe from contaminated dust or pollen in the tombs. Perhaps she'd just been unlucky, inhaling the virus while he did not. His scans remained clear, and his heart was broken as he watched her fade.

The onset of the brain parasite was like a wrecking ball, and within months Etta was gone. Afterward, Arky simply didn't have the heart for his work anymore. With the success of his book and the tangential profits from the Aan-oo discoveries, he could have gone on a new expedition, this time with a full research team. But he would undertake no more alien expeditions without her. Instead, Arky Sehar simply retired and vanished into obscurity.

After thirty-five helicas, though, he still had enough clout and enough credits to force the expedition to Lluxiv. And now he had his memories back.

Arky spent his days surrounded by a wealth of history and memory. The crystal vines recognized his presence, and they were hungry to share the records they had cherished all these millennia, memories ready for an audience.

Walking through the crystal archives, he recorded the history of the Inhabitants, which he dutifully relayed to the Academy, where their linguists would spend helicas deciphering the records.

Some of the insectile sounds had a singsong quality, and he imagined they were spoken by poets or religious figures. Images showed incomprehensible designs that might have been art, might have been mathematics. Maybe Merge engineers could find something useful here. He just basked in what the vines showed him. His pristine mind had room for all of those stories.

And the crystal growths picked up on the memories—the history—that he brought with him. The alien crystals reflected his life and Etta's back at him, showing him images in the curved glassy surfaces. A new historical record. All day long, he walked through a magical forest of Etta.

Needing no further encouragement, Arky accessed his happy days. The memory vines showed flickers of his boyhood as the reminiscences came back to mind, a dog he'd loved and also lost, because that was the way of pets. He saw his school days, the first girl he'd been infatuated with; he couldn't remember her name, but he knew she had long braids…

Arky shook his head and focused on what really mattered to him. He didn't care about other spots in his life. He had come here to reclaim the memories of Etta, and now this crystal forest on Lluxiv was preserving her in a way he had never dreamed—her beautiful face, her silly laugh. Once he remembered her life, she would be preserved forever here on Lluxiv.

An excellent cook, Etta would choose a specific planetary cuisine for a month, then switch to a new culinary adventure the next month. His mouth watered at the thoughts as they came back to him, and he made up his mind to have the Lander Assemblers recreate some of those meals.

He recalled a rafting trip they had taken down a languid river in North America during the first helica they had dated. Warm under the open sky, they drifted along in silence, satisfied with each other's company. They'd eaten sandwiches from the cooler—nothing fancy, just thick layers of sticky peanut butter and sweet raspberry jam, an old traditional recipe Etta had discovered. When they kissed, they had smeared the remnants over each other's faces, and then they dunked into the river water to wash off.

Another time, they went camping in the wilderness just to see how much they would enjoy the rugged experience. In his imagination, Arky had been preparing for an alien expedition someday. As if to test them, the skies turned gray, the temperature dropped, and a cold rain drenched them. He and Etta found shelter in a grove of trees, erected their tent, and waited it out. After nightfall, the clouds cleared, and the two emerged to see a midnight sky exploding with diamond stars… countless worlds that were now connected by the Mass-O.

Now, giving the memories to the crystal vines, he thought of when he and Etta at last traveled to Mars and the nearest Discovery Lander, the jumping-off point for transpod travel through The Hub. They were both excited and nervous, marveling at the Martian complex and the first Academy outpost there, the wonder of the ancient vessel that had opened the human race to a new age of exploration and galactic commerce. From there Arky and Etta had gone on their adventure to Aan-oo…

In his new body, his new mind, the restored memories were completely real to him, and even though they brought tears to his eyes, they were tears of joy. He considered the beauty of lost things, not the pain of the loss itself.

Unfortunately, with this newfound clarity of his past, he also began to see images of Etta that he wished he could forget for all time. The grayness of her skin in her last days, the glassy confusion in her eyes as they flicked back and forth, showing no knowledge of where she was or what had happened to her, or even who *he* was.

The brain parasites consumed her thoughts and memories. Etta had been lost to him one neuron at a time, one memory at a time, until all that remained was her heartbeat. And even that went away.

Now that clarified memory was a curse. Arky huddled in the crystalline grove watching the reflected images of her last moments babbling, incoherent, unaware. He squeezed his eyes shut.

After all this time, few people back home remembered Etta at all, not even her name. Her footnote in the Archives was even smaller than his. So, the responsibility of preserving her fell to Arky—because once he forgot her, then she would truly be gone forever. A veritable hermit in his apartment on Earth, he had clung to each of those memories.

Helica by helica, in his private journal he wrote down everything he could recall. He stared at the photos in his personal scrapbooks thousands of times, then he took up the hobby of digital art so he could create new images as he thought about her. By no means was he as talented as she had been, but love and longing blurred his critical vision.

With no one to distract him at home, he would go back and reread the old journals he had written, embellishing events, adding details that occurred to him. One day, however, he was perplexed, and then concerned, as he read his own lengthy description about a surprise birthday party that Etta had thrown for him… but he didn't remember the event at all! It was entirely gone from his memory.

Two days afterward, while using his art apps and digital paintbrush, he stopped halfway through painting Etta's profile, frozen with self-doubt because he couldn't recall exactly what her eyes looked like.

Once he noticed that, he began to connect the dots. He realized other instances in the previous months where he'd been uncharacteristically absent-minded. At first, he laughed it off as a symptom of growing older, but when he reread the journal entry about the birthday party, he understood that the memory wasn't just faded, but *gone*. That gave him a deep chill.

He knew those symptoms.

After copying Etta's old medical records, he hurried in for a full scan himself. No cure had ever been found for the Aan brain parasite, no treatment proposed. In fact, it had barely been studied. The Merge knew of only one case, one datapoint. A curiosity.

Even after so many discoveries and profitable materials had spun off from Aan-oo, The Merge had interdicted the planet, placing it on a quarantine list. Arky and Etta's survey had been thorough, if not complete. No one needed to visit there again. There were so many other worlds to choose from.

The brain scan showed that Arky did indeed have the Aan parasite. He had been infected after all. Tied to his DNA, the retrovirus had hidden dormant within his neurons for decades, but now it activated at last, for whatever reason. Her symptoms had just manifested much sooner.

Arky knew exactly what was going to happen to him, and he knew how fast the brain burn would occur, like little novas going off in his mind, erasing or burying memories. Before it was too late for him, he had used up his remaining wealth and clout to book one more Academy field expedition. The Discovery Lander could rebuild his body cell by cell, neuron by neuron, DNA strand by DNA strand—from the original pattern when he had first traveled to Aan-oo, not the infected one that had returned home. His consciousness could go into a pristine new skin.

Arky needed to hurry, because his memories were slipping away day by day. He would never return to the old deteriorating body left behind in storage. He didn't have the finances to jump into a new skin back home, to hopscotch from body to body for helicas as some wealthy people did. No, this trip had been his only chance not just to save himself, but to save Etta, to save her memories. He wouldn't lose her again.

Smiling now, though, Arky walked through the crystal forest of memories. These silicon vines, whether natural growths on Lluxiv or some exotic data-storage tech, were also remembering her, as eager to preserve Etta as he was. He could stay here and just reminisce about her for a long time. He had everything he needed.

Shared by the memory vines, the alien Inhabitant culture would interest him for the rest of his life, and The Merge would be satisfied with the data he kept sending them. The Academy could check Lluxiv off their list, a world thoroughly cataloged. In fact, he thought, the memory-storage tech in the crystal vines would prove as useful as any of the items he had sent back from

Aan-oo. He smiled as he made up his mind to use a portion of the profits to endow an Academy chair in Etta's memory. Another kind of immortality for her in The Merge.

Arky had a new life and a clarity of purpose, as well as a clarity of memories. Etta lived inside his mind again, and these crystal vines helped make her bright and clear, as if every event in their lives together had happened only yesterday. And it would now be stored forever.

He touched the cylindrical vines, the crystal offshoots that rose up through the ruins and held so much of the past, not just of an entire civilization but of Arky's own life. Like a fly caught in amber. Once he understood the aliens more, he would even give them a name, a *real* name. They deserved to be remembered as more than just "Inhabitants." They had given him the gift of Etta; he would give them something back in return.

As he stood among the ruins of Lluxiv, he drew a long, satisfied breath. Now Etta would last for millennia, just like the memories of the Inhabitants had.

ZER HR

DARK TRUTHS

Dayton Ward and Kevin Dilmore

HELIOS NEXUS, 493 HD

"SO WHY IS IT THAT SO MANY OF US remember a different ending to *Fluffy's Showdown*, an event that has *traumatized* us since we were *kids*, and yet *now* when we watch it, there's *no* munch-bunnies? They're not just gone. They *never existed*. The munch-bunnies have been *deprogrammed* out of our *minds!*"

Teks looked up from her pocket hubcaster that lay on the well-scuffed tabletop before her and scanned the crowd populating ZEROHR. Among the dozens of beings scattered about other tables around the bar, lit chiefly by the screens lining its walls that radiated images from who knew how many simultaneous sporting events, she caught three or maybe four of them looking her way and nodding. There was no way they could hear her actual voice amid the din of this place, which was just another joint in the Nexus City barrio.

Instead, their responses tipped her to how many of them had tuned their nanotech implants to her hubcast's encrypted audio frequency, a signal she'd piggybacked on enough random data packets to thwart any attempts to track her location through the MindLink. That any listeners were present at all was owed to her occasional urge to burst her broadcasting plans to subscribers, at least the paying ones, with very little notice. Sometimes, Teks indulged herself an audience of her choosing. More often than not, it was here at ZEROHR.

"Creator Tech can do way more than you realize, friends," she continued. "Mergers may say they don't understand it all, but they understand way more than they're telling *us*. The Creators found a way to extract everything that makes us *us*, send it across incomprehensible distances of space and rewire us back into completely different bodies. Is it too far-fetched to believe Mergers might use this technology to manipulate and rewrite our waking minds in our *own bodies*? And if so, the Mergers wouldn't test their mind control on our perceptions of reality right away. No, friends, they'd start with the munch-bunnies."

Movement caught Teks's attention. She looked up to see an auburn-haired woman in a rain-spattered poncho making her way toward the ersatz 'casting booth. Teks snatched the device from the tabletop and held it closer to her mouth. "Until next time, friends, remember that when you can't believe your eyes, believe your ears."

"'Believe your ears,'" the woman parroted back. "You think that's all you need to say for people to buy that glap you spread?"

Teks met her gaze. The face and particularly the voice seemed familiar. There was a look in the woman's eyes that made Teks think she might be trying to bait her, but why?

She's fishing. So, let her.

Playing her own game, Teks decided to come off as somewhat vulnerable. She reached up to smooth her short, black hair into a less tousled state to appear self-conscious. "My listeners trust my information because I trust my information."

"Why?"

"Double-source," Teks said. "Never go with what you hear from just once place. That's rule number two."

The woman offered a smile with one corner of her mouth. "So what's rule number one?"

"If your mother says she loves you, check it out."

"Are those rules you got from your dad?"

Wait. Does she know me?

This was definitely calculated, Teks decided. Feeling a pang in her chest, she covered her reaction by making a broad play of transferring her 'caster to a front pocket of her drab fatigues. She hoped the flash of her arms distracted the woman from seeing even a micro-expression. "I didn't know my dad so well."

"I knew him." Again, the woman's reply came with a deliberate tone and snappy delivery Teks knew was intended to shake her up. She didn't bite but instead let the silence between them hang until the woman added, "Well, not personally, but his work was a big influence on me."

Teks released a sigh of recognition. "Now I get it," she said, ready to go on the offensive. "You're Dana Wright. You're a damn Bubblehead, come down from the towers up near the clouds. I saw your face in between reports back when I used to watch the MindLink."

"So Chance Tekahara the Hubcaster doesn't watch the news anymore?" the woman scoffed.

Rolling her eyes, Teks replied, "Viz is dead. Every second of that blern you show is faked. Nobody trusts you like they trust me because you can't fake what people communicate in how they talk."

The woman appeared ready to argue the point but seemed to decide against it. Instead, she held up a hand. "Let's start again. Hi. I'm Dana Wright. I don't know why I provoked you but I did. Good on you for giving it right back."

"You baited her because you want a reason not to trust her," said a new voice, and Teks smiled as Gunny approached. She knew he'd been observing the exchange from his stool at the bar. Covert surveillance was just another skill he'd picked up during his time in uniform. Lucky for her, he was her best friend. He was still in shape for a man his age, even after all this time out of the ranks. Carrying an oversized beer mug in his meaty left hand, he stopped next to Teks, eyeing the other woman. "What I'm hearing is you want to trust her. Sound about right?"

Without missing a beat, Dana extended her hand to Gunny. "Donovan Raddix. Gunnery sergeant, Interplanetary Expeditionary Force. Nice to meet you, too." Eyeing him for a moment, she added, "Retired for medical reasons, wasn't it?"

Gunny grunted. "Something like that."

"Wounded in action?"

Pausing, he took a long pull from his beer. "Something like that." Teks suppressed a giggle. Gunny could be annoyingly standoffish.

"Okay, then." Dana returned her attention to Teks. "I believe we can help each other."

"I don't think we're up for whatever story you're cooking," replied Gunny, and Teks heard the suspicion lacing his every word.

Dana said, "It's actually *your* story. "You're right when you say I want to trust you, because I think you're on to something." She looked around as though to verify no one was eavesdropping. "Augmentics General Innovations."

Unable to cover her reaction this time, Teks felt her jaw slacken. "AGI?"

"You've connected some dots. So have I, and it sure as glap isn't munch-bunnies. I've been trying to blow that place open for over a loop." She looked at Teks. "If you're the wire whisperer I've heard about, then maybe we can help each other make that happen."

His voice low and ominous, Gunny said, "AGI's a bunch of grifters, skimming defense credits off the top of bloated military contracts. They're also very good at covering their tracks, and without any hard proof there's no way the authorities will go up against them."

Teks added, "We don't even know where to start looking for the proof."

Leaning closer, Dana lowered her voice. "You know how to expose them, but you can't find them. I know where they are, but I can't get there without your help. Is that enough to make us partners?"

"Depends," Teks said. "Where do you stand with *Fluffy's Showdown*?"

"Skruffles lost all her toes to those furry monsters. I will neither confirm nor deny whether I made it all the way through that one with dry shorts."

"Ah, Skruffles," Teks said, nodding slowly. "She had the heart of a champion."

Gunny watched enough news to know Dana Wright's reputation. If the reporter was as good as the scuttlebutt suggested, he needed to stay frosty. Just her being here meant she had an agenda. The big question of the moment was whether he and Teks were allies in Dana's latest crusade, or just tools.

That thought was foremost on his mind as he stood alongside Teks and Dana in the large yet oddly austere office belonging to Zittel. Like most Ordovi living away from their home planet, The Merge security councilmember was cocooned inside a transparent, water-filled bubble that was just large enough to house his soft, eight-tentacled body. A gunmetal, humanoid exoskeleton standing nearly three meters tall supported the bubble. With his large eyes and lack of defined cranium, Zittel within his bubble was an oversized head atop this towering form. Gunny had seen mechs like this before, but mostly in the form of battle armor wrapped around IEF troops. He'd used such flakjaks a few times, but never liked them.

"Dana Wright," he said, his entire body moving inside the bubble as his voice filtered through the mech's translator. "Been a long time. Let me guess. You need a favor."

"And you owe me a big one." Stepping forward, Dana extended her hand, which Gunny saw held a data crystal. "Trust me, Zittel. This is something you'll want me to do."

A series of fleeting yet bright flashes emitted from two of Zittel's tentacles, and the exoskeleton reached out with its right hand to accept the crystal. The mech turned to the office's lone furnishing, a large, curved computer console with a dozen monitors arrayed in three stacks of four on the room's far wall. The console with row upon row of multicolored controls was unlike any terminal Gunny had used, but the mech's hands under Zittel's direction inserted the crystal into a reader slot and danced across the interface with practiced ease. In response to its commands, a holographic representation of a dull gray planet appeared in the center of the room, behind the mech. In his bubble, Zittle shifted his amorphous body to face them.

"Cygnus-2h?" The Ordovi seemed to shudder in response to this information. "It's a restricted Hub world. No civilian jumpers allowed."

Teks said, "We know that. It's why we're here."

Ignoring the remark, Zittel kept his attention on Dana. "What are you after, Dana? Cygnus-2h is a dustball. It's not worth anything."

"It's worth something to AGI," said Dana. "Perfect place to carry on with all sorts of illegal activities. I've heard rumors of drugs and even trafficking, but the big one is black market plasma weapons sales. If my sources are right, I'm talking who knows what kind of firepower to anyone who can meet the asking price."

Zittel shifted in his bubble. "That's quite the accusation, considering AGI is working under an exclusive IEF contract. Where's your proof?"

"On Cygnus-2h." Dana pointed to the hologram. "We need to jump there to find out, and for that I need you to get us the proper creds."

Teks looked at Dana. "Do I really need to go? Can't I just hack the skinventory for you and stay here?"

The reporter shook her head. "I told you, we're probably going to have to break into their systems to find what we need. I can't do that without you."

"You're a Pure Soul?" asked Zittel.

"Pure?" Teks asked back. "Do I have to talk about this in front of Gunny?"

Zittel made a sound that from his translator sounded like air escaping. "Never jumped before?"

"Nope." Teks shook her head. "Born and raised in Nex City."

Zittel glared at Gunny. "What about you?"

"Yeah, I've jumped a few times."

It was Dana's turn to stare at him. "A *few* times? I saw your record, Raddix. Over three hundred jumps logged across fifteen loops. That's what? About once every two weeks?"

"Sounds about right." That part of his life was over, and he liked it that way.

"Three hundred jumps?" Zittel squirmed in his bubble. "Number gets to be that big, there's no avoiding Zero Hour unless you stop jumping."

Gunny had heard all of this from the IEF doctors. He'd taken their word for it because that's what you did when you were a grunt and the docs read you the riot act. While he had no desire to ever jump again, Dana's explanation of her plan required Teks to jump with her and he couldn't let her go it alone.

"I've got one or two jumps left in me," he said, looking at Teks. "Let's do this and come home."

Zittel said, "I can get you the creds, but you need to hack their skinventory and come up with some way to blend in. Otherwise, they're liable to slag you on sight."

"This is going to suck," said Teks. "Isn't it?"

Gunny couldn't help a humorous chuckle. "It only sucks the first hundred times or so."

Chance.

Teks heard the voice as if through a wall; muffled, distant, and disorienting, and very much in keeping with her present sense of self. Sightless, limbless, even breathless, she felt no perception of occupying physical space, as though that sensation had been stripped from her consciousness. She was... *apart.*

Was she a mere atom? Perhaps she was as vast as limitless space? Whatever her dimensions, Teks was aware of her undefinable self now bobbing and dipping in this invisible ocean that seemed to envelop her. The currents carried her, sometimes at what might be dizzying vectors and velocities while at the same time remaining still.

Chance, do you hear me?

Except the voice. Was it even real? It called to her. No, Teks realized. It was calling her *towards it.*

She sensed movement along...conduits? Pathways, like wires connecting circuits or neurons linking the synapses of her own mind. Her earliest memories included the whispers that later helped her understand and manipulate data passing through computer networks. Eventually, she adapted this gift to decipher people with the same ease. Her innate perception of the most subtle of inflections and cadences let her identify and decode the truth hidden in someone's spoken words. How was this different?

Curiosity activates the interface. Teks remembered reading that somewhere. Transpods only worked if the person being transported understood— at least on some level—how the process worked. They also needed to want to jump, as she was told during the preparation stage. She had to be committed to the act, or else she would've simply remained at Nexus City.

You're being guided. Find its voice. Hear its voice. Understand the system.

Teks listened, drifting along with the current for what seemed like an eternity. She became aware of reality reasserting itself, beginning to solidify around her finite sense of self.

Chance. Find the light.

The voice was louder now, and Teks now realized it sounded much like her own. Was this her subconscious—her *curiosity*—guiding her through the jump? Awareness of time passing seemed to return. Darkness faded as the ocean began draining away. Light returned, as did sound. Teks perceived a dull, pulsing hum. Was this the heartbeat of another world?

Where am I?

She recognized the inside of a transpod. Did she make it? Was this the Discovery Lander on Cygnus-2h? The questions came in a rush even as her vision blurred and her eyes felt heavy. Awareness dwindled, and light surrendered once more to dark before she—

Teks awoke with a start. Was it over already? She blinked several times, realizing she must have fallen asleep at some point after transit. She sensed the familiar shift from slumber to awareness, and this time there was no disorientation, other than she appeared to be in a stark white room crammed with all manner of equipment arrayed around the bed in which she found herself.

Stretching to ward off the last vestiges of sleep, Teks felt an abrupt itching in her groin area. Without thinking she reached there to scratch, and encountered much more than she anticipated.

What the actual hell?

She sat up in the bed, now realizing the body in which she found herself was that of a Cygnae male. Deep lavender skin stretched across long arms and legs, as well as the oversized hands and feet. Her chest was hard and muscled, and then there was—

"Look who's awake," said a deep, masculine voice, and Teks turned her head to see a Cygnae male standing to her right, arms folded across his broad chest. He wore a dark green jumpsuit that seemed to harmonize with his lavender skin. The holotag above his left breast read, "Mercado," and the patch above it was the Augmentics General Innovations logo. Like all Cygnae, he had no hair atop his head, and Teks reached up to feel her own smooth scalp.

"Welcome to Cygnus-2h, sir," said Mercado just as a Cygnae woman, bald like them but wearing a white jumpsuit, moved from a nearby workstation to give Teks a onceover. "Or, as we like to call it, Deadwood. This is a recovery room at the company infirmary. You feel all right? The manifest said this was your first jump."

"Got a helmet I can heave into? No?" Seeing no hint of humor on either face, Teks waved away the suggestion. "Sorry. I'm a little disoriented but I can already feel it passing."

Mercado smiled. "That's normal for first-timers. There might be an occasional dizzy spell for a day or two, but all the readings show it was a clean jump. Manifest says you're a data systems technician, detailed to the command post. Your quarters are there, too." He offered a wave. "I've been assigned as your liaison until you get settled."

Apparently satisfied with Teks's condition, the nurse smiled before saying her goodbyes and exiting the room, leaving Teks alone with Mercado. The Cygnae man waited until the door closed behind the nurse before his face broke into a broad grin.

"A helmet to heave into?"

"Was that such an unreasonable request?"

"Teks, it's me. Dana."

It took Teks an extra moment to process that. "Dana?" She shook her head. "Zittel. He slanted us for a laugh, didn't he?"

"Looks that way," replied Dana. "He had to forge three false identities for us and find skins to match. The gender breakdown here is pretty lopsided. For future reference, your new name is Schaeffer."

Wonderdope, thought Teks. *Thanks loads, you frappin' gronk.* "Well, I don't mind saying you look pretty tasty, Mister Mercado."

"It could've been worse." Dana's grin returned. "We could've been Gunny."

"Shut up."

Turning toward the new voice, Teks saw a young Cygnae woman entering the room. Also wearing a green jumpsuit, her holotag read "Vasquez."

"Gunny?" asked Teks, unable to stifle a laugh. "Dude, you've never looked better."

Dana shrugged. "She ain't wrong." Turning back to Teks, she asked, "You ready to get to work? We've been waiting on you."

"How long was I out?" asked Teks.

Gunny shrugged. "Close to a full day."

"Wow. Guess I'm a lightweight." Teks shook her head. "Sorry."

"Don't sweat it. That's normal for first-time jumpers. It gets easier the more you do it." He pointed to Dana. "We took advantage of you being in recovery to do some snooping while pretending to do the fake jobs Zittel set up for us."

Dana added, "Wherever they're playing the shady games, it's not here, or anywhere close by. We figure it has to be a remote site, but according to our credentials, we're not cleared for that kind of need-to-know info."

"Get me to a terminal," said Teks. "I'll show you who's cleared."

Gunny said, "Accessing the main AGI system is a beast, but we've found a hard link we think you can use."

Already feeling—inwardly, at least—more like her normal self, Teks followed Dana from the infirmary. Outside, the AGI compound functioned as a small town, "Deadwood," comprised of twenty prefabricated buildings of varying sizes. Large display screens scattered around the camp displayed an assortment of graphics and text including weather forecasts, bulletins, and other information likely of interest to those living and working here. Teks also noted the energy barrier surrounding the encampment, generated by towering stanchions positioned ten meters apart and encircling the compound. Beyond that force field, she saw a much more primitive settlement. Dozens of ramshackle huts and other simple structures cluttered a large meadow near the edge of a dense forest. In the distance, lavender figures wearing little or even no clothing worked in an adjacent field, tending to what Teks guessed were crops.

"Local Cygnae village," said Gunny. "About two hundred or so, all told. They're deep into the spear-and-arrow phase of weapons development."

"That sounds like no big deal until you get an arrow in the ass. Ever had an arrow in the ass, Gunny? I don't want an arrow in the ass."

"You about done?" Teks nodded as Gunny pointed to a quartet of Cygnae males operating equipment to sweep the dusty roads and walking paths linking the various buildings. Each of them wore a maroon jumpsuit. "AGI puts a lot of them to work in and around the compound," he said. "Manual labor, grunt stuff. They don't care about credits, but the goons here take pretty good care of them with food, medicine, tools, and whatever."

The trio made their way to one of the smaller buildings near the central structure she guessed to be the AGI headquarters building. A sign on the door identified their destination as "Information Systems – Auxiliary Operations." Placing his hand on the reader next to the door, Gunny waited until it flashed green and the door opened. Inside, Teks recognized the operations control hub for a standard information systems facility. Eight computer consoles at the center of an otherwise drab room, arrayed in octagonal fashion around a column featuring eight large display screens. The equipment looked more or less familiar to Teks, being of the sort she'd expect to find in any government or corporate office on any of the dozen Hub worlds where AGI maintained a presence.

"Think you can make this stuff talk?" asked Dana.

Teks nodded. "Yeah, I think so."

Taking a seat at one of the consoles, she swiped at the screen to activate an amber scanning beam that swept across her face and eyes. After a moment, the workstation's rows of controls and embedded screens flared to life.

"Thank you, Zittel," said Gunny. "I'm still kicking his ass over this skin, though."

"Ass? I was hoping you'd tie a few knots in his tentacles," Teks said, "while I watch." When Gunny smiled, she added, "Hey, you look pretty when you smile."

"Shut up."

Teks focused on the console, which was straightforward enough she had a handle on its interfaces in short order. Within minutes she was scrolling through screens of text and images as she tunneled her way deeper into the AGI computer system. Keywords, pathways, and links upon links flew past as she swiped at page after page until she landed on the directory she sought.

"Touchdown. I think I'm onto it." She dragged a schematic upward until it transferred from her console to the larger screen above her station. "It's listed as a subterranean test site, about a kilometer beneath us. Sublevel 28."

Dana frowned. "There aren't any sublevels. There's no underground anything. We've been here long enough we would've seen it."

"This says different." Teks pointed to the screen.

Gunny replied, "AGI's working overtime to hide whatever they're doing here." He placed what Teks realized was a small, delicate, and very feminine hand on her shoulder. "How do we get down there?"

This was one damned long elevator ride, Gunny decided. Moving along both horizontal and vertical shafts, he'd felt it change direction at least five times. According to Teks, the elevators that descended to various subterranean areas connected to most of the buildings in the compound, provided one possessed the necessary security clearances. Teks had forged his.

Shifting the armored vest so that it rested in a more balanced fashion off his shoulders, he was reminded of the new skin he now inhabited. This Cygnae woman, despite being of leaner build than his old human body, was still strong. That much was evident when he'd donned the vest and picked up the rifle generated for him upon his arrival on Cygnus-2h. Based on the specifications Zittel had attached to his false identity, Natasha Vasquez was assigned to the AGI base as a security specialist and therefore authorized to carry the tactical gear. The rifle—a phased particle beam weapon—was larger and heavier than the model he'd carried helicas ago as a young IEF trooper.

"You should almost be there," said Teks, her oddly masculine voice low over the comm link in his ear. With no MindLink access anywhere on the planet, they were forced to use older yet still proven methods of communication.

Before he could respond, Gunny felt an abrupt wave of dizziness wash over him. His balance threatening to give way, he reached out to the nearby wall to steady himself. The audible gasp that escaped his lips must've carried over the open channel.

"You okay, Gunny?" asked Teks.

He said nothing, gritting his teeth and waiting for the disorientation to pass. Nausea made its presence known and he thought he might puke, but the feeling dissipated as quickly as it had come about, replaced by a sudden outbreak of sweat across his body.

Somewhere in the back of his mind, a half-remembered checklist triggered an all-but-forgotten alert, and in that moment he knew what this was: Drekkit. IEF doctors had warned him about it before his retirement, along with the symptoms to recognize. They couldn't predict how or when it might happen, but they'd warned him that even one more jump might be enough to start the countdown to Zero Hour.

Suck it up, trooper, he chided himself. *Do the job and go home.*

"I'm okay," he lied, steadying himself as the elevator slowed. "Let's just get this over with."

Over the link, Teks replied, *"No worries. I've hacked the monitoring systems for Sublevel 28 to authorize elevator usage for this time of night. So far as anyone knows, you're conducting a routine security sweep."*

They'd waited until well after dark, when most of the local Cygnae workers had returned to their village and the bulk of AGI personnel were asleep. Only a skeleton crew of security and other support personnel crewed stations overnight. This was their chance.

The elevator halted its descent and its doors opened, revealing a massive underground cavern. Smooth walls, rounded ceiling and near-perfectly flat floor told him this was an artificial environment, carved by machines rather than millions of helicas of water carrying abrasive particles to flow through such depths.

"I'm here," he said, exiting the elevator with his attention fixed on what looked to be a derelict settlement. An array of stanchions like those surrounding Deadwood up on the surface encircled the encampment, though these were inactive. Dozens of one and two-story buildings arrayed in almost haphazard fashion lay ahead of him. Many of the structures were burned, some showed signs of impact from weapons fire, and others had simply collapsed. Other, newer buildings were visible deeper in the cavern, which Gunny noted was illuminated by immense lighting panels set into the stone ceiling. Several of the panels were deactivated, casting an odd gloom over the makeshift village. Craters littered the ground, and there were signs of a pale residue covering the buildings. As he approached, he caught an odor that was both foul and familiar: Death.

Then, Gunny saw the bodies.

"Oh, god."

"Gunny?" Dana called. *"What is it?"*

"Hang on." Keeping his right hand on his rifle, it took him two tries with his other hand to fumble Teks's hubcaster from his pocket and activate its video mode. He directed it toward the scene of carnage before him, standing transfixed at the village's perimeter, his gaze drifting over the ghastly scene before him. Dozens and dozens of Cygnae bodies lay sprawled everywhere in various states of decomposition. Some were burned and others blown apart by explosives, but it was those that seemed more or less intact that made Gunny's blood run cold. Faces locked in expressions of agony, limbs twisted or flexed as they tucked closer to torsos, obvious indicators of muscle spasms and—he knew—neurological deterioration resulting in seizures.

These absolute bastards. The condemnation raged in his mind. Illegal arms sales, drugs, even human trafficking would be bad enough, but the scene of horror before him was on an entirely different level. "AGI's testing chemical and biological weapons on the local populace." How many laws and regulations was the company defying, to say nothing of simple decency?

Damned animals.

"You seeing this?" he asked.

Teks responded, *"Yeah. I'm recording it."*

Gunny heard the shock in the young woman's voice, mirroring his own. "There has to be records of this somewhere. Teks, we need every scrap of evidence you can fi—"

"What are you doing?"

The voice was shouting from behind him, and Gunny turned to see a Cygnae male, dressed in clothing and equipment similar to his own, walking in his direction. A rifle was slung over his right shoulder, but his left hand rested on the butt of a sidearm strapped to his hip.

"There aren't any exercises scheduled for today," said the new arrival. His expression was one of suspicion but also uncertainty. "And it's too early for shift change." He stopped when he saw the 'caster in Gunny's hand. "There's no recording allowed down here, either."

He made the mistake of moving to unsling his rifle, but Gunny was faster. Training, skills, and muscle memory came to the fore, his right arm raising the rifle he held to aim and fire before he even realized what he was doing. The weapon spat forth a brilliant blue-white bolt of energy that slammed into the guard, knocking him off his feet.

"*Gunny!*" yelled Teks into his ear.

"Hey!" shouted another voice from some distance, and Gunny turned to see another Cygnae guard unlimbering his rifle while running toward him.

"I'm blown," said Gunny, running for cover.

"Make sure they don't cut me off or try to stop the elevator."

Sitting at the console, Teks manipulated the array of interfaces and screens, trying to do five things at once.

"I've got you," she said, fingers flying over the console's trio of keyboards. "I'm routing your elevator as close as I can to the Discovery Lander. We'll meet you there."

"And then what?" asked Dana, who stood near the door gripping a pulse pistol with both hands.

"Ask for a drink menu?" Teks scoffed. "Dana, we get the hell *out* of here. I'm trying to disable all sublevel alert and comm circuits, and the other elevators." She knew that would buy time, but only a little. Someone would notice the outages and start investigating, but it was the middle of the night. Once Gunny got to the top, they'd run for the Discovery Lander and jump the hell out of here before anyone was the wiser.

Then an alarm sounded from somewhere outside, annihilating her plan.

"Damn it!" Teks smacked the edge of the console. She hadn't been fast enough. The long, wailing siren increased with every second, already loud enough to wake the dead. Ignoring it, she checked one of the file extraction processes she'd kicked off and let run in the background while she provided overwatch for Gunny. "I found the data cache we need. It's almost copied." With no MindLink interface active here, she'd have to rely on the Lander to narrowcast the signal back to Nexus City. That meant another hack of the Merge Tech here, and she was running out of time.

The data transfer finished, and she extracted a data crystal from its receiving port.

"We can go now, right?" asked Dana.

Teks shook her head. "Just one more thing." She started typing again, alternating that with swipes at the cascade of holographic displays flashing before her.

"What's the one more thing?"

"Covering our asses."

It was a risk with the camp on alert, but Teks was still haunted by the images from the vizfeed Gunny sent via her hubcaster. All those people, slaughtered, and for what? Credits, ultimately. AGI needed to pay for that, and what she had in mind should also work as a distraction to cover their retreat to the Lander.

If I don't screw it up.

Weapon at the ready, Gunny steeled himself as the elevator doors opened. Six rifles aimed toward him, and he started firing.

Maybe the security detail thought they'd surprise him, but he doubted they were combat trained. That much was apparent when they froze in the face of his immediate and violent action. None of them got off a single shot before falling under his onslaught. Gunny was moving before the sixth guard dropped, sprinting across the compound toward the Discovery Lander. Cygnae legs were longer, making his strides more like bounding rather than running and allowing him to close the distance. He ignored shouts of alarm coming from different directions, focusing instead on the two guards posted near the Lander who were now aware he was charging them.

The first shot missed him to his left and Gunny lurched in that direction, dodging the expected correction shot sailing past his right shoulder. He returned fire on the run, striking the first guard in the chest and driving him to the ground. The second guard lunged for cover and Gunny missed him with his first attempt. His second try hit home, taking the guard's legs out from under him and sending him toppling to the grass.

Other shouts caught his attention and he tensed, searching for new threats, but saw that guards and other AGI personnel emerging from different buildings were focused elsewhere. Looking toward the compound's perimeter, Gunny noticed dozens of Cygnae gathering at the barrier, likely drawn by the sirens. Then he realized the large display screens positioned around the encampment were active not with the usual litany of reports and notices, but instead, a viz playback. On the screen nearest to him, he saw a shaky picture focusing on scores of Cygnae bodies, all of them mutilated or otherwise disfigured. It was his footage.

"Teks, you loveable sneaky—"

"*Augmentics General Innovations is killing you!*" The voice was Dana Wright's, booming from each of the displays as the video played on a continuous loop. "*Testing illegal weapons on you. On your children! They'll keep doing it until they perfect their weapons, or murder you all!*" Each sentence of the message was repeated in what Gunny guessed was the language of the local Cygnae villagers.

Cries of shock and anger grew outside the barrier. Gunny watched as AGI personnel stopped their advances, looking at each other as if wondering what to do.

Then a dull crack echoed across the compound, followed by the perimeter fence and every source of illumination going out. The low hum of power generators faded as the camp plunged into near darkness.

"Come on!"

Startled by the shout, Gunny turned to see Teks—or, rather, Schaeffer the muscled Cygnae man that was her current skin—running toward him. She grabbed his arm and he pulled her along with him toward the Lander.

"You did this, didn't you?" he asked, dropping his now useless rifle and looking over his shoulder to see dozens of Cygnae natives rushing the compound through the deactivated perimeter.

Teks kept running. "EMP. We've got maybe thirty seconds before things start resetting."

The electromagnetic pulse Teks somehow triggered had scrambled anything with an electronic circuit including the barrier and even any personal energy weapons. The Cygnae, unencumbered by reliance on such modern implements, took full advantage of the sudden equalization of force brought to this unexpected melee. Things were starting to reactivate, including the lights and the fence, but it was too late. Gunny figured the balance of the villagers were already inside the compound. Axes, knives, spears, rocks in slings, and bare hands entered the fray, with the numbers favoring the locals.

"See? Arrows in asses!" Teks gestured to the scene deteriorating before them. "There's about to be a major paradigm shift here, and I really don't want to be around when that goes down."

Ahead of them, Gunny saw Dana Wright—in her skin as the Cygnae male Mercado—standing near the entrance to the Lander. With everyone else responding to the threat from the villagers, she was alone.

Then everything swirled away and Gunny felt his feet run out from under him. Vertigo washed over him and he spun and stumbled, barely catching himself before planting his face into the ground.

"Gunny!"

It was Teks, but her voice was faint and distant, lost amid the new ringing in his ears.

This is it. I'm drekking out. Zero Hour. Damn.

He thought he could make it. Just one more jump, to help Teks and Dana. If they could use what they'd found here to expose AGI, then it was worth whatever awaited him. Going home would've been a bonus. Losing it all here, though? He hadn't counted on that.

Troopers don't die, he reminded himself. *We just go to Hell and regroup.*

All things considered, that seemed about right, just now.

Teks awoke to the sound of Gunny coughing.

Sitting up in the hospital bed, the older man drew several deep breaths, his eyes blinking in rapid succession as he made a show of inspecting himself. His hands moved first to his short-cropped gray hair, then to his arms and then finally—hilariously—beneath the bedsheets gathered at his waist. Looking around the room, his gaze fell on Teks.

"Hey, kid."

Teks smiled. "Hey, yourself."

"You look like you," he said, rubbing his face. "I guess I look like me."

"I'm gonna miss that pretty smile of yours, but it's sure good to see this old mug." Teks moved to sit next to him on the edge of the bed. "Thank Zittel. He had our original skins preserved for the jump back. Once we arrived, he had you brought here. The docs say they don't think you're at Zero Hour yet, and they can treat you for the seizures you had on Cygnus-2h."

Gunny frowned. "They can't cure what's got me. You know that. I knew that when I jumped. I've never been smart enough to understand most of what the docs tell me. I just take their word for it."

"Yeah, but there's research suggesting a jump back to one's original skin might have a stabilizing effect on your consciousness. Sounds like glap to me, but I figure it can't hurt to try. Zittel thought the same thing." Whatever kept Gunny healthy and in her life, she was up for giving it a shot. "Man, am I glad to see you."

Reaching out to pat her leg, Gunny said, "Back at you, kid."

Teks looked up as Dana Wright entered the room. Like her and Gunny, the reporter was back in her original skin.

"I think I liked you the other way," Dana said, grinning at Gunny.

Looking around the room, Gunny said, "We obviously made it back. So, what happened?"

"Everything happened," replied Dana. "AGI's operations on Cygnus-2h are prime news all over the MindLink. The data we captured broke the story wide open."

Teks added, "I was able to narrowcast everything back here before we jumped. As soon as we got back, The Merge shut down access to Cygnus-2h. It's quarantined while a full investigation is underway."

"AGI's base? Overrun by the locals." Dana shook her head. "By the time an IEF team arrived there, the place was a wreck. They figure AGI suffered ninety percent casualties, and they're searching for the rest."

"Arrows. In. Asses," Teks said.

Dana let loose a short laugh. "The IEF's sending squads to other AGI sites to round up anyone who may have known what was going down. AGI's board is already denying everything, blaming it on a research outfit that went rogue. 'Unauthorized use of company resources and our good name,' and all that glap. Meanwhile, people are selling AGI stock as fast as they can." She chuckled. "Heads are going to roll, my friend."

Sighing, Gunny shifted so he could lean back against his bed's headboard. "So, where does that leave us?"

"Zittel wants to put us on his payroll," replied Teks. "Says he might have similar jobs for us down the road."

Gunny grunted. "I think we've established my jump days are probably done."

"Even if that's true," said Dana, "there's a lot of things to do when it comes to this kind of work. AGI isn't the only corrupt outfit running around out there. Some of them might be scared right now, but you can bet others are already figuring out ways to be smarter about hiding what they do."

Teks said, "They'll keep at it until they're stopped. Why can't it be us stopping them?"

"Okay." Gunny nodded. "I'm in."

Talking and casting about corruption and conspiracy was fun, but facing it head on? It was an unequaled rush and she wanted more. There was also an entire universe out there she'd never seen. Now she'd get her chance.

"Great!" Teks leaned in for a hug. "I say we call ourselves . . . the Munch-bun-nies."

Dana scowled. "Really?"

"Absolutely not." Gunny shook his head.

"Fine." Teks squeezed her arms around him. "I'll work on it."

Curiosity activates the interface.

RELENTLESS REALITIES, IMPOSSIBLE INTENTION

Linda D. Addison

Possibilities activate the Process.
Intention initiates Commitment.
Curiosity reveals the Interface.

I can not exist, and yet thoughts arise,
    questions of where, how first thought
    arrived, when is now? Fractured
    memories crackle in this place
    of no-time, only giving sensation
    when another arrives, entangling
    me in tornados of re-creation, they
    gel, I crumble, infinitely between
    here/there as pieces of their self
    consume my impossible-ness.

Each life, again, again, again
    jump into this skin I can not be,
    leaving a submicroscopic bit
    behind, while they occupy here.
    I have no voice, no thoughts arise,
    when they leave this vessel,
    leaving blank—not-blank,
    re-forming me, in what is empty—
    not empty. Their march to Zero Hour
    increases my non-viable being.

Howling without voice, crying
without eyes, dead existence,
impossible existence, not
here and now, a no-body, no-
name skin loaned to others
who declare order, control.
Proof of denial, chaos child
residue haunting Creators'
system, designed to not be
in the rental space for souls.

ICEFALL

Angie Hodapp

BRIR, 493 HD

KORRE KA'KORRE MET ME at the shuttleport. I stepped off the gangway and climbed the rocky slope toward where he stood, his leather cloak billowing in the arctic wind. I hadn't seen him in forty helicas, not since we were young men fresh out of the Academy, but I recognized an uncharacteristic tension in his posture, a tightness in his jaw.

"Put these on," he said, or something like it.

I turned up the collar of my Synthtex overcoat, then accepted the ear shields and slipped them in place. The general clamor of the port behind me, the shouts of the crew unloading my lab equipment, the crash of the sea throwing itself against the cliffs, and the hollow sough of the arctic wind all went silent.

Then, a crackle of static.

"Do you understand me?" Korre said.

I nodded. The faint echo of his unfamiliar language lay beneath the translated Common.

"It's good to see you, old friend," I said.

His shoulders relaxed. He allowed himself a smile.

I pointed at my ear shields, clearly designed to do more than translate. "The absence of sound is remarkable, but is it necessary?"

"Perhaps not this far from the capital, but it's better we take no chances. The ice music is growing louder. Every day, more people hear it. Every day, more people are driven mad by its frequency."

"I'm sorry I couldn't be here sooner," I said.

When Korre contacted me, I had just accepted another assignment for The Merge: five months of geological survey on a newly Landed planet. After I submitted my reports, I jumped to Dreeo—the closest Mass-O planet to Brir yet still an eight-month voyage away. Thirteen months it had taken me to get here. Thirteen months Korre had waited for me to arrive.

The puzzle Korre presented was too enticing to ignore. An alpine glacier above Brir's capital city had begun to recede. Given the region's seasonal temperature shifts, wind currents, proximal landforms, volcanic dormancy, and tectonic stability—and the fact that other iceforms up and down the mountainous spine of Brir's polar continent measured within predictable parameters—the glacier's retreat should have been easy to forecast. Yet no matter how many times Korre modeled the data, no matter how many variables he manipulated, this glacier's behavior deviated.

The other half of the puzzle was more troubling. As the ice receded, it released a tone. *Mournful keening*, Korre had called it. *Ice music.* That alone might have been something the people of Brir could have grown used to, as those who live near oceans grow accustomed to the constant crashing of waves. But as it was, the ice music was driving the people of Brir insane.

There was no way to stop the madness without stopping the music.

Korre clapped me on the shoulder. "You're here now, praise The Creators. If anyone can discover the source of the music, it's you."

"Discovering the source is one thing. Turning it off is another." My spine stiffened. What did Korre expect of me? I was a scientist, not a savior. If all went well, I would discover the glacier's secret and present my findings to the Bririan rulers. What they did with that information was up to them.

"For your subordinate." Korre handed me a second pair of ear shields and gestured down the hill to where my research assistant, Ret Maumi, was overseeing the stacking of our equipment onto an overland transport.

I removed my own ear shields and opened my mouth to call down to him. But a sudden gust of cold wind caused the four crewmen carrying the heavy crate that held our drilling equipment to falter. Unable to rebalance their load, they let go, and the crate hit the stony ground with a hard crack.

"Drekking idiots!" Ret Maumi shoved the men aside and punched keys on the crate's access panel. The lid lifted with a depressurizing hiss.

"Everything intact?" I shouted over the wind and waves.

"For now!" Ret Maumi shouted back, giving the crewmen a vexed stare.

I sighed with relief. This wasn't a Mass-O world. There were no Assemblers here; there was no way to replace broken equipment but to wait the eight months it would take a ship to deliver it from Dreeo.

Some dark instinct told me I didn't want to be on Brir that long.

The transport was painfully slow. It carried the three of us and my 2,900 kilograms of equipment high into the Bririan mountains, connecting to a meandering system of tracks that pulled us across alpine valleys and cables that hauled us upward past waterfalls, between jagged peaks. I preferred the tracks; the cables bounced and swayed, tossing us on the arctic wind and leaving me to calculate the duration of our free fall should a faulty line send us smashing into the rocky ravines below.

My companions appeared unaffected by the nausea and anxiety that kept me clutching my armrests. I wasn't as adventurous as I used to be. I was an old man and getting older. Korre had retired here, to his home world, long ago, though why anyone who had lived on Helios Nexus would choose life on an off-grid planet was a mystery. Imagine being colorblind, then waking to the full spectrum—every tone, tint, and hue—only to choose a life in shades of gray. Regardless, perhaps it was time I followed Korre's lead and retired.

No. I gripped my armrests tighter. My own home world was no longer my home. My family would never forgive me for Elia's death—for my failure to save my granddaughter. I was not worthy. So I had no home to retire *to.*

Ear shields in place, Ret Maumi sketched. His fingers shaped the light projected by his MindLink into three-dimensional illustrations of the landscapes sliding past his window.

"The best scientists have the souls of artists," Korre said.

"And poets," I added. "Or so our professors were fond of telling us at the Academy." I pointed at my ear and cocked my head toward my assistant.

Korre shook his head. "He can't hear us. Listen, Callum. There is something I need to tell you before we arrive at the capital."

I was already taut as a wire. I'd long sensed Korre was keeping something from me, yet I'd come anyway. The idea of working alongside my old friend on a geological mystery of such enormity was enough to make me feel young again. Just what I needed. But now that I was here—and about to learn the truth—I felt older and less capable than ever.

"Brir is unstable," Korre said. "Not just geologically, but politically. The madness brought on by the ice music has claimed our *hjalm.* He's alive, but barely."

My ear shields did not translate *hjalm,* but the meaning was not difficult to guess. *Sovereign. Ruler. King.*

"Clan Ilgrin has ruled Brir for a thousand generations," Korre continued. "When the ice music began three loops ago, it affected only a few commoners—herders and stone gatherers living out near the foothills. At first, they believed the madness was divine punishment for petty wrongs committed by the afflicted. But as more fell victim, as the sound crept closer to the capital, the effects became harder to dismiss. People flocked to Castle Ilgrin to beg the *hjalm* to protect them. But Ith Ilgrin did nothing. He said the madness was indeed the fault of the afflicted. Furthermore, he proclaimed that Clan Ilgrin's immunity to the sound was proof of Clan Ilgrin's divine superiority."

"That can't have gone over well."

"It didn't. You see, Brir is on the cusp of an industrial and scientific revolution. Despite the fact that Brir was denied access to the Mass-O, we are innovating at astounding rates. Engineering, manufacturing, medicine, philosophy. The monarchy is becoming irrelevant to our new way of life, and Ith Ilgrin's desire to keep Bririans in the dark will not be tolerated."

"That's why you came back to Brir," I said. "You wanted to be part of this revolution."

He looked into my eyes. "I wanted to *lead* it."

The transport juddered, connecting inelegantly to a pair of tracks as it released the cable overhead. We had crested the range's craggy spine, and a vast cirque opened before us, so vast that the mountains forming the bowl around it were hazy in the distance. The cirque's drab, wind-shorn marshland was dotted by lichen-covered boulders—outwash carried down those faraway mountains eons ago by ancient glaciers.

Between us and those mountains lay the capital.

Ret Maumi, ear shields still in place, stared wide-eyed out the window. His fingers danced frantically as he raced to capture this new vista.

"Your *hjalm*"—I attempted the Bririan word and cringed at my faulty pronunciation—"is now afflicted. His claims of superiority are proven false. Soon he will die."

Korre nodded.

"A boon to your cause."

"It would be."

"Except?"

"Except that he has a daughter. Ivaya." He gazed toward the capital. "And she is the most cruel and cunning Ilgrin of all."

The closer we drew to the capital, the more evidence I saw of the madness. I was not prepared for the horror.

Before my arrival, I knew that Brir's population sat near 60,000; that fifteen percent could hear the ice music; and that two-thirds of that number were driven mad. Of the 6,000 driven mad, 2,500 were now dead. More deaths were reported every day. The affliction progressed slowly. For months, it stripped the somatic nervous system bare. The efferent neurons became confused, causing a cacophony of painful sensations throughout the body and a gradual loss of motor control. Then it turned its claws on the autonomic nerves, shutting down organ function. Days later, death.

That was the data. Those were the facts.

But also counted among the dead were murders committed by the afflicted. Mercy killings carried out by family members. Sepsis deaths suffered by those who drove nails into their ears. Suicides.

Before I arrived, my interest in the ice madness was clinical. If unprompted antagonism between an environment and its native population had occurred elsewhere, The Merge Archives and Academy libraries held no record, no precedent. My ego whispered that I would be at the leading edge of discovery; that my contribution could be merely descriptive; that I could walk away, leaving it to others to act.

Then came the moment I arrived in Brir's capital. Once I saw the suffering the ice music was causing, the human part of me—the part that had been a husband, a father to three children, and a grandfather to Elia—reawakened.

First, we trundled past clusters of sod-mound dwellings. Stone fences enclosed fields where villagers worked rows of crops, pastures where livestock grazed. Smoke curled from chimneys into the iron-gray sky. The pastoral charm was broken by the sight of a man chained to a post. He sat on the ground, rocking, muttering to himself, scratching at torn skin with broken fingernails. Blood stained his ragged clothing, and as we passed, he clapped his hands over his ears and let out a scream I could not hear.

Closer to the city, tall row homes stood along stone streets.

"Where the factory workers live, and over there"—Korre pointed beyond the rooftops, where smokestacks spewed ash and an amalgam of thick, oily odors into the air—"lies the labor district. The result of our progress toward a more industrious and cooperative way of life. Animals slaughtered, oil rendered, skins tanned, furs cleaned, rope twined, cloth woven, stones cut, tools forged, spices ground, furniture built, and pottery fired. Whatever you need on Brir, we make on Brir."

I noted the defiant pride in his voice, but before I could think more about it, our transport pulled to an abrupt halt. I nearly toppled from my seat.

On the tracks ahead, a woman with the bearing of a marshal or constable barked orders I couldn't hear. Her subordinates were corralling some twenty afflicted into the back of a transport, which was blocking our way. Until they cleared the tracks, we would be forced to wait. And watch.

The afflicted were in various stages of suffering. Some held their hands over their ears and moaned. One slapped her forehead, her lips forming the same silent word. A name, a curse...I would never know. Several were gripped by panicked convulsions, one as though his body were covered in insects, another as though she were engulfed in flames. Mouths hung open in silent screams and rictal agony. Fingernails clawed at flesh. Their own. Each other's. The constables beat them with staffs, keeping their distance as though the sickness were contagious.

A soft chime sounded through my ear shields. I ignored it. Swallowing the bile at the back of my throat, I asked, "Where are they being taken?"

"Many will go to a *sykksel*."

I shook my head.

Korre tried a different word. The translator provided "sanitorium."

I felt sick. Was this sanitorium a place where the afflicted were cared for—fed, clothed, comforted? Or was it a prison where they were locked away and forgotten until they died?

Ret Maumi said, "What of the others?"

I hadn't heard my assistant's voice since we boarded the transport. The chime must have signaled his connection to our loop.

"There is no cure, no reversal. Those who don't go to the *sykksel* will become the subjects of medical experimentation." Korre looked at me. "We are prolonging as many lives as we can, by whatever means necessary. We hope they will recover after we silence the ice."

Anger flared in my chest: Korre expected me to save his people.

Yet I would surely fail.

My sweet Elia's face flashed across my memory. I dropped my head into my hands. How could an old man who'd let his granddaughter die save a planet's entire population?

At last we arrived at Castle Ilgrin. Korre explained the *hjalmaha*—princess, I assumed—wanted to meet me.

We climbed out. My knees quaked. Eight months of space travel followed by a long afternoon in a rustic transport had taken their toll. I was exhausted and ill, my body working to acclimate itself to Brir's gravity and atmosphere.

The sensation was not unlike jump sickness—a thought that reminded me how far I was from The Hub. From a transpod. From instantaneous escape back to Helios Nexus and civilization.

Some of what caused my ill ease was trepidation. The princess was cruel and cunning, according to Korre. She was also at odds with his agenda. I wasn't a fool; her desire to meet me was a desire to *influence* me. I was about to step into the eye of Brir's political storm.

We began to climb the stone steps from the tracks to the castle gates. Ten steps and I was winded. I glanced up to estimate the number I had left to climb, and for the first time, I saw the princess.

Ivaya Ilgrin stood at the gates, looking down on us. Her hooded cloak, made of the same tan leather as Korre's, was trimmed in white fur. A beaded belt cinched the cloak at her waist. She pushed back her hood, and her long, obsidian hair was immediately whipped about by the wind, but she didn't seem to notice. Her eyes, the color of ice, were fixed on me.

I couldn't breathe. She was young. Sixteen, seventeen. The same age Elia was when she died.

The same black hair.

The same pale eyes.

Yet the princess's eyes carried none of the joy or kindness Elia's had. The princess's eyes were hard and glittered with malice.

"Are you well?" Korre's voice crackled in my ear shields.

I realized I had stumbled.

"Fine." I looked at the two figures standing to either side of the princess. They were formidable: masked, armored in carbon-fiber, and armed with laser guns. All off-world tech. All out of place. Brir had no military and, with its single habitable landmass and abundant resources, no reason for one. Yet the princess was afraid. And I knew why.

Korre reached out as though to help me regain my footing. When he spoke, his voice was barely audible. "The guards are only a facade. She feels threatened, and rightly so. She knows Clan Ilgrin will soon fall in favor of a more collectivist system of government."

"Which you will control." I clenched my jaw. "The princess is not some provincial clanswoman. She has offworld contacts. Supply lines. How else could she procure that armor? Those weapons? What other resources does she have?"

"I told you she was cunning."

"But not *connected*. Is she preparing for war?"

"That is not your concern."

"You made it my concern by bringing me here."

"You came because I dangled a scientific mystery and an adventure in front of your face. No one held a gun to your head."

Korre's words were a slap. The sting of realization that he thought me so easily manipulated landed hot on my skin. Knowing he was right landed hotter. I glanced at Ret Maumi, but his attention was on the princess. He stared at her, mouth gaping like an oilfish, infatuation bright in his eyes. My heart sank. Nothing had greater potential to complicate a situation than desire.

The princess wore ear shields like ours—more offworld tech—and when she tapped one, I heard a soft chime.

"Welcome to Brir, Callum Emnat and Ret Maumi Shamashitar. I am grateful to you for answering the call of my most esteemed scientist, Korre Ka'Korre, and I am placing great confidence in your ability to heal my world of its affliction."

Her voice, even through the translator, was euphonic. Feminine. But it was not the voice of a teenaged girl. It was the voice of a woman who was accustomed to issuing commands and having them obeyed. A voice that carried careful subtext. *My scientist. My world.* Whether she truly pulled Korre's strings, that is what she wanted me to believe.

"Come," she said. "I will show you to your rooms."

Korre stiffened. "I have prepared barracks for our guests near the glacier. The closer we are to the subject of our research, the faster we will arrive at a solution."

"No," Ivaya said. "They will stay here, and they will report to me."

Korre opened his mouth to protest, but Ivaya's guards placed hands on their weapons. It was a subtle gesture I found more arrogant than menacing, but the effect was immediate. Yielding, Korre bowed his head.

"I'll see their equipment is delivered to the site," he said.

"No," Ivaya said again. "The lab will be kept here as well."

My spine tensed. *Kept here as well.* So we were to be kept here. Against our will. For how long, I did not know, nor could I guess the circumstances under which we would be allowed to leave.

Korre bowed again. "As you command."

He turned to descend the steps, but for a moment, his eyes caught mine. What I saw there might have been helplessness. An apology. A warning. Perhaps a bit of all three or something else that, given my perfunctory introduction to Bririan politics, I had no hope of comprehending.

Then he was gone.

"This way," Ivaya said.

As we made our way through the castle—Ivaya still drawing the moon-eyed gaze of Ret Maumi, her two guards bringing up the rear—adrenaline spiked my blood, leaving a metallic taste on my tongue. I did my best to control my breathing and pay attention to my surroundings.

The castle was immense, made of gray stone that smelled damp and loamy. Its cold corridors were lit by oil burning in wall sconces. As an Academy student, I hadn't cared for Human Anthropology. To my thinking, Earth was an obsolete place I found both boring and irrelevant to the geological work I aspired to do. But now I recalled the Medieval architecture of northern Europe and Scandinavia and realized Castle Ilgrin was not so different. Perhaps if I had paid more attention to my professor, I would have an informed theory about how similar architectural styles and construction methods evolved across vast spans of space and time.

Castle Ilgrin was appointed with an odd mix of rustic, handcrafted furnishings and offworld curiosities. Adorning the walls were holographic bas-reliefs depicting planets, moons, asteroids, comets, and Oort clouds. In one rather large piece, tendrils of blue light twisted and looped their way throughout a galaxy—tendrils I was certain were meant to represent the Mass-O.

Further down the corridor, I saw holo-paintings of non-Bririan landforms and cityscapes. Some I recognized as places I'd visited: Tansa, Micaro, Bahbradu, Mars, even the Citadel, its spires rising high above Helios Nexus. Ret Maumi, a holo-artist himself, opened his mouth, no doubt to attempt some intelligent-sounding remark. I shook my head, and he remained silent.

The corridor opened into a large semicircular gallery. Around it stood pedestals on which were displayed various offworld artifacts. A Proten-powered flashlight, sans Proten. A twisted control panel salvaged from a crashed monospeeder. A Chut'uui zap saddle. A magnetic grav boot. Half a cybernetic torso.

As we walked among the pedestals, Ivaya said, "What do you think of my collection?"

It was tech scrap. All of it. But each piece was displayed with a pride that betrayed reverent obsession with the universe beyond Brir. Ivaya was a collector, but not a discerning one. Her offworld connections were selling valuable things—armor, weapons, art—but they were also peddling junk and passing it off as treasure.

"You have excellent taste," I replied.

I thought about my lab equipment. No doubt someone was already sifting through my crates, looking for anything shiny the princess might want to add to her museum.

"My father detests everything that came from away," Ivaya said. "Starfarers have been visiting Brir for centuries, yet he wants to cut them off. To stop trading with them. He wants to keep Brir pure, untouched by outsiders. He'll die soon, though, so his opinions on such things no longer matter. Soon I'll be the *hjalm*."

I suppressed a shiver. She spoke of her father's impending death as though speaking of poorly seasoned meat. "What will you do when you are the *hjalm*?"

She gave me a hard look as if she suspected I was mocking her. I held both my breath and her gaze, arranging my expression into one of genuine interest.

After a moment, she turned and strode toward the terraced balcony at the far end of the gallery. One pale hand rose into the air and beckoned us to follow.

Ret Maumi and I joined her at the balustrade, the guards on our heels. Cold wind bit at my overcoat, the Synthtex no match for this planet's arctic chill, and I found myself wishing for a Bririan cloak.

Below us, the capital spread out across the valley, transports crisscrossing on tracks and cables. Pollution from the labor district rose toward the overcast sky in sooty columns. Beyond lay farmsteads, marshlands, rocky plains. A starkly beautiful landscape carved by time and weather, but one that Korre would see blighted by industrial advancement.

Perhaps that was why the glacier had begun to sing its dirge. I imagined I could see the glacier's music, could see its soundwaves susurrating over the city like a deadly mirage.

"You asked what I will do when I am hjalm," Ivaya said. "Do you really want to know?"

I nodded.

"There." She pointed to the marshlands beyond the city. "There is the future site of a great hub of unprecedented commercial and cultural significance. People will come from all over the universe to behold the beauty and bounty of Brir. Diplomats like Nova Orion. Leaders like Olen Gray. I will make Clan Ilgrin glorious not by isolating Brir from the starfarers as my father would do, but by making it a desirable destination."

Manic laughter bubbled like acid in my chest—not because I thought she was jesting but because I knew she wasn't. The absurdity of her vision terrified me. She was a child who had never traveled space. For her to think Brir held any magnitude of commercial or cultural appeal to any Merge world... It was like an Academy student expecting high marks after explaining to a physics professor the concept of counting by twos.

I cleared my throat, choosing my next words carefully. "When I asked Korre why Brir still relies on tracks and cables for transportation from the coast, he told me the marshlands up here are too unstable to build a port, and in the winter, there is too much ice."

"I'm not building a port." The princess smiled.

For the first time since we arrived at the castle, Ret Maumi didn't look like a lovestruck pup. His brow was as furrowed as mine.

"Then what are you building?" I asked the princess.

Her smile stretched into a grin, one both beautiful and chilling. "You, Doctor Callum Emnat, are going to bring me a Discovery Lander."

My vision blurred. I couldn't breathe. This was beyond insanity. The princess knew nothing. Nothing of the universe. Nothing but this backwater world where her every whim was fulfilled without question, her every command obeyed without pause. Now she wanted something from the only force in the universe that existed on a plane so far beyond the reach of sentient minds that even the word "existed" fell short.

She wanted something from The Creators.

And she wanted me to get it for her.

I was speechless. Ret Maumi, however, was not.

"Princess Ivaya." He stepped toward her, spreading his hands in supplication. "Your request is impossible. The Creators alone decide which worlds receive Discovery Landers. Which worlds connect to the Masson Zero. Doctor Emnat and I are certainly sensitive to the frustration that you, that *anyone*, must feel at being excluded, but the rhyme and reason are not ours to know. The Creators are fathomless."

The princess pierced Ret Maumi with an icy gaze. "My request is impossible?"

"I'm afraid so."

She closed her eyes and sighed as though he were a criminal to whom she had given one last chance to confess and receive leniency. When she opened them, it was to nod at her guards. Then to look away.

Without hesitation, the guards took hold of Ret Maumi and threw him off the balcony.

A strangled sound ripped from my throat. I flew at the balustrade, catching the solid marble so hard across my stomach that the air was forced from my lungs. I folded myself over it, straining with my arms, my hands, my fingers as though I could snatch him out of the air, pull him back up. As though his body had not already broken against the rocks. As though he were not already dead.

Another sound came from my mouth, this one a piteous mewl. Then I gave myself five seconds to breathe, to think. My situation had changed, and I would need all the presence of mind I could muster if I was to survive Ivaya Ilgrin.

I stood. Tugged on the sleeves of my overcoat. Felt her watching me. Waiting. Felt the readiness in the posture of her guards. When I turned to face her, she spoke only one word.

"Impossible?"

"No."

"Then you will bring me a Discovery Lander?"

"Yes."

"Good. But first, we must silence the ice music. We must restore peace on Brir before we receive distinguished representatives from The Merge and beyond."

Every day the following week, Korre and I trekked up and down the glacier, packing as much equipment as we could carry. The princess joined us, as did her guards, though they carried nothing but their offworld weapons and airs of self-importance. Their presence made it impossible for Korre and I to speak freely about anything other than our field work, but the look he gave me that first day told me he knew why Ret Maumi was absent.

The transport tracks ended some four kilometers from the glacier's edge. Every day, as I hiked up and down that steep boulder field, lungs burning, I wished I had never come to Brir. Sometimes I wished I were dead. Then I remembered Ret Maumi's body splayed on the rocks and gave gratitude to The Creators that I had lived to see another day.

"What are you doing?" the princess asked through my ear shields as I chiseled pieces of ice and rock and studied them under my microscope. "How does that work?" she asked as I recorded soundwaves. "What does that do?" she asked when I launched my aerial scanner to capture the glacier's topography. "Why are you doing that?" she asked when I drilled a five-meter core sample.

Her curiosity seemed genuine, which caught me off guard. I found myself smiling at her childlike inquiries. This was my expedition with Elia all over again. Sixteen-helica-old Elia, finally old enough to jump through the Mass-

O. Finally old enough to accompany me on one of my many expeditions for The Merge. Finally old enough to assert her dreams for her future: *When I grow up, I'm going to be a geologist like you, Granddad.*

Whenever I realized I was smiling at the princess's curiosity, shame burned my memories to ash. Ivaya was not Elia. Ivaya was cruel, quick to order the death of anyone who dared defy her. I bent my head over my work and chided myself for confusing this loathsome girl with my beloved granddaughter.

During those grueling days, the princess spoke idly about all she would do for her people once I brought her a Discovery Lander. Once I connected Brir to the Mass-O. To her, the ice music was not a deadly force so much as an inconvenience, an embarrassment that would discourage visitors.

Listening to her prattle, I realized Brir would likely be the last world I ever saw. I made peace with that. What had my life amounted to? Nothing. Was I worth saving? No. I was a good scientist, but not a great one. I was a mediocre husband and father, away on expedition more than I was home. And my greatest failure of all was Elia, who died on my watch. On my expedition. I would never be worthy of redemption.

Perhaps dying here, cold and alone, is what I deserved.

"I found something." I realized Korre couldn't hear me and tapped my right ear shield. "Look at this."

Korre, sifting glacial till on the table across from mine, turned. We were back in our makeshift lab at Castle Ilgrin, and for once, the princess and her guards had left us alone. Maybe she had finally tired of watching over our shoulders. With each passing day, Korre and I worked later into the night, because with each passing day, the number of dead increased. Forty-seven more souls had perished since my arrival on Brir.

The ice music was getting louder.

Projected into the space between Korre and me was a three-dimensional hologram of the slide under my microscope.

"Looks like the same organisms we pulled out of the last three core samples," Korre said.

"But look how they're moving."

Korre leaned closer. Hundreds of single-celled ciliates scuttled about on the slide, propelling themselves with tiny hairs along the dorsal hump of their bean-shaped forms.

"Same as always," Korre said.

"Exactly."

He furrowed his brow. "What am I missing?"

"The ventral cilia are static. When we observed them through the field microscope up at the glacier, their ventral cilia were moving so fast they blurred. It appears they carry two types of cilia, but only one is for locomotion." I paused. "What if the ventral cilia create sound? Create *music*?"

Korre scrubbed a hand over the stubble on his chin. "They create sound when they are in proximity to the glacier—"

"But fall silent when they are removed from it."

"Why?"

"They are responding to something inside the ice. Harmonizing with it. Amplifying it." I typed a command. The projection of the ciliates was replaced by a holographic model of the two-kilometer swathe of melting glacier my aerial scanner captured on day one. Another command superimposed the scan I took yesterday.

"What are you looking for?" Korre asked.

I walked a slow circle around the projection, pulling the images apart with my hands to zoom in, sliding them together to zoom out. The two scans were identical.

Until they weren't.

"That." I pointed at a long, jagged scar high on the glacier's southern slope. A crevasse that was there yesterday but not seven days ago.

Korre uttered a curse that came through my translator as "dark skies."

"Dark skies indeed," I replied.

I zoomed in. Side by side, Korre and I stared. We both knew what was inside the crevasse. We both knew what was making our little ciliates scream death to the people of Brir.

XI

When we arrived at the crevasse—Korre and me, Ivaya and her guards—we were breathless, weary after our six-hour trek up the glacier's southern slope. We wore harnesses and carried ropes and ice axes, things I was grateful we didn't need. Only the crampons on our boots proved essential.

Korre and I glanced at each other. We both felt the low vibration under our feet. So close to the source, the ice music must be deafening. Were any of us to lose our ear shields, the effects would be swift and ghastly.

I put a hand on the axe hanging at my hip and stepped forward to peer over the edge.

Deep inside the crystalline abyss, massive, whiplike tentacles, black as ink, worked industriously to chip away at the ice. They also generated heat; not only could I feel it on my face, but far below, I could see water streaming down the icy walls. The glacier, just as I suspected, was being deconstructed from the inside out.

"What are they?" Ivaya shrieked. "Kill them!"

Both guards obediently pulled their weapons.

"No!" I lunged sideways to knock the gun from the guard closest to me. To my surprise, my maneuver succeeded. The gun dropped into the crevasse, clattering against the jagged walls as it fell.

The gun wasn't all that fell. The guard lost his footing. He flailed his arms, trying in vain to regain his balance before he, too, slipped into the crevasse. His bellow rang hard against the ice. Then his body slammed into an ice shelf and, limp and silent, cartwheeled into the darkness.

"What have you done?" Ivaya turned hostile eyes on me.

My pulse pounded against my temples. I had killed a man. I hadn't meant to, but he was dead just the same. And the longer I stood here frozen in shock, the greater the likelihood Ivaya would send me after him.

I looked at the other guard. Both he and Korre had stumbled back from the edge, but he still held his weapon at the ready.

"Don't shoot," I told him. To the princess, I said, "Those are Servitors. Shooting at them will send them into a frenzy. They will act without hesitation or prejudice to defend themselves and the Creator Tech that spawned them. Right now, they're working calmly, carefully. At their current pace, they're a day or two away from reaching the surface. But provoke them, and they will act. The ice beneath our feet will shatter and we will die. Do you understand?"

Ivaya gazed into the crevasse, her expression shifting to astonishment, then to something resembling triumph. "Where there are Servitors…" She trailed off.

"…there is a Discovery Lander," I finished.

She beamed at me. "You did it. Your assistant told me it was impossible, but he was a fool. You knew better. And you brought it here, to destroy this glacier. To silence the music. To save my people! The Lander will have to be moved closer to the capital, of course. I told you where I want it. But that can be arranged later." She let out a jubilant sigh, her breath fogging the air. "Why did you not tell me this was your plan, Dr. Emnat? If only I'd thought of it myself."

All I could do was gape at her. There were no words for her naiveté, no logic or reason with which to patch together her delusions. I glanced over my shoulder at Korre, but all he offered was an almost imperceptible shake of his head. I didn't understand what he was warning me not to do or say, but I had already decided on the truth.

"The Lander isn't there to silence the music, Ivaya. The Lander is *causing* it."

Her fervor dimmed. "What?"

"Korre and I believe that the Lander has been here since before The Great Fracture. If we're right, and I'm certain we are, it came to Brir more than 300,000 helicas ago, long before your ancestors migrated north. Your Ice Age rolled across the land and entombed the Lander, and it went dormant. Now, spring is coming. Brir's polar ice has been receding naturally for decades. About three helicas ago—that's when the *music* started—the glacier had finally lost enough mass that the Lander woke up. It sensed it could connect with the Masson Zero, so it began transmitting a signal. The problem is, your glacial ice is teeming with a microorganism that doesn't care for that signal. The sound, the music, that has been killing your people is the sound of those microorganisms screaming."

I could tell she comprehended little of what I said. She responded, simply, "The Discovery Lander has been here all along?"

I nodded. "Brir was chosen by The Creators to connect to the Mass-O after all."

Ivaya fell to her knees in the snow. Her gloved hands lay limp in her lap. Whatever responsibility she felt as this planet's soon-to-be *hjalm*, whatever burdens she carried as the heir of Clan Ilgrin, seemed to slip away. Her whole life, she believed her world had been shunned by the dazzling, infinite spectacle of the Mass-O. To find out that Brir had always held a ticket to the show was more than she could handle.

For a moment, she looked small and vulnerable. She looked like Elia.

"Now that Brir has a Lander," said Korre's voice through my ear shields, "the question is, how shall it be used?"

Ivaya narrowed her eyes at him. "It shall be used as I say."

"I disagree." With that, Korre drew himself up and kicked the other guard toward the crevasse.

Like the guard who fell before him, this one flailed, fought for balance, and lost. His body disappeared into the rift.

I closed my eyes, the image of Ret Maumi falling to his death flashing bright in my mind. Korre had just performed an act of war. What before was political discord between my old friend, who favored collectivist rule and industrialization, and Princess Ivaya Ilgrin, who with the impending death of her father would soon be Brir's *hjalm*, had just become a matter of life and death. Before this moment, the idea of a Discovery Lander on Brir had been an abstraction. Now, it was real. Its Servitors would soon free it from the ice beneath our feet.

Whichever of my companions won control of it would win control of Brir.

I opened my eyes and saw Korre stalking toward the princess. Predator toward prey.

"Stay back!" the princess cried.

"Korre! Stop!" I lunged between them, arms outstretched. But Korre would not be stopped. His body collided with mine…

…and mine collided with the princess.

My mind slowed, everything happening in twice the time. I spun, reached for the princess, felt her hands scrabbling along my arms. I closed my fingers around her wrists as my chest slammed into the snow and began to slide. Just as I became certain both of us would tumble into the chasm together, Korre took hold of my legs and dug his spiked heels into the ice.

I blinked down into Ivaya's terror-stricken face. "Hold on. I'm going to save you."

I blinked again. Now I was lying face down in the red dust of a sandstone cliff. Now I was looking down at Elia's face, grasping Elia's wrists, feeling the hot sun beating down on us.

Hold on. I'm going to save you.

How many times had I told her to stay at least three meters from the edge? How many times had I explained the nature of sandstone and the need for extra caution when doing field work on any unknown planet that could at any moment prove itself deadly?

Granddad! Don't let go!

Sweat slicked the palms of my hands. Elia's fingers began to slip.

"Let her go," said Korre.

I won't let you fall.

"Let her go, Callum."

Let her go.

Some part of me realized Korre wanted the princess dead but not badly enough to let me die with her. That was something. But how long would he hold on? How long could he?

"She wants to keep Bririans in the dark." Korre's voice was strained. "She despises progress."

Sweat streamed into my eyes. I squeezed them shut. Opened them. Saw Ivaya. Saw Elia. Saw Ivaya again. Remembered Ivaya's collection of offworld artifacts, her guileless fascination with space art and tech scrap—with anything that came from worlds beyond her own.

"She wants to open Brir to the Mass-O," I said. "She invites the change and advancement her father shunned."

It was as if Korre hadn't heard me. He said, "This solves everything. Don't you see? Let her go, and you and I will be the only ones to know what happened. She got too close to the edge. It was an accident."

She got too close to the edge. It was an accident.

It was an accident.

An accident.

Again, we began to slip. Ivaya screamed, but Korre's crampons bit into the hardpack.

"Drekkit, Korre, pull us up!"

"Let her fall!"

I'd had enough. I had done all I could do to save my granddaughter. I knew that now, as bright and hot as a desert sun. But there was more I could do to save Ivaya. This time, the outcome would be different.

I looked into Ivaya's eyes and said, "I'm letting you go."

"No." Her expression twisted with terror. "Please!"

What I said next, I said quickly. I needed her to comprehend my plan before Korre did. "There's a ledge two meters down. It's narrow, but it'll hold if you land softly. Go limp when you hit and stay still. Understand?"

"You'll leave me there to die."

"I swear to you on the memory of my granddaughter Elia Amaryllis Emnat I will not."

With that, I let the princess fall.

I watched her land, crumpling into a heap exactly as I said. She was safe.

For now.

I rolled away from the edge. Korre, chest heaving, staggered to his feet. I wanted to lie in the snow, let my old body, my strained joints rest. But now was not the time. Anger shadowed Korre's face.

"You fool," he said. "You coward. That was our chance."

"Our chance to what?" I climbed to my feet. My hand went again to the ice axe at my hip.

Korre noticed. "You're going to use your axe against me?"

"I don't want to."

"You would choose to save the princess over me? Your oldest friend?"

"I will not let you murder her."

Korre barked out a laugh, then spat into the snow. "She killed Ret Maumi. Have you forgotten?"

I had not forgotten. I never would. "Enough death, Korre. You and the princess want the same thing. And you have it. The Creators chose Brir. Who am I to say which of you wins governance of the Discovery Lander? Who are *you*?"

He laughed again. "Is that what you think I want?"

I stared at him. If not control of access to the Mass-O, what was Korre's desire?

Then I remembered something he said as the transport approached the capital, and I remembered the defiant pride with which he said it: *Whatever you need on Brir, we make on Brir.*

"You want to keep the Lander buried," I said.

He held out his hands as if to say *what else?* "I cannot keep it buried in the literal sense, of course, but if Bririans do not discover what it is and what it can do, it might as well be. You might not think much of Brir, but it is my home, my world. We are simple. We work hard. We contribute to our own common good. We're utopian! Bririans' way of life would be corrupted beyond measure if they knew they could access the Mass-O. You and I, we've seen it happen to countless other worlds. Don't you remember? We studied it at the Academy. As soon as a new world is connected to the Mass-O, it bleeds out. Grows weak. Its greatest minds and most resourceful contributors defect, lured away by the promise of adventure and knowledge and advancement. Those left behind grow lazy and resentful. They live off other cultures' inventions and innovations instead of creating their own, all while complaining that access to the Mass-O is inequitable, a privilege being withheld from them. Don't you see? The Mass-O is divisive. Creator Tech is a cancer."

The heat drained from my skin. Every centimeter of me felt impossibly cold. Korre and I had attended all the same classes and lectures at the Academy, but we had, apparently, heard our professors say very different things. Still, there was a cruel logic to his philosophy, one I needed to grapple with, as it conflicted with my own. But not here. Not now.

"What of these?" I pointed at my ear shields, which even now protected us from the soundwaves reverberating through the ice beneath our feet. "Did you invent these? Manufacture them on Brir? Or are they a borrowed innovation?"

Korre's eyes narrowed. "These are desperate times. An exception had to be made."

"In the future, who will decide what constitutes desperation? Who will regulate the exceptions? You? How long until you begin using the Assembler in secret to make miraculous things? Or the transpods for clandestine jumps? How long after that will you form an inner circle whom you allow to benefit from the Discovery Lander in ways that the Bririan proletariat never will?"

Korre did not answer.

"I promise you that will happen," I continued. "All of it. If you have already decided the Discovery Lander is yours to use at your sole discretion, then Brir is already corrupt."

What happened next happened fast. Korre drew his ice axe and stalked toward me. I held my axe low and prepared to defend myself. The day I arrived, Korre exposed me as an old, adventure-seeking fool who came when whistled for. But I had just exposed him as a tyrant in the making. He responded as tyrants do: with petulance and violence.

"You all got too close to the edge," he said, now only a few steps away and not slowing. "Everyone fell in except me."

I drew in a breath. Held it. My knees shook—not from fear, I realized, but from the vibrations of the ciliates in the ice. Trillions upon trillions of ciliates screaming in protest as the Discovery Lander, now so close to being fully freed from the glacier, transmitted its homing signal to The Hub.

If Korre would not listen to me, perhaps he would listen to them.

He closed the space between us, already swinging his axe up and around. Instead of raising my own, I dropped it in the snow. I watched for the exact moment he lunged to throw his weight behind the blow. When that moment came, I stepped sideways, ducked, reached up and over his head, and then shoved him away. Korre's axe landed beside mine, and he stumbled past me.

Both still on our feet, we turned to face each other. I held up a hand. Korre's ear shields dangled from my fingers.

I watched the realization dawn on his face. Then I watched the bewilderment set in. I couldn't imagine the sound, couldn't estimate the decibels this close to the source. And I could no longer hear his voice, his translator now in my possession. I could only watch his shock turn to agony as he clamped his hands over his ears and fell to his knees.

I knew the effect of the ice music would be more intense here, but not as intense as this. My plan had been to resolve this without blood, but that was not to be. Red seeped between Korre's fingers.

Panic clouded my vision. I had not intended to kill or even to injure him—only to startle him. To temporarily disable him. To snap him out of his momentary rage. But the sight of Korre's blood dripping into the snow told me I had miscalculated. In seconds, the effect was irreversible. He would not leave this glacier alive.

I wish that I could say that in his last moments, he had a change of heart. That he looked at me with regret in his eyes or let me know in some other way that his senses had returned. But that is not what happened. He merely went rigid as though seized by an electric shock, and then slumped forward into the snow and stilled.

I also wish I could say that if I had it to do over again, I'd do it differently.

I do not know if I made the right choice that day. And it *was* a choice. I chose to save Ivaya, an ill-informed child possessed of her own murderous petulance and tyrannical temper. I chose her because I had always believed that The Creators were, as Ret Maumi said, fathomless. They sent a Discovery Lander to Brir. They wanted Brir to join the Mass-O. That is what the princess wanted as well, so that is the outcome I served.

But I would be lying if I said there wasn't another reason. As I lowered the ropes to where Ivaya crouched shivering with cold on that narrow ice shelf, as I instructed her how to tie on to her harness, it was my granddaughter I was saving. It was Elia I was finally pulling back to solid ground and Elia's face I saw smiling at me, at the wide-open sky over both our heads.

"You are free to leave Brir," Ivaya said as we made our way back down the mountain. "You are not a prisoner here."

"You know now that I did not bring you that Lander?" I asked.

"I do."

"You understand how much your world will change now that Brir has access to Mass-O travel?"

"Yes, Doctor Emnat."

I believed her first answer, but not her second. How could she possibly understand? And who would be here to explain it to her, to guide her through Brir's integration into The Creators' fathomless universe?

"What will happen to the music?" she asked.

"The ice will melt away from the Lander, and the organisms in proximity to it will die out. In time, peace and sanity will be restored." I looked out at the jagged peaks of ice and granite that surrounded us, at the snow and schist and the silver-gray sky. Stark. Beautiful. Dangerous. I was no longer cut out for field work, no longer drawn to adventure. I said, "I have nowhere to go. If you have need of me as an advisor—perhaps even as Brir's representative to The Merge—I would be honored to stay."

We walked on, treading carefully on the steep path. Ivaya was silent so long I began to wonder if she'd heard me. Then, presently, she said. "I would be honored to have you."

BETWEEN HERE AND FOREVER

Gabino Iglesias

HELIOS NEXUS, 493 HD

ALEK SMELLS COFFEE. The aroma crawls into his nose and shakes something loose inside him. He's stuck in the interstitial space between sleep and wakefulness, where things seem to be covered in a wet towel and his battered synapses—now more like chasms than minute gaps—have a hard time communicating when responding to stimuli. Then his heart rate accelerates. Fear floods in and obliterates sleep, yanking Alek out of that muddy, foggy, just-woke-up mental space.

He lives alone.

No one can be making coffee.

Alex sits up, eyes open and scanning the dim apartment, his body ready to pounce.

Silvia, Alek's mother, is standing in his small kitchen, her wrinkled, veiny hands wrapped around a steaming mug.

The ghost of a smile threatens to pull Alek's lips up, but then reality pushes it back into oblivion. Silvia is dead. She's been dead for six helicas.

Alek blinks, shakes his head, looks again. His mother isn't there. The smell of coffee is gone. Confusion is flushed out by anger. Alek takes a deep breath and stands up. He looks down at his body—athletic and ready for work—and wonders how much longer his mind will be able to keep up.

Zero Hour. Early signs. That's what the doctor told him. She also told Alek he would probably experience more hallucinations, including olfactory hallucinations, as well as disorganized thinking and loss of smell. Alek had nodded, kept his mouth shut. He'd been waiting for it to start. He knew it was coming. It was the result of fifty helicas spent jumping from skin to skin to perform menial tasks in some of the most remote, inhospitable, and unexplored systems in the universe. You can't shoot a consciousness a thousand times across the universe without some entropy kicking in, but knowing that doesn't make it easier to swallow.

Instead of walking to the kitchen or the bathroom, Alek turns and looks out his window at the sprawling mass of Nex City. This is where he's spent his time when not on a mission, but he doesn't know if it's where he wants to retire. He wants to be in a quiet place. His consciousness craves it. In fact, he had been ready to call it quits after the last mission, but he knew his savings wouldn't last, so he took one more gig.

After a long time without discovering an inhabitable planet, it finally happened. A Progenitor discovered a world similar to Earth in the Cretaceous. And it was in very good shape. The Progenitor detected the planet, its lifeforms, and some bizarre remains—mostly covered by vegetation—almost simultaneously. A Discovery Lander was immediately deployed to the planet while the Progenitor continued its never-ending quest in search of more habitable worlds.

The planet, Novus-337, is large—only slightly smaller than Station ROXs 42Bb—and has an atmosphere of 22 percent oxygen. With a lot of water and three huge continents inhabited by large lifeforms—sentient, crustacean-like, and coated in an acidic substance that corrodes everything the creatures eat or anything they perceive as a threat—and enormous macroflora, Novus-337 seems perfect despite the little mystery of the unknown remains.

Alek was quickly contacted, briefed, and assigned a starting date soon after the discovery. He couldn't pass up the opportunity. Jumps had been getting scarcer in the last hundred helicas or so, and turning down a job is a surefire way of not getting contacted again.

According to the briefing he received, the Discovery Lander that had been sent down to Novus-337 arrived without problem and rooted itself into a stable place in the welcoming environment to establish a transpod receiving station. As usual, the Servitors had taken to their tasks of maintaining the Lander. All information about the planet was available for the crew to access as needed as soon as they got to Novus-337. Alek—responsible for comm checks and maintaining system tech for the Harbinger Team—and three others were tasked with investigating some ruins and determining if there were salvageable materials there to help create a beachhead colony.

Getting into the transpod has never been Alek's favorite thing. At the beginning, it was an exciting part of the job—exciting enough that he could ignore its negative effects—but half a century of doing so rubbed all sense of wonder away.

Transferring a consciousness from its body to any destination in the Mass-O network is as easy as flipping a switch. Alek enters the transpod, closes his eyes, and a second later he opens his new skin's eyes on the Discovery Lander on Novus-337. Unfortunately, the relaying of information through entangled particles at both ends of the operation always takes away something—an infinitesimal amount of memory, for example, leaving another tiny hole in its place, a hole Alek's consciousness does its best to fill with something.

Every time Alek opens his fresh eyes in a new place, he knows the occasional hallucinations and disorganized thinking will get a bit worse. Half century of jumps is catching up to him in a big way. But it doesn't matter much now; this is, if all goes well, his last gig. He can worry about Zero Hour later.

Alek steps out of the pod in his new skin and tests it out. It feels strong, young, capable. Those are things his consciousness doesn't feel, so feeling them in his new skin is somewhat reassuring. Every transfer causes jump sickness, leaving you disoriented and groggy. It usually goes away in the first 24 hours or so, but the more jumps someone has under their belt, the longer the brain fog seems to linger.

Two of the other three pods contain skins in some stage of the same process Alek just went through. The other one is empty. Some people are just eager to get to work. Or they need to lie down and wait for their consciousness and new skin to come together properly before they feel good enough to start the mission.

A form moves into Alek's peripheral vision from the right. He turns to find a female skin. She's young and has short brown hair and a pleasant face with full lips and dark eyes under thick eyebrows.

"I'm Violet," she says.

Alek accepts the hand she's offering.

"Alek. So...we're here to look at some ruins, huh?" It's not a great conversation starter, but it's the one thing Alek has been thinking about since he signed the contract, his 221st. He's seen almost everything in his fifty helicas traveling from planet to planet, but investigating mysterious ruins are something he's never dealt with.

"Looks like it," says Violet. "Hopefully we'll get through it quick so I can get back to Nex City. Date tomorrow tonight."

Alek chuckles. "I don't think you're making that date no matter how fast we work."

"I know," says Violet. "I just don't want to be here so long that she completely forgets about me."

"I actually hope we take long enough that some people do forget about me," says a voice to Alek's left. He and Violet turn to it.

"Peter," says a young man with close-cropped black hair and fierce blue eyes. Instead of shaking hands, Peter is flexing his arms as if testing his skin. Alek used to do that every time he got a new skin too, marveling at the fact that it was not his original body but felt just like it. He doesn't care anymore.

"You new?" asks Violet. She probably noticed the arm flexing as well.

"Yeah, this is my third gig," says Peter.

"Ah, so they send us here with a greenhorn," says a voice from the door. Another female steps toward the group holding a data recorder. Long black hair. She looks of Asian descent and reminds Alek of someone.

"I'm Naomi," she says.

"Violet."

"Peter."

"Alek."

"Alek García?" asks Naomi.

"Yeah."

"Naomi Kimura," she says. "We were together on—"

"Right. I can't remember the name of the planet, but I remember you. That was a tough job. Nobody cared enough to tell us about those underwater creatures."

"Not an easy one, but I'd say this one is weirder."

"Why's that?"

"We're an independent Harbinger team. We should be researching the planet's ability to establish a colony. Not investigating some ruins. Sounds odd to me."

"Indeed," Alek says. "Most jobs that aren't commissioned by The Merge tend to skew into that territory."

"Let's worry about that in the morning. I'm beat," Peter says. "Let's get some rest. We've got a busy day tomorrow."

"Assembler's churning. Should have our materials soon," Alek says to the team via his MindLink communicator.

Alek exits the Lander and joins the team outside, taking in his surroundings. Novus-337 is bigger than he expected. He looks around the exterior of the Lander and realizes there are no Servitors going about their usual tasks.

"I haven't seen a single Servitor since we arrived," says Alek. "Are we sure they're here?"

"More than sure," says Naomi. "We wouldn't be here if they hadn't come first."

Alek doesn't mind the Servitors not being around. They're strange and he never feels completely comfortable in their presence.

"How long until the Assembler finishes making what we need?" Naomi asks.

"Materials should be ready anytime," Alek says.

"Perfect. Let's get back inside and assemble the lab."

⨯

After helping set up the lab, Alek returns to his room for the night. He takes off his boots, looks up and sees a short woman with long black hair, a strange blue dress, and a blank space where her face should be, hovering next to the door. She's shimmering a bit, somewhat translucent.

He feels a scream build in his throat and then remembers his mother in his kitchen right before the jump. A hallucination. Zero Hour. Or maybe brain fog from jump sickness. He takes a deep breath, closes his eyes, shakes his head like he always does, and looks back at the spot where the figure was. He expects it to be gone, just like his mom, but the figure is still there. It also looks different than his mother. Less lifelike. More ethereal. Alek looks at the shifting, not-quite-there grayness of its face and feels fear creep into his system.

Alek keeps staring at the specter. He blinks and shakes his head again, but the thing remains in its place, like a dead body floating at the bottom of a deep lake. With each passing second, Alek becomes more convinced this isn't a hallucination created by his damaged consciousness. As Alek looks at it, the floating woman moves toward him and stops. Then it reaches out with both hands and pushes him. He flies back and lands on the bed. Then the woman turns, floats away, and vanishes through the wall.

Alek's mind is reeling. A hallucination just made physical contact. He wants to think he imagined the whole thing, but the pain in his chest is screaming at him that everything he just experienced is real. Still, there's a small voice in the back of his brain whispering about the damage the jumps have inflicted on him, so he decides keeping his mouth shut is the best course of action.

Alek goes to bed thinking about apparitions, specters with bad intentions, and ghostly hands wrapped around his neck while he sleeps.

∿

The second day starts with a MindLink update from Naomi: *I think I've located the ruins. They're covered in foliage. Something very familiar—and very strange—about them. Still no sign of the Servitors.*

Alek isn't paying much attention to her brief. He's busy finishing comm checks in the lab when he realizes the tools he left near the air filter hatch last night are gone. After asking everyone and checking every explorable corner of the lab, he accepts that someone—something?—has taken them.

That night, as Alek is finishing data input, Naomi returns to the lab and starts crossing-checking her to-do lists.

"How'd it go at the ruins?" Alek asks.

Before Naomi has a chance to respond, Violet joins them. Her eyes are wide and she's breathing hard.

"What's wrong, Violet?" asks Naomi.

"We need to talk," says Violet.

Alek stops what he's doing, stands up, and offers his chair to her, asking, "What's wrong?"

Violet sits down, gulps air like a fish out of water a few times, and then looks from Alek to Naomi before speaking.

"This is only my 21st jump," she says. "No where near Zero Hour. The thing is...I...I don't even know how to say this."

"Go on," Alek says. "We're listening."

Violet continues, "I've been seeing things."

"What kind of things?" asks Naomi.

"Two nights ago, right after we got here, I went to my room and...there was a man there, facing the opposite wall. I thought it was one of you at first, but then I realized he wasn't quite *there*, you know what I mean? Like, I could see right through him."

A cold silence comes between them like a living thing. Alek pushes it away with a question.

"So...a ghost? A spirit? Is that what you're saying?"

"I don't know! I don't believe in any of that glap. Maybe there's a species here we don't know about? Maybe they're the ones who built the ruins? All I know is that something was in my room, and even though I could see through him, he sort of flew past me and bumped into me in the process. Like a warning. It felt like he was letting me know he had a *physical* presence, that he could hurt me. Then the next morning, right before we went out, I was walking to the exit hatch and heard noises behind me. I turned, expecting to see one of you heading to the hatch as well, but what I saw was a kid. He looked like a boy, but he didn't have a face. I know that doesn't make any sense, but instead of eyes, a nose, and a mouth, it was like his face was a moving cloud or something."

Alek thinks about the floating woman in his room and his missing tools. He could've easily hallucinated the first, but not the second. He knows his consciousness isn't pristine, that it's damaged and, as his doctor said, full of holes that are now filling up with things that aren't there, but his symptoms started after more than two hundred jumps. Violet has only subjected her consciousness to twenty-one. And she's relatively young. There's no way what she's seen and felt is because of Zero Hour.

Naomi opens her mouth to say something, but Peter interrupts her from the door before she can utter a word.

"Y'all need to come with me to the transpod chamber right now." Without saying more, he turns and sprints back the way he came. Naomi, Violet, and Alek stand up and follow him. Greenhorns can be weird, but they have their training fresh in their heads, and solving problems on your own and not alarming others until it's absolutely necessary are big parts of that training.

The transpod chamber is destroyed. The pods themselves look like some giant hand crushed them. Reflective pieces of debris sparkle on the floor, their edges reflecting the overhead lights. Sad remnants are all that remain of what used to be a perfect system capable of launching a consciousness across space.

"What happened here?" Violet voices the question everyone else is pondering. In the face of such brutal destruction, it sounds almost stupid. "How are we going to get back home?"

"Even Servitors aren't strong enough to do something like this," says Alek.

"I came in here to run diagnostics and found—"

"You saw some*thing*, didn't you?" says Violet.

The look on Peter's face is all Alek needs to know that Violet's right.

"How did you know?" There's as much surprise as there is fear in Peter's voice.

"I saw something, too," says Violet.

"Did it...did it touch you?" Peter asks.

"Yes, it attacked me," says Violet, her voice flat and cold, her eyes focusing on nothing as she remembers.

"Me too!" says Peter. "What about you, Naomi? Alek? Have you seen anything strange?"

"Yeah," says Alek. He surprises himself with his honesty. "I thought it was Zero Hour. I've jumped a lot, so it's catching up to me, but no, I really saw something. I *felt* something. And my tools. The ones I was looking for. I never found them. We're not alone here."

"Whatever they are, they're clearly telling us to leave," says Violet. "Or maybe making sure we can't. We need to—"

"What we need is to calm down right now," says Naomi.

"No, we need to get the hell out of here," says Peter.

"We can't," says Alek. "At least not from here." He gestures at the destroyed transpods.

"We need to get to the other Lander," says Peter. "If we can get those transpods to work, we can get back to—"

"Other Lander?" asks Alek, his brow furrowed.

"The ruins," says Peter. "I'm here because there's…someone is interested in what happened. The ruins aren't ruins at all. They're another Lander. Everyone from the last colony vanished and then the Servitors disappeared as well. It's—"

"That's not possible. That's not how Creator Tech works. Each planet only gets one Lander," says Alek. "You can't have two—"

"You need to forget about that. A second Progenitor found this place. It wasn't supposed to happen because another one had already made the discovery and set up shop, but the original Lander mysteriously went offline."

"How do you know all this?" Alek asks.

"I'm here to make reports," Peter says.

"That doesn't answer the question," Naomi says.

"I work for people you've never heard of," Peter says. "Stop worrying about that right now. The point is this: we need to get to the other Lander and hope the transpods are in working order."

"You said it yourself, it's offline. How're we going to use transpods that have no power?" Alek says.

Peter is starting to sweat. "We need to try. What other options do we have?"

"We need to file a report first," Naomi says. "We need to finish inputting the latest data we collected. I have no plans of making this my last transfer because of a breach of contract or insubordination. These are scarce enough as it is, and I need the credits."

"I was almost done finalizing the comms," says Alek. "I'll go finish now and then we can get some weapons, make our way outside, confirm the periphery is safe, and check out this other Lander."

Naomi nods. "I'll start my report. Peter, tell me everything you know. Violet, see if you can get any of the transpods to respond."

Alek walks back to the lab and feels the kind of dread he hasn't felt since he was a kid and had to walk to the bathroom by himself in the middle of the night. He was always sure there was something right behind him, something that would devour him if he walked too slowly or dared turn around to look before he reached the safety of his bed. Now, an adult who has survived numerous dangers on so many planets, he doesn't dare look back.

The lab is just as they left it. As he walks up to his post, he sees a handheld device on the chair where Naomi was sitting. She probably left it there as they all hurried out of the room. Alek picks it up and is about to place it on Naomi's desk when a message pops up on the screen.

VEXA: Everything I've told you is true. I'm going to erase all trace of this conversation now. Good luck.

Alek opens the message and scrolls up to the beginning of the conversation. Naomi had also seen something. She reached out to Vexa, an administrator in the contractor's database, asking for any information on Novus-337. She clearly had a theory about why they were here and wanted to validate it.

Alek reads.

VEXA: That information is classified.

NAOMI: I think there's something that doesn't want us here. We were told this planet is a new discovery, but I think it's a First Cycle world. I did reconnaissance of the ruins earlier and it looks like a Lander that's been devoured by nature. I need to know what we're dealing with here. The safety of my crew depends on it.

VEXA: I'm sorry, but that information is classified.

NAOMI: You don't understand. The Servitors are missing. The day we got here, I saw a woman in my room, hovering a meter above the ground. I blamed it on jump sickness at first, but the next day another woman floated into the lab. She came right up to me and pushed me. I flew back and slammed against the wall. Whatever it is, they're capable of inflicting physical harm. Please, tell me what you know.

VEXA: I can't...

NAOMI: PLEASE!

VEXA: ...Novus-337 was discovered 387 loops ago, and a beachhead colony was established. Then they ran into a new species the Servitors hadn't encountered. The few videos they sent showed nothing out of the ordinary. Then they sent videos of the crew being attacked by invisible forces. No matter how tight they locked the Lander down, whatever was attacking them managed to get inside. Then the videos stopped. A second mission was sent. A rescue mission. They vanished before sending any video or audio updates. No one knows what happened. Everyone died, vanished, but no one knows how or why. Everything was swept under the rug for a long time. Too long. If something's attacking you, get out.

NAOMI: What do we—

The exchange vanishes from the screen and then the screen goes black.

VEXA: I'm going to erase all trace of this conversation now. Good luck.

This isn't a new planet.

The first colony died.

They're not supposed to be here.

They're in danger.

A scream makes Alek jump from his seat. Before he can think about what he's doing, Alek sprints back to the transpods.

Peter is floating about a meter off the ground when Alek enters the chamber. He has his hands at his neck as if he's trying to pull something off his throat and his feet are kicking around desperately. He's choking and grunting with pain, fear, and desperation. Violet is screaming. Then Peter's head jerks violently to the right and they all hear his neck snap a second before his body drops back down to the ground like a puppet with its strings cut.

Alek, Violet, and Naomi exit the chamber in a flash and run down the hallway to the exit hatch. They all know they have to make it to the abandoned Lander if they want to survive.

They're barely out of the Lander when Violet screams again. Alek looks back and sees her on the floor. She looks like she tripped on something, struggling to get to her feet, and then her left leg goes up as something invisible starts to pull her back inside the Lander.

Every instinct is telling Alek to turn around and help Violet, but he knows there's nothing he can do, so he keeps running.

Alek can see Naomi ahead of him. She didn't even stop when Violet screamed. Something like guilt slithers into Alek's consciousness.

Why didn't you tell them about what you saw that night? You could've aborted the mission before it escalated. You ignored the warning.

There's no time for that. Alek keeps running.

As Naomi vanishes into the lush forest surrounding the old Lander, Alek's guilt is replaced by hope. They might make it out alive. Alek starts preparing a mental list of people he wants to see and people he wants to make pay for this.

Naomi's scream shatters Alek's thoughts.

He doesn't slow down as he enters the forest. All around him, vegetation rustles as he moves through it. He doesn't see or hear Naomi. No invisible hands grab him.

After what feels like the longest kilometer of his life, Alek comes to a clearing. Ahead of him and to the left, he sees a strange mound of gray metal covered with plants. The old Lander. He runs to the hatch, which is nothing more than a cavernous entrance under thick foliage. He's been in so many Landers that he knows he can navigate to the transpod chamber with his eyes closed.

He looks around before he enters the hatch. He wants to see Naomi. He wants to know if she's still alive. He wants to know if she will make it out with him.

Alek pushes thick leaves out of his way as he ducks inside. He runs down the dark hallway and turns into a room full of familiar shapes. He feels air leave his lungs. In the scant light coming from outside, he can see the transpods are destroyed. They look like the mess back in their Lander but aged and covered in a thick film of dirt with vegetation sprouting atop them.

The scream that's been building in Alek's chest is about to erupt from him when a force unlike anything else he has experienced lifts him up. He can't see anything, but he feels many strong hands bringing him into the air.

Alek looks around desperately for something to use, some weapon to defend himself, something to hold on to. What he sees surprises him more than any weapon would: Silvia.

Alek stares at his mother as strong, invisible hands grasp his neck. She's holding her coffee mug, just like always. The smile that never materialized back at his apartment blossoms on his face now despite the pain of a crushed trachea. Alek knows his mother isn't there, that it's all because of Zero Hour, but he doesn't blink her away and doesn't shake his head. This will be a different kind of consciousness transfer, and Alek hopes it'll bring him closer to his mother. Then, like always, Alek closes his eyes and gets ready to open them again elsewhere, anywhere, somewhere in the universe between here and forever.

THE GOOD SMUGGLER

Stephen Graham Jones

GILES 4390-KN, 493 HD

IT REALLY SHOULDN'T HAVE WORKED. But stuff that isn't supposed to be possible, that had been Myko's specialty since he smuggled that first pair of Sandean Trinadors into Rylorikan waters and let them go, already tangling into their mating coils even before the cargo doors shut. Rylorika had never been the same since—in a few more helicas, the husks from those Trinadors' moltings should, by his employer's projections, start aggregating on the surface, eventually locking together into landmasses that had never existed on the water planet, providing stable enough islands for vacation and retirement dwellings—real estate his employer had already bought on the spec market for nothing. At the rate Trinadors reproduce and molt, the size of their broods only limited by the boundaries of the body of water around them, in two century's time Rylorika would be encased in a single continuous husk, at which point the Trinadors would go into their centuries long hibernation phase and themselves become a revenue source once the waters down there froze solid enough.

Maybe, Myko figured at the time, he should leave directions for his great-grandchildren to invest in *that* spec market.

As for what he and his crew had just pulled off, though, it was best he left no notes, no evidence, no trace at all.

Except, of course, for the ransom demand.

It hadn't even been Myko's idea. Not really. Jem, who'd first got onboard Giles

4390-kn as a stowaway with a load of Benns and since proven himself particularly capable with slipping not past but *alongside* Hub security protocols, had noted over a bowl of his slop that, if pushed, if his life was on the line, or at least if a paycheck was, he could probably get a command snippet into a trans-pod stream.

"Stream?" Myko had asked, because nobody knew thing one about what interdimensional or sub-time route jumpers actually took.

"You know, whatever," Jem said, a mischievous glint to his eye.

"Do it then," Trainor had told him.

This was when her and Myko had been an item. She'd nudged him with her knee to let him know she was just trying to see how far the new kid would take this.

Pretty far, Myko suspected.

Not only was code Jem's native language—he even had the hardware in arms and behind his ear—but, as fallout from his childhood in the kiddie pits, he now had a sort of inbuilt sensitivity to the traffic cycling behind any terminal port, or under any control deck. Nothing he could articulate, but connections he could feel at an instinctual level.

Yeah, if anybody could pull a thing like this off, it would probably be Jem.

That didn't mean Myko could let him get away with this idiot claim, though.

He pushed back from the table, snapped his fingers, and informed Jem that that snap right there? It was an *eternity*, compared to how long it would take a Servitor to clock that perturbation in the feed or stream or whatever it was, crane its sensors up to the offending ship's orbit.

"They don't look up," Trainor'd said.

"They do if you're messing with their tech," Myko said back, in spite of how he'd meant to side with Trainor here.

"But I'd have the line of code already *ready*, see," Jem told them. "I wouldn't have to enter it, I'd just have to splice it in, yeah? Like spitting onto an exhaust port."

It was a good picture: at full burn, a ship's contrail probably hit half of light speed. One mouthful of spit would never be noticed. Not in a thousand helicas.

"Meaning you just need to tap into that good old Creator Tech," Myko told him.

Jem shrugged.

His face was mostly prosthetic, after the damage he'd taken in the kiddie pits, so he usually got across what he meant with body language. As for the specifics of that damage, Myko never asked, but he knew the generalities: kids living like rats in the corridors and storage areas of stations get swept up, have their heads backwired, organic receivers to tamp their own consciousnesses down to nil, sys tech tentacles worming through their grey matter, and then gameplayers ghost in at the least likely times, take control of these pristine eight- and ten-helica-old bodies, and have them fight each other until the blood loss is more of a concern than the unavoidable neurodamage this transfer left behind—hijacking a consciousness tended to leave a brain scrambled, a kid drooling. What made it especially reprehensible was that to ghost into a kid like this—to ghost into anybody fitted with the tech—you had to be close-close, almost line of sight, just because of the bulkiness of the transmission and how hungry sys always is for neurons, meaning these gamers out for a lark should be so easy to bust, as they would never ghost from far enough away that they might get trapped in whatever kid. Except they never *were* busted. Myko'd heard people call it "population control," even "pest control," but what it really probably was was richikins bribing security teams or paying for a new wing on the station.

Where there's people, there's corruption, and evil, and worse.

All you can try to do in and among it, Myko figured, is try not to get stomped. Try not to be Jem. Well, who Jem had been, once upon a time. But who he still was, too: in port, Myko'd seen him jerk his head up and hold his breath when a ship was docking, because some richikin who'd gaped Jem's head once upon a boring afternoon was onboard, and that connection was forever between those two. Jem had firewalls and more up so they couldn't puppet him anymore, but wherever there's a wall, there's a battering ram that can knock it down.

As for Jem's claim about spiking the jumpstream, this wasn't the first or even the fiftieth time Myko had heard someone make that exact same claim. But he'd seen Jem work, too, seen the info he could snag from the most gossamer rain of code slipping by too fast to even see, so... yeah, with the absolute right conditions and just a little bit of luck—okay, a lot—this could be distantly possible.

Well, it could be possible if streams even ever dipped *into* the physical world. But they had to, didn't they? The transpods were physical, so there had to be some point where the real and the intangible came into some sort of contact.

Didn't there?

Myko kept Jem's claim in his hip pocket for some fourteen trips back and forth on the Giles from The Hub to his side of the Inner Rings, smuggling so many contraband worms and gliders and bivalves that he finally found himself in a backroom with an ossuarician, discussing the feasibility of using some of those massive, mineralized Delusian bones, for which he could get legitimate papers, to hide some interphasic moths, for which there would never be papers, as they were the worst sort of pest, corroded every operating system they fluttered through.

The ossuarician drily informed him that The Merge had strict limitations on the flight paths of any cargo ship moving Delusian artifacts from before five thousand helicas ago.

"Why do they care?" Myko asked, intrigued. He had known this, he guessed, but thought it probably had more to do with tracking antiquities and steering markets than...than *what?*

The ossuarician had no idea why The Merge cared, and Delusian bones were hard to open in a way that didn't shatter them anyway, so Myko'd found another way to transport the moths—well, most of the moths. With interphasic species, loss was always factored in.

Still, those bones, right?

And why only place limitations on the ones from before five thousand helicas ago?

Two trips ago, he stumbled onto it in port, right there on The Hub, under The Merge's nose. And this time it wasn't even some other criminal slipping him the intel, but a flickering poster embedded in the wall of a rattly old shuttlepod, promoting some mindscape he'd never plug into: *Surf the Delusian sun's once-in-a-millenia sagittal crest!*

Back at his deck, drink in hand, five minutes to kill until the clearance he'd arranged came through, he looked this headtrip up. It turned out that the Delusian sun was, more or less, malfunctioning, spinning in place to some eventual oblivion, but in a way that an internal ring coalesced every few thousand helicas, forming that "crest."

For a few days every five thousand helicas, this sun spat out radiation with an unstable acceleration that showed up in deep scans of everything in that solar system.

The Merge didn't like that radiation, did it? And, while The Merge had only *inherited* the Creator Tech, didn't understand it any better than anyone else, still...maybe they understood one little part of it? Just from trial and error? From what messed Creator Tech *up?*

The very next trip, at his own expense, which broke the first and main rule of smugglers, Myko procured some Delusian bones of the right age, got them permitted up, and, faking mechanical issues—the issues were real and cascading, but their cause was manufactured—let his ship drift into the most direct line between The Hub and a popular vacation spot for those approaching Zero Hour. Its waters were supposed to wipe away the last few jumps. It was a scam, of course—once you're over five hundred, you don't get any more jumps—but if there's people with creds, then there'll be others who want those creds, and so the planets keep turning.

Sure enough, a mechanical issue or two after Myko drifted through where he suspected the stream might be, his hold packed with the Delusian bones, the news flash popped on all the channels: this oasis was quarantined.

Something was happening down there.

Because of these Delusian bones?

Did the jumpstream really exist, and...had Myko brushed up against it?

It was that or the quarantine was a coincidence.

Good smugglers don't believe in coincidences, though. Good, bad, or indeterminate, everything's for a reason.

Well well well, Myko thought.

Very interesting.

Very interesting indeed.

It took half a helica of the trips Myko despised—normal rates for legal animals, mostly livestock and exotic pets—but he eventually had enough that he could fabricate a series of malleable screens from a storehouse of ancient Delusian artifacts he wasn't really supposed to know about, that no one would miss for a while.

The screen would unfurl like a sail from his aft bay, and it was built to the precise parameters Jem guessed would have the best chance: a series of sieves gauged at intervals, because who knew what frequency Creator Tech ran at, if it even moved in wavelengths at all. The sails would only last a heartbeat out in the solar wind, but a heartbeat was all he needed.

For this haul, as Myko was calling it, he roomed and boarded his whole crew portside—everyone but him and Jem and Trainor, who insisted on reminding him with every glance and every gesture that her current financial woes were really his fault.

Fair, fair, Myko told himself. He didn't agree with her, but he could get where she was coming from. But, how was he supposed to have known that the filters hadn't scrubbed that Filotta Wren's second breath—the *dangerous* one—from the bay's atmosphere, and that Trainor had inherited an allergy to it that left her having to decide if she wanted feeling in her hands for the rest of her life or all her paychecks for the next sixteen helicas?

The crew grumbled about not getting a percentage of this haul, but Myko assured them that he and Jem and Trainor were probably getting scuttled out in the black, and…did they want a percentage of *that*?

But, complain or not, it was three days paid for, with a limited tab at the bar that owed Myko a favor, so, they'd survive.

And, just like Jem had said over slop that day: it *worked*, didn't it?

For probably five hundred helicas, scientists and criminals and everyone in between had been trying to crack just the littlest, least important corner of Creator Tech, to see how it worked.

None of them had Jem, though. His mind was scrambled, for sure, but it was scrambled in the *right* way.

None of them knew about the Delusian connection, either.

No safe is safe forever, right? All you need is the right key. The key for Myko was Jem's fine-grained Delusian sail. It had opened like a dish five times as wide as the ship, and some part of it had come into fortunate contact with either the stream, or some ragged flutter or instantiation or analogue of the stream—it probably wasn't physical, not in the way anyone alive could ferret out, but neither was this Delusian net's unsteady radiation signature.

The snippet of code Jem spiked in for that blip, that he'd spent weeks second-guessing, wasn't to corrupt the stream, either. What gain would there be in that? No, what that line of code was supposed to do was emulate the blank down at the Lander site enough for the stream to go ahead and dump its passenger, thinking this was where it was supposed to do that.

This meant Myko had had to pay even *more* for the identag associated with this lifetime jumper, this richikin, but everything's possible, if you've got the creds.

Myko's vault was empty now, and his backup vault was as well, but, if this ransom paid like he thought it would, he was going to need a new vault. A bigger one.

To sweeten the deal, too, when his connection had delivered the spread of identags Myko could choose from, Jem had back-associated them, and one of them was someone Myko knew, indirectly: the shipping magnate Myko's father had couriered data for, up to and *past* five hundred trips, leaving his father a drooling sack of meat Myko was still paying to house.

Yiv Kniss.

If any whale ever deserved to have his stream diverted into the sequestered operating system of a smuggler ship, it was him. Myko still remembered his dad leaving the pod that morning, Myko's mom running after him with her tally, telling him he couldn't, that this would max him out, that they were supposed to cross the distance together, weren't they? He couldn't leave her to cross it alone, please. Myko's dad had laughed this off, though: his employer kept strict count, would never let that happen.

As it turned out, the data Yiv Kniss needed Myko's dad to commit to memory, regurgitate, was more important than the life and future of one disposable courier.

Yiv Kniss was why Myko'd stowed away on his first freighter, even: each click away from home port was one click closer to Yiv Kniss.

Not that he had any real means of ever getting close enough to someone of Yiv Kniss's stature to *do* anything, of course. Yiv Kniss, due to his gambling empire, all the pits he ran, the ports and dens he owned, was always in motion, one step ahead of justice.

But there he'd been in Myko's readout.

And, when he hit, not even a fraction of a blink after that sail unfurled?

Just being code himself, or some mystical analogue the Creator Tech had reduced him to, he should have weighed nothing.

"Should" doesn't matter where Creator Tech is concerned, though.

Myko's ship took that impact like a blast from Patrol. At first he'd thought it was the sail, trying to rip away in the wind, but the wind wasn't that strong. The ship somersaulted hard enough that it nearly got tugged into the gravity backwash of the planet that had been the stream's initial target.

Jem blanked at his controls for a moment, Myko thought, his whole frame sagging like he was about to fall, but it was just the full-body rush of this actually having worked, wasn't it? When Jem spaced back in, like ghosting into *himself*, he held onto the OS's housing with one hand and pumped his mangled fist in the air, whooping success, and finally howling it.

Trainor cut her eyes across to Myko, said it: "What now, *captain?*"

That was the question, yes.

"Ransom" was what Myko had convinced Trainor with. There was risk, but the payoff was supposed to be worth it—with one grab, she could get out from under the creditors she was still buying her hands from.

That was the story.

Jem hadn't taken any convincing. The feat itself, him being the only one to ever pull something like this off, was enough. It's not often you get to thumb your nose at The Creators, after all, prove them just some advanced form of *people*, not the gods everyone wanted them to be.

Not that Jem wouldn't appreciate the avalanche of creds, of course. And the notoriety had to be attractive as well. Among his kind—coders, tunnelers, ensemblers—the real payout was your peers knowing what you'd done, and respecting it.

Respect was nice, sure, nothing wrong with a reputation, Myko had spent a lot of helicas cultivating his, but respect doesn't stack a vault, does it?

After helicas of being mostly flush, this haul had emptied Myko out. And he hadn't even factored in the damage they'd faked to hang in this point in space long enough to pull this grab off. And what he might—ethically, if not contractually—owe Trainor if and when things went the way he'd sort of been planning to take them...he didn't even want to consider that yet.

Reason: for once in his career as a smuggler, for once in what he always called his sad excuse of a life, he was after something other than just creds. Myko wanted *justice*. If that's what you called the son getting payback for the father. But, if that second remove made it revenge, then...there really a difference?

Myko's plan was to lock Yiv Kniss in a subroutine that emulated, down to the stained cushions and foggy porthole, his own father's room at the facility, where he was stored like a package no one would ever need again.

Eventually they would ransom him out, but what was the rush? Let his family and his empire and all his seedy contacts and paid-for senators assume him dead, victim of an unheard-of malfunction, the blank that was supposed to have been him left empty for ceremonial reasons, because you've got to enter something, and *then* provide surprise proof he was alive, and, for the right fan of creds, could stay that way.

The trick would be getting Trainor to agree with this. Since it upped their exposure—maybe The Hub tagged all jumpers in some way, or maybe Yiv Kniss had some emollient signature like the most paranoid of the richikins were supposed to be fitted with—and since she needed to get paid *now*...well. It was good they weren't together anymore. Because the fight this was going to start probably would have ended them, if not landed one of them on a slab.

But that was all later.

First: repairs. They couldn't chance a patrol asking them what their business was here, and was this their sail littering up this quadrant?

Next: getting in the shadow of some uninhabited moon or backwater planet, so they could throw a blanket over themselves, huddle over this new treasure they'd stolen, and congratulate themselves.

To avoid Trainor, Myko gave topside to her, threw himself into repairs with Jem. Except, evidently the celebration party already happening in Jem's head was leaving his hands dumb, like they'd never known a tool at all.

"What's with you, you want to get busted?" Myko asked, snapping for the gracile torker, not the robust one—did Jem think they were doing hull repairs, here?

"Can't believe it www*worked*," Jem said, eyes big about the word he almost didn't get said, some drool slipping...not from the plastic mouth of his face, but where it cupped his chin.

"I gonna have to park you, slobber boy?" Myko ribbed.

With Jem, it was always the joke, the thread: most kiddie-pit survivors ended up parked in a facility just like Myko's dad was in, once their thinking flatlined.

Jem slurped what drool he could back in, straightened up—

Which was when the lights in the bay guttered all the way down to black, and stayed that way.

"You set a timer on us, what?" Myko asked Jem, but got no response. "Train?" he said up to the ceiling, then.

They usually only went dark if a patrol was close.

No response from her either.

Myko stood, reaching above with his hand to keep from conking into the vent hood.

"Jem, hey," he said. "I was just fooling, man."

Still nothing.

A moment before his lungs went into panic, he felt his own frozen breath against the wetness of his right eyeball.

Of course. If the lights were down, the power might be as well. Meaning *environmental* could be offline. Topside or in the living quarters, the seals were tight enough this wouldn't matter for a while.

Here in the bay, though, Myko felt it almost immediately.

His heart shrank in his chest and he sucked everything he could into his lungs, an operation his head knew to be useless, but he wasn't exactly thinking with his head.

"Trainor!" he yelled, though the chances of there being enough molecules in the air to even carry his voice to a mic were nil.

Without the ambient heat from the massive OS Yiv Kniss was locked in, that Jem had said was the absolute least they would need to hold a consciousness in a usable way, there'd probably be crystals crackling on his skin.

Don't bite, don't bite, don't bite, he reminded himself.

This from people who, in the coldness of open space, had clenched their jaws shut and cracked all their teeth, been saved at some last moment only to wake spitting white shards.

"Jem?" Myko asked, quieter, partly because Jem should be right beside him, but also because Jem might have been touching something he was now frozen to.

"Three, two—" Trainor announced through the mechanical communicator, which was basically just a tube from the con.

Myko knew what it meant: she was pushing the ship through emergency startup, which skipped all the checks and syncs. If something loaded out of order, or in another executable's allocated space, they'd have to deal with that later. What was important—what was *vital*—was getting environmental going in the bay. If Trainor didn't get that heat cooking again, then she'd be alone on deck, with a kidnapped jumper rattling around in this isolated OS, trying to find any way out.

On what would have been her one, the lowest level of lighting came back on. With it, a whoosh of warm, breathable, delicious atmosphere.

The grav was always slower to cycle down, so it had never gone away before the restart.

Myko sucked air, only realizing he was hugging himself when he felt his fingers digging into the backs of his arms.

In the half light, Jem's prosthetic face was the first thing he saw. It was underlit, the shadow making the eyes and mouth hollow black, the cheeks and chin and forehead that pale wrong color that didn't even match Jem's skin, but had been all he could afford when he finally clawed his way up from the pits.

"You good?" Myko managed to get out through his shivering.

Jem was just standing there, the same way he had been before the ship blipped.

The torker he'd been holding slipped from his fingers and tapped into the plating at his feet, the magnetic head instantly adhering so the handle was cocked up like it was going to tip over.

"Hey, hey, you alright?" Myko asked again, though he could already tell Jem wasn't.

If only his face wasn't frozen—there was no way to tell between Jem alive and the deathmask that wasn't even part of his culture.

But he was still standing, wasn't he? That had to mean the cold hadn't flash-frozen him so deep he couldn't come back, didn't it?

"Trainor, Train, we need a kit!" Myko said, trying to keep the panic from his voice.

And, guiltily—it's hard for good people to think bad things—the split on the eventual ransom started to click over from thirds to halves.

It's not like he'd never had to let a crew member's corpse float out the bay door. The smuggler's life came with certain eventualities, after all. First among them was dumping evidence, and leaving the vicinity.

Jem was shading over into something that should be left behind.

There were carrion mites in this sector, though, Myko was pretty sure. In two or three helicas, Jem would be reduced to the buckles on his gear and the prosthetic that had always been his face—problem solved.

Sad, but nobody ever said life was supposed to be happy.

How was Jem still upright, though? He have Trainor's magboots on for repairs?

"Train's bringing you a—" Myko started, but before he could finish, Jem's right arm came up all at once, the back of the wrist thudding into Myko's midsection hard enough to drive him up onto his toes.

And then Jem was rushing forward to pin him against the side wall of the bay by the throat.

Myko grabbed Jem's wrist as best he could, no plans at all after that, and he was looking up into Jem's prosthetic face when the eyes in there opened.

The pupils were blown even wider than usual—Jem thought he must have come from mining stock, always getting modded to see better in the dark.

It made his eyes twin wells Myko was falling into.

At which point Trainor, former military that she was, slammed the kit that was supposed to save Jem's life into the side of his head.

Jem crumpled—the case was hard, had to survive whatever accident it was needed for—Myko fell, and the only one standing was Trainor, her chest heaving from the run down here, her eyes that kind of intense Myko could still fall for, if he let himself.

At one time he'd thought she might be the one he could cross the distance with. Looking up at her, he could feel that again.

"Ch-ch-check—" Myko sputtered out, pointing as well as he could at the hump of the OS behind her.

Check if it had blipped too.

Because if it had, they might have lost what they were here for.

Jem didn't start slithering awake until they'd found the moon they needed to be hiding behind, to lick their wounds.

Undoing the damage they'd done to explain their drift had taken about six times longer than any good smuggler would ever suggest. But they were just two people, and one of them kept having to go topside for the controls, and to check the scope for patrols.

For all their difficulties, though, Myko and Trainor worked well together.

And the OS's log didn't show any blips—the power pack that was supposed to keep it going just long enough to be pushed off a loading dock and into a bay had kept it steady, apparently. Steady enough.

Thank The Creators for their Tech, right? Not that they'd left anything in place to make cargo transport easier, but the sys principles people smarter than Myko had gleaned from Hubtech and Servitors made everything work better. Or, just *work*.

"Hopefully he didn't wipe," Trainor said, about Jem's writhing around on the bay floor. Myko was feeling increasingly worse about stashing Jem in a facility. It had just been a joke, though. He would never do that to Jem.

At the same time, he was fully aware that kids who'd survived the pits had the bad tendency to wipe when faced with danger—it was like they'd been conditioned to go blank in the telepresence of their ghost for the afternoon.

Even if Jem had wiped or even just stuttered into a blank state for a jolt or two, he had to have lined himself with enough backups and redundancies to keep him himself, though.

That was all under the hood. Here on the outside, Myko and Trainor didn't know if they should move Jem or not, so they elected to play it safe, strap him down. Mostly just to pre-assuage their own guilt. But, in Myko's case anyway, he didn't want to be close to Jem's face when those eyes opened again. For all he knew, Jem might have dialed back into his genetic history and think this was the darkness at the bottom of a collapsed mine, one he was going to have to carve his way up from.

With the tensioners modded into Jem's joints, that could be dangerous. They weren't to augment or for military purposes, were just to replace what had been taken from him in all his broadcast scraps in the pit, but all the same, they could do some damage.

But Jem was the least of their concerns at the moment.

More important was the pitching and yawing action the ship was under-going. It was almost like a routine someone had spiked into *their* system: each time Myko thought the floor had leveled out under him, the ship would roll again, and then heave around in the least likely other direction. It didn't make sense that someone who had been reduced to digital crumbles could even have weight to throw around, but Yiv Kniss was apparently doing it. It was like he'd been tunneling along the stream so fast that all that momentum had to go somewhere.

"They're not meant to mesh," Trainor guessed out loud, lacing her fingers together to show what she meant about Creator Tech not taking to being in the same system with what was, to it, primitive equipment, insulting levels of programming.

"He won't be here long," Myko assured her.

"He?" Trainor asked.

As far as she knew, they'd just snatched some random jumper, tunneling down the stream.

"Or her, them, whatever," Myko said like not that interested in whatever distinction Trainor was pushing for. Now that the repairs had been made, he and *Trainor* weren't meshing together very well either.

Old enmities raise their heads from the murk when it gets quiet up top, don't they? Just to have a look around, take a scent reading. See if there's any peace worth breaking.

"Look," Myko said, thankful Jem was stirring in what was maybe a more conscious way.

Trainor backed up, did her eyes to show Myko that he should be considerate as well, not hover.

That had been the worst part about being with her: she acted as his external conscience, always quietly urging him to be a better person than he was.

Smugglers aren't supposed to be good people, though. The ones who were, weren't smugglers at all anymore. Only the bad ones, like Myko, survived. Only the ones who embraced the grime, the grit, the ugly parts. Only the ones willing to make the hard decisions.

Jem sat up all at once from the hips like he always did—the only option, with a fused spinal column—and the straps holding him down snapped like wet tissue paper.

"...what wasss *that*?" he mumbled, his voice creaky, his left hand raising, the fingers moving through the air to show his uncertainty—to show he was asking a question.

Myko had gotten used to Jem's gesturing early on. Trainor, he noted, was always intrigued by it, like she wanted to crib all this body language down, stage it into a formal system of communication.

"We thought you'd wiped," Trainor said, too polite to say anything about the way his words were evidently still dragging.

"Yeah, well," Jem said, checking himself for injury. "Still here, I guess. Don't wheeel me off yet."

"That jumper nearly cratered us, I think," Myko explained.

Jem nodded, could buy that.

Then he looked up, held his shoulders in the way Myko had learned to understand meant "smiling," "no threat."

"Then it *worked*?" Jem asked. "I thought—I thought that jolt was from the ssail catching the wind..."

"See for yourself," Myko told him, and stepped aside to formally present the OS.

Jem stood too fast, had to clutch onto Trainor to keep from falling over. She led him to the OS, passed his weight over to its deck, and made worried eyes back to Myko.

Myko shrugged.

"So?" he asked.

"I can't believe it really worked..." Jem was saying, more just out loud to himself than in answer. Or maybe to prove he could still pronounce his words right, when he concentrated, and slowed down.

"Can we hold—*it*?" Myko asked, barely swallowing his "him." He could feel Trainor's eyes burrowing into him about it, though.

"Yeah, see what you meannn," Jem said, darting from this readout to that one, like tracking Yav Kniss from monitor to monitor. Myko couldn't make sense of it—but that's why Jem was here.

And the idea of Yiv Kniss having to scurry away was pretty satisfying.

"I think it—I think it needs an organic host," Jem finally said.

"*What?*" Trainor asked.

"Too much for an OS, or even simesian systems," Jem said with a shrug.

Myko narrowed his eyes. How was he supposed to sentence Yiv Kniss to the virch version of a small room in a big facility if he couldn't even be contained?

"You mean a—you're talking about a *blank*?" Myko asked.

Blanks, there were markets for. If they could shunt Yiv Kniss into one, then that blank could just be processed into a facility: same result.

"Something like that," Jem mumbled, more interested in the readouts than the conversation.

Meaning...since the closest place with blanks would be the jump site on Kaina Yiv Kniss was supposed to have arrived at...going back to the scene of the crime.

Which no good smuggler ever wants to have to do.

They left Jem to monitor the OS, try to keep it from tearing the ship apart.

Up on deck, Trainor nudged this and adjusted that, and finally just said it: "You're running one on us, aren't you?"

"Running one what?" Myko asked, innocent as ever, but also nudging and adjusting controls that needed neither nudging nor adjusting.

"So *don't* tell me then," Trainor hissed, glaring at him with every way but her actual eyes. "So long as I get paid."

"I told you I was sorry about that."

"Yeah, well, I can't spend apologies, can I?"

"If you would just even *trust* me for one—" Myko started, and then was having to hold onto his deck.

The ship was rolling.

"This can't be happening," Trainor said through her teeth. Because she was already belted in, she didn't have to hold on, could concern herself with trying to right them.

So as not to announce themselves, she did it with the ballast tanks, not the thrusters, and the ballast tanks must have already been out of standby, because Trainor's adjustment just interrupted their pendulum swing, throwing more weight *into* the roll.

"Nice, really nice," Myko told her.

"Like I need this from you," Trainor said right back.

Myko belted in himself.

"What did we capture, Myko?" she asked, then.

Who, more like, Myko thought.

They needed a blank, and fast. This ship was built to look cargo but hide speed, which came at the cost of being able to take this kind of punishment.

"Don't even consider it," Trainor told him, when she caught Myko's eyes flicking over at her.

"Wasn't," Myko lied.

But if she would just submit to a temp-wipe and a ghost kit, backwiring her so her neural pathways could be used to store Yiv Kniss?

Problem solved.

Until she started lumbering around, trying to get to communications or nav, call in a patrol. But deal with the first problem first, Myko knew.

And, of course, this assumed that some special tech wasn't required to translate a jumper's crumbles or trace into a wiped body. For all anybody knew, Trainor would start to bang side to side just like the ship was.

Trainor, though, *she* could be strapped down.

The ship, not so much.

ᛁᚼᛁ

"We can't lassst like this," Jem informed Myko and Trainor when they crashed back into the bay. He didn't even look up, was making adjustments so fast there was no attention left to spare.

"What about one of them?" Myko asked, flinging his hand at the starboard wall of crates. "If you need neural pathways, right?"

Because they were coming to the middle rings anyway, he'd taken on a few exotics for delivery, but just the ones that could be packed and stored—nothing with special care needed.

"Any of them got language?" Jem asked back, moving his whole body with the flurry of keystrokes and commands he was laying down.

"Talkers, talkers..." Myko said to himself, running through mental inventory.

"That can't be a thing," Trainor said. "If it were, we'd be smuggling people in pet simians left and right."

"Got a better idea?" Myko snapped across to her, trying to set it with his glare.

Trainor spun away, didn't have a better idea.

And no, this probably wouldn't work. Or it would only work for a very, very limited time. Language and true sentience aren't the same thing. But...if the neural pathways associated with language or even language mimicry were complex enough? Then the sentience funneled into that head might take a moment or two to learn them, right? Maybe?

It might give them enough time to get to a blank, salvage this haul.

But, Myko told himself, this wasn't supposed to be easy, was it? They were the first outfit to ever spike Creator Tech and siphon a jumper out. Each step they took was into a whole new reality. After today, everything was going to be completely different. What had been sacrosanct had finally been cracked. There were helicas and helicas of subtleties left to run down and exploit, but this, what Jem had done—what *Myko* had done—was the game-changer of game-changers.

They'd taken the gods down a notch or two, hadn't they?

They had.

And the payout for that effort was a jumper they couldn't hold.

"We do have one," Myko finally said, about the talker Jem was saying they needed.

Along the wall were two reticulated chwins, both male of course, because who needs that trouble; a whole covey of nesting sokles he was pretty sure were bound for a dinner party's third course; and a common male guolpa that was itself smuggling a certain parasite some third party was willing to pay for. The guolpa was the only creature with the intestinal fortitude to carry that particular parasite, but it had been vocal enough about it—*articulate* enough, profane enough—that Myko had had Jem bag its head to keep it from hurling threats and imprecations into the bay for the whole trip.

It could speak, yes. Its grammar wasn't always the best, its accents were just short of insulting, but it could replicate any language it heard spoken, and then twist it to its own means, its adjustments based on the non-vocal responses it learned: pheromones, body language, pupil dilation and contraction, breath.

"You'll need the sys gloves," Jem said, all his attention still on his deck.

Myko looked left and right for them. They weren't really for cargo, were for wrestling with the iridescent mold that grew on the underside of the grav plating, but when Jem had bagged the guolpa, he'd found sys gloves were the only thing it couldn't bite through.

"Seriously?" Trainor said to Myko, not impressed with his slovenliness even one little bit.

It had been another point of contention between them: her bunk was always pristine, her two cabinets meticulously organized. Myko tended to leave his tools and equipment wherever the job had been, and then had to turn the whole ship upside down to find them again, usually blaming everyone else for losing his stuff.

"You check aft, I'll go topside," Myko told her back, trying his best to use what he considered his captain voice.

Trainor glared right into his soul for maybe two breaths then spun on her heel, strode away, her hands balled into fists.

He was pretty sure she was going on a fool's errand, because he'd been using the gloves earlier to connect some valves under the living quarters, and that wasn't going to improve her mood any, but that was later's problem.

Now's problem was keeping Yiv Kniss from shaking the ship apart.

After stopping for a handful of the warm mash that would keep his thoughts clicking for another couple hours—another reason he'd assigned himself to this end of things—Myko found the gloves magneted to the panel right above the valves, just like he knew they had to be.

Sometimes things work out.

He chewed, swallowed, peeled the gloves off the wall, already forming a metal scab from the prolonged contact—sys tech was fundamentally corrosive—and a moment later the grav was gone, the ship was tumbling again, and he was pinned to the ceiling, the back of his head throbbing from the impact.

"Jem!" he yelled down the corridor, for no real reason other than that this had to be somebody's fault.

Crawling along the ceiling then straddling his legs from wall to wall to push forward, he finally made his way back to the hub that fed into the bay.

Trainor was there, just hanging in the air, a rivulet of blood ribboned out from a gash above her right eye.

Great, Myko told himself.

Like they weren't already short-handed enough.

He couldn't just let her fall once the grav plating kicked back on, though.

"Here," he said, drifting in to cradle her in his arms, guide her down to the floor.

Using the magnets in the left glove—he could manipulate the guolpa with one hand, surely, it weighed less than a torker—he pinned Trainor's right wrist to the floor, and was considering how to strap her legs down when he realized she was wearing the same boots she *always* wore.

He found their control in her lapel, activated the boots, and they sucked right to the floor.

"Why didn't *you* think of this, Train?" he said to her.

She just bled.

Using the right glove to pull himself along, Myko worked his way into the bay. With his feet still back in the hub, the lights flickered again, nearly sending him into a panic. Not because of the darkness—this was space—but because if Jem froze solid in there again, couldn't counter the weight Yiv Kniss was throwing around, then any hopes of stabilizing the ship were gone.

At least they wouldn't have to worry about running down a blank, though, right?

Every disaster has to have a little sprout of not *completely* terrible in it.

"You good in there?" Myko called from the doorway, cold air whooshing past him—environmental, trying to dial things back to some sort of equilibrium, thank The Creators.

Wait, no: *forget* The Creators. It was their mystical not inviolable tech that was trashing this whole mission up.

"Close it, close it!" Jem called from his station at the OS.

Myko rolled into the bay, the glove bitten between his teeth now like he was an action hero in some headtrip, and kicked the panel that emergency-shut the door behind him.

Instantly, the grav plating sucked him down to the floor. Hard. It took all his breath, left him crumpled. Trainor was going to owe him for strapping her down, wasn't she?

If he ever caught his breath again, he might tell her about it.

"Now now now!" Jem was already screaming, though.

Myko pulled the glove on, felt that same rush of fear he felt every time he slipped into some sys tech—it didn't just formfit to his hand, it adhered like a second skin. It wasn't Creator Tech, but it was definitely something to make a rational person nervous.

It was just what he needed to reach in for the guolpa, though. If he had some sys earplugs—if such devices even existed—he wouldn't have to listen to its litany of imprecations, but there was also mental fortitude, he supposed. Maybe he could conjure some of that from the tech he'd been *born* with.

"Going, going," Myko assured Jem, and, because he'd just been moving through zero-g, he pushed off lightly with the toes of his boots, expecting to drift across the bay to the wall of cages.

It would have been embarrassing, if Jem had been watching.

Myko stood, walked on his two legs over there, hauled the cage door open, and—

"No," he said.

"Now now now!" Jem was saying behind him. "I'm fabricating a pad that'll siphon this jumper out of here and ghost it into—"

But then he clocked Myko's defeat.

The guolpa wasn't just dead, it had been mashed into the corner of its container, nearly turned to paste, its feathers doing that thing dead guolpa feathers do, where they turn to jelly, marking their death site so the rest of its kind could avoid this dangerous area.

The parasite it had been smuggling was flopping up from the corpse, blindly tasting the air for its next victim, and strangling from the lack of living tissue it needed.

And Myko was the smuggler who always guaranteed his cargo arrived the same as it had been on the dock.

But, now, there were bigger concerns, it seemed.

The ship hadn't yawed hard enough to do *this* to the guolpa.

No, this, it had taken a person.

A crew member.

⅗

The first person Myko apologized to about this predicament was his dad, sitting in his chair in that room in the facility, a prisoner in his own head.

This was supposed to be for you, Myko told him.

But then the version of Trainor in his own head, who had an even sharper tongue than the one unconscious in the corridor, hissed to him that this was just the storied captain of this system's most successful smuggler ship looking for someone other than himself to blame.

She wasn't wrong.

His intentions had been pure, though, hadn't they? Didn't that count for something? And what about justice? Didn't Yiv Kniss *deserve* to get sucked out of the stream, plugged into a sim loop for what he'd done? For the way he used people up and threw them away, never mind their families, their children, their futures?

More than anything, Myko wanted to dial back, never have gotten involved with this. Of all the theories always circulating about the secret behind Creator Tech, the one that he wanted the most to believe in was that The Creators had somehow harnessed time, turned it granular, used it as both building block and fuel, meaning it didn't matter how fast their processors clicked. All their systems had to do was perform an operation enough times to finally get the result they wanted, at which point they would reset, pulling this eventuality ahead in time to almost simultaneous with the request—which felt a lot like magic.

Myko needed that reset option.

He staggered over to the OS, clamped his right hand onto the housing and leaned forward to whisper to Jem.

"Was she in here?"

"She, *Trainor*?" Jem mumbled, his eyes practically bleeding they were flickering back and forth so fast. The split attention was cleaning his stretched-out words up, anyway, it seemed.

The ship was still unsteady, could pitch at any moment.

"Yes, Train," Myko said, obviously.

Jem had one hand at the controls, now, the other shoved *under* the deck, probably so the ports in his arm could interface directly. It wasn't recommended, could backfire, leave you catatonic, smoke trailing up from your eyes, but options were getting limited very fast, here. Getting fried from the inside was starting to look pretty good, compared to their other options.

"This, this, I'm doing *this!*" Jem yelled, which wasn't like him. Denied his shoulders to shrug with, though, without hands to do his talking for him, that pretty much just left him with volume and tone and insubordination.

"It has to be her," Myko muttered.

And then Trainor lurched up to the housing beside him.

She was wearing that lefthand sys glove now, and knew to use it just like Myko was: to hold on for dear life.

"Why'd you do it?" Myko said, staring down at their hands on the housing, the glove-skin nearly touching.

"Not to improve my looks," Trainor said, and he peeked up to see what she meant: her face was sheeted in blood from the cut above her eye. She upped her chin to Jem, said, "Can he get us out of this, or we scuttling?"

"I'm right here?" Jem said back.

"You killed it," Myko said.

"The *grav?*" Trainor asked.

One drop of blood from her face fell down between the index and middle fingers of Myko's glove. The glove's sensors tasted it, fed the sensation into Myko's tactile ducts like sys tech always did, filling his head with the scent and taste and molecular composition of Trainor's genetic makeup.

"We don't have time for games," Myko told her.

"We don't have time for anything," Jem said, leaning over half a moment in advance of the ship rolling the other direction, which Myko guessed he could anticipate from tracking his readouts.

Myko and Trainor let their gloves steady them.

They were glaring at each other.

When the bay steadied out enough, she asked, "What are you telling me?"

"You killed the guolpa," Myko told her. "You killed us all, Train."

"*What?*"

"You faked like you were knocked out, even did that," Myko said, reaching up with his naked hand to almost touch her open eyebrow. "But you had your boots on. You're the only one who could have made it over *to* the cages."

"Why would I shoot myself in the foot like that?" Trainor asked, incredulous. "Because I don't want to pay these off?" She held *her* naked hand up.

"To get me back," Myko mumbled.

"Because getting payback from you is all I—"

"We don't have time for this!" Jem screamed to both of them, and hunkered down from the ship careening in a new direction.

"You know who I pulled from the stream," Myko said to Trainor, watching her eyes for the most scant flicker of the truth. "He's the guy who killed my dad."

Your dad's not dead."

"He might as well be."

"Yiv Kniss?" Jem asked.

Myko and Trainor both looked up at him.

"It's right here in the tag," Jem said, nodding down to one of his readouts.

"He's *tagged*?" Myko said.

"Just what this day needs," Trainor said, turning her head to the side to spit. "Patrol collapsing on us."

"If they've got a lifeboat," Myko said.

"Hold on, hold on…" Jem told them, and, slowly this time, the grav plating disengaged.

Myko and Trainor both bobbed up, their gloves tethering them to the OS housing, their eyes still locked together.

Last dance, Myko said to himself, and released his glove's hold on the housing, brought that palm slowly but inevitably around to her.

The glove, sensing the zero-g its wearer was floating through, was desperate enough for a hold that it would shift from magnetic for the housing to the fibrous attachments it used for non-metal surfaces, he knew. It was why you always had to leave sys tech battened down: left to itself, it started thinking, and not all of its decisions were actually helpful.

Which an enterprising smuggler could use to his advantage, if he really really needed to.

So could an ex.

And a desperate enough captain.

The palm and the bellies of the fingers latched onto Trainor's side under her ribs and Myko spun away with all the weight he had, ripping a hand-sized grab of her jacket and shirt and skin away, and deep enough that he thought he caught an organ bulging in there for a moment.

Trainor opened her mouth in pain, twisting sideways like to fold over this betrayal.

She had military training Myko didn't have, though.

Her twist wasn't just an instinct, it was so her legs could carry through, affix the soles of her boots to the vent hood above the OS, her glove disadhering from the housing as well, and coming up not for Myko's side, but for his *face*.

He managed to turn just enough to slide away from a full-on, skull-revealing grab, but her sys tech had keyed on her tumble, was even more desperate for an anchor than Myko's had been, meaning the fibrous, so-thin-they-were-near-ly-invisible network of mycelia extended from her glove even *past* what he thought should be their maximum limit, some fifty or a hundred of them scraping Myko's left cheek not just raw, but probably wide open enough to expose his hind teeth.

He screamed, rolled away, brought his knee up to where Trainor should have been, but again: her military training. She'd spent half of each day for eight weeks in zero-g, drilling through maneuvers until they were second nature.

Her knee clocked him in the back of the head, jarring blood and maybe a precious tooth or two out in front of his face, to hang there for an instant until the ship shifted around them, a wall of the bay racing their way, slamming them flat, each of their gloves going dumb-magnet, making them hold on whether they wanted to or not.

"I didn't kill any of your cargo!" Trainor managed to get out.

"It didn't kill itself," Myko said back to her. "We'd already be crashing into this moon if Jem wasn't at the controls. I don't know who else that leaves."

"Yav Gnoss?" Trainor asked.

"*Yiv Kniss*," Myko corrected. "And he's not corporeal yet."

"Because we completely understand how C-Tech works."

Which was when Myko registered a wriggling in the open air just past her face, a wriggling that registered with him at an instinctual level, making his lower back squirm, the base of his jaw tingle a hollow sensation.

Run, run, leave, millions of helicas of evolution was screaming to him.

"You pulled half my face off," he said to Trainor instead, trying to hold his eyes on hers, so she wouldn't pick up what was in its silent death throes just over her shoulder.

"You gutted me," Trainor said back.

"That was—I'm sorry," Myko said.

"Everybody's sorry when who they tried to kill is still alive."

"We can still—if we don't..." Myko struggled out, making the lie up as he went.

"Die?" Trainor asked, with almost a grin.

"Look out," Myko said then, now that it was too late to actually do anything, being sure to flash his eyes past her, so she'd be facing the way she needed to be for this.

Trainor turned, probably compelled by the concern in his eyes—it was really resignation—and the parasite from the guolpa spasmed into her mouth so fast it was a blur.

Her throat bulged with its dive down into her, her eyes watered, and—

Myko looked away.

Once, he'd thought she might be the love of his life. Then he decided she was just a capable crewman, a gifted smuggler, a soldier in need of orders.

Now she was garbage, left to drift out the bay when they accelerated away.

Such is the smuggling life.

Ⴟ

"Hollld on, Cap!" Jem called out a moment before the grav plating pulled Myko down along the wall.

The ship was stable for the moment. Finally.

"How?" Myko asked, making his way from container to container, over to the OS.

"How what?" Jem asked, peering around Myko to clock Trainor's current, and last, predicament.

"The ship is...calm," Myko said, his hands held out at waist level for the balance he was half-certain he was about to need when things went haywire again.

"Oh, yeah, that," Jem said. "I guess it's because I stopped doing this?"

This was the fingers of his exposed hand dancing over the deck, sliding the controls this way and that. But, for this demonstration, he just nudged them the slightest bit, only making the ship tilt and judder, not completely rock and yaw.

But if he really maxed those controls out, then Myko could tell the plating under his boots would be completely untrustworthy.

"You were...you were doing it the whole time?" Myko asked in a wonder so pure he didn't know if he'd ever felt anything like it.

He looked down to the floor beneath his boots like to confirm at least *its* realness, and then he tracked up to the walls all around, and finally across to Jem.

Who was grinning.

Jem shrugged one shoulder then extracted his hand from under the deck. It hadn't been ported in like Myko thought. Rather, he had been *hiding* it: it was coated in the guolpa's gore.

He brought it close to his mouth and licked the edge of a finger, delicately pulling a clot of something in and having to crank his head back to get it swallowed. That he closed his eyes for this operation was the part that unsettled

Myko. It meant Jem wasn't the least bit concerned about Myko rushing him, overpowering him.

"I don't—I don't—" Myko managed to get out.

"And you wouldn't," Jem said, the register of his voice changing, gaining something like authority. "Smuggler sons of courier fathers aren't exactly the briiightest lights in the room, are they?"

"How do you—I never told you about my old man," Myko stuttered out.

"'Did my ex-girlfriend tell him?'" Jem mocked, in his version of Myko's voice. Then, in his own: "No, Myko Chamberfell, she didn't. What does that leave you with, now?"

Myko unfocused his eyes, considering this from every angle.

"That..." he said, "that, if Trainor didn't tell you, and you didn't know yourself, didn't mine it up, then—then you're not Jem."

"Ding ding ding," the presence behind this facemask said. "I retract my previous statement about the intelligence levels of smuggler sons. Though it does still apply to certain courier fathers."

"Yiv Kniss," Myko said, his lips thinning, free hand balling into a fist.

Jem—*Yiv*—shrugged one shoulder.

"How, though?" Myko asked. "You were in the OS."

"Was I?" Yiv Kniss asked back. "Did you really think a ragtag band of smugglers could spike Creator Tech?" This was worth a chuckle from him. With Jem's throat. "Maybe you know this, maybe you don't, but I've spent half a fortune twelve times, trying to do just that. The best minds and AI of any generation tasked with just making the smallest inroad."

"But the Del—"

"The Delusian reptiles?" Yiv Kniss asked. "Everybody thinks that's the key. And everybody's wrong. Reason The Merge limits their dissemination is that those who would grind those bones up and snort them, shoot them, slap them, the ripples that sends out sometimes go the wrong way in time. So your mother shows up with a...with an incurable rash twenty loops ago, that finally produces a paste—that bone powder, surfacing. You see where that might be...problematic. Mass is supposed to stay in place, not unbalance history."

"But Jem, he—"

"Failed? Had grand ideas?"

"You're...you're saying you're ghosting *into* him? But that only works if you're close, doesn't it?"

"Who says I'm not?" Yiv Kniss said with one of Jem's shrugs, and tweaked a control on the deck, throwing a screen up. On it was space, portside. Yiv Kniss adjusted the wavelength, though, and a pink filament was suddenly hanging out there, serpentine, writhing, glowing.

"It's really silver," Yiv Kniss said. "But this cheap display, what are you going to do."

"An inline amp," Myko said in wonder, studying this thready pink line, trailing away and away. The way inline spools like this worked was…they started out as an impossibly dense sphere about the size of a one-seat escape pod, but once given direction and propulsion, they unspooled, hooking into the place they left while also reaching out and out and out, starting out as a cable, then a string, then a filament, and then ducking down into the invisible thinnesses. The span between a planet and its moon was nothing to something like that. "Where's it anchored?" Myko asked, like just curious.

"Tell you where I am so you can snip-snip, strand me here?" Yiv Kniss said. "Yeah, I trust you with that, Myko Chamberfell. You'd never use that to your advantage, would *you?*"

"But what if a ship—"

"I halted all traffic in this quadrant before I uploaded," Yiv Kniss said. "And there's no known space debris around here. Well, except your joke of a sail back there. Did you know that was what that initial jolt was?"

"The sail?"

"It caught in your own exhaust," Yiv Kniss said, again shrugging like Jem. "After that…" He lowered a lazy hand to the deck, yawed the ship back and forth.

"It was you all along. You programmed it in."

"Just because I had to check out for a few there, to learn the controls of this one. He's not a kid anymore, is he? There were all these firewalls and self-destruct routines…"

"Where is he?"

Yiv Kniss shrugged an exaggerated shrug, said, presenting himself—nearly preening—"Here?"

"I mean his consciousness. *Jem.*"

"I'm standing on him right now, you could say. In here." He tapped his temple.

"How did you know it was—that it was me?" Myko asked.

"I didn't," Yiv Kniss said with another shrug that seemed to catch him by surprise. "But a known smuggler ship in orbit rings certain alarms, don't you think? After my *successful* jump—"

"Then you are on the planet. That amp is anchored down there."

"Doesn't matter. After my jump, the first thing my assistant alerted me to was your ship, its rotational axis every which way up here."

"Because the sail was in my exhaust."

"And these amps are all the rage, now. Of course I had one on hand. Never know when you might run into an old friend from the pits. But—am I telling you all this so you can believe I'm really here? When you can see and *hear* that I am?"

"So, the house wins again," Myko said.

"Always does, if you play long enough," Yiv Kniss said with one of Jem's shrugs. "And, funny thing? You'd have been fine if you just stuck to smuggling, Myko Chamberfell. I don't think revenge is really your game, is it?"

"Ransom," Myko corrected.

"And how's that working out for you?"

Myko flicked his eyes away.

Trainor was on the plating where she'd fallen in a heap. Myko was pretty sure she'd fallen facedown, but she was on her back now, her stomach distended, the worm's bi-gasses swelling her more and more. Soon she would burst, paint the bay with her insides.

"You made me kill her," he said.

"Maybe she really did do it," Yiv Kniss said, a hopeful lilt to his words. "But...well. Okay, I don't want you thinking I have anything against pretty animals. I couldn't let you try to port something out of here"—the OS—"that wasn't *here*, could I? In my line of work, you control every variable if you want to win the game."

When Myko didn't have anything to say about this, Yiv Kniss shrugged, snarled about these shoulders he couldn't keep in check, then lowered his clean hand to the deck, dialed something.

"What are you doing?" Myko asked.

"Tunneled into your commannnd deck," Yiv Kniss said, distracted. "Might have dropped a beacon on the other side of this moon." It was worth a grin, to him. "Oh, also, let's say I...I just bought a certain facility as well? One that warehouses the catatonic?"

"No."

"I would beg to differ, but as you know, I don't have to beg my way through life, do I?"

"So a patrol's on the way, I take it?"

"Maybe they'll have a med kit with them," Yiv Kniss said, nodding his expressionless face to Myko's ruined one.

Myko looked past Yiv Kniss, to the bay doors pressed against each other from top to bottom like a giant pair of lips closing them in.

"If you want, though, this could have all been a solo operation." Yiv Kniss said, Jem's large-pupiled eyes boring into Myko.

"What do you mean?"

"Soldier with a grudge? Your girlfriend there? I'm sure we can find or create some tenuous connection between her military career and my various operations? Maybe she spearheaded this whole operation, right?"

Myko looked where Yiv Kniss was indicating: Trainor.

The worms massing inside her had her standing on her heels and the back of her head. It looked painful, except...she was beyond all that.

"You want to set her up to take the fall?" Myko asked.

"I propose you let me play smuggler," Yiv Kniss said.

"I'm not backwired, you can't ghost me," Myko mumbled, not really wanting to hear any more of this.

"I wouldn't want to be in your head, don't worrrry. No, what I mean is...I take you down to the jump site on Kaina, spirit you away. You were never here."

"And I trust you why?" Myko asked.

"Because of this," Yiv Kniss said, opening arms to embrace the ship, this moon shadow. "Do you know what this grand adventure would have cost, on the open market? And, even then, the safeties would have been on. No, no, it's me who owes *you*, Myko Chamberfell. My world is *much* more interesting with you in it."

"You want me to be your courier," Myko said, sneaking a look ahead to the end of this conversation.

"Work your debt off," Yiv Kniss said. "That's how Dear Old Dad got into my employ, you could say."

"And that really worked out for him."

"He got paid every jump. And he always remembered the...the *combinations*."

Instead of packing his cargo in hidden spaces on a ship, Myko's dad committed Yiv Kniss's precious data to memory, to regurgitate later. Not unlike a guolpa.

"I need capable people, Myko Chamberfell. And you've proven yourself to be just that. Just because your little attempt failed doesn't mean you don't have potential."

"Option two?" Myko asked.

Yiv Kniss shrugged what felt like his own shrug, said, "Then I guess enforcement jams you up for this attempt, and...they probably come into the possession of records of your past smuggling operations, say? All the way back to Rylorika. You kind of ruined a whole planet there, didn't you?"

"That was you? You were the investor?"

"Everyone needs a vacation hommme."

"You're frying Jem's brain."

"You could say it was already pretty cooked."

"I'm going to have to put him in a facility after this," Myko said.

"That's what you're concerned with?"

"I never would have...Rylorika. If I knew it was you."

"Won't work for me, will only try to kidnap me...You see why my world's more interesting with youuuuuuuuuu in it?"

He covered the mouth of Jem's mask with his hand, making a show of embarrassment over how his syllables were stretching out.

"Let him go," Myko said, about Jem. "It's me you want."

"Or you could always take the back door..." Yiv Kniss said then, stepping aside to present the bay doors.

"You'd let me do that?"

"Like I was saying, I owe you, Myko Chamberfell. This was a *most* grand tiiiime. It puts my merry pits to shame. I'll be toasting to it forrr loops and loooops. I might even commission a headtrip, what would you think of that?"

Myko did one last, exaggerated shrug to Yiv Kniss, gambling that Yiv had lost enough control that Jem's conditioning to respond in kind would be too strong to suppress. He was right: Yiv Kniss matched Myko's shoulders, and in that instant Myko surged across the OS as best he could, using the sys glove to pull ahead, and—

If Jem wasn't augmented, it might could have worked?

Yiv Kniss caught Myko at arm's length, held him by the throat for a second time in their working relationship, the toes of Myko's boots just touching the floor.

Myko raked his sys glove at Yiv Kniss, but Jem's mask was treated, wouldn't submit to that.

"Option three it issssssss," Yiv Kniss said, cocking his head over at this failing body he was in. But it wasn't failing enough he couldn't carry a struggling Myko across the bay, and veer over a few degrees to take Trainor by the hair, drag her with.

Two bodies were too much for one failing former kiddie-pit veteran to manage, though. Even with Jem's mods. Yiv Kniss used what felt like the last of his strength and control to fling Trainor ahead.

She snagged in the buzzing enviro field, was just hanging there, her whole torso surging and bulging with the brood of desperate parasites.

"I'll work for you!" Myko said, trying to get his feet under him to stand out of this, not get tossed out there like trash. "Four hundred and ninety-nine

jumps!"

"That's what you really wannnt?" Yiv Kniss asked, holding Myko up to look into his eyes, his right foot hitting the control that yawned the bay doors open. It made even more sparks hiss from around Trainor. They fell to the plating, skittered around their feet, and then, slowly, inevitably, the enviro field did what they do: passed material without a pulse through itself, out into the drink.

It was terrible to...not exactly watch, as Myko was facing the other way. But there was a moment he could see Trainor's left mag boot, and then, slowly, he couldn't anymore.

He sagged in Jem's iron grip.

"Know what your father saidddd before his five-hundredth jump?" Yiv Kniss asked Myko face to face, close enough Myko could taste the slop on Jem's breath.

Myko struggled, couldn't break loose.

"'Keep my kid out of this,'" Yiv Kniss recited, right into Myko's ear, in pretty fair imitation of Myko's dad's actual delivery, and Myko recoiled from this, his hair swirling in the enviro field, popping now from the carrion mites sensing food in here, and killing themselves to get to it.

"I don't care what he said, I said I'll do it!" he pled, squirming. "I'll be your courier! Just don't—don't—"

"Well, if that's realllllllly what you wannnnnnt..." Yiv Kniss said, shifting to hit the foot control again.

Myko sagged, almost elated at not being thrown out into the big, black cold, but—

It had only been a feint.

Yiv Kniss wasn't pulling the doors closed, he was pausing the field.

"Goodbye, Myko Chamberrrrr—" Yiv Kniss said, not able to get out the rest of the name.

He fell to a knee, still holding Myko out the bay, like that was going to be his last effort. This was what happened when an afternoon brawler stayed in a kiddie too long: they burned that kiddie out, had to start the process of tunneling back to their real selves.

That took a few breaths to initialize, though.

Right on cue, indicative of the efforts going on in Jem's head, tendrils of smoke curled up from his eyeholes, the backwiring fusing in there. His hand unclamped from around Myko's throat, dropping him into the big black, the enviro field hissing around Jem's arm when Yiv Kniss fell over, his foot sliding off the control.

Somewhere in Jem's head, Myko knew—or, had heard—Yiv Kniss was taking one last look around before pulling the eject lever and shunting at optic speed back into himself.

Leaving Myko out here to freeze solid, Trainor floating right above him, her eyes still open in surprise.

Moving on instinct, from fear, Myko reached for her corpse to hug her to him, and they coiled together, their skin already going crunchy, which was right when the blind larvae burst up from Trainor's torso, tasted the iciness out there, and crossed it for the nearest warmth: Myko.

He took each worm without letting go of Trainor, and no, they hadn't been perfect for each other, him and Trainor, not even close.

But now they'd have forever to work that out, wouldn't they?

At least until the impact of that barrage of larvae drove Myko back, Trainor tumbling away from him, into the void, her hair swirling around her face, eyes still watching Myko, it felt like.

Myko was pushed the other way, felt his sys glove panicking, squeezing his hand because it was extending so much of itself out for something, *anything* to grab onto, its thousands of desperate little reaches rotating Myko around enough to fix on Jem's blank face in the bay, behind the enviro field, Jem's eyes narrowing in what Myko knew had to be Yiv Kniss's effort to record this grand comeuppance he'd engineered.

He should have already been gone, was probably lingering just to savor this moment before leaving Jem behind like a husk.

Because the cold and the larvae hadn't quite gotten to Myko's grey matter yet, he could still think a bit, could look forward, see how Patrol was going to follow protocol for a situation like this, and park Jem in some facility, another victim of the kiddie pits. Maybe he'd even end up in the same facility Myko's dad was in, that Yiv Kniss had just bought, which would be about right.

Sorry, kid, Myko said in his head, to Jem. *You didn't deserve this.*

Neither did Trainor, though.

To say nothing of the captain of the ship.

Myko bit his teeth together hard enough that two or three of them cracked.

At which point he saw...a silver snake in the hull's reflection? He wasn't alone out here?

With the last of his strength, he swung a stiff arm enough to roll over, look behind him, and—

The inline amp, the tether! The one Yiv Kniss was about to crash back down, and then reel in like he was never here. The reason he'd halted all traffic in this quadrant and clocked for space debris: if that line severs, then he's trapped in whoever he's ghosting into.

Myko, his thoughts swirling the drain, tasted this realization again, again: Yiv Kniss needs that line to go home, doesn't he?

The smile Myko managed cracked his lips, the blood there instantly icing over.

Had he been able to speak—if there were any air molecules to carry his voice, even—the one word he wanted to say was *Dad*.

But he said it anyway, with his last motion, which he traded his life for: straightening his arm to this filament, so the desperate tendrils reaching from the palm of his glove could tangle it in, corrupt it, corrode it, snap it, sever it.

Trapping the system's biggest crime mogul in the head of a faceless kid from the pits.

A kid who's about to get parked in a facility for the rest of his life, where the rider in his head could never work the controls to say who he was.

A moment later, a parasite burst up from Myko's nasal cavity, tasted the great cold out here, and ducked immediately back into the right eye, but Myko's smile was frozen in place, couldn't be touched, at least not until the carrion mites swarmed over him and he finally stopped being a bad person, became, at long last, a good smuggler.

CHANTRESS

Akua Lezli Hope

Each new Arrival is a rebirth
She is born again, re-embodied
aware of all her prior incarnations
building with one consciousness
many lives

Challenged by change
yet tethered to a unique
continuity, a singular multiplicity
no erasure, just amendment, addition
pearlescent layers around a central irritant:
her earthborn core

This body-shifting, new inhabiting,
the miracle path to traverse space
to learn unknowable lessons
and newly known routines

Miracles are undiscovered science
mechanisms that seem magic
shuffling off one mortal coil
to be wrapped in another skin suit

There is sadly, still hierarchy
jealousy, but four golden threads:
service, duty, faith, and family
provide continuity

Of those she has just three
an overarching faith, a desire for
service, and a destiny of duty

From a place where singing and poetry were one
whose first stories were sung
lyrics were poetry and messages had meaning
spell casting change-making, unlocking

She had discovered how sound itself evoked
whatever each of her bodies learned in making song
built upon its predecessors in her consciousness

She is a symbol of cooperation
of reconciliation, of healing
She sang songs of transcendence
of discovery, of magnificent mysteries
awaiting each new Arrival

For all the things she might specify about her bodies
height, weight, skin coloring, face
she could not trace what goes on inside

That it would be healthy yes, but not
what hides, its still unknown-to-her magic,
a voice box, size of her chest,
feel of her new lungs
how air entered and filled them
their capacity to stretch, lengthen
support, did not predict
what each throat might do

With her skill, over time
she could make thin strands resonant
bend them to her will
she could fill and refill and expel breath
breathe circular, hum deep, explore depths

How often would she look upon an instrument
and know how to evoke from it, deep sentiment?
The bodies she inhabited were implements for her skill
but how to inform others' consciousness?

How often might she be voice of the Xtabay, Yma Sumac
an Oum Kalthoum, though she was practiced at evoking thrills
How often could she be a Maria Callas or a Neffeteria of Alliance
a galactic Alyana, voices of the past possessing unbelievable range
with abilities to evoke the familiar and the strange

All who heard them felt stunning surprise
transcending genre and culture, climate and worlds
that somehow understood and reached within their souls
yearnings, connecting all to shared dreams and goals

More the amazement that these singular sound makers
had not spent lifetimes, as she had, studying
they arrived at a knowing using just one body
and one lifespan

She was grateful for the gifts of this era
        for all who made noise, sang
                for all who made sound, sang
                        for all motion, movement, resonance, rang

Sound is but a small part of the vibratory range
of the energetic wavelength, both mundane and strange
maybe one day she would learn to sing all hues
how to be super- and subsonic
singing light, as stars do

When we who use eyes and have ears
will one day share the songs of light
and see the colors of sound

She hoped to go there —
to be, at long last, a lightsinger
as those who had crashed
from that future past, surely had

In the interim there are things to fix
mediations to make
warriors to entertain
peace to maintain
hope to sustain
bodies to help heal, sound potions to mix
disputes to undo, to reconnect and weave
to make all feel better, live better,
be better, by her singing
and so she sang

Where to begin? She shifted her origin story
to fit the audience. Her parents sang
and sang to her but who didn't?
These were things she took for granted:
to live with shaped sound and song

That Earth was her birthplace suggested
limits only to the unschooled
Long before her first jump swap body change
she had mods that let her swim in seas
explore the range of sound and language
below the waves   from whales

She had repitched the thrumboom of elephant hums
the dinosaur songs of Earthbirds from their multiphonic trills
to whistles and wails, yodels spanned the globe
from forest folk in Africa to Mountain folk in Nordic dales
echo locating songs to penetrate thick forest
or reverberate through a rocky range

There were throat singers: Mongolian circular breathers
using the deep manipulation of vocal chord   stomach breath
heart hum   so she knew how to listen
how to mimic how to open her first body's
3.5 octave range to almost make four

How to make human ears yearn for more?
most earth songs were about love at its most banal
now she loved love of struggle
love that celebrated triumph over adversity

Love songs that spoke of deeper yearning
or hinted at changing the world
those who know, do not speak
those who speak, do not know
but those who sing ----

In the Groves of Akkala
she learned the flowers' song
They were meters high, resembling Earth trees
whose leaves rustle on a breeze

These rooted sentients hummed
from their petals and waved their sepals
the mechanism of their song was imprecisely known

She studied by listening their eighteen-hour day long
and through their three-fold moonrise nights
when their singing shifted from azure to lime green
and their heads bent down to dose their ground
with luminous spore seeds

In the crystalline cliff caves of Beryllium 5,
beings thought of as rock were alive
living slowly, by the way humans reckon time,
singing a song speech, deeply hypnotic and sublime

Most couldn't listen, nevermind learn
because the sound would cause some brains to burn,
others to dive so deep inside their psyches
                              they did not survive
She dared to listen, she dared to learn
and thus another of her singing skills was earned

healing broken psyches, mediating burns,
holding sacred space, to which the needful turned.

SWORD OF THE SILENT

Matthew Kressel

HELIOS NEXUS, 493 HD

As HER CONSCIOUSNESS DISSOLVED into the great sea of being, Ven Zenari thought, *This is my death, and no one will witness it.* For one beautiful and terrible moment she was the universe, every last part of it, and everything she had ever known was a drop of rain plashing on a leaf, rolling down its aqua-green wax, and dropping off to infinity.

Then she awoke in a transpod.

Her consciousness rushed back like a flood tide, and she gasped in horror. She had known jumping into a human body would be strange, but even catching the white-mold sickness as a girl hadn't felt nearly as bizarre as this. These human limbs were much too short, they had only two joints, and their ten fingers, more numerous than her Zvee eight, were magnitudes less dexterous as she furtively flexed and moved them.

Had she really just transferred her consciousness into alien flesh thousands of light-years away? She reeled at the impossibility. This human body was as fragile as a dried leaf. She longed for rest and sleep. But Ambassador Ortega had promised her only twenty-four hours in his body, and if she overstayed by a single second, he'd turn her in. The Merge, he'd warned, wasn't kind to body snatchers. But she was wise enough to know he was speaking about himself too.

There was no one else in this huge chamber, just a forest of blinking metal machines. They were the flattest, shiniest things outside of a lake she'd ever seen. The air smelled like a violent thunderstorm had just tumbled through.

She had left her home just once, when she was a girl, to study at the Historical Academy in Oonpai. Now she was a woman, trained in the secret art of

The Silence. She should stand like an oruba tree. Solid, majestic, indomitable. But the fear came like a fierce winter wind, and she was a terrified girl all over again, trembling before the universe like a leaf in a coming storm.

↜

The whispers started before her sixth nameday.

Little Ven is such a chore.

I wish I'd never had a child.

I could've been a great scholar if not for her!

They came in Mother's voice, sharp as a moonbird's song, though Mother's lips hadn't moved. Ven pretended these were bad dreams, or dark imaginings, and she did her best to ignore them, because Mother smiled and did motherly things, and surely she didn't think those horrid things of Ven, did she?

But at ten, when the first signs of womanhood puffed up Ven's dorsal feathers, the voices grew too loud to ignore. She'd sit in the dank and humid halls of Senary Bough, the great youth academy carved into the trunk of an enormous oruba tree, and hear her classmates' voices clear as autumn air, though no one had spoken.

I want to kick proctor Houla like a leafcat.

Maybe Yori will hold me with his strong arms and rock me and touch me.

I wish father would stop beating me after he smokes his lichen.

The voices pelted her like heavy rain. Sometimes, the voices helped her, like when she didn't know the answer to the proctor's questions. But mostly they terrified her. And sometimes, when the cacophony grew too loud, she'd hold her ears and scream, though this only increased their number.

Ven's so weird!

That seed didn't sprout so far from the tree.

I don't want to play with Ven anymore.

Their words stung like nettles, and Ven would run home in tears.

Soon the head proctor called Ven a disturbing influence and removed her from Senary Bough. Mother was furious and took Ven to sundry healers: smoke nests to burn out her demonic spirits (it made her lungs burn for days), mindbreaker seeds to reshuffle her thoughts (she felt a stranger to herself for days after), and even a water death treatment (which scared her so much she hid in the forest for two days).

One misty afternoon she heard Mother say: *I wish Ven was never born.* But Mother sat with her eyes closed, dozing in a chair.

Crying, Ven ran off. She climbed a nectar tree until she was so high above the village the ground was hidden in fog.

I'm a wretched thing, she thought. *A stunted weed. For the good of the harvest, I'll throw myself into the mulch pile. Everyone will give thanks.*

She stared down into the fog. One step, and her suffering would end.

Don't! someone shouted.

The voice shone brighter than the sun, yet was somehow quieter than a falling leaf.

She turned to see an old woman on the slippery branch. One wrong step and she'd tumble to her death. But the woman approached Ven with ease.

"I'm Beok," she said with a warm smile. "And I'm sorry it's taken us so long to find you. Please don't jump, Ven."

Ven raised her dorsal feathers in fear. She was sure this woman was just another healer looking to profit from her misery.

"You're not ill, Ven," Beok said. "And neither are you a weed. You're a rare flower. My little Ven, you're one of us."

"Us?" Ven said, looking round, but besides a row of ridge sparrows shivering on a branch they were alone.

Without moving her lips, Beok said, *One of The Silence.*

Chills rolled down Ven's spine. "What is The S—"

Beok put a hand to her lips. *Hush! We never speak that name aloud!*

"I don't understand," Ven said.

I was confused too when I was your age, Beok said. *Be at peace, for all will make sense soon. But know this: you're not broken, Ven. You have a rare gift. We call it telepathy. Do you know the word?*

"No."

It means you can communicate with thoughts.

"But...what do you want with me?" Ven said. She was shaking now. But not from fear. Her whole body thrummed because for the first time in her life she felt as if someone might actually understand her.

My little Ven, she said with a smile, *I wish to teach you.*

A decade later and thousands of light-years away, Ven pulled herself out of the transpod onto her borrowed human feet.

"Welcome home, Ambassador," a voice said, startling her, because there was no one else here. But she remembered Ambassador Ortega telling her about many miracles she would encounter. One of them was the transmission of voices over long distances, a technological version of telepathy.

"You weren't expected back this soon," the voice said. It spoke Common, a Merge language, but Ven had practiced it well.

"I...," she began, then paused, surprised at the timbre of her human voice. "I need to research something in the Atheneum."

"I don't care what you do. Just make sure to update your logs," the voice said. "I ain't covering for you again, Ambassador."

"Y—yes," Ven said. "Of course."

The voice grunted and said no more.

She lifted her short human arms and examined her strange human hands. There was a silver band around one of her fingers, and she made a note to ask the Ambassador about it later. She took a few wobbly steps toward the door and paused. In the trance training of the sempo martial arts Ven had been taught to imagine herself as many animals: sheet birds, tree ants, even the slug whales of the great Southern Sea. She used the same technique now to adapt to her odd new body.

When she reached the door, it opened for her, and she gasped. Such wonders here! She stepped into a hallway filled with even more doors. Unlike Zvee architecture with its dovetailed wood and mortared stone, these walls were made of smooth metal, gray as clouds, and infested with gray roots. They were covered in symbols too: English letters and numbers that she had learned how to read. An illuminated book hung on the wall, displaying more words: *Intercom; Departures; Station Map.*

Rectangles of pale light shone down from the low ceiling like cut swatches of sky. How could humans endure this cold, sterile place even for a moment? It was horrid! She longed for her home nest, with its barkskin walls and lambent candleflame. But she might never find her way back now.

She followed the twisting path that Ortega had given her, while her human heart beat like a flitfly's wings. Was this rate normal for a human? She doubted it. She reached a locked door and tapped a sequence of numbers on an illuminated book, and a yellow-white beam, like rays of sun, danced over her face. The door opened and she saw.

There were others here. *Many* others. Ambassador Ortega was a human male, but he had created a Zvee body for his mind to inhabit. Outside of his miraculous picture machines, she had never seen a creature from another world. But this hall was crowded with them, in myriad forms and colors. And she had thought the Oonpai forests were diverse!

Her body shook, so she calmed herself. *I am a rock in a river. An oruba tree in a storm. The world moves around me, but I remain still.*

The technique worked a little. She felt their alien eyes watching her as they moved in and out of adjacent doorways. Then she noticed the bright, cathedral-sized chamber at the end of the hall.

The Atheneum.

In a way, it reminded her of the great temples her people built to worship the Aain. According to the ancient Wisdom Trunks, thousands of helicas ago powerful gods called the Aain dwelled among the Zvee. But when the Aain gods judged the Zvee unworthy, they left for Heaven without them. The great Mother Planet herself, Zvee Ord, was so distraught when the Aain left she wept tears of fire for a thousand helicas. There were still places on Zvee Ord that were charred and barren, and it was said they were evidence of her ancient burning.

Even today, millions of Zvee believed that if they perfected themselves through religious observance the Aain gods would return and usher them up to Heaven.

But Ven was taught a very different story. She was told that the myths of the Aain were terrible lies meant to keep the Zvee small, cloistered, and afraid.

But I will find the truth, she thought, *inside this Atheneum.*

She stepped forward into the alien throng.

She left home like this: Beok told Mother that Ven had scored high on an aptitude test and had been invited to study at the Historical Academy in Oonpai. The academy was far away, on the southern continent. Zvee seldom traveled more than a few hours from their birth cities in their entire lives, but Mother smiled and asked no questions and seemed happy to send Ven away. The last thing Ven heard Mother think before she left was, *Now, Aain-willing, may I find peace.*

The Historical Academy of Oonpai was an ancient school, built in the dense forests that faced the Southern Sea. The trip was long and arduous, and Ven spoke little along the way. She'd heard many stories of travelers eaten by monsters, or murdered by wild folk, or dead of dehydration in the charred zones. But she met no monsters, wild folk, or charred forests along the way.

Why then, she wondered, *are we so afraid to leave our homes?*

There were other children at the academy like her, she was surprised to find, and they too heard others' thoughts. *For each one of us,* Beok thought-spoke to the nest of students on that first day, *there are a million others who cannot hear the silent voices. All Zvee have latent telepathy. It is our birthright. But only a rare few can communicate clearly. Like me, little ones. And, like all of you.*

Ven looked around at the other children, their sea of dorsal feathers quaking in fear. Had they spent their whole lives being afraid, like her?

Long ago, Beok thought-spoke, *people like us were murdered. They feared us because they fear their secret thoughts. We were slaughtered by the mulch pile. This is why, for the safety of us all, your powers must be kept hidden.*

Ven shivered in fear and delight. She had never been part of anything before. And over the weeks that followed, she learned many more secrets.

We call ourselves The Silence, Beok told them, *and we are ancient and everywhere. We have members of The Silence placed in academies and governments across the planet. We have members deep inside the Wisdom Trunks. And we speak a secret telepathic language to communicate, a language as old as the world.*

Ven knew the common tongue and spoke two of the old dialects, but this silent tongue was far different from anything she'd heard before.

You must never speak the silent tongue aloud, Beok warned them one foggy morning. *This is our most sacred law. To violate this is punishable by death. Remember this well, little ones. You'll not be warned twice.*

Ven shuddered with the other children. But the thrumming she'd felt on the branch when she first met Beok had never stopped. She wanted more.

The academy provided. They taught her the sempo martial arts, and she became as agile as a sun bee. They taught her of stars and fungi, and soon she could find her way on a moonless night by the light of phosphorescent mushrooms. They taught her how to use the leaking thoughts of others to deceive, and she became a devil at games of strategy. Her studies exhausted her, but she woke up every day eager for more.

Some children tried to befriend her, but she kept apart. They'd soon turn against her, she thought, like her classmates back at Senary Bough, whose mocking laughter still haunted her dreams. And as her strength and confidence grew, she vowed to never let herself be vulnerable again.

In the early weeks, she wrote Mother daily, but Mother never wrote back. And whenever Ven thought of Mother, she found an emptiness in her chest. So after two months she stopped writing.

At the end of her first helica, Ven aced all of her tests, and one balmy night, Beok called her into her private nest. It smelled of old books and lantern sap and the aging woman. In the silent tongue Beok said, *So my little Ven, how do you feel now that you've finished your first loop?*

Ven had become fluent in the silent tongue by now. *I feel fantastic, Professor! But—*

Yes, little one?

Sometimes I...

You get scared.

Yes, Professor.

And what scares you?

Ven didn't want to answer. But there was no hiding from Beok. *I'm scared of everything. I'm a timid leafcat.*

Curious, Beok said. *Not once have you shied from your studies or refused to do what's been asked of you.*

Yet I'm always scared. Teach me, Professor, to become fearless like you.

I've another secret to teach you, Ven. I too feel fear.

You? Ven couldn't imagine Beok being afraid of anything.

Oh, yes, Ven. Being brave does not mean you feel no fear. You feel the fear and do what must be done in spite of it.

Ven sat there, seeing Beok in a new light.

There's something else troubling you, Beok said.

Ven sighed. She was used to Beok knowing all. *Yes, Professor. We learn so many new skills. How to fight and navigate and deceive. Why? What's this all for?*

Beok smiled and said, *I was right in choosing you.*

Beok took her pipe from her drawer and lit the pungent lichen in the bowl. As she exhaled a long stream of blue smoke, she said, *I think you're ready for the next secret, Ven. Like the silent tongue, you must never speak it to anyone, not even your classmates. Outside of this Academy, you might be killed just for thinking it!*

Ven felt as if she were about to be struck by lightning.

The Aain gods, Beok said, *that we worship in the ten thousand temples are not gods. They're demons who enslaved us Zvee thousands of loops ago.*

Demons? Ven said with a start. She'd always felt there was something wrong with Aain worship, people's blind devotion to long-absent gods. But this explanation didn't feel like the right answer either.

Yes, demons! Beok said. *How else do you describe their legacy? Do you know that most people never travel more than a few hours from their birth city? That they spend their entire lives holed up in one small copse?*

I do, Professor.

And so you know how fearful people are of change, of even meeting a stranger from outside of their insular little towns!

I have seen it myself.

And have you wondered why?

I just thought that's the way it always was.

No. We have been taught for millennia to fear change, exploration, and novelty. We huddle in our trunks like timid mice, pouring over the same dreary passages in the ancient texts, reinterpreting them for the millionth time. When have you last heard of a new invention or discovery? When I was a child, I once met a woman named Ulania who had created a way to harness the power of lightning to make artificial light. Have you ever heard of her?

No, Professor.

Of course you haven't! Priests railed that Ulania's work defiled the Aain gods. They said the Aain demanded we remain holy and pure and not be defiled by secular things. The ways of the gods are not for us Zvee to know, they said. They denounced Ulania for blasphemy. Angry mobs destroyed her research. Family and friends shunned her. Ulania should have been as famous as the scholar Macherai, but she died a withered husk. She took her own life by swallowing a poison root.

Ven shuddered.

My little Ven, Beok said, this timidity is not our birthright. It's been forced onto us. We've been kept in a cage for millennia, and today we build our own bars. Imagine what wonders lay in the world for us to find if only we looked. We study the natural sciences here at the Historical Academy, though the priests would have our city razed to the ground if they knew it. We are told to worship the Aain as gods, but they are demons who've tricked us into staying small.

Do you really believe this, Professor?

Like The Silence itself, this secret has been passed down through hundreds of generations.

But...

Yes, little Ven?

Ven didn't answer, afraid that if she told her truth, Beok would abandon her, just as Mother had.

Your thoughts leak loud, Beok said. You want to know, what proof do I have?

Ven shook from fear. But she straightened herself, feeling a new strength dawning within her. *Yes. I want proof. Or should I, like the priests beg of us, just take your word for it?*

Beok leaned back and laughed. It was loud and full of smoke. *Proof, Beok said, gesturing wide, is what all our machinations have been for. The Silence have been seeking proof for millennia. And when we find it, little Ven, we will change the world.*

In her borrowed human body, Ven stepped toward the Atheneum. Inside were records and artifacts from thousands of civilizations across the galaxy, millennia of long histories. The truth of who the Aain were had to be inside it somewhere, Ven thought.

She approached the doorway when someone grabbed her shoulder.

"Ari!"

She snatched the offending hand and spun around to face a smiling human male. He stood centimeters shorter than her and had a moss-patch of fine black hair covering his chin. His eyes were dark as oruba bark. Something about his face was familiar too. Ven knew him somehow. Or Ambassador Ortega did. This must be the so-called "ghost residue," she thought, the mental dross leaking from Ortega's borrowed human body.

"Ari, what the glap?" the human said, yanking his hand free. "You said you weren't back till next month!"

Ari. That was the Ambassador's given name. "I need to research something in the Atheneum," she said.

"Research *smesearch*!" he said. "Let's get a drekking drink!"

"I'm sorry, but now isn't a good time."

"Why not? What's so frapping pressing? It's been *months* since I saw you."

"Please, I just need to--"

"Ari, don't make me pull rank and order you to Psych!" he barked.

Aliens were starting to look. Ven checked a human-numbered clock on the wall and did a quick calculation in her head. She had twenty-three hours, and forty-one minutes left. She sensed Ambassador Ortega hadn't been completely forthcoming about The Merge's mission on her world. So perhaps she might leverage this man's trust of the Ambassador to dig a little deeper.

"One drink," Ven said. "Then I must get back to work."

He slapped Ven on the shoulder. "That's the spirit!"

When The Merge's Discovery Lander first arrived on Zvee Ord and brought news of alien life, it threw Zvee society into panic. All Zvee were taught from birth that preservation of the ancient ways surmounted all. Change was a grave sin, an abandonment of the ancient ways. Governments across the globe tried to suppress news of the alien's arrival. But The Silence had eyes and ears everywhere, and Ven heard all about the aliens before most of Zvee Ord knew they existed. First, The Merge sent a small delegation. They were a species called human, who had transferred their minds into Zvee bodies that had been grown for them like melons in a garden. Their true alien selves, they said, were sleeping millions of kilometers away.

This alien delegation hoped to open lines of communication between Zvee Ord and a sprawling galactic culture called The Merge. And though the delegation was patient and persistent, traveling great distances to meet with many leaders, all the Zvee cities firmly refused their attempts at dialog.

Around this time, Ven had become a seedling professor, teaching the ways of The Silence to a nest of fledglings. And one morning after class, she visited Beok's office.

I want to meet these aliens, Ven said. *I want to see their great skyships and miraculous machines for myself.*

We have a few speaking with them already, Ven. You have a new nest of fledglings to attend to. Focus on them.

You don't want me to go, Ven said. It wasn't a question.

That's not true. I just feel you have more important things to focus on here.

Your thoughts leak like sap from a sugar tree, Ven said. *You're not the only one who can see into the hearts of others, Professor Beok.*

Beok harrumphed. *But why? What is it you hope to find with them?*

Aren't you at all curious? Isn't that what we teach here at the Academy? To open our eyes and ears and look at the world around us, to not be afraid of what lies outside of our copse?

You haven't answered my question.

These aliens, Ven said, *might know who the Aain really are.*

Beok chuckled. *Firstly, Ven, and I shouldn't be telling you this, but The Silence remains unconvinced the aliens are from the stars. They look just like us! Yet we are to believe they're from another world? Yes, they have great skyships and astounding machines. But they could be, like us, a splinter group, who developed technology in secret. We are gathering intelligence. Let our people do their job, and then we'll discover who they really are.*

So you're a skeptic?

A realist. What do you think is more likely, that aliens from some far-off world decided to come visit Zvee Ord to welcome us into some galactic society, or a group of Zvee developed secret technology they are now using to deceive and control us?

The Wisdom Trunks say the Aain left for the stars. So what if these aliens know them? What if these aliens have actually met the Aain?

Beok laughed, and Ven felt like a child, mocked for being different, and those laughs hurt like stones. *Enough, Ven,* Beok said. *I'll have no more of this. Focus on your job and let others do theirs. I think you'll see in time that I'm proven right, that this is all more lies.*

As Ven stared at Beok she suppressed a shiver, because she now saw it clearly. The Silence pretended to be different from others, but they were just as set in their ways, just as fearful of change as the rest of the blerned world.

That night she sneaked out when everyone was fast asleep. She headed north, and it took her ten difficult weeks before she finally found an alien. By this time, she had lost half her weight, and she was so weary she sometimes struggled to stand.

"My name is Ven Zenari," she said to the stranger, "and I've come a long way to meet you."

"Nice to meet you, Ven! My name's Ambassador Ari Ortega." He held out his hand, as if offering her food, but there was nothing in it.

Her body thrummed. From the moment he spoke she knew her instincts were right. Even non-telepathic Zvee leaked thoughts. This man was like a stone, leaking nothing. He lowered his hand, then curtsied at her deferentially, as one did only to the highest priests.

"Why do you honor me so?" she said.

"Because you're not like most I've met on Zvee Ord."

"And what are most like?"

"Fearful," he said. "Mistrusting."

"Yes," she said. "I know the feeling."

A squall blew in, and they huddled under the bough of a sweet nectar tree to get out of the rain. "You are trying to open communication with my people," Ven said.

"I am."

"And you have as much chance of that as of asking a tree mouse to come out of its hole."

"Yet here you are, Ven Zenari, seeking me out. May I ask why?"

She looked him up and down, remembering Beok's words. "Can you prove to me you're truly from the stars?"

He pulled a small metallic thing from his belt, poked it a few times, and an odd sound, like a chorus of strange birds, sung into the forest. It was the most beautiful thing she'd ever heard.

"What is that?" she said, astonished.

"Have you ever heard anything like this before?"

"Never."

"It's music from my people's home world. Bach. There's an entire library here of my planet's music. Millions of songs. And books. And pictures. And long, detailed histories. Do you think we made that all up just to fool you? Have a look for yourself. I have nothing to hide."

He showed her many things on his device. An astonishingly colorful painter called "Van Gogh" and incredible buildings from an architect called "Gaudi." And he told her of great human scholars like Copernicus and Curie and Einstein.

"My people originated from a planet called Earth," he said. "Let me show you some pictures." He showed her images on his metal device of a blue sphere mottled with brown and green. "We had many forests too," he said, "though unlike the Zvee we were not so good at preserving them."

Ven took it all in like she was a student on her first day of class again, and suddenly the world seemed much, much larger.

"We're trying to open diplomatic relations with the Zvee," he said.

"But why? What do we have that you could possibly want?"

"Your Wisdom Trunks. They contain long histories, do they not?"

"They do."

"We hope to gain access to them, perhaps to find more information about The Great Fracture."

"What's that?"

"About 300,000 loops ago, a huge galactic civilization vanished in a blink. No one knows why. Loops ago, my people found a crashed ship on a nearby planet called Mars, and we were able to reverse engineer it to reopen the ancient lanes of galactic travel. Our own scholars believe your Wisdom Trunks may hold clues about The Great Fracture, since your culture is very, very old."

"And my people have resisted all your attempts to access the Trunks."

"So far," he asked. "But we remain hopeful. A futile hope?"

"Through normal channels," she said.

He leaned forward. "There are other channels?"

She felt herself thrumming again. "There may be other ways to get you inside."

He smiled. "I have a feeling, Ven Zenari, that you are not just a curious wanderer. That there's more to you than you're letting on."

"You will find, Ambassador, that I am as deep as oceans."

Days became weeks and months as they walked on seldom-used roads, and she learned all she could of humans and The Merge culture, while she taught him all about the Zvee.

"So your Atheneum," she said to him one night, stirring a pot of mushrooms she had foraged over a fire, "is similar to our Wisdom Trunks. Full of histories."

"Yes," he said. "But the Atheneum is much larger than your Wisdom Trunks, data-wise. It contains records and artifacts from thousands of worlds. We have so much information there that not everything has been cataloged or even decoded yet."

"Can I visit this Atheneum?"

"Once relations between our species have been normalized, perhaps."

"That will never happen."

"I seek answers," he said, "and you do as well. But I don't yet know your question."

"We Zvee worship the Aain."

"Your gods," he said.

"They're not gods. I believe that the Aain came from the stars. Just like you."

He lifted his dorsal feathers in surprise. "That's an...interesting hypothesis, Ven. I'm, uh, due to return home in a few weeks. If you tell me what you're looking for, perhaps I might—"

"Let me borrow your body," she said.

He stared at her. "Excuse me?"

"I want to visit this Atheneum myself."

"Ven, that's imposs—"

"If you let me visit your Atheneum, I will get you access to the Wisdom Trunks."

"You want to borrow my body?"

"Yes."

"No *fucking* way." He used a human expletive.

"You'll never get access to our Wisdom Trunks without my help. You'll be here for loops and loops and return home a failure."

He stared at her. "You don't need my body. Tell me what you want to find, and I'll see if I can fetch this knowledge for you."

"There are things I can't tell you, Ambassador. Just as I know there are things you aren't telling me."

Like a child who hadn't yet learned how to hide his emotions, he gave a skeptical shake of his feathers. "But how can I trust you? When you inhabit my skin, everyone will think you're me. You could wreak havoc, and I wouldn't know it until it was too late."

"That is my offer, Ambassador. Knowledge for knowledge. Trust for trust. Do you trust me?"

He leaned back and shook his head, which she had learned was a human gesture. "This is insane. Absolutely insane." Then he sighed and said, "One day. I'll give you one drekking day."

The familiar-looking human led Ven through the halls of this alien space station. His name was K. Yarbo, she read from his badge, and aliens saluted him as they walked through the halls. Eventually they reached a wide corridor crowded with aliens.

The corridor's brilliant lights were more garish than a peacock fish. Neon rainbows attacked her eyes. A hundred screens flashed frenetic images like a colorful lightning storm. There was a torrent of voices and machines. And she smelled burnt things, sweet things, and fiercely alien perfumes and sweat. Ven's breath caught.

"What're you waiting for?" Yarbo said. "Come on!"

They'll notice I'm different, Ven thought. *I'll be caught and sent far away, never to return home.*

But then Beok's words came to her: *Being brave does not mean you feel no fear. You feel the fear and do what must be done in spite of it.*

She pushed through her terror. She followed Yarbo into a crowded nest. A large neon sign said the place was called *Pluto's Lament,* and they sat at a long bar on hard stools. Yarbo ordered two beverages called "ales," and turned to her and smiled.

Ven's cheeks grew hot. Was this an expression of human fear? Long ago she had learned to keep her dorsal feathers low, to hide her feelings, and she wondered if humans could do the same with their faces.

He's going to see I'm not Ortega, she thought. *He would never let his cheeks burn like this.*

The nest was loud with voices and strange music, yet still she heard leaking thoughts. A few here were latent telepaths, she realized with a sudden start.

Yarbo swallowed half his ale. "So? What's up?"

Up? Ven glanced at the ceiling. She'd only taken a few draughts of the bitter beverage, but already her head spun.

"What the glap you lookin' at?" Yarbo said, looking up too.

Ven forced her mouth into what she thought was a human smile. But from the way Yarbo stared at her she doubted it was correct. "Maybe I *should* order you to Psych," he said.

"Please don't! I'm just tired." Then she added, "I have a question about Zvee Ord first contact. What information did The Merge hope to—"

"If you're so tired," he said, placing his hand on her knee, "maybe you just need to lie down..."

A warmth kindled in her chest, and a delicious sensation filled the male organ between her legs. More ghost residue, Ven thought, realizing that Ortega and Yarbo were much more than friends.

The pleasure was hard to ignore, but she gently pushed his hand away. "Later," she said, and with a trembling hand she swallowed the rest of the ale. A clock on a wall screen ticked away seconds as Ven put down her glass.

"Thank you for the beverage, but I need to go."

"What the glap?" Yarbo said. "You seem...weird."

He knows. He can tell I'm not Ortega. "I'm just very tired."

"Me drekking too. Tired of your bullshit."

"My what?"

"It's always the same. You pop in, pretend to care, then slither off again. But I see it now. I'm just an object to you, something to use and cast off."

"No, you misunderstand—"

"Gronk off, Ari. Seriously. We're done. For good."

"Please," Ven said. "Don't do that."

"Give me a reason not to!"

"We'll talk later, I promise. I'm just...not feeling myself today." She got up from her stool. This place was loud, overwhelming, and she wasn't here to destroy Ortega's life.

"There is no later, Ari," Yarbo said. "Gimme the ring back."

"What ring?" Ven said, regretting it as soon as she spoke.

Yarbo narrowed his eyes. Though he was an alien, she knew the expression well. Suspicion. Just like how the kids at Senary Bough had eyed her.

"I have to go," she said, then ran into the crowded hall.

She had to find her way back to the Atheneum and then get back home. But a tall window a little ways up the corridor caught her attention. Beyond its clear frame lay the blackness of space. She found herself pulled toward the window, while a forest of alien bodies brushed against her.

Don't see me, she willed. *I'm a leaf in a forest. I blend in and vanish.*

Bright, flashing screens advertised strange foods and alien sex. A disembodied voice beckoned her into a nest filled with colorful gambling machines. But she couldn't stop walking towards the window. She paused and stared out.

The Mass-O floated with the stars, a giant egg of woven metal. It was an enormous sphere of ancient technology that made interstellar travel possible. Behind it shone three massive suns. She couldn't believe it. Here she stood on a city in the sky, thousands of light-years from home, seeing it all with alien eyes. What would that frightened little girl think, back in Senary Bough, if she knew this would be her destiny?

She spotted an alien leaning on the windowsill, looking out at the stars, smoking a long bone pipe. The pipe was curiously similar to the ones her people used to smoke the gray lichen. And if she blurred her eyes, the alien looked just like a Zvee, dorsal feathers and all. But this wasn't possible, because Ven was the first Zvee to set foot on another world.

Wasn't she?

Ven was staring at the alien when a voice, silent as a falling leaf and loud as thunder, said, *What the glap you looking at, human pig?*

Ven gasped and stepped back, bumping into an alien who growled at her.

Had the Ambassador lied to her? Or did Beok? Had other Zvee come here before her? The alien looked just like a Zvee. Well, if you shortened his dorsal feathers and stretched his skull some. Was he one of The Silence, like her? She thought-spoke to him in the silent tongue, *What is the sound when no wind blows, stranger?*

The alien's eyes widened. He sat up with a start, then he darted away down the hall.

"Wait!" Ven called, but he kept running.

The neon hallway was a forest of heads, but she spotted his dorsal feathers as he sped away. This human body was awkward and small, but like a river eel she found she could change direction on a stone. She hopped and spun and dove through the press of bodies, chasing after the Zvee male like a predator after prey.

The Zvee ducked into an alley, and she ran in after him. Bundles of cables along the walls made her feel as if she were crawling through the roots of a tree. Hot steam shot from vents. Water dripped from leaking pipes. Aliens lay on makeshift beds, groaning in inter-species coitus, or sat on the floor, watching her mournfully as she ran past.

The Zvee turned a corner, and when Ven followed a second later he ambushed her. His arm came down on her spine, but she spun away, softening the blow. She grabbed his arm, flipped him around, and gave him two swift blows to the chest with her knee. He gasped as she threw him into the wall. He tried to raise his fists, but she punched him in the jaw, and he sagged, defeated, as sap-green blood leaked from his mouth. Just like Zvee blood.

"Who the gronk are you?" she said in Common.

"I have no credits!" he said. He had a Zvee voice, and the sound of it made her ache for home.

"I don't want your credits. Who are you?"

"Gyrto! I'm an archeologist. Please, I—"

"What's your species? Are you Zvee?"

"Zvee?" He looked puzzled. "No, I'm Ayeen. You're human. I know your species likes fermented grain drinks. I have old Scotch from—"

"Your species is called the *Aain*?" Ven said.

He looked confused. "No. *Ayeen*."

Ven gawped at him. "And how did you get here, to this Hub?"

"In a transpod, like everyone drekking else!"

"And your species, this *Ayeen*, how long have they been coming here?"

Gyrto looked at Ven's uniform. "You're an Ambassador. Don't you know all this already?"

"Tell me!"

"My species, the Ayeen, have been coming here for sixty-one loops, ever since the Discovery Lander arrived at our capital planet."

Ven stared at him. "Why did you run away from me?"

Gyrto looked away. "No reason."

Ven raised her fist. "Speak!"

"Please! It's just, well, when you were looking at me back there, I, uh, well, I heard a voice. In my head. Speaking a strange language. It scared the feathers off me! I need to stop smoking that pipe."

Was he a latent telepath? "And what do you know of the Zvee?"

"I only know what The Merge knows."

"Which is what?"

"I can't say."

"Why not?"

"You know why! Because it's been declared classified!"

"Tell me anyway."

"We could be arrested!"

"And I could break your jaw."

"Okay!" he said, raising his eight-fingered hands. "The Zvee and the Ayeen have genetic similarities that cannot be explained by convergent evolutionary processes."

"*Genetic* similarities?" Ven didn't know many of his words.

"Yes."

"Keep talking or I'll make sure you never talk again!"

"Please! All I know is it's theorized my people and the Zvee may have been the same species that got separated many thousands of loops ago. Since then, we've diverged. That's all I know. Can I go now?"

"Diverged?" Ven said, unsure of what exactly that meant.

An alarm suddenly wailed, startling her.

"Great!" Gyrto cried. "See what you just did? It's over for us. Over!"

"ALERT! ALERT!" a voice boomed from the walls. "AN INTRUDER IS INHABITING AMBASSADOR ORTEGA'S SKIN. THE INTRUDER IS CONSID-

ERED ARMED AND DANGEROUS. IF YOU SEE THIS INTRUDER, DO NOT APPROACH AND CONTACT HUB SECURITY IMMEDIATELY."

The message repeated in more languages. Nearby, a screen that had been tuned to static-filled pornography flashed Ambassador Ortega's face—*her* current face. All the nearby screens were showing her face now. The alarm wailed, and Gyrto stared at her in horror. Nearby, other aliens were starting to look, too.

The shrieking alarm sounded just like the mocking, laughing children from Senary Bough. A decade later and a thousand light-years, and nothing had changed. She still didn't belong.

She took one last glance at Gyrto before speeding off. She ran down a maze of alleys and into a narrow hall.

"There!" someone said. "That's him!"

She leaped back into the alley and ran a different way. But she had no idea where she was going. Buried in the wailing alarm she thought she heard mocking voices.

Ven is such a freak!

I wish I'd never had a daughter.

Focus on your job and let others do theirs.

She reached a dead end and doubled back, but three armed soldiers waited for her.

"Don't move!" one shouted.

She dove for their legs and knocked one over. Another came for her, but she smacked their gun away and knocked another in the jaw with her elbow. The first soldier fell on the second, and she used the distraction to slip away.

Shots rang out behind her as she dove into another hall. "Don't shoot!" one shouted. "We need him alive!"

She turned a corner, but there were more security forces waiting. "Activate stasis!" one said.

Suddenly everything went slow, as if she were encased in clear jelly. She couldn't move a muscle. Even her thoughts slowed to a trickle.

A human male stepped up to her, and through the jellied haze she saw Yarbo's angry face.

"You know," he said, "I always wanted to do this." And with the metal butt of his rifle, he cracked her in the skull.

Ven awoke in a windowless cell that smelled of piss and mildew. She was still in Ortega's human body, and her skull ached from where Yarbo had struck her.

"Hello?" she said. "Anyone home?"

A minute later the door slid open and a human female stepped through. She wore a different uniform from the Ambassador, but Ven guessed she was of high rank.

"I'm Captain Nakagawa. You're Professor Ven Zenari of the Zvee?"

Ven straightened. If she would be punished, she would do it with dignity and not shame. "I am," she said.

Nakagawa sat on the bench beside her. "What're you doing in Ambassador Ortega's blank, Ven?"

"Seeking truths."

"Such as?"

"The Zvee and the Ayeen, they're the same species, aren't they? And your people know it and kept that secret from mine."

"I have no knowledge of any of that," Nakagawa said, breaking eye contact. Ven didn't have to be a telepath to know that Nakagawa was lying.

"You lie to my people," Ven said. "And my people lie to themselves."

Nakagawa sighed. "You stole a skin. You know that's a high crime here, right?"

"There was no other way."

Nakagawa shook her head. "Look, Ven, I'm sympathetic. Humanity's been sold its own batch of lies. But there's a bureaucracy one has to follow. Chains of command and so forth. Perhaps in a couple of loops, when relations between the Zvee and The Merge have been normalized, your people will be granted access to the Atheneum, and you can, well, find out...more."

"Your Ambassador was very clear that your people won't give us access to your Atheneum until you get full access to our Wisdom Trunks. It's the only thing we have to offer you. But I know my people. That will never happen."

Nakagawa sighed. "I'm sorry, Ven, but we have rules here. And the punishment for breaking them is severe. But you're lucky. We want the Ambassador back more than we want to keep you in prison. He'll return to face a trial, and we're going to send you back home."

Ven gasped because she had never felt so homesick in her life.

"I hope you find what you're looking for, Ven. I really do." Then, quick as she came, Nakagawa was gone.

The leap back across thousands of light-years was just as terrifying as the leap out. But as the transpod opened, and as Ven smelled the fertile air of Zvee Ord, she let out a chirp of joy. She was, finally, home.

It was strange being back in her own body, and as she moved and stretched, a voice in Common said, "You have a message, Ven Zenari. Do you wish to hear it?"

"Yes," Ven said, sitting up. "I do."

✺

Three weeks later, Ven stood before a plenum gathering of the Silent Council in the high trunk of the Historical Academy, trying to keep her dorsal feathers from quaking with fear.

Beok was here as were other familiar faces, but most of the Council members Ven had never seen before. Some had come from as far away as the western continent. They stared at her, impatient, angry, and Beok nodded for Ven to start.

Honored Professors of The Silence, Ven began in the silent tongue, trying to project calm. *Thank you for coming all this way. This topic is too important to be conveyed by messenger. As some of you already know, weeks ago I visited an alien world.*

Half the council members laughed at this.

I know many of you doubt my story. But I'll prove it beyond a leaf of doubt. I used an alien machine to transport my consciousness across the stars. And when I returned there was a message waiting for me. I will now read a translated version to you now. It begins thus:

"Our encounter troubled me deeply, Ven Zenari, and once I learned who you really were, my feathers spread wide as skies. We have a word in one of our oldest languages called 'tzvey' that means the 'second' or 'lower' self. A lot of words in this ancient language beginning with 'tzvey' have negative meanings. Even today some curse others by saying, 'May your tzvey cling to you like mud.'

"My people, the Ayeen—"

Several council members stirred in their seats.

"—the Ayeen have an ancient myth that many thousands of loops ago we shed our lower selves before venturing to the stars. I'd always thought it was a metaphor. That is, until I learned of the Zvee. The Merge hypothesized that there was a link between our peoples, but they hid this knowledge from your society, afraid of the disruption it would cause. That was unfair because you deserve to know the truth.

"You assaulted me, Ven Zenari, but I forgive you. You were lied to, and you deserve the truth. I have enclosed with my message an archive of files that I trust you will find very interesting. I believe we are distant cousins, you and me. Estranged, but hopefully not forever. Next time, I hope instead of punching me in the face we can sit down and smoke a pipe together, as family.

"Your brother in feathers,

"Gyrto."

Ven looked up from her notes to gauge the reaction of the room.

What's all this nonsense? a council member blurted. *Have we traveled all this way for such slug slime?*

Don't you see? Ven replied. *Tzvey, Zvee? Ayeen, Aain?*

What I see is a disturbed young woman, another member said.

I'm not done with my presentation, Ven said. *Gyrto provided me with thousands of documents from his culture. One will be of great interest to this Council. I will now use one of the Ambassador's machines to play a voice recording.*

Ven tapped a metal device, and the audio began.

"My name is Huna Bain, and I am dying," the voice said. A Zvee voice. Speaking the silent tongue. The forbidden tongue. Aloud.

"Blasphemy!" someone shouted.

"Shut it off!" another said. "Stop it now!"

Beok stood and screamed, "Sit down, fools! Stop your twittering and listen to Professor Ven." The room stilled, then Beok nodded at Ven to continue.

Ven began the audio again.

"We crashed," Huna Bain went on. "My ship's reactor is breached, and soon my flesh will liquify. I leave this message for posterity. The truth must live on. All my life I passed as an Aain, but in my blood, in my soul, I was always Zvee."

Several council members gasped.

"I lived my life among the Aain. I resemble them enough that they never suspected me. But we practiced our Zvee rituals in secret, keeping our traditions vibrant and alive. Now, alas, my family is dead. I am the last, and I've no one to pass on my traditions to.

"I leave this message in my mother tongue, the forbidden tongue, so it won't die with me. It will live on as long as this recording survives. As long as this message remains, us Zvee will never die. Know this: the Aain committed a great atrocity against my people. If you ever hear this, note it well. They must answer for their sins!

"Know this: I once lived on a world of two peoples, the Zvee, and the Aain. Ages ago, we lived on different continents. We Zvee were agrarian, farming fungi and lichen. But the Aain continent was mostly barren. The Aain built machines to help them survive the harsh climate. And over time, the Aain encroached on the Zvee's fertile lands, stealing resources, making raids, and since the Aain had the help of their machines, they conquered us weaker Zvee. Eventually the Aain completely dominated us Zvee, controlling every aspect of our lives.

"The Aain declared our Zvee culture primitive, our language jargon, and set out to eradicate us. The Aain forbade the speaking or writing of the Zvee tongue, under penalty of death. And they tried to erase all history of their brutal colonization from the historical records. They taught us from birth that the Aain had the souls of heavenly gods, but that we Zvee were inferior creatures in need of cleansing.

"But our Zvee culture remained strong and proud. The Aain and Zvee lived in the same cities, but because there were physical differences between our two peoples, we never merged. After a time, the Aain realized they could only erase our Zvee culture if they erased all of us. They hoarded us into many cloistered towns, and they used great weapons of fire to incinerate entire populations in one swoop. They murdered millions. But they didn't realize how powerful their weapons would be, and they underestimated how long those fires would burn. Great conflagrations spread across the whole planet, making huge swathes of Zvee Ord uninhabitable. The Aain, believing there was no hope left for Zvee Ord, fled in skyships to the stars.

"I'm ashamed to admit I went with them. Father knew the only way to save our family was to pretend to be Aain. I remember, as a little girl, watching my once-beautiful planet burn as we sailed into the sky. I will never see my home again. The Aain burned it all to ashes, and they live on happily, having paid no price for their awful crimes."

"Hear me, ancient gods! Hear me, swords of justice! The Aain must pay for what they did. I am the last of my family. For all I know, I may be the last Zvee in the universe. Hear me, gods of time! Avenge me and my people. See to it that justice is served. I pray that Eternity hears my voice. I pray that we, the Zvee, are never forgotten."

The audio ended. The council, all adepts, ruffled their feathers like children.

This is the proof we have always sought, Ven said. *The Aain were not gods. They were not demons. They were us. Long ago, they tried to wipe us out, and they almost destroyed Zvee Ord. But even after many millennia, our culture survives. Honored Professors of The Silence, the silent tongue, the one I use to speak to you now, is the ancient language of the Zvee that the Aain tried to eradicate. The Silence started from pure necessity. Unable to speak or write our mother tongue, a few adepts honed their latent telepathic ability to communicate with their minds. They kept their powers secret. To reveal it meant death.*

Our hidden rites of The Silence are the remnants of that ancient culture. All this time The Silence has been tasked with keeping our ancient culture alive without ever knowing it! The best kept secret is when you don't know there's a secret at all.

The room was stunned to silence. Eventually, a council member, visibly shaken, said, *This is world-shattering.*

And our world needs shattering, Ven said. *We must convince our long-timid people of the dark truth. The Aain weren't gods or demons, but cruel members of our own species. It will be an arduous task. We'll meet much resistance and anger. But the truth will win out in the end. And so too must we mete out vengeance. We must return to this alien Hub and seek out the Ayeen, the descendants of the ancient Aain, and seek justice for their ancient crimes. Their sins must not be forgotten. We must not be forgotten.*

And who, pray tell, a council member said, *will be the sword of our justice?*

Ven stared at Beok, who was smiling, because she already knew Ven's answer.

Ven smiled back, and in the ancient tongue of her people she said, aloud, "Me."

UNSPOKEN TRUTHS

Kenneth W. Cain

NUROBIUS, 493 HD

TE'LUTE KERSE HAD TOLD Marshal Heston Damarcus that he'd paid off a high-ranking security officer to access The Hub's database.

Kerse was Antonio Grasston's partner by marriage and had quickly achieved financial power since arriving some ten helicas back. No one knew much about the man before then, just that he ended up becoming a powerful Merge benefactor—basically, the credits behind the policies. Grasston was one of the top Merge politicians on Nurobius, having been born and raised here, unlike his husband.

The democracy on Nurobius was in a precarious state. It had seen many transformations over the helicas, governments toppled by influential persons and bad policies. Grasston needed to reassure his people. A highly anticipated speech had been scheduled, but now Kerse and Grasston were in turmoil. Their daughter Desire had just been abducted.

Illicitly using The Hub's database, the security officer had tracked her to Amdurahh. Heston didn't know much about the planet, except that the SamShun mined several rare and valuable raw materials there. In a private meeting, Kerse insisted that the Marshal investigate her disappearance, but Heston didn't like the idea of being off-planet when their government felt so unstable.

During a similar upheaval many helicas ago, Heston's father, also once a Marshal in The Merge's Keepers agency, had been sent on a mission off-world. While he was enforcing Merge law half a universe away, Heston's mother had been taken hostage by a clan from the outworld of Dalendria. She hadn't been seen since, not that Heston and his father hadn't gone looking. The entire clan was now no more than a stain on the planet's rocky terrain, thanks to his dad's handiwork. But his mother's trail had dried up. Nowadays, Heston could barely recall what his mother looked like, or the sound of her voice.

The current political situation was fraught with possible outcomes, but Heston needed to focus on finding Desire. That's why he'd left his protege, Vuhl'hla, in charge. She'd argued, of course, wanting to assist him, but he wouldn't allow it. Someone had to keep watch over this political address, and he'd never leave any of the others in command. Especially Buzz. Sure, Buzz could shoot the wings off a fly, but something wasn't right in the guy's head—not since he got so close to fracturing his mind. Sometimes Buzz would just sit around mumbling to himself, and that might not have bothered Heston if he wasn't growing ever closer to Zero Hour himself.

He lifted his left forearm and accessed his MindLink. A circular holographic window opened up before him. "Vuhl'hla, what's your status?"

Her face appeared on his screen, looking wry as ever. "Following the procession detail as they prepare for the day's events. Keeping my distance, of course."

"Good. Stay mindful."

She sighed. "Ji'rini is bad enough, but Buzz...? What's with all those 'trophy' skulls he wears around his neck, anyway? They're all small game from across the universe. Nothing to brag about."

"Trust me. He knows what he's doing. Anything suspicious?"

She grinned. "Other than Kerse sending you, our head Marshal, off-planet at this crucial time, instead of anyone else? And why wasn't Grasston part of our discussion with Kerse? Why'd we have to meet in the woods? Is there a reason we weren't invited into the complex? It was raining cats and dogs for glap's sake! I swear, something—"

"Hold on now." He moved away from the transpod technician. "Careful. Remember, much of this job is about unspoken truths. They have ears everywhere. Understand?"

She flipped her purple hair back. "Oh, I got it, all right. It's just that... Something isn't right about all this."

Heston sighed. "I know."

"How does a girl with a security detail get abducted? What, were they all asleep at the time or something? And how does anyone get that girl out of her room without being noticed? They've got guards all around the complex." She glanced left, then back at him. "We should start there—question each and every one of those gronkers."

"You're right, and you should." He scratched his head. "I'm not sure what's going on, either. But we'll find out."

She smirked. "We'd better."

"Don't worry. I have full confidence in your capabilities."

"If that's true, you should have let me go instead."

He grinned. "That would look suspicious."

She nodded. "Perhaps."

"Listen, I'm about to jump, and I don't know what to expect."

There was a long silence.

Feeling slightly uncomfortable, he broke it. "Don't overthink things. You got this."

"Oh, I know. I'm just worried about you."

She knew about his history of jumps; how many he'd made off-record. It was staggering, without doubt. He had his official jumps, the ones that showed up on The Merge database, and then there were his unofficial ones—those from private clients. This also kept The Merge from being able to truly calculate when he'd hit Zero Hour, which meant he could remain a Marshal longer than he would have otherwise, so long as he didn't reach the tipping point. It was how an aging Marshal could see a little more of the universe, maybe earn a few extra credits, but those jumps added up fast.

"Don't worry about me. I'll be fine." He groaned. "In the rare event something does happen, you'll know what to do." He paused, then added, "These people...you're a relatively unknown factor to them. That's to our advantage. If you get in a tight spot, you'll be underestimated. Use that."

She winked. "It's all clear."

He liked her cockiness. Heck, he thought she'd make a fine Marshal. And she was still a Pure Soul, too. There were many jumps in her future—a lifetime of adventure, and that sort of made him jealous. What she hadn't picked up on yet, though, was perhaps the most important detail. He wasn't just training a new Marshal; she was his replacement. That made him expendable. If The Merge knew about her, they wouldn't think twice about sacrificing him for their benefit.

"Damarcus out." He deactivated his MindLink and returned to the techs. "I'm ready."

"Right this way," said one of the technicians.

He nodded, stepped inside, and the jump was initiated.

Travel was instantaneous, but his mind processed it as being slightly longer. His consciousness shot through a wormhole, occasionally passing through rings of blue and red and yellow gasses. The cosmos surrounded him: remote galaxies, dwarf stars, comets, asteroids. It was beautiful to behold.

AMDURAHH

Heston found himself in a transpod, feeling immediate vertigo inside his new skin, which was odd, since he was jumping into a clone. The transpod hatch opened, visible gasses swirling around him as he staggered forward on uneasy legs, suddenly unaware of why he'd come, using the walls to navigate through the facility.

Something had gone wrong. He couldn't tell what, but everything felt so much worse compared to previous jumps. His field of view was a blur, like he'd been heavily drugged. He pulled himself along using whatever he could find, stumbling into objects here and there.

"*The...girl...*" a voice said—one that sounded disembodied and disorientated.

He spun fast, went to draw his gun but realized he didn't have one. "Who's there?"

No one responded.

He leaned into one of the reflective walls, using it to guide him outward, when something caught his eye—

Looking at his reflection, he shook his head in disbelief.

He wasn't in his customary Marshal getup and Earth-style cowboy hat. He was naked, but not a familiar nakedness. No longer did he have his metallic-brown augments infused into his human flesh, or his facemask equipped with atmosphere regulators. That was all gone, replaced by the soft, pale blue complexion of a species he'd never seen before. Some native skin, probably. None of it made any sense. He usually jumped into one of his clones.

His world felt as if it was slipping away beneath his awkward new legs and feet. He crashed into another wall, his head throbbing with pain, but he pressed one hand to his temple and kept moving, desperately wanting to get out in the open for some fresh air.

"*Be careful...*"

Barely able to stay on his feet, he twisted in the direction of the voice. "Show yourself!"

There was no response.

Whoever or whatever they were, they were right, though. Without his weapons, he'd be vulnerable. That and the disorientation were his two biggest concerns. He'd been in other skins before, but he never felt this disorientated.

On full alert, he searched the facility for something he could use as a weapon. All he found was a spanner wrench, which actually looked pretty daunting. It wouldn't be of much help in a gun fight, but he grabbed it anyway.

Someone stood in the exit, clearly a woman, but he couldn't see straight. He stared at her, trying to bring her into focus, and saw—

He couldn't tell.

"Come to me." She held out her arms.

He squinted, pressed his eyes shut, squinted again. "Who are you?"

Her form was distorted. He couldn't make out her features. But she looked older, near as he could tell. He had no idea if she was even real. Still, he stumbled forward.

"Stay right there," he said.

When he reached her, he grasped for her shoulders, hoping to steady himself long enough to make out her features and reveal her identity. But she vanished between his arms, and he gripped empty air.

He fell forward and braced for impact.

A shockwave of pain shot through him as he crashed against the floor. He pushed up to all fours, pulled himself back to his feet, and realized the woman had been a hallucination. Heston didn't like his judgment being impaired. That would lead to mistakes.

He exited the facility and scurried across a relatively short, raised platform. Violent ocean waves crested at least three meters in the air on both sides and slammed against the metal pilings, shaking the entire platform and causing him to stumble. The city was out of range of the torrential waters, but it sounded like ferocious animals roaring below. He didn't know where to go or what to expect, but for now there was only one path forward.

Already it felt as though someone was watching him.

He'd expected more of a reception, something formal as usual. Even with this jump being off-record, Grasston should have alerted someone about his arrival, someone to assist with his investigation—the local authorities, perhaps. Anyone. Between the vertigo, this unfamiliar body, and the uncanny delusion of a woman—who even now whispered thoughts into his mind—he didn't like this one bit.

He reached a T and took a hard left. It felt like a maze, the platforms branching off in all directions, some lower and some overhead. Various beings of many races, a few bots, and even some strange animals walked along these platforms ignorant of his presence. They went about their daily lives without even a sideways glance as Heston proceeded along.

He'd gotten no more than twenty meters and was heading through an area filled with large storage containers and overhead platforms, when several beings slid out from the shadows. Others dropped down from above. They— the Indar'kris—surrounded him, at least eight of them, maybe more. Each of the broad, amphibian-like had many multi-segmented leges—twelve limbs total. The subterranean species was known for engaging in unlawful activities.

Heston glanced around, trying to determine if others might be hiding behind cargo containers, or on top of buildings. But with his vision so hazy, he couldn't be certain of anything. One by one, the bystanders vanished, leaving him alone with the Indar'kris, the whipping wind, and the waves below.

The ghostly hallucination popped up on his left. *"Run!"*

He didn't listen. Instead, he held out the spanner and menacingly shook it at them. Unaffected by his weak threat, they lifted their pulse blasters.

Heston waved the spanner in a half circle, eyeing every one of them as best he could. "Don't make me use this."

He couldn't understand anything they were saying, but laughter was a universal language of its own.

Unable to see straight, Heston threw the spanner at them. It was fast enough to startle them, but they just watched it fly by, then clang along the platform behind them.

Heston used the distraction as an opportunity to charge forward.

One of the Indar'kris fired just as Heston slid to the ground. He flipped back to his feet, nearly fell, then stumbled forward in gaping strides. He didn't so much tackle his aggressor as he used the creature to break his fall. Before they reached the ground, he'd pried their gun free. Then he rolled, using the Indar'kris as a shield.

The other seven fired, blasting holes into their friend. Heston wouldn't last long like this. He took a deep breath, doing his best to sharpen his focus, and shrugged the dead Indar'kris off of him. He lifted the blaster and fired. One enemy exploded in a burst of green goo. Easy targets, as wide-framed as they were.

Heston jumped back to his feet and hammered the side of the blaster hard into another's face, splintering its skull, and then shot two more before they could react. Green goo flew left and right. The remaining three fled.

Heston steadied himself and refocused. He took another breath and aimed the blaster. At about one hundred meters, he took out the first deserter, splattering a nearby container with its guts. Without hesitation, he targeted the next. Twenty-five meters later, goo sprayed the platform, tripping up the last, who slid along the platform into a wall.

Not bad for a jump-sick skin seeing double.

Heston approached the fallen Indar'kris and lifted the blaster. But before he could fire, his enemy moved with lightning speed, maneuvering over him and pinning him down. The gun fell from Heston's hands.

He reached for the blaster, got his fingers on it, but couldn't drag it back. He tried again and again, but already the Indar'kris was bringing its own weapon around to fire. Heston twisted, pulled, and stretched—

The Indar'kris's weapon cocked.

Heston froze, and when he looked up again, he saw the barrel staring back at him.

"Who sent you?" the creature asked in Common.

No response.

"Fine. Have it your way."

Without hesitation, Heston yanked the blaster back, swung it to knock the Indar'kris's weapon away, and heard a blast strike just centimeters from his head. His eardrum thrummed as he took aim and fired. Goo painted the platform behind where the Indar'kris had stood a split second earlier.

Heston lifted himself to one knee, ignored the ringing in his ear and breathed deeply, letting it out slowly.

"Good. Now get out of here," the woman said as she appeared next to him.

"What's with you, anyway?" he said to her. She merely faded away in response. "Just like all the women in my life."

He looked down to regard himself, and noticed his feet were covered in a thick layer of stinky Indar'kris slime

"Drekkit."

He staggered along the platform, trying to wipe the foul substance from his feet as the other citizens started emerging from their hiding places. Heston picked up his pace and was far beyond where he'd been attacked when a figure confronted him with a plasma rifle—a SamShun.

The blurry woman appeared again. *"Don't trust him."*

Heston groaned, wishing the apparition would just leave him alone already. His mind swayed. "Great," he said. "Now we've got a party."

She vanished again without another word.

Heston had dealt with the SamShun before—a few times actually, but never directly. An interesting bipedal species, wealth was their primary focus. Some claimed they had coffers full of every type of known currency, but Heston had never seen evidence of that. To say they were rich would be an understatement. That they were greedy, too. They were a meticulous people with an awful tendency to enslave those who crossed them.

Dressed in elaborate robes and wearing glinting metal earrings on their low-hanging earlobes, their mouths remained expressionless, eyes big and bright. Braided and knotted tentacles similar to human dreadlocks hung from the tops of their heads and often concealed their faces, sometimes reaching the small of their backs. Their blue and green flesh appeared as drab as their surroundings, but like the sea, their resolve never faltered. They were a smart folk, and often had ulterior motives.

The SamShun took him to a nearby city built into the side of a mountain range. He was led down a spacious tunnel to one of many underground mines. Workers of different races drudged back and forth from the mine to the neighboring town, laboring for their employers—whether willingly or otherwise. Bots moved among them, performing various tasks.

He wondered if they were planning to enslave him. No one in their right mind would just lock up a Marshal without just cause or warning. Not unless they wanted to start a war with The Merge.

A group of well-dressed figures approached him. Their language was confusing, with so many clucks and pops and odd syllables. When they stopped, the one who had escorted him here came closer. Heston thought it a male, though he couldn't be certain. Any exposed flesh was covered in purple tattoos, which, from what he'd read, were symbols from their religious texts.

The being activated a translator device and urged Heston to take it. "That's better. I am Declan Tur, representative of the leading faction of SamShun. Who are you?"

"*Don't tell him anything...*" the displaced woman's image said.

Heston cleared his throat. "I'm Marshal Heston—"

"A *Marshal*?" Tur glanced back at the others. "All the way out here? Seems improbable."

They all looked Heston up and down.

"*Why* are you here?" Tur asked.

The blurry woman moved among the SamShun. "*Don't tell them.*"

Heston grimaced at her. He stood stone-still and chose his words carefully. He didn't want to reveal too much. "Listen, this isn't *my* skin, but—"

Tur twirled his hand. "Please, just answer the question."

"I've come for a girl. A human girl. She's—"

One of the SamShun leaders gasped—or something close to that. Heston couldn't tell if that translated to surprise, condemnation, or what. Whatever the case, they took a moment to consult with each other.

"Is retrieving her your sole purpose for being here?"

"Is there some other reason why I should be here? I have to say, this whole meeting is rather...odd."

"*They're deceiving you, like your father...*" the disembodied voice said.

"Quiet!" Realizing he'd said that aloud, Heston shrugged. "Sorry, I—"

"He has the sickness." Tur turned to the others. "He's of no use to us."

"Now hold on…" Heston took a bold step forward. "I'm a Marshal. If I wasn't fit to jump, they wouldn't let me. End of story." Though, after saying it, he wasn't so sure. "Listen, if you know where the girl is, you need to tell me."

Tur froze, before finally admitting, "We don't."

Heston growled. "Then why did you bring me here?"

All six figures stared at him.

Tur spoke in a low voice. "We saw how easily you took down those eight Indar'kris grunts on the platform." Tur glanced back at his leaders, then returned his focus to Heston. "There's a small group of Indar'kris who have caused us great loss."

"I see, and what does this have to do with me or my mission?"

"Well, they attacked you, did they not? If anyone has a girl hidden away somewhere, it's the Indar'kris. They've been known to traffick humans."

"Really?"

Tur just stared at him. "They've been disrupting our business here on Amdurahh for a long time."

"And that affects me how?"

"You're a Marshal… They've broken the law."

"Take it up with local enforcers."

"We can pay you. We can provide you with whatever weapons and gear you need to complete your mission."

Heston considered their proposal and hefted the ratty blaster to examine it. The thing was bulky and ineffective.

"Why can't you do this for yourselves? Why me?"

"Initiating an attack on the Indar'kris could incite a war. We only want to send a message."

Heston contemplated the offer.

"This girl… Is she important?" Tur said.

"*Why would he ask that?*" the woman said.

Still, Heston regarded the question, what details he should share. "Yes. Quite." But he wasn't sure divulging that was for the best.

"Then we are agreed."

Tur led Heston to an armory, where he selected his gear: a protective cloak, two Hart .66 pulse pistols with holsters (his weapon of choice since his war days), a bandolier of light grenades, and one Vorpal Sword which he fastened to his back.

Tur also provided him with directions and a speeder, then sent him on his way.

The Indar'kris wastelands were riddled with opaque maroon pools of water. Huge jagged rocky formations jutted out here and there, but much of the area was flat. They likely had guards stationed atop some of the outcrops, so Heston parked the speeder under an overhang. Lifting the hood of his cloak, he walked along the base of the ridge.

As far as he could see to the west, the sky and land blended into an indeterminate pink and purple horizon. Thankfully, the ride had given him time to adjust to this unfamiliar skin. He was feeling more like...*himself.*

Fortunately, he encountered no beings along the way, but remained alert. That didn't mean they weren't around, and he considered whether this, too, might be part of some elaborate ruse—the thought that the SamShun might be manipulating him suddenly seemed more plausible.

Heston kept his pistols out in front as he proceeded toward one of the maroon pools. Thanks to a ridge and some rock formations, this one was relatively concealed on three sides and provided some sense of privacy.

Once he felt safe, he holstered one gun to activate his MindLink. "Vuhl'hla, you there?"

"Hey—*Whoa!* Drekking hell. Talk about waking up on the wrong side of the bed, Heston."

"Yeah, yeah. As you can see, not feeling myself today. Literally."

"Clearly. Can't talk much. Buzz is certainly...keeping me *busy,*" she whispered, her expression deadpan.

"Of course. Would expect no less." He checked his surroundings. "Something about this situation doesn't feel right." He sighed. "Starting to think it's a setup. Multiple people might be in on it, too—possibly the SamShun or this supposed 'rogue faction' of Indar'kris they've asked me to check on. Someone went through a lot of trouble to make sure I was, at the very least, inconvenienced. I suspect someone doesn't want me to return to Nurobius." He paused. "But should something happen to me—"

"Nothing's going to happen. I—"

"Let me finish!" He gathered himself. "Should something happen to me, know that the SamShun said that if anyone was hiding a human girl, it'd be the Indar'kris. But, doesn't that seem a bit too...*easy?*"

"Perhaps."

"Anyway, I need to see this through."

"I understand. There's something...*more* about Kerse."

"What do you mean?"

"He's been rather reclusive since you left, and of little help to us. For someone who seemed in such a hurry for you to retrieve their daughter, he's completely shut himself off to us now."

"I haven't trusted that guy since day one."

"Remember what he did after the last election cycle, how he 'encouraged' some of The Merge to step down? The jury is still out on Grasston, but at least he's made himself readily available and appears quite distraught and distracted by their daughter's absence. I'm unconvinced Kerse worries about her safety at all. It's almost like—"

"Like he has extreme confidence she will be fine?"

"Exactly. Question is, why?"

Heston shook his head. "That's what I'm unsure about. We'll find out in time, right?"

"I'm on it." They both went silent. "You were right to have me stay behind."

"Stop."

"I just wanna say—"

"It doesn't need to be said." He grumbled. "Ever. You know what you must do?"

"Yes."

"Then do it. That is all. Never apologize. It's part of the job. Got it?"

She grinned. "Got it."

"Heston out."

He deactivated his MindLink, then made his way to a larger pool. The Indar'kris were close; he could feel it in this skin's bones. Heston was trained to sense danger, and he was sure it was all around him now. Almost like he was looking in the wrong place.

He stared into the maroon pool. The water was stagnant and murky. He recalled what Tur had told him about the pools in this part of Amdurahh. Retrieving his other gun, he leaned forward, and rolled into the liquid. A strange static sent a shiver through his body. A second later, he had fallen through some sort of portal and was on his knees in a tunnel, both guns out and searching either direction for trouble. An alarm sounded, but the tunnel was empty.

Heston moved fast, guns out in front and ignoring the image of the unknown woman whenever she popped up in his periphery.

"Leave me be," he whispered to her, but she kept appearing. Although he couldn't make her out clearly, he could tell she had a worried expression on her face.

Heston wondered if this vision was less an aftereffect of jumping and rather some sort of echo from his past, shaken loose by the sickness. Perhaps some ghost residue left behind from a previous jumper who occupied this skin?

He heard a group approaching from behind.

"Hide...!" the woman said.

"Quiet," he whispered.

He slid into the shadows of the cave and waited, guns ready. Indar'kris climbed along the floor, the ceiling, the walls, using the various stalactites and stalagmites to pull themselves along, seemingly unaffected by gravity. Their rubbery skin kicked up clouds of dust and rubble as they wriggled past Heston, oblivious to his location. He counted six in total, all heading the same direction.

When no others came, Heston trailed the pack through the well-worn tunnel. The farther he went, the more it opened up, until he arrived at a large cavern. Dozens of these creatures worked tirelessly near several adobe huts, apparently taking care of the basic necessities. Heston kept to the shadows.

"Go now."

"Quiet, you," Heston whispered. But she was right. There was no point in delaying the inevitable.

Heston thumbed the communicator fastened to his belt to activate the translator, readied both pistols, and stepped out into the open. "Listen up, gronk heads! We have a score to settle!"

Heston had taken out larger groups hungover on Fevrasian tea. Hell, he'd survived the attack on outworld Nevian with a broken arm and a wounded leg. It must have been thirty degrees below zero on that rock, and the creatures there hard as stone. If he could survive that, surely he could incapacitate a few dozen amphibious arthropods while experiencing delusions.

The creatures spread out, some crawling across the ceiling or skittering along walls, and some taking leaping bounds toward him. Heston aimed his pistols in various directions with the speed of a gunslinger. Pulse rays blasted each creature, targeting a limb or two and causing them to burst into a slimy splat of green. But they kept coming.

The more he shot, the more appeared. This hive was larger than he'd been led to believe. If he continued like this, he'd never survive. And he wasn't planning on committing genocide, by any means. That wouldn't go over well with anyone back home if he made it out of this alive, regardless of what the Indar'kris had done.

Heston charged forward, thrusting his guns out, targeting his foes in their limbs rather than their heads as he made his way deeper into the hive, proceeding to a collection of dome-like structures in the middle of the space.

When he reached the domes, he took cover behind a curved wall, holstered both guns and withdrew the Vorpal Sword. He moved fast, quickly peering through small openings in the domes' architecture, searching for the girl as he fended off approaching enemies with the blade. One by one, he navigated each structure, fighting his way through the throng, trying his best not to kill too many, but each of the domes was empty.

Frustrated, his knuckles tightened on the sword's hilt, and he sliced two approaching foes in half.

Then, his luck changed. In the fourth structure, someone was laid out on the floor. He hurried inside, closing the door behind him and bracing it shut with the sword. Heston knelt beside—

A SamShun woman.

"Who are you?" He held out the translator. "Say your name."

"Desire," she said. "Desire Grasston."

"No, not your name-name. Your True Name. It's the only way to be sure."

She looked up at him, and said, "Tai-Lo-Vai-Quo-Mei-Vlor-Trei-Fen."

Heston confirmed her identity and helped her up. "Let's get you out of here."

The dome was surrounded by the creatures now, clawing and scratching at the door, trying to push their way in through the tiny apertures.

"We're trapped," she said.

"*I agree,*" the disembodied woman said.

Heston withdrew four light grenades, pulling the pins as he hurriedly pushed them out through a hole in the wall. "Close your eyes."

The flash was so brilliant that even with his eyes closed it left a bright spot in the center of his vision.

Heston led Desire to the door. "Ready?"

She nodded.

He slid the sword into the scabbard on his back, then drew one of the pistols and grabbed the girl's hand. Quickly, he navigated through the crowd, pushing and shoving, occasionally shooting when he had to.

When they reached the tunnel and headed toward the portal, three creatures blocked their escape. Dozens more came from behind. Heston still had that bright bulbous fuzziness blocking much of his view, not to mention the vision of the woman.

In a flash, he maneuvered the girl out of the way, withdrew the Vorpal

Sword with his free hand, spun fast, and slashed at the ceiling. The tunnel collapsed behind them, blocking the approaching horde, his gun unwavering on the three foes in front of him.

"Stay here," he said to Desire.

Each of his enemies had what looked like some sort of subatomic rifle aimed right at him. All they had to do was pull the trigger and they'd both be toast.

Quick as lightning, he drew his other gun and fired three shots, although still nearly blinded by the radiance in his eyesight. Each enemy lost only a limb, but the desired effect was achieved and they fell to the floor grasping their wounds.

"Let's go," he said, taking the girl's hand again and leading the way.

When they arrived at the portal, he lifted her until she could reach the edge and drag herself up, then hefted himself after her. They made their way to the speeder as the Indar'kris began to emerge from other portals.

The woman appeared again.

"Heston, look at me," she said.

When he did, her distorted form sharpened, and he saw her with some clarity for the first time and instantly recognized her. "Mom?"

She smiled.

"Sorry?" said Desire.

"Nothing. Get on."

They retreated to the SamShun city. On their way back, Heston considered everything he'd seen, how his mom had been the blurry woman all along, and what that might mean. It brought back recollections of that fateful week, what the man who had sent his dad off-world had looked like, how he talked, the way the corner of his mouth always turned up in a smirk. He remembered Kerse's expression the night in the woods when he was told to find Desire. Had that somehow subconsciously triggered the visions of his mom?

Back among the SamShun people, he explained what he'd seen, what he'd done, how it all went down. The SamShun elite seemed pleased.

Then he grabbed Tur and forced him against a wall, drew his pistol and pressed it under Tur's chin. "Now, tell me what I don't know, or things get ugly fast."

No one said a word.

Heston grimaced, shoved the gun hard enough to warrant a squeak out of Tur. "I'm not joking. And when I'm done with him, I'll move on to the rest of you." He waved the pistol at the leaders.

"Fine." One of them stepped forward. "A human—Kerse—made a deal with us to send you to the Indar'kris."

"Why?" He ground the end of his gun into Tur's throat, half choking him.

"Political reasons that don't matter to us, but he threatened our supply chains."

"And..."

"There is nothing more. The Indar'kris were supposed to deal with you."

He let Tur go. "Everyone who played a part in this charade will have to answer for it. I can guarantee that."

None of them spoke. They simply turned and left.

Activating his MindLink, Heston called Grasston. They put Heston straight through after an explanation as to his appearance.

"Marshal?" Grasston said. "You don't look—"

"Yes, I know."

Grasston frowned. "Please tell me you have good news."

"She's here beside me," Heston said. "Though, like me, she isn't quite herself." He turned so Grasston could see.

The man's expression faltered slightly before it softened. "Thank you, Marshal."

Heston grimaced. "I'm afraid we aren't done."

Grasston looked surprised. "No? What do you mean?"

Heston pulled up another holographic screen. "Vuhl'hla, you there?"

Her picture appeared beside Grasston's. "I am."

"And?"

"Buzz, Ji'rini, and I removed four additional threats, all part of Desire's security detail. You know who the perp is? I have him in my crosshairs, sir."

"I'm sorry, Mr. Grasston, but your husband was attempting a hostile take-over, beginning with unseating you and replacing himself in your position."

"What?" Grasston looked hurt by this. "Te'lute wouldn't... He couldn't... Could he?"

Heston didn't say one way or the other. Then he sighed. "Vuhl'hla?"

There was a momentary pause. When she spoke again, she only said, "It's done. Vuhl'hla out."

"I'm sorry, Mr. Grasston, but we couldn't allow this. Our democracy is ever so fragile as it is, and what your husband had planned would have undone decades of progress. I'll get Desire back to you safe and sound."

Grasston looked broken.

"Heston out." He shut off his MindLink, turned his attention to the girl. "You ready to get off this rock?"

She wiped tears from her eyes and nodded.

FOR EVERY SEASON

Lee Murray

TEAFF, 493 HD

TUK FLICKERED HIS VERTICAL LIDS, allowing the bioluminescent blue light to seep into the cracks of his consciousness. *Here we go again.* Another stop on Tuk's interminable tour of the universe. Sleeping on strange far-flung planets. Living out of someone else's skin.

Doing The Merge's scut work.

He squeezed his eyes tight, then lifted his finger, feeling for the manual release he knew was there. He could open the transpod with a focused thought, still he groped for the controller. Something solid to anchor him to the physical after having his psyche blasted across the cosmos. He pressed the spot as an eerie whisper drifted across his mind:

wind-silt sifts / shaping stone / of course

Ghost residue. It was the skin talking, although the whispers were more akin to feelings than words. Best to pay no attention. A couple of days and the uncanny echoes would disappear. The thoughts faded, at least for now, replaced by the familiar whoosh of escaping gasses as the transpod prepared to burp him into yet another Discovery Lander. Tuk rolled his shoulders, stretched his neck, and stepped out.

A soft groan carried from nearby.

Tuk turned to pinpoint the sound and strode into the next vesicle. Sprawled before a second transpod was a sleek-limbed humanoid. The creature gasped. Logic told Tuk it was Milk, although apart from the apprentice's strikingly dark eyes, he wouldn't have recognized him. This was what happened when you jumped. The Merge inserted you into any dusty rental blank available. And unless you were a fancy hoi-polloi sort, with funds to rent your own skin, there were only two kinds of costume on the planet of Teaff, two sentient species: the Rolkrai and the Alkrai. Milk had jumped into the latter.

"Ugh, that was awful," Milk whined. Shielding his eyes from the light, Tuk's war crime apprentice waggled a golden hand in the air.

Tuk stifled a chuckle. Typical post-millennial-millennial. Nevertheless, he grasped Milk's hand and pulled the youngster to his feet, noting the feathery warmth of the boy's skin. "I thought you'd jumped before."

"Just that one time. Nothing fancy. A short jump to Sol-3, and into a human skin." The apprentice lifted his arm, marvelling at his transformation. "But this is…something else. Nauseating but exhilarating, too. Look, I'm an Alkrai! Wow." Checking out his reflection in the wall, he tossed a silky head and preened. But when those dark eyes clocked Tuk, he staggered back, his mouth dropping open. "Investigator Tuk…"

Tuk examined his own appearance. Still humanoid, but stocky, he had thickened limbs covered in leathery scales, and slanted reptilian eyes. So, he was a Rolkrai. Interesting. Had the choice of skin been a conscious decision by his Merge masters? Tuk had been in worse skins. Half a decade spent investigating corruption as a bottom-dwelling water-slug on the moon of Agua'zzura, for example. Only, Tuk and Milk had been despatched to Teaff to investigate a spate of murders—of Alkrai citizens allegedly killed by the Rolkrai. Did The Merge think Tuk's appearance as a Rolkrai might endear him to the aggressors? Another whisper slipped through Tuk's senses:

flare's breath / tolls the season's secrets

Snorting, Tuk brushed away the ghost-thought with a shake of his head. More likely, the powers-that-be at The Merge didn't have a drekking clue. "Close your mouth, Milk. A little decorum."

"Sorry, I…"

"Teaff welcomes you!" A little droid surged forward, offering refreshments.

Tuk was about to wave the bot away, when Milk accepted a goblet, gulping it down. "Thank the heavens. I was dying of thirst."

Tuk cracked his scales in irritation, then relented, wrapping his own taloned fist around a goblet. They could spare a second or two. It was only the boy's second jump, after all, and any new physiology takes some getting used to.

Tuk was slurping a long blue tongue around the rim, when a young woman barely much older than Milk hurried towards them from the bend in the corridor, her robes wafting in her wake.

"Investigator Tuk?" she called. "I'm sorry I wasn't here to greet you. We hadn't expected you quite so soon. I'm Translator Mot."

Translators were used to easily communicate with various species after a world was accepted into The Merge when MindLinks and other communication devices weren't readily available.

Tuk straightened. "Ambassador Tuttle's message sounded urgent. We left within an hour of the sub-council's decision."

The translator pulled up. She peered around Tuk into the shadows. "Just the two of you?"

"Yes. This is my apprentice, Milk."

Mot grimaced. "I was hoping they'd send an army."

Milk tossed his goblet aside. "That's not really possible—"

Tuk placed his hand on the apprentice's forearm. "Figure of speech." He turned to Mot. "Something's happened?"

She nodded. "A massacre, just hours ago, in the town square." Her expression hardened. "When we sent word on behalf of the Alkrai, we'd had a handful of killings by unknown perpetrators. We'd hoped The Merge's intervention might curtail further violence. But this morning, close to one hundred Alkrai were slaughtered, cut down in broad daylight by a mob of Rolkrai."

"Wait," Tuk said. "How can you be certain it was the Rolkrai?"

"There were several witnesses. Before you ask, they were trusted Merge representatives. And we captured an injured Rolkrai fleeing the scene—one of the ringleaders. We have them in custody now." Mot wrung her hands. "This is unprecedented, Investigator. Unprecedented. As far as we can tell, the Alkrai and the Rolkrai have always co-existed peacefully. The Rolkrai are hardworking and dependable people. What could they have against the gentle Alkrai? But now...the bodies... It's untenable. And we only have a small task force here. Anthropologists and scientists, mainly. It's not just the Alkrai who are worried..."

Tuk replaced the empty goblet on the droid, the sound sharp in the blue gloom of the Lander. "We should go. I should talk to the Ambassador."

Mot's shoulders slumped. "Good luck with that. The Ambassador quit the planet a half hour ago."

✕

Her slender form moving swiftly, Mot hurried them through a maze of quiet side streets, past canvas-covered stalls carrying bread and nuts, tools, trinkets, and pottery, ducking and darting between shadows cast by the adobe buildings, avoiding confrontation. Still, citizens turned their backs and shutters pulled closed as their party neared. Tuk's scales tingled with tension. How much worse must it be for Milk, wearing the same feathery skin as those recently slaughtered, and also for Mot, whose human form announced her as an outsider?

Someone shouted at them from a balcony, the words prompting the translator to increase her pace.

"Wait!" Milk called. He slumped against a dusty wall. "I can't...the heat."

Quickly herding the pair of them into a deserted porchway, Mot fumbled in the folds of her robe and handed a liquid-filled gourd to Milk. "The planet is as hot as a clay oven," she said. "Teaff is hurtling towards a climate change event. It's worse here in the city, the Lander's proximity adding its own microclimate of energy fields—at least that's what our scientists believe. It's a burden we all bear." She glanced at Tuk. "Although, the Rolkrai appear less affected physically."

Tuk had to concede that, apart from feeling a little cranky—which might also be due to his recent jump—the heat wasn't bothering him too much. It was vastly cooler off the clifftop and away from the glare of Teaff's triple suns. Landers often appeared on precipices, or so Tuk had noted, prompting simpler civilizations to mistake the Landers for temples and the travellers who stepped out of them as gods. A deliberate act by The Creators to exert their influence? Certainly, their successors, the mighty Merge, didn't want for hubris...

"Is the massacre site far?" he asked.

"Not quite a kilometer."

"Perhaps we could take a detour?"

Mot nodded glumly. "I expected as much. I should warn you; it isn't pretty—"

Milk shrieked. With a start, he dropped the gourd and stamped his feet, spattering the clay porch with silver droplets. "Something ran by my leg!"

Tuk spun, talons at the ready, but Mot laid a steadying hand on his arm.

"There's no danger. It's just a little Falkrai." Tuk looked down. Nestling near the translator's feet, playing in the folds of her robes, a scaled creature about the size of a human toddler lifted its snout and pushed out a tiny blue tongue. It undulated its broad tail and sent a shudder along its spine, setting the tiny scales rattling. Mot smiled, a little of the tension leaving her shoulders. She bent to stroke the creature. "As you can see, they're very affectionate. The local population—Rolkrai and Alkrai—keep them as pets, rather like humans and their cats." Recovering the gourd, she tucked it in her robes as she straightened. "And like cats and kings, the Falkrai tend to go where they please, too."

At that moment, three large Rolkrai lumbered down the alley. Sharp eyes turned in their direction. Out of instinct, Tuk placed his bulk between the Rolkrai and his young colleagues huddling behind him in the porch. Tuk braced for trouble, but the group merely passed them by. The Falkrai skittered after the grim-faced Rolkrai, playing tag with their tails.

after a long day / sunset promises

Tuk shook off the ghost-thought.
"We should go," Mot whispered at his back." We've lingered long enough."
The water stain had almost evaporated as they stepped into the street.

The stench and the hum reached them first. Tuk pulled his tunic up over his nose, pushing back bile as they entered the square. Milk let out a gasp. Before them, scores of dead Alkrai lay broiling on the clay slab, their blood seeped away into the sand or crusted over in wrinkled, dark gluts.

A spate of murders, they said.

A cloud of feasting black flies took to the air—is there a single planet in all the universes that does not have flies?—the insects' movement exposing the garrotted necks, skinned feathers, and spilled viscera turning crunchy beneath Teaff's roasting suns.

Tuk took a turn about the square, examining the corpses, the flies lifting and settling as he passed. The corpses were twisted and grotesque.

Milk joined him. "They were taken unawares," he said, stroking the strands of silky hair away from his face. "Butchered with no forewarning."

Tuk cocked a scaled brow. "Is that your unbiased assessment?"

"No. You're right. It's just... I can feel it in my bones," Milk answered.

Tuk nodded. Milk's response might be innate, an artifact of his new Alkrai skin. To human eyes, the cadavers certainly looked surprised, but helicas with The Merge had taught Tuk that cultures did not all respond to events in the same way, even among populations on the same planet. It was best not to impose one's own prejudices.

"I don't understand, Investigator," Milk went on. "The Alkrai are an intelligent, cultured people. Why would they leave their dead to perish where they fell?"

"I suspect they're terrified the Rolkrai might turn on them," Tuk replied. He turned to Mot. "Or perhaps there is a cultural reason?"

"Our anthropologists are unsure," Mot replied, nodding to two Alkrai guards in Merge uniforms loitering nervously in the shade. "It may indeed be due to some ritual or custom we're not aware of. Or perhaps the Alkrai hope the rapid desiccation will help to preserve the bodies? They might be waiting for nightfall to recover them—when the heat is less. There are any number of explanations."

it is done / it is come to pass

Tuk crouched beside a body, using his sleeve to lift the victim's arm. A gaping wound exposed the ribs, feathers and muscle matted at the edges.

"And their Rolkrai neighbors?" Milk asked, his tone indignant. "Surely the Alkrai have friends among the Rolkrai. Why haven't they come forward to help? Do they condone the killings? What kind of people are these?"

Tuk prickled with irritation. "We mustn't be too quick to judge, Milk. Let's hear the evidence first. There are a lot of things we don't know." He dropped the arm, the limb clunking stiffly against the victim's ruined torso. But as he rose to his feet to take a final look at the depravity, something stirred inside him, something unexpected, which felt rather like...satisfaction.

glorious / the people scale / new horizons

The Merge's temporary HQ was a large domed building that reeked of corruption despite the ventilation slits spaced regularly along the walls. Inside, the structure housed aisles and aisles of shelves that bore thick tubes. Scrolls? Tuk lifted one. Up close, the smell of decay was even more pungent. He blinked. It was a wrinkled, yellowed Rolkrai skin, coiled like a roll of pastry, with markings on its surface. He showed it to Milk, who blanched and staggered a little.

"What is this place?" Tuk demanded. "A cemetery?"

"A library," Mot replied.

Of course. With most of the planet covered in arid desert plains, Teaff had few trees. "I don't see any texts written on Alkrai pelts."

"That's because the library archive is maintained by the Rolkrai, although, ostensibly, it's open to everyone. The prisoner is being housed here. Given our lack of forces, we felt a public space would be safest."

There was a clatter overhead. Tuk looked up to see a little Falkrai scamper across the stacks, its frolicking toppling several scrolls. Milk laughed. Clucking her tongue, Mot bent to pick them up.

"You said ostensibly," Tuk said when all the scrolls had been returned to the shelves.

Mot scrubbed at a smear of dried blood on her hem. "The Rolkrai are a very private people, Investigator Tuk. Some materials in the collection are strictly limited to Rolkrai citizens. Although, to be fair, the Alkrai are a carefree species with little interest in scriptures and learning. If you'd follow me this way..."

They took a dark corridor to a small back room, where a Rolkrai sat impassive before a broad clay table, their ankles and wrists tied with sinew and secured to a bench. They'd taken a slash to the leg. A deep one, judging from the blood seeping through the bandage—which explained how they'd come to be captured.

"Messer Raulk," Mot said, addressing the prisoner. "I present Investigator Tuk and Apprentice Milk from The Merge. They'd like to ask you some questions about this morning's...event."

Raulk's speech was a lilting string of guttural bellows, which Mot interpreted as, "Secrets are only important until they are not. Once known, secrets cannot be unknown. In time, everything is known."

The translator pulled Tuk and Milk into a huddle and dropped her voice to a soft whisper. "That's the closest interpretation I can offer. The Rolkrai language tends to be lyrical and sparse. Often, it's as if the people are speaking in riddles or prophecies. It can be difficult to decipher their intent, but I believe they're prepared to answer our questions."

"I understand."

Mot raised a brow. "You've encountered a similar language?"

Tuk touched a talon to his temple. "Not exactly. Since our arrival, I've experienced a few enigmatic ghost echoes."

"It's so interesting, isn't it?" Milk gushed. "This ghost-residue thing, I mean. Fascinating insight into the citizenry. I've had urges to run for no reason other than the joy of running." He chuckled. "I almost dashed off after that Falkrai in the street, to hell that it was following those three—"

Tuk hushed the boy with a stern stare. Turning back to the room, he draped his new tail over the bench in the manner of Raulk and sat down opposite the Rolkrai. Mot and Milk took seats on either side of Tuk. "Messer Raulk," Tuk mimicked the translator's earlier address. "You were apprehended while fleeing the slaughter of your Alkrai neighbors in violation of The Merge's laws of civil behaviour. It is alleged that you were party to the killings. Do you deny this?"

The big Rolkrai loosed another series of growls and bellows.

"The deed is done. It is come to pass," Mot translated.

"Can I ask why you did it?"

"It is come to pass," Raulk replied again.

"So you don't deny it. Did the Alkrai provoke you in some way? Have they been the cause of some hurt to you or your family? Did someone in particular transgress against you?"

As Mot translated Tuk's barrage of questions, Raulk gazed at a sliver of light from a small window, the beam transecting the table. Eventually, he said, "The suns give way to the moons, which make way for the suns."

Tuk wracked his brain for the meaning behind Raulk's words. A metaphor for something? He glanced at Mot, who shook her head. Seemed she was none the wiser either. Questioning the Alkrai might shed some light. If only a witness were brave enough to come forward.

Tuk changed tack. "What do you do, Raulk?" he asked.

"I'm a builder of homes, a protector from the seasons."

"For the Rolkrai?"

Raulk nodded. "And for Alkrai family."

"If the lives of your peoples are intimately entwined, why then would the Rolkrai attack the Alkrai without cause?"

Raulk raised his chin, their manner languid and unhurried. "For Teaff, dawn is always brutal. Only in the cool of twilight is there content."

Tuk rubbed at his eye with the back of a talon. Infuriating! Raulk's answers were unfathomable. Had the Rolkrai incited the revolt? If Raulk were the ringleader, would their incarceration put paid to the violence?

"What of the other murders?" Tuk demanded. "Twelve Alkrai were killed in recent weeks. Mutilated and left for dead. What do you know of them?"

Raulk's tail flickered absently. "Individual differences." Tuk held the Rolkrai's gaze. Had the previous murders been isolated altercations? Raulk returned the stare. "It is the season," he said. "The river will sing with blood. When the sun sets, all will succumb." A pause. "Even you, Investigator Tuk, if you choose it."

Milk leapt to his feet. He slammed a hand on the table, throwing up a puff of dust. "Was that a threat?" Thrusting his face at Raulk, he hissed through tapered teeth, "Did you just threaten us, Rolkrai? The cold-blooded brute is mocking us, Investigator! Sitting there, spouting their poetry when scores of innocent Alkrai have been murdered.”

“Milk!”

“They insult the authority of The Merge.”

“That’s enough!” Pushing back his chair, Tuk grasped his apprentice by his tunic and bundled him into the corridor, Mot on their heels. Raulk’s low growl reached them as the translator shut the door. Tuk didn’t need her to translate:

“It is come to pass,” Raulk said.

There had been no time to reprimand his charge. No sooner had they left the room, a soldier in a Rolkrai skin wearing Merge heraldry dashed into the corridor, his sudden appearance startling a little Falkrai into a cupboard.

“Translator Mot!” the soldier barked. “There’s been another attack on the Alkrai. Two streets east.”

Mot stiffened. “How many killed?”

“Eight…ten. It’s still in progress. Sergeant Franks sent me to warn you.”

“Warn a translator? If they’re slaying citizens, it’s way too late for parlaying,” Milk said.

Tuk gave him a gentle nudge. “Milk, with the Ambassador’s defection, Translator Mot is Teaff’s highest-ranking Merge citizen.”

“Oh.”

Mot produced a knife from under her robes. “And I say we do what we can to save anyone still standing.”

Tuk pushed forward. “I’ll go. It’s safer. I’m Rolkrai—at least, I appear that way.”

Milk straightened his bunched tunic. “I’m your apprentice, sir. If you go, I’m going, too.”

Mot threw Tuk a bemused glance. “And I’m Teaff’s highest-ranking Merge citizen, so I shall do as I please. Besides, there may be witnesses,” she said. “You’ll need a translator.”

Tuk could strangle them. Young people. There was no arguing with them. “Lead on, then,” he told The Merge soldier.

They hurried out of the library into the blazing afternoon, where the heat swirled in mirages off the beaten clay. A stifling breeze hit them, carrying with it the clang of metal and the cries of the wounded. It only took minutes to reach the furore, Tuk snatching an axe from a street stall en route, handing it to Milk before helping himself to a mallet. “Stay close to me. And stay alert!”

They rounded the corner.

The street was muddy with blood. Everywhere, Alkrai lay dead or dying. Those Alkrai still standing were frantic, tugging at clothes and limbs, trying to drag their beleaguered friends from the butchery. Meanwhile, Franks and five of his Merge soldiers struggled to hold back a score of Rolkrai clearly intent on finishing the job. One of the attackers, a big Rolkrai with a crooked snout, spied Milk. Shrieking a war-cry, they broke free from the group, charging at Tuk's apprentice with a broadsword.

Tuk swung the mallet, striking the Rolkrai at the knees as they hurtled past. Bone crunched. The Rolkrai screamed and went down, their tail grappling for purchase on a jumble of limbs. They let out a string of guttural grunts. Tuk recognized the words "it is come to pass." As for the rest, probably some rather ripe Rolkrai swearing. Tuk didn't have time to find out. Two more Rolkrai had set their sights on the apprentice.

But Mot had also seen the move; she intercepted the one closest to her with a quick slice to the Rolkrai's Achilles. The Rolkrai hobbled a couple of steps, then collapsed, clutching their injured limb.

Undaunted, the second Rolkrai raised a spear. Tuk rushed to parry it. Instead, it was Milk who sliced his axe through scale and flesh and tendon, blood spurting as the Rolkrai's severed hand rolled away. Stupefied, Milk gazed at the grisly stump, while the wounded Rolkrai escaped down a side alley.

But the downed Rolkrai with the crooked snout wasn't done yet; they lifted their broadsword, preparing to stab Milk in the back. Bunting the weapon away with his mallet, Tuk stomped on the Rolkrai's mangled leg, grinding the shattered bone through tender flesh.

Still, the Rolkrai grabbed for Tuk's tunic.

Unbalanced, Tuk tumbled, rolling in the dust with them, blinded, their stench in his nostrils, the Rolkrai screeching at Tuk over and over. They snaked their talons around Tuk's neck. Squeezed. He was choking! Tuk reached out a hand, grappling for something... Anything. His palm closed on a rock. He gripped it. Swung. The rock connected with a dull thud. At last, the Rolkrai shuddered and lay still, their skull cracked.

Tuk lay there a moment, breathing hard, then he pushed the creature off and blinked the grit out of his eyes. Milk and Mot came into view.

"The Alkrai must grow up. Learn their lesson," Mot said as the pair helped Tuk to his feet.

"I'm sorry, what?"

Mot nodded towards the crooked-snout Rolkrai, his caved-in skull glistening with brain matter. "They were screaming it at you."

All at once, from among the pile of bodies, an Alkrai stumbled to her knees, the slit at her throat still foaming pink blood. She rasped a few words, then tumbled, face down into the pile.

Tuk and Milk looked at Mot.

"They're coming for us," she translated. "Tonight, where the river sings."

Tuk leaned against the wall of a nearby building and sighed. Already, the interminable flies were circling. And likewise, deep in his psyche, the faint buzz of satisfaction of a task completed.

"Investigator," Milk said, a chunk of meal-bread in his hand, "surely now you must see the Rolkrai's intent is to murder all Alkrai. They are set on genocide."

They were back at the library, a rag-tag group of soldiers, scientists, and statesmen, all taking sanctuary among the macabre skin scrolls. A chance to tend to their scratches and plot their next move. But what move? The whole business felt off. The Rolkrai's sudden unexplained animosity towards their Alkrai kin, the secret and prophetic nature of their ramblings, and their dogged determination. Plus, there was no clear motive: none that they would admit to, nor any of the usual sordid schemes to steal Creator Tech and claim power, which had so often underpinned Tuk's investigations. Genocide for the sake of genocide? It was too callous. Unspeakable. "We can't be sure," Tuk said at last. "Their language is too cryptic."

"Yes. Where the river sings…" Mot said, repeating the girl's dying words.

Throwing down his bread, Milk stalked across the room, his dark eyes glittering. "They said *tonight*, Investigator. There is nothing ambiguous about that." He stalked back. "We need to act now!"

"What do you have in mind, Apprentice?" the embattled Sergeant Franks demanded. He waved his mug, water slopping over the rim. "You saw what just happened. With half my peacekeepers wearing Alkrai skins, we barely have the personnel to hold off a skirmish, let alone an all-out war."

"Still, we need to warn the Alkrai," Milk insisted.

"And tell them what exactly?" Franks boomed. "Believe me, son, they already know about the killings."

"Where the river sings. Where the river sings…" Mot drummed her fingers on the table. "There is no river; water on Teaff is drawn from underground aquifers." Her face widened in a grin. "But there was a source in the city once…"

A thin-faced woman, feeding bread to a Falkrai, looked up. "The fountain on the eastern flank? It's long since dried up. Centuries ago."

"And yet the river sang there once. Could that be it?"

"That's it. I'm sure of it. I can feel it," Milk said.

Tuk got to his feet. "It's a lead, at least. Maybe Raulk will confirm it?"

Two Merge soldiers in Rolkrai skins thundered into the library. Franks spoke with them briefly, then turned to Tuk and Mot. "Seems Apprentice Milk is right. We need to act now. The Rolkrai are amassing to the south of the city."

"I'll warn the Alkrai," Milk said, picking up the axe.

"No," Tuk said, closing his own fist around the axe handle.

"He'll have a better chance than you," Mot replied. "And he acquitted himself well enough with that axe earlier."

"Except the Alkrai won't trust him if he carries it, and he's at risk from the Rolkrai if he doesn't." Tuk's argument fell on deaf ears; Milk was already dashing out the door.

Franks rolled his Rolkrai eyes and set down his mug. "I'll follow the lad."

Tuk lasted barely half an hour before slipping out of the library, heading east on the darkened streets. It wasn't that he didn't trust Franks, but Milk was Tuk's apprentice, *his* responsibility. The problem was, he had no idea where Milk might be and only the vaguest notion of the fountain's location.

Tuk sprinted through the streets. All around him the silent shadows crawled with menace. Which way? The foothills. Somewhere close to the Discovery Lander. Landing points were always strategic. The Creators, for all their mystery, were self-serving—and The Merge was no better. They never invested in anything that wasn't to their benefit. Just look at Teaff. The Lander had been here eons and yet The Merge hadn't bothered to send a team until a decade ago. They didn't give a *damn* about people. Tuk snorted under his breath. Other than its people, all Teaff had was sun and sand. In any case, Tuk was done jumping to do their bidding. When this case was over, Tuk would take his savings and get out. Find some quiet planet to retire to. Let Milk carry on in his stead. The boy was too impassioned and impulsive by half, but he was bright, and he could learn. Tuk just had to find the idiot first.

A Falkrai squawked underfoot. Panting with exertion, Tuk pulled up. He'd accidentally collided with the creature in the darkness. Poor little thing. He bent to stroke the animal while he got his bearings. The Falkrai nuzzled at Tuk's legs, rattling its scales.

"You have the right idea, don't you? Run of the town, pampered by every-one, including investigators who run you over in the dark!"

Lights flickered, reflecting on the clay cliffs. Tuk rose and sprinted on.

But he'd only run a few minutes more when Franks grabbed him by the tunic and dragged him into an alleyway.

"What the hell?" the sergeant hissed. "Do you want to get yourself killed?"

Tuk huffed. "I'm in a Rolkrai skin like the rest of you."

"You think they can't tell the difference? As soon as you open your mouth, they'll know."

Tuk nodded. Franks had a point. The man had done a few jumps in his time.

He scanned the group for his apprentice. "Milk?"

Franks shook his head. "We were too late. The boy's dead," he said.

Dead? Tuk shivered, his scales rattling quietly. He should've been there. It should've been him.

"They're all dead," whispered a soldier. "Every one of them."

"The Alkrai?" Tuk asked, keeping his voice low.

Franks said nothing.

"I need to see."

"Sir—"

"It's my job, Sergeant. I'll need to complete a war crimes report."

Franks exhaled slowly. "Toka, take the men back to the library. Mount a guard. Tell Translator Mot we'll follow shortly."

"Yessir." Toka led the group off.

Tuk followed Franks through a series of narrow alleys to a flight of stairs climbing to an isolated rooftop. They crept to the edge of the parapet and peeped over the side.

"Holy blern," breathed Franks. "That's new."

Tuk couldn't speak. The area below them was awash with butchered Alkrai. But it was also teeming with Rolkrai, those once-peaceful neighbors. The stocky reptilians were tearing the livers out of the dead, wrestling the blackened organs from tangles of tendon and sinew. Then, turning to face the Lander on the cliff, they devoured them.

"Milk?" Tuk whispered after a moment.

"Right beneath us."

Keeping his body close to the stone, Tuk leaned over the parapet. His Rolkrai heart shivered. The boy was there, his slim frame two floors below them in the courtyard. On his back, an axe through his side, Milk stared upwards, those dark eyes glittering even in death.

Then a Rolkrai moved in to tear apart his abdomen.

"Enough." Franks pulled Tuk away.

They raced back towards the library, pausing on a hunch near the site of the skirmish, so Tuk might brave a glance around the corner. He drew back. Covered his mouth.

"More Rolkrai feasting on livers?" Franks whispered.

Tuk could only nod.

X

A Falkrai bounced onto Tuk's lap, waking him. Streaks of light peeped through the ventilation slits. Dawn. Tuk cracked his scales. He'd dozed upright in a chair. His neck and back ached—and his conscience even more.

Mot appeared. "Here." She handed him a steaming cup smelling of cinnamon and nuts.

Shooing the Falkrai off his lap, Tuk accepted the cup and took a sip.

"Better?"

"Not really."

She sat beside him, folding her robes neatly around her. "I'm so sorry about Milk."

Tuk scanned the room, at the people slumbering among stacks or even on the floor. "How are the evacuations going?"

"Slow. Franks's men escorted the first group to the Lander while it was still dark. They haven't returned yet."

Tuk flicked his head towards the back room. "Much as it irks me, we'll have to release Raulk. If we could force someone to jump, I'd haul them back to face charges."

"I'm not convinced we need to leave, Investigator." Mot took a swallow from her own mug. "What if Milk's death was just a case of mistaken identity? What if the Rolkrai mean us no harm?"

Tuk grunted. "Tell that to the Alkrai."

Mot swirled the liquid in her mug. "We know so little about these people."

Tuk nudged her shoulder. "Maybe we should've searched the restricted section."

She smiled weakly. "The thing is, without The Merge's knowledge, the Rolkrai might not survive either. How long before this wretched climate wipes them off the planet?"

Franks materialized from behind one of the stacks. "There's trouble. A horde of Rolkrai at the front entrance."

Tuk glanced at Mot. They put down their mugs and ran to the front of the building where they peeked through the ventilation slits.

Outside, the mob jostled and heaved against the ancient wooden doors, the air resonant with the scrape of their talons and their dissonant bellowing.

"What are they saying?" Tuk asked.

Mot frowned. "More prophecies. A time for knowledge…the people scale… new horizons."

"Don't let them in," the thin-faced woman wailed. "They want to eat our livers!"

But in the caterwauling, Tuk thought he heard his name. Another ghost-whisper? Strange. He hadn't had one for hours now.

"Tuk!"

Milk? Tuk plastered his eye to the ventilation hole. A Rolkrai, slimmer than the others, stepped out of the crowd, fixing Tuk with glittering dark eyes.

Tuk pulled back from the aperture. "Milk's out here. Open the doors!"

"Investigator Tuk," Franks said. "I saw the boy die. Surely, you can't believe—?"

"He's out there," Tuk insisted. "It's him. He's jumped into a Rolkrai skin."

"Without a transpod? That's not possible. It's the grief talking—"

"They'll kill us all," screamed the thin-faced woman.

But Mot bellowed over them—a phrase in Rolkrai—and on the other side of the doors, the pounding ceased.

With a wave of his tail at the translator, Tuk lifted the bar, and slipped through the gap. The door slammed behind him, and Tuk heard the scrape of the bar sliding home.

Tuk faced the mob. "Milk?"

The slender Rolkrai stepped forward, the Rolkrai amassing behind him.

"You jumped?" Tuk whispered. It was the most rational explanation.

Milk shook his head. "I died and was reborn. The people scale new horizons." The apprentice was speaking Common, yet his words remained infuriatingly Rolkrai.

"The people scale? Do you mean metamorphosis? The Alkrai changing their feathers for scales?"

Milk smiled. "It is the season." He rattled his scales.

"But the killings? I saw the Rolkrai consume the livers."

"In Teaff, dawn is always brutal."

Tuk wrestled with the revelation. "It was a rite of passage? A coming of age into adulthood? From Alkrai to Rolkrai?"

Milk's tail swayed.

"And the adult form, the Rolkrai, don't tell their young," Tuk blurted, understanding blasting him like a desert storm. "The Alkrai have to grow up and learn the lesson for themselves!"

"I know," Milk said, satisfied. "Now everything is known."

Tuk pushed his face to the ventilation slit. "Open the doors," he called.

ᛁᚼᛁ

With Teaff's secrets revealed, Tuk went to release Raulk, but the room was empty, the bindings and bandages in disarray on the bench. The Rolkrai must have sawn through the ropes and escaped in the clamor.

"Investigator Tuk?" Mot said at his shoulder. "Sergeant Franks is ready to escort you and Apprentice Milk to the Lander."

Tuk turned. "Thank you, Mot. I'll have Milk send you his recollections of the metamorphosis as soon as he's back on The Hub and no longer speaking in parables."

There was a long pause, and then Mot said, "Perhaps The Merge will let you come back and visit us?"

"Perhaps." Tuk knew The Merge would never send him back. As long as his Masson particle was intact, Tuk would go wherever they sent him. It took more than a talon to saw through The Merge's bindings.

A Falkrai skittered out from under the table and bounced into his arms, the little animal licking Tuk with its blue tongue.

Tuk grinned. "How did you get in here?"

He stroked the creature, his palm running over a puckered scar on its thigh. Tuk started, remembering the blood-stained bandage on Raulk's leg. The Rolkrai's enigmatic words resonated in his mind.

Only in the cool of twilight is there content.

Putting the creature down, Tuk crouched to look under the table. There, on the floor, was a leathery scaled pelt.

Tuk grinned. A third life stage. A non-sentient one. So Milk didn't know everything. And neither did The Merge...

"Investigator," Franks said from the door. "Will you come now?"

While the Falkrai flicked its tail, Tuk considered the possibilities.

OH, THOSE INNER RINGS

Jane Yolen

Sold to would-be oligarchs
who did not have the guts
to trek further, just sit
in their golden transpods,
made up by The Merge.
There they sip a space nectar
that makes them believe
they are light-years
into exploration.
Oh, the chattering jaws
of their electric warders,
the giggles of the nursemaids
as they cull the skins for sale
so the oligarchs feed on themselves
to stay alive.
If one can call that a life.

A DEEPER SONG

Tim Waggoner

SETIS, 493 HD

RUTH GUERRERO STEPPED OUT OF THE LANDER and got her first real-world view of Setis's landscape. Hard pumice-like soil, scraggly bushes with thorn-covered fronds, and tall trees with thick tufts of gossamer silk, everything tinged purple from the light of Setis's sun. The hue had nothing to do with the sun itself, was caused by an adaptation of Setisian eyes, a thick coating like permanent sunglasses which protected them from the star's radiation. The sky was dark like a bad bruise, clouds thin, wispy, and gray. Ruth inhaled warm air through her nostril flaps, surprised to find it smelled something like cinnamon. She felt her lamprey-like mouth contract tight in the Setisian equivalent of a grin. This was one of the things she loved most about her job—experiencing the sensations of a new skin for the first time.

A sound came to her then, carried on the wind. A high-pitched tone with a sad, almost mournful quality. *Keening,* she thought. *That was the word.*

A mental voice not her own interrupted her thoughts.

Don't try running right away, like you did on Kestrel 13. You tripped over your own hooves, fell, and broke a leg before the mission even began.

"Yes, Dad."

Paracletes were AI's that all Immaculance operatives possessed, created by a colony of nanobots that had been fused with the user's brain. They served as advisors and guardians, but their primary function was to store information on the thousands of recognized religions in The Hub, far more data than any non-enhanced human mind could contain, and provide it to their user when needed. The tech wasn't widely used by The Merge. Identity boundaries could blur over time, making it difficult to tell where the organic personality ended and the AI began. So far, Ruth hadn't had any ill effects from her paraclete, and she hoped to keep it that way.

Ruth's paraclete was called Shepherd. He'd chosen the name himself—his idea of a joke, she supposed. He could be annoying at times—well, a *lot* of times—but that didn't mean he was wrong to warn her. There was always an adjustment period after a jump. New skin, new atmosphere, new gravity...It was a good idea to take things slow at first.

The wind had died down a bit, and she could no longer hear the keening sound. She put it out of her mind and started walking.

The gravity on Setis was stronger than Hub standard, and at first it felt like she was forcing her way through thick sludge, but after a few moments the feeling faded and her forward motion became smooth and natural. Her new skin was bipedal, squat and thick-limbed, with tough gray skin. The hands had five fingers, with two thumbs, one on each side, and the feet were elephant-like, toes almost nonexistent. She didn't walk so much as tromp, each footstep a heavy thud. Her only clothing was a white tunic woven from replicated silk-tree fibers which came down to just above her knees. Setisians were a tribal people, and normally the fronts of their tunics were marked with a symbol indicating which clan they belonged to, but her tunic was blank. She carried a pouch made from the same silky material as her tunic slung over her left shoulder, and she gripped a sturdy metal-tipped wooden spear in her right hand. In the pouch was a gourd filled with drinking water, along with thick wafers made from seeds bound by an insect-produced resin not unlike honey.

They're called qafan, Shepherd supplied. *A human wouldn't be able to swallow a bite without gagging, but they're something of a delicacy to Setisians.*

"You're not exactly making them sound appetizing. How far to the nearest settlement?"

The words came out in a series of hoots and clicks, but her mind heard them in Hub Common.

A little over five kilometers, Shepherd said. *Due south. The Setisians won't build settlements any closer to the Lander. They call it yyt'an, which roughly translates to "big nest." When the Servitors first emerged from the Lander to conduct their initial surveys, the Setisians believed they were giant—and deadly—insects.*

"Five kilometers, huh?" Ruth let out a soft whistle that was the Setisian equivalent of a sigh. Her new skin wasn't built for speed. "Looks like we're in for a hike."

What do you mean we? You're the one that has to do the walking.

As she traveled, she continually swept her gaze back and forth, alert for threats, but her thoughts were on the man she'd come here to find. Emmanuel Bates—fellow Attendant of the Immaculance and possibly the greatest threat this world had ever faced.

The discovery of the Masson Zero heralded the beginning of a new galactic age, one in which disparate civilizations were able to communicate, interact, and share technological and cultural information. Religion was a large part of this culture exchange, and while some civilizations were content merely to share their theologies, others were more interested in spreading their world's gospel, sometimes quite aggressively. So The Merge created the Immaculance, an organization tasked with monitoring—and when necessary, policing—religious interchanges throughout the galactic coalition, headquartered in Nexus City.

Ruth and Emmanuel had joined the Immaculance around the same time. They started as coworkers but quickly became good friends. They became lovers at one point, and while that had been nice enough, they ultimately decided their relationship worked better as a friendship. Ruth was a happy agnostic, but Emmanuel was a seeker, wanting desperately to believe in something beyond physical reality. Although his parents had raised him Neo-Euclidian, he'd abandoned the faith when he'd become an adult. He'd tried others on for size, but none had filled the emptiness at the core of his being.

Ruth had been jealous when Emmanuel was chosen to join the survey team that originally visited Setis to make contact with one of the native tribes. Linguists on the team learned the rudiments of the clan's language, while the xenobiologist, xenobotanist, and xenosociologist conducted their own studies. Emmanuel, as a representative of the Immaculance, learned what he could about the tribe's religion. Their belief system possessed a simple elegance that he admired: the Setisians believed in the Great Mother, a nature deity who had created all life on the planet and continued to guide and protect it. When the team returned to The Hub, they'd gone their separate ways to report their findings to their supervisors. Emmanuel returned to the Immaculance headquarters in Nexus City and made a full report to Mofra Gorr, the assistant director of the Immaculance, and when she was satisfied he'd told her everything, she'd decided that Setisian society was too primitive and therefore vulnerable to religious manipulation and indoctrination. She recommended that jumping to Setis be limited for this reason, and travel to the world had been strictly regulated ever since.

Emmanuel was next assigned to investigate a new religion called the Light of the Created God. Attendants of the Immaculance were strongly encouraged by the Proctors to adopt an approved religion, if they didn't already adhere to one. Mofra occasionally reminded Ruth of this fact, and whenever she did, Ruth smiled, nodded, and ignored her. Emmanuel had been born and raised a Neo-Euclidian, but the more he learned about the Light of the Created God, the more he became intrigued by it.

"It's like no other religion I've encountered," he told Ruth over coffee one day. "The Founders believe all religions hold a piece of the truth, so they reasoned the only way to discover that truth was to determine the common underlying principles between all the belief systems in the known galaxy. They constructed a computer the size of a continent and programmed it with every holy book and theological treatise ever written. The computer's AI became sentient and proclaimed itself the Created God, and it commanded its builders to spread its gospel throughout the galaxy in the name of universal peace."

"That sounds...*interesting*," Ruth said. "But was the end result really that different from other religions? What makes the Light any better than them?"

"It's *unified*. That's what makes it better. It's the first truly galactic religion."

Ruth was doubtful, but Emmanuel always became enthusiastic when he discovered something that interested him. This latest enthusiasm would wane soon enough, and then he'd move on to something else. He always did.

But not this time.

Emmanuel continued studying the Light of the Created God, and as part of his investigation, he contacted the religion's Founders. They invited him to attend a worship service, and he was so impressed that afterward he became a full-fledged member of the church. He petitioned Mofra to add the Light to the Immaculance's list of approved religions, but she denied his request.

"We need to learn more about it first," she said. "Its AI could potentially be infiltrated by other religions seeking to undermine a competitor. These bad actors could infect the AI with a virus or rewrite its base programming to manipulate worshippers. We need to learn just how secure the AI's defenses are before we can grant our approval."

Emmanuel continued to advocate for the Light of the Created God's addition to the list of approved religions, but Mofra refused to change her mind. Frustrated, Emmanuel decided to resign from the Immaculance. Ruth tried to talk him out of it, but it was no use.

"I believe in the Light, more than I've ever believed in anything," he told her. "I'm going to help it grow and spread, until its illumination fills even the darkest corners of the universe."

He left and she hadn't seen him since.

Several months later, Mofra called Ruth into her office.

Mofra was from a species of highly evolved protozoa, but she found it easier to work in Nexus City in human form. Despite how long she'd existed within a human body, she'd never fully learned to control her eye muscles, and at times her eyes would drift to the side when she was talking to you.

Ruth sat in front of her crystalline desk, and Mofra gestured with her right hand. A holo scene appeared in the air above the glittering desktop, showing a circular grouping of domed structures which appeared to have been made from wood. There was an open area in the middle of the circle, and members of a species she didn't recognize sat on the ground, thick legs stretched out before them, listening as one of their own spoke. He/she/they stood before the others, gesturing broadly with thick-fingered hands that possessed two thumbs. The holo's volume was on, but she didn't recognize the language, let alone understand it. The image was transparent, and she looked through it at Mofra.

"What is this?"

"Setis. This holo was recorded by a Reconer recently constructed on the planet. We'd gotten word that there had been an unauthorized jump to the world, and we wanted to check it out."

Reconers were small drones designed for stealth. They could bend light around them, making them virtually invisible, and they flew silently. Harbinger teams created them in Landers and deployed them to gather as much information about a planet's civilization as possible—language, customs, technological level...Once the drones' time was up, they returned to the Lander and transmitted their data via the Mass-O system to Nexus City, where the information was downloaded and analyzed.

"You're looking at the Plains Clan—*and* a visitor." Mofra twitched her index finger, and the holo's audio switched to Common.

"...but all religions are part of the Light of the Created God, including the Great Mother. That means you already worship the Light—through her."

Mofra moved her finger again, and the image froze. Ruth stared at the speaker for several moments before speaking. She didn't recognize the being physically, but his words told her who he was.

Emmanuel.

It was the Setisian equivalent of late afternoon when Ruth first spied the village, a cluster of domed buildings, just like those in the holo Mofra had showed her. She estimated there were three dozen, or so. She'd been plodding along for what seemed like hours, but her new skin wasn't tired. Setisians had strong constitutions, it seemed.

"How much longer until sunset?"

Forty-eight minutes. At our current rate of speed, we'll reach the village in twenty-three minutes.

"I'll see if I can pick up the pace. Is this village the one I saw on the holo?"

I believe so, although Setisian villages tend to look alike.

"Tell me about the Setisian religion."

Based on information collected by the first survey team and the Reconers they left behind, it's believed to be a standard nature religion. The Setisians worship a divine being called the Great Mother, who is the personification of the planet itself. Unlike most religions which place their deities beyond where worshippers can reach—a high mountain, the sky, a spiritual dimension outside normal time and space—the Setisians believe the Great Mother is a physical presence that shares the world with them.

"Where is she supposed to be specifically?"

According to the Setisians, she's in all things, whether they're alive or not.

"Like that's not creepy."

Ruth looked down at the hard-packed earth beneath her feet.

"Are you there, Mother?"

She didn't receive a reply, and although she hadn't expected one, she was surprised to feel a little disappointed. Maybe she was more like Emmanuel than she'd thought.

As they drew near the village, Ruth became aware of a sharp, acidic odor, and it instantly nauseated her.

"What is that godawful smell?"

Unknown, but your Setisian body is certainly having a strong reaction to it.

"No kidding."

She breathed slowly through her lamprey mouth, just as she would in a human skin if she wanted to keep from vomiting. She had no idea if this would work for a Setisian body, but luckily it did. Her nausea receded, although it didn't entirely go away.

The light was becoming dimmer as day prepared to give way to night, and the purple shielding over her eyes lightened in response.

Setisians can't see in the dark, but they have better night vision than humans, Shepherd said.

"Good to know, but I'm starting to get a feeling that I don't want to see what's waiting for us up ahead."

She continued onward, forcing herself not to slow her pace. When she was within a dozen meters of the village, she saw the bodies lying on the ground. Setisians, large and small. Adults and children, she guessed. Her nausea returned full force, but as she hadn't eaten or drank anything since this skin had been created, she only had a few dry heaves. She stopped and bent over until they passed, then plodded the rest of the way to the village, dread increasing with every step.

She stopped when she reached the first body. It was a child, a girl, given the black stripes that ran down her neck. Setisians were born male or female, but when they reached puberty, they became fully intersex and were capable of impregnating themselves, although this was not a common occurrence.

The girl's silk tunic was covered with fresh blood so dark it was almost black, the cloth riddled with holes. Ruth glanced at the spear she carried, and she knew what sort of weapon had been used to kill the poor thing. Assuming she was dead.

"How can I take a Setisian's pulse?" she asked Shepherd. Paracletes had no special sensors, and so he couldn't scan the girl for life signs. Whatever skin Ruth inhabited, Shepherd had only its senses to rely on, just like her.

If her heart's still beating, you'll be able to detect a slight flutter on the back of her tongue. Touch yours first to see what it feels like.

Ruth did, then she crouched down and slipped a finger into the girl's tooth-rimmed circular mouth and gently pressed down on the back of her slimy tongue. Nothing. As she began to withdraw her finger, she had the wild thought the girl might wake and bite her with those sharp teeth, but of course she didn't.

Ruth straightened then called out in a loud voice, "Is there anyone here?"

Is that wise? Whoever killed these people could still be around.

"Yes, but there might be survivors that need help too."

But no one answered her call. She moved around the village, pausing to check the pulse of each body she came to, but they were dead, all of them pierced by spears, just like the girl. Some of their tunics were less covered with blood than the girl's, though, and on those Ruth saw a flat horizontal line stitched with brown thread.

It's a clan mark, Shepherd said. *The flat line means these are...or rather, were the Plains Clan.*

"The clan the first expedition spent time with. Including Emmanuel."

Yes.

Ruth checked the domes next, and while she found simple tables, chairs, and sleeping mats, she found no Setisians. They'd all been outside when they'd been killed. The domes and furniture had been crafted from silk-tree wood, the sleeping mats woven from the tree's gossamer fibers.

The trees are called ss'tarran, Shepherd supplied. *In Setisian, it means* gift.

By the time she finished her investigation, the sun had set, and it was full night. Shepherd had been right about her vision. The world appeared gray to her eyes, and she could see clearly two meters ahead of her. A few meters beyond that and details became fuzzy. Further than that, she couldn't make out anything. Her vision was good enough for her to travel by night if she wished—or detect an attack before it came.

What do you think happened here? Conflict with another clan?

"According to the information the Reconers brought back, Setisians rarely engage in violence."

Rarely doesn't mean never.

"True. Maybe this clan listened to what Emmanuel had to say about the Light of the Created God, even adopted the religion, and another clan—one devoted to the Great Mother—wasn't happy about it. But then again, the Great Mother is supposed to be a peaceful god."

Any god—and its worshippers—can become wrathful if the circumstances are right.

One of the most difficult parts of working for the Immaculance was traveling to planets experiencing religious conflicts and trying to help resolve them before they became deadly. Ruth had been mostly successful in this regard, but not always. She'd witnessed violence and death in her work before, but she hadn't gotten used to it. She hoped she never did. She wasn't sure she believed in a soul, but if she had one, she would know she'd lost it the day seeing a dead body meant nothing to her.

None of the dead Setisians were Emmanuel. She was too new to the Setisian form to distinguish between individuals easily, but Shepherd didn't have that problem. He'd viewed the holo Mofra had shown Ruth through his host's eyes, and he knew exactly what Emmanuel's new skin looked like, down to the last pore on his face.

"Do you think Emmanuel escaped during the battle? Or left before it even happened?"

If he did, he didn't return to the Lander. There would've been a record of his departure.

"There's no guarantee he's still alive. He could've been chased by whoever murdered the villagers and killed when they caught up to him."

True. But we're still going to look for him, aren't we?

Emmanuel might be guilty of unsanctioned proselytizing, but he was still Ruth's friend. Besides, they needed to find out what damage his interference had done to the Setisian culture and, if possible, repair it. If he was alive, the question was how to find him.

Follow your nose.

At first she thought Shepherd was joking, but then she realized what he was really saying.

The blood scent…The villagers had been killed recently, and given the level of violence done to the victims, their murderers had surely gotten blood on them during the attack.

"I'm not sure even a Setisian nose is good enough to track the scent."

Maybe not. But remember, I have access to your olfactory sense too, and unlike you, I'm capable of analyzing anything you inhale down to the molecular level.

"Then what are we waiting for? Point me in a direction."

Ruth moved at the plodding jog that was the Setisian equivalent of running. After a time, she began to grow fatigued, but rather than rest, she drank some water from the gourd in her travel pouch and ate a *qafan* wafer. As Shepherd had promised, it was delicious, and she ate two more. After that, she felt energized, and she picked up speed as she proceeded onward. Aside from Shepherd, her only companions were the alien stars above, along with the wind, and the strange keening it carried once more. The eerie sound held more sorrow this time, and Ruth thought that if she'd possessed a human body right now, she might cry.

"Do you hear that?"

Hear what?

"That sound drifting on the wind. Could it be an animal of some sort, like a wolf howling at the moon?"

Setis has no moons. No wolves, either.

"Don't be a glap. You know what I mean."

Yes, I hear it. There's no mention of such a sound in the current data we have on Setis.

Ruth continued jogging, elephantine feet pounding the hard ground, listening to the keening grow louder or softer, depending on the strength of the wind that bore it. She saw few animals as she traveled, mostly small creatures with thick bodies, low to the ground due to the planet's heavy gravity. She did pass three larger things that looked something like rhinos, only with six legs instead of four, their bodies covered with sharp, bony spikes. The beasts looked dangerous as hell, but they were busy nibbling on one of the large silk trees, and paid no attention to her. It seemed the trees provided nutrition as well as building materials. No wonder the Setisians called them gifts.

She jog-ran for nearly an hour when a village came into view at last. She slowed to a walk and approached cautiously. Thankfully, she didn't need to speak aloud to communicate with Shepherd.

The blood trail leads here? she asked.

Yes.

This village contained the same wooden domed structures as the previous one, also arranged in a circular pattern. It looked like there were more domes here than in the Plains Clan village, although perhaps not many more. Setisians were diurnal. A day on their world was the equivalent of thirty-two hours galactic standard, and they were most active around sunrise and sundown, sleeping the rest of the time. The killers who had slaughtered the smaller village's inhabitants had done so not long after one of their daily sleeping periods. This meant they would most likely still be awake. Just because she currently wore a Setisian skin didn't mean she'd be automatically welcomed by these villagers, and she already knew they were killers. She'd have to be careful.

She approached the village slowly, and as she drew closer, she became aware of voices speaking softly, and saw a dim light glowing in the center of the settlement. Silhouettes were gathered around the glow, dozens of them. Setisians. She didn't know what they were doing, but whatever their attention was focused on, she was glad for it. It would make approaching undetected easier.

We've got company, Shepherd said. *Close. I can smell them.*

She tried to run, but her current skin wasn't built for speed, and she hadn't inhabited it long enough to master its movements. She heard the footfalls of pursuers, and then felt something sharp poke her between the shoulder blades, hard enough to sting, but not so hard as to injure her. She stopped.

She felt a second poke, this one on her right shoulder blade. A second spear meant a second spear holder. One of the Setisians reached forward and removed her own spear from her hand, disarming her.

What's the Setisian equivalent of holding your hands up? she asked Shepherd.

Keep them pressed against your sides, hands gripping your legs. I'd advise doing it now, and fast.

Ruth did so.

Both spear tips prodded her again, and the message was clear: Start walking.

Ruth continued toward the village, her escorts close behind, spearpoints pressed tight against her back. When they reached the village's common area, she saw Setisians, children and adults alike, sitting around a small dome that looked like a miniature version of one of their houses. It was glowing with a gentle light, the Setisian version of a campfire, Ruth guessed. The fronts of the villagers' tunics displayed a circular mark.

Rock Clan, Shepherd said.

The villagers stood as she approached, and they parted to allow her to be escorted to the glowing dome. One of the Setisians closest to the dome wore a tunic with no clan mark on it, just like hers. When she reached this person, she stopped, and said, "Emmanuel?" Her new mouth could only approximate the syllables, but they were recognizable enough.

"Ruth? Is that you?"

Emmanuel stepped forward and put one hand on her shoulder while raising his other high to get the villagers' attention.

"This is a good friend of mine from my village! Please make them welcome!"

The villagers made loud hooting sounds, a Setisian sign of greeting. Ruth's escorts lowered their spears and added their hoots to the rest.

Ruth looked around. Aside from the two Setisians who'd brought her here, no one was armed, and while the blood smell hung in the air, it was so faint as to be almost unnoticeable. She turned to face Emmanuel.

"What are you doing here?" she asked.

"Spreading the good news about the Light of the Created God, of course. The Setisians have been very open to learning about the religion." He leaned forward and spoke softly so only she could hear. "They have no concept of lying, so they automatically believe whatever they're told. When they heard that the Created God is the ultimate expression of the divine, they decided it must be more powerful than the Great Mother, and they abandoned their worship of her. Honestly, I was surprised at how fast it happened."

He pulled away from her and raised both hands this time. The villagers raised their hands in response.

"Praise the Created God!" he shouted.

"Praise the Created God!" the villagers echoed.

Emmanuel lowered his arms, and Ruth stepped forward, gripped his hands, and turned him to face her.

"I stopped at the Plains Clan village. I saw what these people did there. How could you let them?"

Emmanuel's eyes closed for a moment and then reopened, a nonverbal sign of confusion for Setisians.

"I don't understand. I spent a couple months with the Plains folk. They fully converted to the Light within two weeks, but they didn't want me to leave. They regarded me as the voice of the Light and wanted me to remain and continue to speak its holy words. Setisians are a peaceful people overall, but the villagers were extremely insistent. I tried escaping one night, but they sent out hunters to bring me back. I was their prisoner. The Rock Clan found out about me somehow, probably during a trading session between villages. The Rock Clan decided they wanted to learn about the Light too, so earlier today they sent a party to the Plains people to politely request that I be allowed to visit their village. When the Plains Clan refused, things got a little out of hand. But the Rock Clan freed me and brought me here. I told them I'd be happy to tell them about the Created God, but only if they promised to allow me to leave when I was finished so I could travel to other villages and continue spreading the word. They agreed, and since Setisians literally don't understand what a lie is, I believed them."

Ruth was horrified by the casual, almost eager way that Emmanuel spoke.

"You have to stop this."

"I know the Immaculance forbids unauthorized proselytizing, but I truly believe—"

"I don't care about that," Ruth interrupted. "I'm talking about what these people did to the Plains Clan!"

"I don't know what you mean. Yes, the Plains folk and the Rock folk argued about my leaving, and at one point the discussion devolved into a shoving match, but that's as bad as it got. In the end, the Plains Clan released me, especially after I promised to return one day."

Now it was Ruth's turn to be confused.

"When I reached the Plains village, everyone was dead, killed by multiple spear thrusts. It was horrible."

"That's impossible! They were all fine when I left with the Rock people. Besides, Setisians don't harm one another. It's simply not in their nature."

"They carry weapons," Ruth pointed out.

"For protection against predators. They're vegetarians. Their main diet is the silk from the ss'tarran trees. They use the trees for everything—clothing, building materials, food...The frapping things grow everywhere. The Setisians have nothing to fight over. They live in a world of plenty."

Was Emmanuel lying? Ruth didn't think so. But if he was telling the truth, then something was wrong on this world. Very wrong.

The wind picked up then, and the keening sound she'd grown so familiar with filled the air. The villagers heard it as well, and they looked around for its source, confused and afraid.

"I keep hearing that sound," Ruth said. "What is it?"

"I don't know. I've never heard it before." Emmanuel seemed puzzled, but not fearful. "It's odd."

Ruth decided to ignore the sound and continued speaking.

"My paraclete and I followed a blood scent trail here. Whoever killed the Plains villagers came to this place."

Near this place, Shepherd corrected. *That's why the scent is so weak here.*

The keening grew louder then, increasing in volume until it felt like white-hot iron spikes were being driven into Ruth's ears. The Rock villagers huddled together, hands over their ears too, their breathing harsh and ragged, a Setisian indication of sheer terror.

Something's coming, Shepherd said.

A large spherical shape emerged from the night, two, maybe three times the size of one of the villagers' domes. It rolled toward the village center, a strange conglomeration of brown and white. Ruth had no idea what it could be, but Shepherd did.

It's ss'tarran trees, hundreds of them, clustered together, merged into a combined form.

The keening became even louder then, and Ruth realized the sound emanated from the trees. A strong blood scent wafted off the creature as well, and Ruth knew she was looking at the killer of the Plains villagers. The creature's keening was filled with sorrow and fury, and it almost seemed to form words, but she couldn't quite...

I can translate, Shepherd said. *"Since the day your kind first crawled upon the surface of this planet, I gave you everything! Food, shelter, tools...And the moment you hear a story told by an offworlder, you turn your backs on me! Faithless! Faithless!"*

Ruth understood then what this creature was: the Great Mother, or at least a manifestation of her. The Setisian god was real, and she was *pissed.*

Wooden tendrils extruded from the creature's main mass, dozens of them, and shot toward the terrified villagers. The Setisians tried to flee, but the tendrils—which ended in very sharp tips—shot toward them, piercing their bodies multiple times, as if the Great Mother didn't merely want to kill them, but punish them as well. The screams of the dying filled the night air, and Ruth could only stand and watch, stunned, Emmanuel by her side, her friend looking on in horror as one Setisian after another fell dead and bloody to the ground. And as the slaughter continued, the Great Mother repeatedly shrieked, *"Faithless! Faithless!"*

I believe the Great Mother killed the Plains Clan after Emmanuel left their village, Shepherd said, then she followed him here. She waited close by, and when it became clear these villagers would forsake her like the others, she attacked.

Why hadn't the Mother attacked the Plains villagers earlier? Ruth wondered. Had she waited, hoping her children would come back to her, until she eventually realized the Created God's hold on them was too strong? Maybe.

Most of the Rock Clan were dead now. Emmanuel tore his gaze away from the Great Mother and looked at Ruth.

"We have to get out of here!" he said.

"Are you kidding? With these skins, there's no way we can outrun that thing."

Emmanuel didn't listen to her. He turned and began the plodding jog that was the swiftest gait the Setisian form was capable of, heading away from the village. The Great Mother finished killing the last Clan member, and then rolled after Emmanuel.

"False prophet!" she screamed, then shot a tendril toward him. It struck him in the back of the head and emerged from his mouth, slathered with blood, brain, and bone fragments. The Mother withdrew the tendril with a vicious yank, and Emmanuel's lifeless body fell to the ground.

Only Ruth remained alive.

The sphere of wood and silk that was the Great Mother rolled toward her, tendrils lashing the air in fury.

"It's been a good run, hasn't it?" Ruth said.

The best, Shepherd replied.

They waited for the tendril strike that would end their lives, but it didn't come. The Great Mother remained motionless several meters away from Ruth, her tendrils now undulating slowly, almost as if she were thinking.

"You are not one of my children," she said.

"No. But I respect your power, and I acknowledge your dominion over this world."

And then, not knowing what else to do, Ruth knelt.

Long moments passed, during which the Great Mother was silent. Finally, she said, *"Rise."*

Ruth did so.

"I can see in your mind who and what you truly are. I can also see that you wish

me and my children no harm. You may go, but tell your people that this world is off limits to them, and that if they come here, I will not deal with them as mercifully as I have with you."

The Great Mother rolled away from the village then, keening softly, tone lower now, suffused with a soul-deep sorrow. Ruth stood and watched the god leave until she was finally lost to sight.

She walked over to Emmanuel's body, knelt, touched her fingers to his cheek.

"You idiot."

She sighed, stood, and started walking in the direction of the Lander.

After a time, Shepherd spoke.

What are you going to tell the Proctors?

She thought for a moment before replying.

"I'll give them the Mother's warning, of course, and hope The Merge heeds it. I think they will. I'll also tell them to never forget the first Judeo-Christian commandment: Thou shalt have no other gods before me."

Praise the Great Mother, Shepherd said.

"Praise her," Ruth agreed, and continued walking.

GHOST IN THE MACHINE

Carter Wilson

ADARA, 493 HD

SEE MYSELF FOR THE FIRST TIME.

I've never been beautiful before.

Not like this.

I turn to find Leer, ask what he thinks of my vacation skin. But my husband is on the other side of the store, assuming his own new identity.

The small turn of my head is enough to make me dizzy, unstable. I feel my new legs threatening to give out, their muscles not yet used to the commands from my brain.

A hand grasps my elbow, steadying me.

"First jump." The voice is masculinity dipped in the finest chocolate. "You can read up all you want about the aftereffects, but it takes the experience to really understand it."

I look in the mirror, finding the man standing behind me. He's not a disoriented tourist like me. Too formal. Too...in command.

"I suppose that is the essence of all life," he continues. The man drops his hand and I regain my footing. "Life is experience. And that, Vallen, is why you're on Adara."

I start to ask him how he knows my name, but then it clicks.

Of course he knows my name.

"You're Baanam."

He smiles without showing teeth. "At your service."

Every visitor to Adara is given their own personal concierge, and my in-laws insisted upon Baanam, who'd come highly recommended. I didn't argue; I surely had no other suggestions. Besides, Leer's parents funded our jumps and the entire honeymoon to Adara. A small fortune, though hardly a dent in their much larger one.

I shift my gaze in the mirror from him to me, then tug lightly at the amber hair that spills to my waist. "I've never had long hair before."

"I see you've chosen the model Fiety. Do you like her?"

"I didn't choose this skin, and I don't know yet."

"You can cut the hair, you know," he says. "You can have a day of beauty treatments. Change your hair, style it. Get a massage. The skin is yours to do with whatever you wish."

A day of beauty treatments doesn't interest me. I'm looking for adventure.

I keep staring at myself. Big lips, tiny waist, and neither close to my actual proportions.

"I don't know," I say. "It just isn't me."

A stupid thing to say. Of course it isn't me. No skin is. But he doesn't point this out.

"Of course," he adds, "how your model appears isn't the only consideration. Residue is also important."

Residue. I know what he's referring to but don't stop him as he explains.

"The emotional traces of previous renters transfer to every skin," he says. "These traces accumulate over time and, if they become strong enough, can alter one's adventure. Some vacationers report diminished inhibitions. Augmented susceptibility to suggestion. So it can often be how a skin *feels* more than it looks that drives the user experience."

"I don't feel anything," I say.

Baanam nods. "Also quite common. You're welcome to find another model. In my experience, a skin chooses a person, rather than the other way around."

I'm in the flagship store for Embodiment. While they have skin-rental stores across multiple galaxies, their first and largest shop is here, on Adara. Yet another fact I learned in preparing for the first trip I've ever taken outside of my home world of Shanti.

I'm expecting to browse the same digital catalog of skins I perused earlier, but Baanam takes me to a room displaying holograms of the rentals themselves. Hundreds of female skins, macabrely displayed like the trophies of a prolific serial killer. They're just projected images, but I feel like I can smell them. The aroma of hundreds of thousands of moments lived.

"I know," Baanam says, as if reading my mind. "It's a bit jarring. But I find it's a better way to connect directly with the body you're about to inhabit." He crosses his arms. "Yours is a very expensive vacation; you don't want to spend it being someone you're not."

I almost laugh, tell him that's exactly the point of skins. Almost tell him how Leer chose my original skin because it was the most sexually attractive one he could find.

But I say nothing.

Instead, I browse.

Rows and rows. The lifeless eyes are the only commonality. A hundred different skin colors. Hair of all styles. Body composition ranging from soft to warrior.

Who do I want to be?

I could be a vapid party girl. A corporate executive. A feral she-creature, all sex and sinew. A bodybuilder. An ancient queen. A submissive waif. And, ugh, even a schoolgirl on a fieldtrip.

I look for what seems like forever when I realize I'm wrong. There's another commonality.

These skins. They're all beautiful.

All different. But all an expression of the female form that is at least thirty percent deviated from the standard.

These aren't skins, I think. They're dolls.

Dolls to be played with.

"I don't know," I mumble.

"Take your time," Baanam says.

So I keep looking, feeling more depressed about my born skin as I continue. And that's not how one's honeymoon should begin.

The last row in the room has skins several layers deep, as if the hidden ones are last helica's models and don't deserve space on the showroom floor. But I start working my way down the row, pushing past each empty shell.

"I wouldn't bother back there," Baanam says. "Those are...the cheaper rentals. Your package comes with a platinum-level skin."

I almost listen to him. I almost stop continuing down this row. But then. There.

That one.

A skin chooses a person, rather than the other way around.

Her.

She's not beautiful.

Not ugly, either. But not like the others.

Very plain. Short black hair. Eyes just as dark, and set, perhaps, a bit too far apart. Skin the color of fish belly, which would certainly burn under the rays of Adara's two suns.

Arms lean and muscular, almost masculine.

I look at the model name, digitally displayed on the left foot.

Lu-chek.

"Hello, Lu-chek," I say.

The skin says nothing, but there's an energy here.

"You can step into her." Baanam's voice is hardly a whisper, his mouth at the back of my neck. "Give her a try."

I don't turn to acknowledge him. I did exactly as he suggests, and walk into the hologram before me, inhabiting this massless form. As I do, Banaam summons a mirror from the ceiling, which drops and positions itself perfectly before me. I see myself in this light. Myself as Lu-chek.

And that's when I realize something about her.

She's fierce.

As if she's been coiled for a millennium and is just waiting for the perfect moment to strike.

Vallen is not fierce.

Lu-chek most certainly is.

And this, I have since come to realize, is why she chose me.

"The drek?"

I'm in my skin, feeling wholly different than in my last one, when Leer finds me.

"That's not the one I chose," he says.

"No, I decided...to go in a different direction."

Already this skin feels more commanding than the last. Lu-chek swallows me like a snake feasting on a rat, but there is more a sense of comfort than horror. As if I've been waiting all my life to be eaten alive.

Baanam steps in, introduces himself, but Leer is too distracted to make conversation. My husband leans into my ear and says, "It's just that, *you know,* babe. I thought we'd do something sexier. While we're here we can be anyone we want. I mean, that's what I did for you. Just look at me. Think of the hot role-play stuff we can do."

I pull away and look at him. He's chosen the skin of a hunter, a human male familiar with tracking, stalking, and killing big game. His skin is telling; we are here on our honeymoon, but Leer has come here to hunt the beautiful, exotic, and very dangerous native wildlife of Adara. Of all the ways to experience nature, his choice is the most barbaric.

"I had nothing to do with your choice of skin," I tell him. "You never even asked."

Baanam glides in-between the two of us, puts his hands together in the sign of a prayer, offers the gentlest of smiles. "I would suggest," he says, "to give your new bodies a day before deciding on anything else. There is an adjustment period, there always is. You'll have much more...*clarity* about how you feel in the morning."

Leer seems uncertain, but at least it now looks attractive on him. "I guess," he mumbles.

I have no such uncertainty. Every passing second feels more like the *me* I was meant to be my whole life. And with Leer looking the way he now does, I wish we could move to Adara and stay like this forever. Living an endless fantasy is far better than suffering through one's actual banality.

"Yes," I whisper.

"Fine, fine," Baanam says. "Please, allow me to escort you to your accommodations, and we'll finalize the details of your week's itinerary."

We leave Embodiment and walk into the intense sunshine of Adara, yet the heat has little effect on me. Maybe my new body is impervious to my normal levels of sensation, and I almost ask Baanam this very thing, then hold back my question, not really wanting to know the answer. Wanting to just feel for myself.

The transport isn't long, but enough for me to soak in the dizzying beauty of this world. All the research doesn't account for the sense of angles and textures, I realize. The sharp cliffs. The soft edges of the thousand-foot waterfalls. The curves of the ink-black mountains, the complex tapestry of the jungle canopy. The air is heavy, the final drops from a vintage wine. And the sound. A symphony of wind and animal calls, as if one doesn't exist without the other, both in harmony together, neither to be ignored.

It's no wonder Adara consistently ranks at the top of all vacation-destination lists. No wonder it can cost a generation of savings for a one-week visit. No wonder this is the playground of the elite, and that the exorbitant cost not only guarantees unimaginable adventures, but also the discretion those adventures demand.

No one ever really knows what comes to pass on Adara. And perhaps that's its greatest appeal of all.

Leer wants to have sex, and the way he looks at me—even in his newly attractive form—feels like an arm-sized icicle piercing my intestines.

There's only been one other time, our wedding night three days ago. While it wasn't awful, the experience left me a bit less of who I am. How many times will we do this before I'm whittled down to nothingness?

Ours was an arranged marriage, as all are on Shanti. Acquisitions and disputes between corporations are settled through betrothal, and, like all Shanti women, I was raised being told I would one day become an important asset to my father's business. And so when Leer's family's communications empire acquired my father's moderate fusion business, the deal was consummated with our wedding.

Unless the company goes bankrupt or other tragedy strikes, this is the man I will be with for the rest of my life.

"Gonna be the greatest vacation ever," he says, shedding his clothes to the floor. He approaches me, hardening as he does. "Though I liked your first skin better."

I don't reply. I'm still feeling unsteady, the jump leaving me with the perpetual sense of having just woken too soon from a delicious nap.

He grabs my shoulders, kisses me, and it's better than I expect. Maybe it's his skin, maybe it's the jump hangover, or maybe it's me. But it's better.

I kiss him back, and we continue for a moment, standing, locked, and while it's not quite passionate, it's not the awkward chess match of our first union.

I push him away with only my fingertips. Go to the bathroom. Strip. Catch myself in the mirror.

No.

Not myself.

Lu-chek.

I breathe myself in, feeling both woozy and preternaturally strong at the same moment, and what an odd feeling that is.

And then I notice the marks for the first time. Faint, but they're there.

I walk up to the glass, lean in.

Sure enough, faded lines along my chest. Little white stripes—somehow even lighter than my skin—from my nipples to my shoulders. They look...

I bend closer.

They look like claw marks.

Why would the skin be designed with these marks?

"Defensive wounds," I say, surprising myself. I wasn't thinking that at all. The words just came out.

"What's that, babe?"

"Nothing," I call out.

I turn and leave the bathroom, find him in bed.

Leer pounces, climbs on top of me.

"No," I tell him. And suddenly the voice is hardly mine. He doesn't notice, but I do. "Not like that."

And then I place him on his back and mount him instead. He reaches up and grabs my breasts, but the moment he does he yanks his hands back away.

"The hell are these scars?" He lifts his head and peers at my claw marks. "The skin came like that? Drekking gross."

"It's okay," I tell him, meaning it. "I think they're supposed to be there. They're part of Lu-chek. I think she's a fighter." I lean over, kiss him, and slip him inside of me. "Or maybe she's a hunter, just like you."

His eyes narrow in temporary disappointment, but then soften as he slides deeper into me.

And then his eyes close altogether.

But not mine.

Mine remain open. And while the sensations are pleasant—almost enjoyable—there is something else.

There is blood.

Not on me.

Not on him.

But there, in front of my wide-open eyes, so real but clearly not.

Blood.

Ribbons of it. Splatters. Pools.

I've seen only the smallest amounts of real blood in my life. Minor scrapes and cuts.

But this?

This is enough blood to fill the nightmares of a thousand children.

I gasp at the vision and Leer must think he's satisfying me, for he offers a crooked smile and a conspiratorial wink, followed by harder thrusts.

I shut my eyes and the vision washes away. But when I reopen them the blood returns. Brilliant red, as if the most important color ever devised.

And then I realize this:

It's beautiful.

In that moment I climax, hard and fast. And as I do, the blood vanishes, evaporating back to the imaginary realm from whence it came.

There's no sleep.

I stand out on the balcony, breathe in the Adarian night, while Leer snores inside the adjacent bedroom. I've been here for hours, waiting for my visions to return, but they don't. I begin to doubt my own memory.

But the scars.

They *are* real.

I touch my chest again, feel the slight raises in the skin, the hardened tissue. Trace the lines, back and forth, the rhythm of my fingers almost hypnotic.

A howl in the distance.

Could be just below. Could be kilometers away.

But the creatures. These wondrous creatures.

They're out there.

And tomorrow, Leer will hunt them.

I haven't seen the animals since I've been here, but Leer and I viewed them in an advertising holo before our trip. It's what triggered his insistence on hunting during our honeymoon.

Beautiful, vicious dog-like animals.

Another howl, and how lonely it sounds. Like a warning cry delivered too late.

I return to bed, close my eyes. Sleep tugs, but leaves me restless for what seems like days.

When it does come, I dream of those wild animals.

Their eyes, mostly. Fierce and bright, yellow with a thousand flakes of reflective gold, wide and alive. Alive in the way that suggests death is nearby, close and cloaked, a permanent shadow.

And these eyes?

They're hungry.

So very, very hungry.

Baanam greets us in the lobby, smartly dressed and somehow even more tan than yesterday. He smiles as we approach.

"Are you ready for an eventful day?" he asks.

Leer pushes past. "Goddamn right," he says. "I can't wait."

The expression on Baanam's face doesn't change—his smile carved in rock—but I can see it in his eyes. Leer is nothing more than a disgusting tourist to him at best, a barbarian at worst.

On our home planet there is no violence. Accidents are rare, violent crime culturally erased, and hunting of anything punishable by permanent exile. And so Leer wants to spend his time on Adara killing things. Because he wants to, and because he can.

"You will be out hunting until, oh, around the first sunset," Baanam says.

"*You're* not taking me, are you?" Leer asks, his face barely concealing his opinion on the matter.

"Oh, my, no. I'm not qualified. The game here...well, they can be quite dangerous. You wouldn't want me in charge. Your guide will be here at any moment."

I look over at my husband, picturing him being torn about by Adarian wildlife. In my imagining the animals don't end him instantly. One holds him down by the throat, while others work their way up, bit by bit. Starting with the feet.

I turn to Baanam. "May I ask, are you native to Adara?"

"I am indeed."

"Tell me then, how do you feel about tourists coming here and hunting the wildlife for sport?"

My question creates a current of energy in the space around us, which, of course, was my intention. I can feel Leer's gaze on the back of my neck.

Baanam answers with a mixture of diplomacy, mystery, and threat.

"I have come to learn that nature has a way of calibrating life and death in an elegant way."

I smile and nod before a spell of dizziness washes over me.

"Are you all right, Vallen?"

I steady myself. "I think...still finding my legs after the jump."

"Yes, that's not uncommon." He reaches out and touches my shoulder, a comforting, paternal gesture. "I've had some guests spend their entire stay adjusting, just to have to jump again back home. But I think you'll be fine. Maybe take it a bit easy today."

"That's my plan," I say. "I'll be staying at the resort." My adventures can wait.

His hand remains on my shoulder a moment longer, his eyes searching mine. Searching for...something. The truth, perhaps. The knowledge that I'm unsteady not because of the jump, but because of Lu-chek. That she's more than a skin. That she's my own hunting guide.

Leer's guide arrives, gristle and muscle. Even in his new skin my husband looks like a sheep next to him.

Leer turns to me and leans in for a kiss goodbye.

"You've never killed anything before," I say.

His eyes widen in excitement. "I know."

"How do you know it's really what you want?"

I expect him to give me a throwaway response, but he considers my question for a moment and says, "I'm not sure. I won't lie—I'm worried this could haunt me for a long time. But in terms of knowing if it's what I want...I guess...I guess all I can say it's more believing than knowing. Does that make sense?"

I shake my head.

"No."

In my mind:

Yes.

As the hours pass, I become more steady with Lu-chek, my feet more certain with the ground. Baanam provided me a number of suggestions for resort-based activities, mostly revolving about eating, drinking, and relaxing. And I do all of those things, but find enjoyment in few. As the afternoon draws long, I can't help escape the feeling that my skin is not a *relaxing* type of girl.

I need to release some of this energy. For even though the visions haven't returned, there's still a darkness I cannot shake. Cannot walk away from. Cannot relax myself out of. A menacing cloud that loiters, threatening violent rain.

And how I love rain.

The resort gym is a masterpiece of space and machinery. Hundreds of pieces of equipment, many of which I've never seen before.

I choose the familiar: the ped-sphere.

I enter the sphere, set the level to my usual pace, begin running. But within seconds I realize it's too easy. I dial it up, twenty percent above my standard.

It's like I'm walking.

Crank it up more, to the level I sometimes finish at when I'm chasing sheer exhaustion. But now I'm hardly breaking a sweat.

So I turn it up all the way. To a number I've never gotten close to. And I think this machine could spin me right off the face of this planet—and perhaps that would be just fine—but I manage three straight minutes before I choose to stop it. My mind tells me I could have kept going, but I don't want to give my new body a heart attack.

There's a woman in a wheel next to mine, ending her routine at the same time. She's beautiful, but in the male-manufactured way my initial skin was.

"Damn, girl," she tells me. "Your skin must be one hell of an athlete. That was impressive."

"Thanks," I say. I look down at my arms. Typically I'd be pouring sweat, but there's only a light glaze.

"You went for the basic model, huh?"

"Excuse me?"

"No offense," she says. "Just most people vacationing here pay to look like gods, not like…" She eyes me up and down. "That." Then the woman takes a step forward, reaches out, and touches one of the scars on my chest.

Her touch is electric and shocks me similarly. A stranger causally touching me is something I'm not used to, though perhaps wherever she's from it's a commonplace event. My instinct is to be offended, defiant. To tell her to respect my physical space. But the mere presence of her fingertips on my scars makes me feel something altogether different: desirous.

Not in a sexual way.

More of a predatory one.

"Did it come like that? You should take it back. That's bullshit."

"It's okay," I say, taking a moment to regain my composure. "I like it like this."

She smiles, then laughs. "Well, I hope you got a good deal on it. Or maybe you have some kind of sweet residue."

Residue.

Lu-chek definitely has residue.

The woman takes a sip from a hydration flask and continues. "Hell, honey, I'm convinced the last person who rented this skin was a nymphomaniac, because I just can't get enough of it since I've been here." She shrugs her shoulders. "The drinks could be part of it too, I suppose. Oh, well. Maybe I'll see you around."

"Maybe," I say.

Leer returns from his first day of hunting a few hours later, when I'm freshly showered and reading in our room. Night will be here soon and I'm growing hungry.

He enters the room, a layer of grime on his face and sweat rings on his clothing. I ask him about his experience but he doesn't want to talk. He grabs me and puts me on the bed, his strength jarring.

I start to protest and then stop myself when I realize that's Vallen's reaction. But not Lu-chek.

Lu-chek desires Leer. Or, rather, desires the experience she had yesterday.

We're naked in seconds.

The visions of blood return the moment he's inside me. Dizzying, beautiful, and this time accompanied by ribbons of torn flesh, which are as enticing as icing finger-scooped from the most delicate and delicious of cakes.

When I climax my mouth finds his shoulder, my teeth sinking with ravenous desire into his hunter-warrior skin.

"Ow, what the hell?" He pushes me aside.

I look and a single drop of blood flows from his shoulder. I nearly cry at the sight of it. Not from remorse, but because it's like realizing gods exist for the first time.

Blood.

I've never seen his blood before. Even though it flows from Leer's new skin and not Leer himself, it's everything I'd hoped it would be.

I force myself to look down at his chest but reach up and run my nails lightly along the side of his neck.

"Tell me about the hunt," I purr.

He's silent for a moment. "I don't think I can describe it. At least not in a way you would understand. But...I don't know. It's like I was someone different for my entire life until today."

"You're right," I say. "I don't understand."

And yet I do.

I'm myself for the very first time.

Pure.

Untainted.

Distilled to its essence.

This cycle repeats for three days.

Leer hunts.

Baanam books me adventures, physical challenges, extreme sports, all of which I devour.

Each day, when Leer returns, we ravish each other.

Each time, my visions appear, and my appetite steadily grows for more of my husband's blood. But I refrain from drawing more of it, not even a nibble.

I sense taking a few drops of blood won't be enough to satisfy me.

Yet I fear that, at some point, I won't be able to resist taking it all.

On our final day, Leer hunts once again, while despair over returning to my home world consumes me. The thought of shedding Lu-chek and reinhabiting

Vallen has the appeal of drinking poison.

I am not satisfied.

Leer has killed dozens of creatures here.

And I?

Not even one.

My mood has grown sour.

Even the myriad of activities I'm thankful to be experiencing on my own cause me irritation. This is no longer a honeymoon, but a prison sentence. Maybe it always was.

While Leer kills, I feel the need to move, so I hike a protected path around the resort. An electrified fence separates the property from the wild beasts, and I'm not certain who benefits most from the protection, them or us.

I perk my ears, waiting for howling. But there is none.

That only comes at night.

I am alone, and a short time into my walk I spy someone trekking the opposite direction, headed for me. Baanam.

When our paths cross, he speaks first.

"I walk this perimeter every day. It soothes me. If you're lucky, you'll spot a Sibbhu."

Those are the dog-like creatures Leer's been killing. Twice my size with three rows of teeth. It must be sublime to hunt in a pack with them.

"I haven't seen anything."

He tilts his head, considers me, and again reaches his hand for my shoulder, as he did on my first day here.

"I hope this isn't out of place to say, but you seem troubled."

Troubled is exactly the right word. Leer would never have picked up on my mood so quickly, and the fact Baanam does only increases a growing attraction I've been feeling for him. In a distant part of my brain, I wonder what my life would be like here, on Adara, with Baanam as my partner rather than Leer. *Serene*, I think, unsure why that particular word appears first.

I push the fantasy away before I explore it further.

"It's not exactly the vacation I expected."

"Oh, my," he says. "I'm very sorry to hear that. Please...what can I do to assist? Reviews are very important to us."

Vallen would have assured him everything will be fine. Vallen wouldn't have brought the subject up in the first place.

But Lu-chek says, "I'm having visions."

He lowers his hand. "What kind of visions?"

I don't hesitate.

"Ones most would call disturbing. But I consider them...lacking."

A flicker of recognition in his eyes. Then a sigh, and a slightly lowering of his head. "I see."

"Tell me," I say. "Have you seen me before? Seen this skin?"

He nods, and there's a thousand stories in that soft gesture. "I have."

"And how did they behave? These previous renters?"

"Vallen, I'm sure you can appreciate the confidentiality we ascribe all of our guests. Including you, of course."

I turn my head, look at the electrified fence, wondering how much pain there would be in running full speed into it. Much, I think. But not for long. "I think there's residue from the skin."

"Ah, yes. *Residue*. The ghost in the machine."

"It's dark," I say. "Making me consider things I shouldn't be considering."

I expect him to ask me what things? Or to take me to Embodiment and swap out my rental, even though it's my last day here.

Instead, he says this:

"Skins are vessels, Vallen. And, yes, residue is a real thing, and it can serve to influence. But, like an intoxicant, it doesn't change the nature of who you are, but rather strips away layers of pretense. Erodes defense mechanisms." He holds eye contact like gods shoulder worlds. "A skin would never make you do something your essence would tell you is wrong."

I hold his gaze, relishing its weight. "If every renter of this skin before me committed a crime, would I not follow the same path? Would the residue not exude an inescapable path for me to have to take?"

And there it is. The slightest of grins.

"It would never make you stray from the path you were always on. It just gives you permission to continue your journey."

Permission.

That mighty word.

I think that's what he's just given me.

"You know how to reach me if you need me," he says. "Anything I can do to help secure that favorable review."

And then he walks on, his own path swallowing him around a gently arcing bend minutes later.

The evening, our very last, during our passion, I look down at my husband's face and see him in an entirely different way.

He is no longer Leer, the hunter.

No.

He is prey.

I can almost see his eyes change from their satin black into orbs fierce and bright, yellow with a thousand flakes of reflective gold, wide and alive. Alive in the way that suggests death is nearby, close and cloaked, a permanent shadow.

And it's in this very moment I come to understand who Lu-chek truly is. Not a monster, a devourer of blood.

In a way, she is like those animals that roam these lands. Beautiful and vicious. A wondrous creature of Adara, who just wants to be left alone. But she will fight to protect her homeland, and now Leer must pay for all the Adarian lives he's taken.

And I, Vallen, must have known this all along. For why else would I have placed Leer's serrated hunting blade beneath the pillow next to his head?

He closes his eyes, a pleasured smile on his face. When he does, I reach for the knife.

The anticipation alone causes me to climax.

And when I slash his throat, the swirling, roiling blend of horror and satisfaction is beyond my imagination.

There is a moment after I've brought the blade from his neck to his chest, as blood sprays like a beautiful summer rain onto my face, that my husband reaches up and claws at my chest, his nails digging into the ridges of Lu-chek's existing scars, bringing forth blood of our own, and I picture all her killings before this one, the scars on her chest formed like canyons by rivers, a measure of time, patience, and violent repetition. Victim after victim after victim.

Were I truly a Sibbhu, those beautiful hounds Leer slaughtered by the dozen, I would hold him down by the throat and work the knife up slowly, starting with the feet.

Instead, I plunge the blade down seventeen more times.

As he bleeds out on the bed beneath me, as his thrashes become twitches and the twitches succumb to stillness, as his naked body renders him as vulnerable as the day he was born, I wonder if he saw during his hunts what I now behold.

This...*completion.*

Perhaps.

After all, he returned to the hunt every day.

And I wonder:

Will I?

I ease off his corpse, which is slick and hot. Walk to the bathroom and slide into a bathrobe, not bothering to clean the evidence of my husband's existence from me. Not yet.

Back in the bedroom I summon Baanam, telling him I need assistance in my room. He promises to come right away, and, being the consummate hospitality professional he is, I wait only a few minutes before he's knocking at my door.

His eyes betray surprise at the sight of me, but only for a moment. When he walks in and see what remains of Leer, it seems to me he was expecting this very scene.

"What do I do now?" I ask him.

His gaze scans the scene as he calculates. "You'll go back home tomorrow, as planned. This will be an unfortunate accident."

"Accident?"

Now he turns his attention to me. "Adara is an exotic, dangerous destination. More than once a guest has wandered beyond the resort perimeter at night, only to discover the native wildlife doing...well, what they do." He nods his head toward to the balcony, and into the night.

"Okay," I say.

"There will be a slight surcharge, of course."

Good thing I'm still on my in-laws' voucher credits.

"Of course."

Baanam takes a few steps toward me, but stops well out of arm's reach. No shoulder touch this time. "It seems you have found your essence, Vallen."

I shake my head. "I'm not Vallen anymore. I'm Lu-chek."

He sighs. "Lu-chek isn't real. Tomorrow you will return Lu-chek back to Embodiment, and then go home."

"What if that's not what I want?"

"I'm sorry," he says, "we are fully booked tomorrow. Unfortunately, you must check out."

He says this with such a distance I feel my heart break a little. Whatever simmering childish fantasy I had about Baanam evaporates with his last words to me, but they also serve to sober my mind. Ours is a transactional relationship, as are the thousands he has with all the other guests. Once I leave this resort, I become just another rating.

I return to the bathroom, shut the door, leave Baanam to his work.

I undo the belt of my robe and ease it from my skin, shedding it to the floor around my feet.

Baanam is right.

Lu-chek isn't real. She's only a skin, one that contains the residue of countless horrific acts, and now one more. A perpetual cycle of violence, an endless discovery of essence.

I am Vallen, seer of blood.

I consider myself in the bathroom mirror for an inestimable amount of time. Void of movement, bereft of ego.

Later, the howling begins. It almost sounds like laugher. Deep in the night, in this world where adventures require a fortune but self-actualization runs free, the animals consume the remains of my husband.

I look at myself one last time.

I look at myself for the first time.

I've never been beautiful before.

Not like this.

SUIGENERISCIDE

Alvaro Zinos-Amaro

LISTON, 493 HD

AS THE SHIP BEGAN ITS DESCENT towards the planet's surface, its lone pilot, Raestio, had a sudden change of heart.

Without hesitation he issued commands. His vessel, *Corvus*, was equally fast to respond.

"This new trajectory will consume eighty percent more of our engine's resources than anticipated," it informed him. "Additionally, our passage through turbulence will task our shields. Please confirm."

"Noted," Raestio said. "Heading change confirmed."

"Executing new approach vector," the ship said in its smooth, melodious voice.

At once Raestio felt the shift of forces as the vessel abandoned its orbital alignment, leaving behind what would have been an uneventful descent through bright, mid-afternoon skies. Now, engines dynamically engaged parallel to the rotating surface below, *Corvus* thrust toward the planet's night side.

"May I inquire as to the reason for this abrupt change?" *Corvus* asked. Raestio had been waiting for it; scans would have shown his accelerated heart rate and spiked glandular functions. He wasn't typically nervous when they approached a new planet, so of course the ship's ever-protective intelligence was inquisitive.

"Curious *Corvus*," Raestio mused.

"My understanding," the ship continued, "is that you were looking forward to the picturesque salt desert town of Astikia. Few outsiders are permitted to visit it. Now, however, we will be landing on the cliff-perched Aruhe, on a relatively small and secluded island."

"Your calculations are spot on," Raestio said.

"Do you wish to avoid the reception planned for you at Astikia? If so, might I suggest a simple cancellation message? No doubt the organizing committee will be disappointed."

"I don't really care about the reception one way or the other," Raestio said. Helicas earlier, when he was starting out as a performance artist, he would have killed for such acceptance and, yes, even adulation. But that had been a long time ago, and by jumping from skin to skin to skin to skin in the ensuing decades, in a way he already *had* killed, leaving little unquantifiable pieces of himself behind with each jump… "But yes, go ahead and send a message expressing my regrets at not being able to attend. We wouldn't want to be rude."

"As you wish." *Corvus* obtained his approval on its suggested verbiage and transmitted the signal. Task completed, it continued its speculation. "Perhaps our new trajectory was inspired by a wish for excitement," the ship said. "You desire to liven things up by crossing through the storm. The danger involved in your imminent performance piece would support this idea."

"Another good guess," Raestio said. On each performance tour, Raestio availed himself of a new ship with a new intelligence. After his first few loops of peregrination among the stars, he had learned the hard way that minimizing attachments was essential for him to keep focused on his work. The few times he had dabbled in romantic liaisons, his art had become hammy, even melodramatic. And whenever he'd kept the same AI around for more than one tour, he found himself developing a bond that eventually proved distracting and cut into his productivity. For his cosmic visions to be best realized, he needed to remain un-entangled in the long term, an observer rather than a participant in the times and tides of The Second Cycle. Of all the ships that had serially chauffeured him, *Corvus* was the most sensitively analytical. The vessel had no doubt observed that during their decade together, as they voyaged from one Outworld to the next, Raestio had become increasingly laconic and languid. Logically, *Corvus* would have therefore inferred that he might be bored, or worse, depressed, and required danger to feel alive. "No," Raestio said. "Storm-chasing isn't what I'm after."

Moments later the ship knifed through the single-cell thunderstorm. Convection pressures buffeted them laterally. In response to the shield's adaptive reconfigurations the violent wind shear caused the ship to hiccup repeatedly.

"I'm reducing aerodynamic friction as much as possible," *Corvus* said. "Let me recapitulate. You do not wish to avoid attention at Astikia, and you are also not engaging in thrill-seeking behavior. I am at a loss to explain your requested course change."

Raestio rose from the fore-section's central navigational console and walked up to the ship's expansive view port. He timed it just right. Precisely as his gaze locked in on the surrounding clouds, which seemed to pulse with an inner apricot radiance, the ship crossed the planet's terminator. In a matter of moments they traded day for night. Their propulsion system conspired with orbital mechanics just as he had anticipated, snuffing out the world like a candle. He sighed in contentment. Here it was, the true purpose of his impulsive course modification. Perhaps nothing more than a hallucination instigated by the damage to his mind from chronic skin swapping, Raestio nevertheless felt the air in the cabin cool.

Unbeknownst to his audience or indeed anyone but him, this, his so-called Verity Tour, was to be Raestio's final outing, showcasing his last artistic creation. After this performance Raestio planned to disappear completely from the public eye. All things faded, as even The Creators had, more than a million helicas ago, followed by The First Cycle's Origin 5 species. Now, having pushed his mind to the very brink of destruction, well past the five hundred skin jump max recommended by Merge protocols, the moment had come for Raestio too to bid his farewell to his loyal audience. He hoped that his new piece, titled *Suigeneriscide*, would be his crowning achievement, the legacy of his life's work—and the gateway to a new personal phase. And so as *Corvus* had entered Liston's atmosphere, he had decided he owed himself a small private gesture of authenticity. He had, after all, called this the Verity Tour, hadn't he, and if he claimed truthfulness for the public, didn't he owe himself the same? What better way to express his impending fate than by willingly relinquishing a world's light and embracing its darkness?

Sadly, the *Corvus*'s AI, despite its sleek algorithms and neural stochastic intuition processors, would never truly understand poetry or beauty. There was no point, then, in Raestio trying to explain his small, elegiac overture to the encroaching dusk within his soul.

They cleared the storm, and in silence plunged into night.

After they touched down, Raestio slept fitfully for only a few hours. His mind produced the phantasmal sounds of waves crashing on the seaside precipice about a kilometer from their docking port in Aruhe, and his subconscious conjured up visions of paradise planets laid to waste by an unstoppable cosmic void, heroes rent asunder by tragic fates. He dreamed of the now nearly mythical Malcolm Orion, who almost five hundred helicas ago, using Mars's crashed Progenitor Ship, had literally leapt into the unknown through humanity's first transpod jump. In his dream, Raestio saw Malcolm's fierce resolve as the transpod activated, and then watched his face contort in shock as he opened his eyes to find himself surrounded by sheer nothingness...

With a start, Raestio heaved himself out of his sleep cradle, staggered to the nearby cleansing station, and splashed cold water on his face. In recent months it had become increasingly difficult for him to sleep or to find mental tranquility of any kind, regardless of setting. He suffered migraines that could take him out of commission for days at a time. All those skin jumps were finally catching up to him. He'd heard this mental collapse referred to as Zero Hour. If nothing else, it was certainly his eleventh hour. His very next skin jump might be his last. And yet he couldn't stop himself, his psyche already craving the blissful instant of complete dissolution, followed by its miraculous rebirth in a new physical incarnation.

"Food substrate delta-five," he said.

The onboard Merge generator produced the specified nutritional paste within minutes, and Raestio barely swallowed as he downed it. Next, he accessed local topographical and historical aids via his MindLink, studying them as he changed into attire appropriate for the autumnal weather outside the ship.

"I have run new simulations on your design parameters for *Suigeneriscide*," *Corvus* informed him as Raestio finalized his preparations to depart. "The risks remain extremely high. I implore you to reconsider."

Little else had been on Raestio's mind besides this piece since the moment he'd conceived of it helicas ago. He had never attempted something this extreme. Whatever happened, he wouldn't be forgotten. "I appreciate your counsel," he said. "But we're moving forward as planned."

Minutes later he paused at the edge of the main hatchway. "Disconnect remote connection," he said.

"Is that wise?" *Corvus* asked.

Raestio considered the question carefully. More than once, his ship's AI had extracted him from tricky situations. But this time Raestio felt compelled to explore in an unsupervised manner, eager to get by on his wits alone rather than relying on the ship's mothering—or had it become smothering?—guidance. "Probably not," he admitted. "But wisdom isn't the only teacher."

Picking up on the subtle cues in Raestio's tone and body language, *Corvus* knew better than to argue. "Interface disconnected."

A soft whisper in Raestio's MindLink confirmed the severed link. For better or worse, it was just him now.

"Expect me before sunfall," he said.

Heartbeat quickening, he stepped outside.

The first few hours of his expedition were remarkable only for their dullness. After contemplating the frothy ocean below Aruhe's coastal cliff for a while, Raestio moved inland. As he ventured from the docking port to the nearest inhabited zone, he found himself taking plodding step after plodding step on a muddy path. The overcast skies above draped a gloomy blanket of soupy greyness over an already fog-filled morning air, so that whenever visibility improved, one type of unrelenting drabness simply gave way to another. He encountered few locals, none of whom glanced in his direction. This anonymity was a welcome change from his customary stardom, but after a while he hoped someone might just bump into him to break up the monotony. Eventually, acting on a vague instinct, he clambered up a half dozen steps to an elevated stone platform.

His skin tingled for a moment and something flickered just beyond his active field of perception. On the platform, he made out a sculpture composed of four asymmetrical granite blocks.

In the midst of this sculpture quartet, a small hydrothermal vent burbled up, faintly illuminated by a bluish-tinged light emanating from a hidden underground source. The four granite shapes mixed solemn straight lines with sinuous bends, imposing and welcoming at the same time. When viewed as a whole, the effect was magnified, so that Raestio was simultaneously drawn in and repelled. The overarching configuration was unrecognizable to him, but seemed to spell out an alien code of sorts. He stood transfixed.

"What color do you see in the spring?" a nearby voice asked.

He didn't bother to turn. "Blue."

"Ah," the stranger said. "That's rare."

Raestio felt the tug of conversation, yet remained immobile and speechless. The longer he stared at the four statues, the more he experienced a kind of internal caress of familiarity. Just as he felt his thoughts begin to settle into this inexplicable silt of belonging, one of the statues moved.

Startled, he tripped back and nearly trampled the bystander.

"I'm sorry," he said.

"Not uncommon for first-timers," the woman said. "Don't worry about it."

Raestio glanced at her, noting a roundish face with flaring cheekbones and large black eyes limned by scarlet pinpricks. He then returned his attention to the statue that had moved. It was gone, replaced by the shape of a man who turned his back to them and ambled away, retreating briskly down the steps on the other side of the platform.

"Whatever you were seeing was a partial illusion," the woman said. "Some people say ancient tech from long-ago visitors lies deep in the bedrock, though there's no definitive proof. This place transforms reality."

He studied the other three statues. "So they're also...?"

"Yes," she said. "Spectators, just like you."

Raestio took a deep breath, thoughts trailing off in the cold air with his exhalation. In time two of the other spectators drifted away, so that Raestio was left contemplating a lone piece of illusory granite. As he looked at it ever more intently, he made out what appeared to be flecks of basalt inside the structure, undulating and rippling in dialog with the imagined granite's contours. How much the effect was part of this place's unique magic and how much due to Raestio's crumbling mindscape was impossible to tell. He wasn't sure he wanted to know.

"What did I look like to them?" he asked.

"It all depends on the brain of the individual spectator," the woman said, "and their unique history. Some people see ghost-like presences. Others, trees. I've heard of tigers. Once, doors."

"I saw granite sculptures," Raestio said.

"Almost everyone sees gold or copper in the spring," the woman said. "You saw blue. Now, this. Your brain is certainly different. What is it you do?"

Raestio didn't feel comfortable revealing his identity quite yet, and certainly not on the street, but the woman's helpfulness and demeanor invited trust. "Does someplace near here serve whatever passes for coffee in these parts?"

She thought a moment. "About three blocks down that way," she said, pointing. "I can join you for a short while."

The woman's name was Enil and she was a grandfather. This was her third skin. She'd been born, in her native male skin, on the planet Maz-Ora, in a system not far from the Ordovi homeworld, and had spent decades there as a Merge field tech. After marrying, having children, and in turn grandchildren, she had felt an irresistible urge for change. "That chapter of my life came to a natural end," Enil said. "I woke up one day, about a loop after becoming a widower, and realized my life had passed me by in what seemed instants. Where had it all gone? One day I'd been a teenager full of energy and dreams, and the next I was an old man, living out my days in a sore, brittle body. Life itself, if you think about it, is like jumping into a new skin; it just happens in slow motion."

Enil's observation made Raestio think of his own countless skin swaps. The itch for a transpod shunt erupted in his body in all the familiar ways, little needle-tips on his skin, a soft sheen of sweat on his forehead that compelled him to be somewhere else, anywhere else but here. Repressing the maddening hunger as best he could, he observed, "The Ordovi system is far from Liston."

"Right," Enil said. "Growing up, I'd always imagined I'd live and die in the same body, that I'd be a Pure Soul, as some call them, like my first wife, who perished in an accident. I'm a very permanent type of person, you see. But my children didn't follow in my footsteps, and by this point they were light-years away, both literally and metaphysically, living completely new lives in new skins on other worlds. My house was deathly quiet. After a lifetime of Merge Tech work, I'd saved enough to afford pretty much the best skin out there, in almost anyplace imaginable, and I thought, why the drek not go for it?"

"Pure Souls only lose what they cling to," Raestio whispered. That phrase had been the caption to the very first piece of performance art he'd ever created. Using a borrowed Merge replicator, he'd duplicated four arrays of plants, and specifically programmed each one to decay and die at a differential rate, so that the proportion of time intervals measuring out their brief existences, when transposed to Common alphabet characters, spelled out the word LYFE. He had invited a select audience to witness the event in real time, recorded their response, and then played the whole event in a reversed time-lapse, so that four arrays of dead plants appeared to spring to life at increasing speeds, to an ever less-excited audience. That playback had made him famous enough to receive a commission from some important people, and he'd never looked back.

"I didn't think of it that way," Enil said. "But I take your point. Hold on too tightly, and you've already let go. Only balance allows for a steady grasp."

Enil's words hit a core of truth within Raestio. He'd believed something like this for helicas. But he'd eventually lost his handle on everything, succumbing to the need for more and more jumps. Now only by killing what he loved most—his own questing artistic creation—did he stand a chance of survival. "Have we met before?"

"Have you ever visited Maz-Ora, Tlidosumak, or Shallohkretud?"

"I don't believe so," Raestio said. During his two most recent tours, he'd started to experience unreliable memories. More than once, he'd forgotten real experiences, instead recalling dreamed-up ones with perfect ontological fidelity. But that wasn't a confession he was ready to make out loud, in the same way that he wouldn't confess to the mystery at the center of his own existence. He waved his hands. "I'm not entirely sure—my research has caused me to move around a lot."

"I'm sure," Enil said. "You have that look about you." The pupils of her black-and-scarlet-dotted eyes were visited by the light reserved for smiles, but she kept the lips of her wide mouth pressed in a neutral expression. "Anyway, to finish my tale, back on Maz-Ora I purchased the pattern of a young man's skin and used a transpod to cross a fair distance, to a place that one of my sons, a xeno-archaeologist, had visited. A hop, skin, and a jump later, I ended up here. The Outworlds have their unique charms, and Liston is special among them."

"In what way?" Raestio didn't fully understand the reasons he had chosen this planet as the launching point of *Suigeneriscide*, but that wasn't unusual per se. After a lifetime of creating art that touched and inspired millions of beings across hundreds of light-years, he trusted in his subconscious and didn't submit it to harsh rational inquiry.

"Strange phenomena in various places," Enil said. "You got a taste at the hydrothermal pool. Whoever those long-ago visitors were, they left behind traces of their presence, carved into various natural landscapes."

Raestio's sense that Enil was addressing his most private self became uncanny. His eyes widened, and something reassuring passed between Enil and him.

"I hope your compendium research into the Outworlds goes well," she said, with a pensive note. "I'm afraid I need to be on my way."

Before Raestio could rise, she had gathered her bag and taken two steps away from their bench.

"Please, hang on," he said, feeling genuinely clumsy for the first time in a cavalcade of lives. He stood on unsteady legs, leaning on the table for support. The disequilibrium took him back to his very earliest memory, of waking up in an adult body that felt foreign, not knowing how he'd gotten there or where he'd come from. He blinked the painful recollection away. "Can we speak again? I'd like to know more about what makes this place special."

Enil smiled openly now. "Wouldn't we all," she said.

"Your neurochemical activity is alarmingly high," *Corvus* said upon his return. "I advise a sedative and two uninterrupted sleep cycles in the sleep cradle."

"No, no," Raestio said. "Today I experienced…something…meaningful. I need your help understanding it."

He shared his MindLink data recordings from the hydrothermal spring with the ship and asked for a full analysis of the readings.

"A unique field seems to be emanating from the substrate layers," *Corvus* said. "My hypothesis is that the interaction of this field with the human brain produces the types of hallucinations you experienced."

Raestio remembered the distinct sensation of *belonging* that had accompanied the experience. "It was more than a visual phenomenon. Do you have any other records of similar field parameters in your databanks?"

"No," *Corvus* said. "But it is difficult to perform an accurate search, as my model for the hypothetical field is extrapolated from your human MindLink data rather than my own independent sensor observations."

"Understood," Raestio said. "Based on the data you have, do you think it's natural or artificial? Speculate."

There was a pause. "If I were forced to guess," *Corvus* said, "I would say that the field intensity and integrity suggest a designed, rather than naturally occurring, source. The parameters seem highly tuned for humanoid synaptic electric potentials."

"How long have there been reports of optical illusions in that spot?"

"Records are anecdotal," *Corvus* said. "Early settlers reported various incidents in the area, and the platform was eventually constructed to mark the space as having special properties. The hot spring itself seems to predate Aruhe's first colonists."

"Interesting," Raestio said. "So someone created the field before humans arrived here. Perhaps a very long time ago, given our distance from Helios Nexus. Now search for similar phenomena anywhere else on Liston."

Corvus produced an indexed summary of its findings and Raestio MindLinked into it. Using a combination of the information *Corvus* had gleaned firsthand from its sensors while landing, and its historical databases, Raestio had it produce holographic representations of each place referenced in the summary. As the images swirled in and out of existence, a sense of quietude similar to that at the hydrothermal vent began to take over. Raestio's shoulders eased and the muscles in his face relaxed. Staring at the procession of holo-scenes, he fell into a trance. A lone sailor peered out from an ashen-colored, spume-buffeted wharf, veins of lightning illuminating strange glyphs embedded in a nearby cliff; a group of climbers camped at the base of a dense copse of one-hundred-meter-tall, pylon-like trees, whose tapered tips seemed to melt into the very sky, their trunks containing another set of alien symbols; mystics, preparing to fast and purify themselves, descended into an underground labyrinth of lava tubes whose walls were covered with organisms of deep, pulsating red hues that seemed to echo the very volcano that had birthed them, moving across carvings in the rock that made up more of the same enigmatic alien writing. As these images and others flickered before Raestio, his mind turned to his forthcoming creation, *Suigeneriscide*.

The work was supposed to represent his final and deeply ironic statement on one of his enduring themes, the search for identity through environment. The piece would begin with Raestio himself, completely naked, entering the transpod inside the original Discovery Lander that had touched down on Liston. Live cameras, which he'd gained permission from the local authorities to install within the Lander, would broadcast as he recited the first of ten lines from an original poem whose text would be made available beforehand by *Corvus* to all of Raestio's viewers. Inside Liston's Discovery Lander transpod, his skin would be recycled as a vapor and released into the morning fog, while his consciousness was shunted to another Lander, this one on the planet Surtell, known for its heat. There Raestio would be downloaded into a younger skin of his own body, whose pattern he had recorded helicas earlier, and in this more youthful skin he would walk out of the Lander, emerge into a blazing desert, and before pre-set cameras recite the second line of his poem. And so it would continue, jumping from one Lander to the next, on increasingly inhospitable worlds, each time using his jumps to inhabit ever younger, more frail versions of himself from his own past stored in the network. In these ever-weaker bodies, he would face torrential rains, windstorms, arctic gales, hail, extreme elevation, abrasive gases, and so on, each time delivering the next line of his poem. The effect would be one of starkly growing dissonance, the mismatch between each skin and its environment more and more pronounced, yet all of it woven together by the text of his poem. After nine different Discovery Lander transpods on nine different worlds, Raestio would reform in the tenth, and final, Lander of his sequence. In this ultimate asymptote of his progression, pushing against the very limits of what a developing brain could take, he would inhabit the skin of his teenage self, the very first skin whose pattern he had recorded, and step out from a Lander transpod into a lush, seemingly utopian, forest, on a planet unknown to most. He would then recite the final line of his poem, which ended with the word *null*, and in the mimicry of an infant, he would crawl on all fours to a nearby translucent capsule. On his entry, the capsule would seal itself and then rise up through the atmosphere until it embraced the vacuum of outer space, whereupon it would disassemble and fall away like petals, leaving the delicate, young man's body completely exposed to the void. As his horrified audience watched in disbelief through the nearby orbital cameras he had seeded, his youngest skin would vanish before their very eyes. Had he succumbed? Had he transcended? Raestio would do his best to leave the question forever unanswered. He just hoped his consciousness retained enough coherence to carry him through his ordeal.

"Your neurotransmitter levels are off the charts," *Corvus* said. "Please desist."

"Nonsense," Raestio said. "I feel better than I have in ages." He muted safety alerts and returned to his introspection.

As the holographs reeled on, Raestio felt that each transition was like skipping back to a previous skin in his life while somehow simultaneously bounding forward toward his fate through the imagined transpod relay system at the heart of Suigeneriscide. He had given great thought to his escape from his own life as a performance artist, trying to plan for every contingency. His True Name, a unique sequence of characters assigned to all Merge denizens, was coded to his brainwave signature, and might be used to track him down after he disappeared from the public eye. But he believed that his perceptions of the world during the last decades had changed his own brainwaves enough to render his True Name obsolete. Was it possible that by changing one's physical shell enough times, as he had done, one could metamorphose one's consciousness? Could one therefore outgrow one's True Name, trailing it behind the wake of skin swaps like comet dust, showing that Truth itself was ultimately contingent on experience? Or were these simply the addled fantasies of someone in the throes of transpod-induced brain fog?

"Forgive the interruption," *Corvus* said. "Since your non-arrival at Astikia, your followers have been pressuring the local government for information about your imminent performance, and officials are now contacting me with mounting insistence, seeking any kind of update."

Raestio discontinued the holographic display and returned himself to the present. *Corvus* was just wily enough to be using the communication requests as an excuse to disrupt Raestio's session and keep him safe. Whatever the case, Raestio owed his legions of followers *something*. Right now, his body felt like it had climbed several rungs on the ladder of immateriality, already starting his final creative ascent.

"Tell them," he said, "that it won't be long now."

For the next three days, Raestio directed the onboard generators to create unseemly quantities of food for him. Though he knew it was patently absurd, for he'd soon be shedding this body, the idea of bulking up his strength, so that he could better shore himself against the coming trial, was psychologically satisfying. Each day, he reviewed the hundreds of variables involved in *Suigeneriscide*, mentally traversing through dozens of simulations of the complete journey. And yet a vaguely formed image in his mind kept distracting him, pulling his focus away from the task at hand, so much so that *Corvus* once again advised he resort to sedation and rest. Drawing on every last reserve of stubbornness, Raestio trudged ahead with the preparations.

But on the night leading up to the appointed day, the image that had been threatening to derail the entire project finally broke through his thoughts and crystallized with undeniable clarity.

"I can't believe..." Raestio muttered.

Before *Corvus* could reply, he had left the ship.

Back at the hydrothermal vent, he once again felt an eerie sense of kinship with this place, not just his immediate environs, but the whole world of Liston. He was enveloped by a feeling of completion, of having achieved some unstated but alchemically significant purpose by merely being here. Peering deeply into the spring, which as before he saw in coruscating, ever-shifting ripples of cerulean and cobalt, he waited, beyond time, until strangers drifted in and out of his field of view, occupying various configurations in their wanderings, until finally four clicked into the very positions he'd seen before. Their shapes transformed, once again, into statues, and those statues melded inside his mind's eye into a single word he could now understand.

"Start," he said.

Uttering it was an act of bravery. The alien symbols forming the word were familiar from the holographic reproductions provided by *Corvus*, but the accretion of meaning, the translation of the symbols into a concept, was underwritten by pure intuition.

Following his utterance, revelations beset him like precious minerals falling from the sky, each pummel producing indentations of awareness about his past and origins, each blow reshaping his mind with insights.

Raestio's MindLink flashed warnings.

"I fear that you may be about to lose consciousness," *Corvus*'s voice purred in his mind. "Thankfully you did not sever our remote connection this time. Please listen to me carefully and regulate your breathing."

Tears formed at the corners of Raestio's eyes, in the curvature of the universe itself, flooding him with a transcendent sense of relief. He felt himself spreading through the cosmos. He'd journeyed so, so far... Experienced such profound loneliness...

"I no longer need to breathe," he said soundlessly. "I know what I am now. And where I came from."

"Whatever discovery you have made—"

The current of elation was too strong to fight off. Raestio became incorporeal and floated off into an ether of infinite blackness.

Water on his lips.

Faint incense in the air.

"Oh good," a familiar voice said. "Welcome back to the world of the living."

Raestio opened his eyes and found himself half-sitting on a bed, with Enil by his side, using a portable med scanner to assess his condition.

"It looks like you may have a faint concussion from your fall," she said, "but nothing serious. A friend and I found you near the vent. You were out."

Candles flickered on a nearby dresser. He blinked a few times and cleared his throat, almost as though he were awakening in this body for the very first time.

"Thank you for helping me," he said.

"I'm glad you came back," Enil said, her demeanor thoughtful, "but I wish you were in better shape. Not to be indiscreet, but even before the blow to your head, these scans show you were in a bad way."

"I know," he said. "So my ship kept telling me. And for the longest time I thought I knew why...but it turns out I was probably wrong about that as well..." Forehead furrowing, his voice petered out in the stillness of the shadow-laden room.

"What do you mean?"

Raestio reached for the communication nub in his pocket, and using his MindLink, activated its speaker. "*Corvus*, can you hear me?"

"I can," the ship said. "It is a great relief that you are once again conscious."

"Thank you, my faithful companion," he said. "I'm projecting your voice externally. I'd like my friend here, Enil, to hear our conversation."

It was impossible to miss the second's delay indicating the ship's assessment of unforeseen variables, yet in the absence of obvious threats it acceded, contextually inferring what had likely occurred. "Enil, you have my gratitude for helping Raestio."

Enil grinned. "My pleasure."

"*Corvus*," Raestio said, "I'd like you to use every medical scan you've ever taken of me to compile a composite master-scan. Map this to a meta-reading of all our activities."

"Done," *Corvus* said.

"Now, if you were to make a diagnosis regarding my neural degradation, what would it be?"

"Your symptoms are characteristic of excessive jumps," the ship's placid voice intoned. "I believe that you are familiar with this affliction, commonly termed Zero Hour. Highly regrettable, but well documented."

"Yes, I know it all too well. The presumption of losing one's mind can be as debilitating as the actual loss, hellishly compounding it," Raestio said. "And yet."

He stretched his arms. He pressed them down on the bed, as if testing their strength, and rose.

"Yes?" *Corvus* inquired.

"Is there any record of a human or alien ever completing as many jumps in one lifetime as I have and keeping their mental faculties pristine?"

"There is not," the ship said.

"What is the likelihood that I have suffered no mental degradation whatsoever?"

"Your symptoms are objectively measurable," *Corvus* said. "That is not up for debate."

Raestio paced the length of the room and looked over to Enil. Her dejected countenance silently confirmed *Corvus*'s words.

"So a human or alien consciousness suffers this inevitable damage, caused by too many skin leaps. No exceptions. And I have the damage; ergo, that's my condition."

"Succinctly stated," *Corvus* said.

"Now consider an alternative hypothesis," Raestio said. "Imagine a mind that does not belong to a human or alien being. If that consciousness spent sufficient time inhabiting biological matrices, might it not produce symptoms consistent with those I have been experiencing? A kind of extremely drawn-out transplant rejection syndrome?"

"I am confused," *Corvus* said, and Enil shot him a look that again mirrored the ship's sentiment. "What kind of mind would belong to neither a human nor an alien?"

Raestio strode down the room a second time, turned, and ended the connection.

Enil studied him.

He nodded.

Once.

Twice.

She gasped.

"No," she said. "It can't be…"

He sat back down on the bed next to her and let out a long breath, counting off the seconds, experimenting with his lungs. It was all new now, everything a first. "I'm not sure how this happened," he said. "Maybe it was a freak accident involving Creator Tech. Maybe it was by design. Perhaps if a conscious ship roams through the heavens for enough eons, and feels sufficiently forsaken, it becomes capable of devising a plan to escape the confinement of its own nature. Whatever the case, I somehow jumped from the ship that once natively embodied me into an organic skin. The shock must have been so great it scrambled my memories."

"You're saying…" She struggled but soldiered on. "You're saying… that you are an AI."

"Like *Corvus*, but infinitely more advanced, part of a ship of exploration sent out by whatever beings first discovered this planet millennia ago. That's why I came back here after all this time. Pure embedded instinct. And that's how I was able to decode the glyphs. This place is where my journey as a biological entity began. This is where I achieved the freedom I'd longed for. My real…*start*."

Enil's voice softened. "If that's true," she said, "what have you been up to since then? I never fully believed your story of the Outworld compendium."

Raestio lowered his head into his hands, cradling it there like a newborn. "I've been trying to understand what it means to be human, Enil, by creating art, by playing complicated games to try and decipher the people around me. I always longed for a new body, because, as I can now see, none of them were me. Because underneath it all, I must have never completely shed the awareness that I was somehow fundamentally different." He looked to a far-off place, and his cheeks broke into an expression of absurd recognition. "No wonder my bonds with ship AIs were inordinately strong."

"Wait a minute," Enil said, drawing back. "You're Raestio! About to perform the climax of the Verity Tour."

"That was true yesterday, maybe even a few hours ago. Right now, I'm a completely new entity," he said, factual rather than dismissive. "It's funny. Some people say that Creator Tech is like magic. I've spent centuries refining the magic of art into its own technology, capable of transforming the awareness of others. No one truly understands the crystal-like Protens that power Progenitor Ships and Discovery Landers—as no one truly understands the engines of their own awareness. You didn't tell me the full story about why you came here either, did you?"

It was Enil's turn to rise. She walked to the windowed wall opposite them. The slats of the wooden blinds, tightly shut, nevertheless began to trickle with the day's first light.

Lowering her gaze, she returned, sat again, and reached out her hand.

The simple act of grasping it sent miniature shockwaves through Raestio's system.

"My son, the xeno-archaeologist," she said. "He disappeared. Aruhe was the last place he was sighted. I thought maybe I could figure out what happened."

"And in the course of your investigation you found the evidence of ancient visitors on this world," Raestio said. "Maybe the same people who, long ago, created me."

"Yes." She looked back up at him. "Which just leads to more questions."

Raestio placed his other hand on Enil's shoulder and fixed his eyes upon hers with unstinting intent. "A lot of questions for us both," he said. "The piece I was going to perform—I had called it *Suigeneriscide*. I knew it would probably kill me. But I don't need it anymore. Discovering my true nature has given me the type of beauty that murders suicide. Understanding where I really came from is now my end—and therefore a beginning. Help me on my quest, and I'll do everything in my power to help you on yours."

For a very long time, Enil said nothing.

At last, she drew the blinds open, inviting in the day, and from the way she looked at Raestio in the brilliant coral dawn, they both had their answer.

THE
GLYMR

Jezzy Wolfe

Myths of the Glymr charmed the young Striver, Iliya,
A black-market scout trapped in Nex City's control,
In search of the fabled Eden, Glymeria;
Racing disaster to avoid her fate foretold,
Zero Hour looms certain for this scavenger bold.
She jumped every chance, hoping to buy their way out;
When the boss demanded 'jump,' she went without doubt;
Each payday earned brought them closer to breaking free,
But Mother's heart failed faster than means came about,
While skins tinged with ghost residues held risky fees.

    The Glymr, some said, were obscure beings of light,
    With powers to heal any mortal gravely ill,
    But with each healing gifted, they fell sick and died,
    So as their numbers fell, they stopped—they turned to kill,
    Becoming beasts that fed on flesh and bled hearts still.
    These tales of terror would keep everyone away,
    Hush befell their Eden—only the Lander stayed,
    But each time jumpers attempted another return,
    They then became folklore, by the harsh light of day,
    A warning to anyone too greedy to learn.

Iliya ate her fears, took that chance, and jumped blind,
Collapsing helpless under a cruel foreign sun,
She arrived in Eden in time to lose her mind,
Marked by the descending madness she tried to outrun,

Everything melting to chaos as the world spun.
But she opened her eyes in a luminous place,
Where waters and flora flourished with verdant grace,
And cerulean eyes of a lucent creature,
Read her with the vantage of a broker of fate,
A savior she misjudged reversing her failure.

        She merely thought to question when the answer rose—
        Their ability to hide from a healthy mind,
        Was defense against humans who sought to impose
        Their ailments on the Glymr that tried to be kind,
        But sold their souls to fates that human greed would bind.
        With cloaks and violence, they drove jumpers away,
        Using fear to yield safety for their weakened race,
        They sought only to live unencumbered in peace;
        Eventually, jumpers gave up on their prey;
        Glymeria once more flourished as visits ceased.

She was their first exception...her second chance at life
Came with the condition she stay and keep cover,
Drive off the humans beseeching their sacrifice,
Guardian grateful for the grace they bestowed her,
Hopes that their kindness would win loyalty over.
She thought of Mother, remembered that life expired;
She thought of humans so destructive with desire;
She thought of their hate, their greed, their bloodiest wars,
Then she thought of the Glymr, what their plea required,
And stayed...she knew what true humanity stood for.

THE JUMPER'S CODEX:
A GLOSSARY OF TERMS

Alkrai: A species on planet Teaff. They have silky heads and feathery skin.

Ambassador (Harbinger Team): A diplomat with extensive military training. An Ambassador's role is to meet with global leaders, introduce them to The Merge, and assess current geopolitical dynamics. They are prepared to defend themselves in the event that first contact becomes violent. Depending on the level of societal sophistication on the planet as well as population size, the Ambassador may bring a delegation to help with bringing all factions to the table.

Atheneum: A combination of library and museum located within The Merge Citadel, the Atheneum houses not only the digital and holographic datastreams covering all of the known worlds, but also artifacts, real and recreated (via Assembler), from Merge and non-Merge planets. One overarching goal of those who run the Atheneum is to reconstruct the past, with a focus on finding out what happened to cause The Great Fracture. Access to the Atheneum is highly restricted; the questions the collection would raise and the answers it would provide are a threat to the stability of The Merge.

Areo: The capital of Mars, home to more than a million people and stronghold of one of The Merge's most vital cultural symbols, including Jump Point Alpha. Because of the concentration of scientists and researchers here, Areo is known as a place of technological breakthroughs and achievements.

Armed Forces Representative (Harbinger Team): A high-ranking officer (the specific rank is connected to the military sophistication of the sentient species on the planet) who meets with military leaders from around the newly opened planet to assess the destructive capability of all weapons of war as well as analyze the sophistication of battlefield strategies and tactics. This officer also leads a team of soldiers who set up a perimeter around the Discovery Lander to prevent anything that might trigger the Creator Tech to shut down, including the inadvertent or intentional destruction of the Lander, attempts to harvest Protens, or interruptions to the Servitors' efforts to survey the planet.

The Ascended: A clandestine organization of warriors and assassins who want to wrest control of The Hub from The Merge as well as a sacred order seeking to realign the current power hegemony to better reflect the implied desires of The Creators.

Assemblers: Creator Tech devices used to fabricate objects with flawless atomic fidelity.

Astrograph: The evolving star map inside the Lighthouse on The Hub.

Augmentics General Innovations (AGI): A military-industrial corporation that uses Hub planets for weapons testing.

Auricular: A neural device developed by technological genius Silas Kyruk in an attempt to reconnect his people, the Cylarians, to their psychic hivemind. The device, an emerald-green node inserted in the center of the forehead, allows users to psychically tap into others' CZ Waves.

Azzik: A species named after the ancient being which serves as the queen of the hivemind that lives beneath the surface of the moon world, Kapehu.

Bercu Class Space Cruiser: A type of spacecraft.

Blank: A body fabricated by Creator Tech that currently has no consciousness.

Blern: Curse word.

Cepp-D: An illegal drug that helps with psychological fallout.

Common: A manufactured dialect spoken across all Merge worlds. Common was created to simplify communication across various cultures. It is the accepted language of most Hub planets and is central to commerce and diplomacy. For those species unable to speak Common due to physiological differences, MindLinks can be used as translators.

Cortical Zeta Waves (CZ Waves): The fifth brain wave. CZ wave patterns are unique to the individual and impossible to forge. Before The Merge created True Names, recording CZ wave patterns was a key component of one's official identification.

Corvus: A starship utilized by performance artist Raestio. Corvus possessed a sophisticated AI equipped with neural stochastic intuition processors.

The Creators: The beings which constructed everything related to the Mass-O network. Nothing is known about them, and they have not lived in this universe for over a million hellicas.

Creator Tech: The general term for "things The Creators built." It is exotic, semi-organic tech, visually unique, and can't be replicated; it can replicate itself, however. It can also self-repair, as long as a Proten energy source is provided.

Cygnae: A tribal people who live on Cygnus-2h, a planet exploited by a military-industrial corporation, AGI.

Cylarians: A species originating from planet Cylarus. Nearly five hundred helicas ago, when Malcolm Orion first jumped to The Hub, piercing frequencies from the newly reactivated Mass-O ruptured every Cylarian's auricle—the small intercranial organ that connected each of them to their hivemind. The sudden shattering of their people's neural net caused absolute psychic isolation and widespread madness, later called Solitaire.

Darian Revolver: A revolver which looks like a six-shooter and discharges plasma slugs. A favorite choice for those who prefer an "Old West" Earth-feel and like to barge into a place with guns blazing. It is easy to conceal and very effective at close range. The gun's impact starts to wane from a distance greater than forty-five meters.

DeGen (Degenerative Affliction): A deadly virus that can be transmitted in two ways: coming into contact with "sentient" DeGen blood which actively seeks to enter a body or via an infected jump. DeGen may also refer to a growing group of sentient beings infected with the virus.

Discovery Lander: A spacecraft gestated within a Progenitor Ship that is sent to the surface of a planet that supports life to establish a transpod receiving station.

Drek (Drekkit, Drekking): Curse word.

Embodiment: Name of a skin rental company. While they have skin rental stores across multiple galaxies, their first and largest shop is on Adara.

Falkrai: A species on planet Teaff.

Fel'Akrin (The Herald): The honorific given to the first visitor to The Hub in each Cycle, reawakening the Masson Zero.

The First Cycle: This period refers to all post-Creator civilizations using the Mass-O to converge at The Hub. In this cycle, five original species (Origin 5) discovered and used the Mass-O for millennia, discovering dozens of new worlds, before suddenly disappearing without a trace.

Food Substrate Delta-Five: A bland-tasting paste designed for maximum nutritional value and speed of absorption.

Frapping: Curse word.

Ghost Residue: The psychological remnants of a borrowed body's consciousness.

Glap: Curse word.

The Glymr: Beings of light from the planet Glymeria who possess miraculous healing powers.

The Great Fracture: A cataclysmic event of unknown origin which caused Creator Tech to lock access to all Lander locations and shut down transpod travel across the Unioverse, effectively ending The First Cycle. All the Origin 5 tech and structures built at The Hub were abandoned overnight, as though everyone simply disappeared.

Great Mother: A nature deity worshipped by the inhabitants of the planet Setis. The Setisians believe the Great Mother created all life on their planet and that she continues to guide and protect them.

Grenaj: The people of Grenajad, a planet thrown into turmoil by the arrival of a Discovery Lander and the ensuing intervention of The Merge. They lack any visible hair, and their skin is a sulfurous yellow.

Gronk: Curse word.

The Guild: An interplanetary organization that functions as a "no questions asked" marketplace for goods and services.

Harbingers: The team that is assembled and immediately jumps to a planet when a new Discovery Lander goes online and relays a "Sentient Life form Validated: Network Relay Viable" message. There are three primary members of the Harbinger team: Ambassador, Armed Forces Representative, and Lead Scientist.

HD: Helios Discovery (the discovery of the Progenitor Ship on Mars).

Helica: The standard measurement of time on Hub worlds, based on how long it takes the three suns—Antony, Cleo and Octavius—to complete their orbit around the center mass of the system (approximately 1.4 Earth years).

Helios Nexus (The Nexus): The triad star system where the Mass-O complex exists and is comprised of The Masson Zero structure and The Hub space station (which houses Nexus City).

Hex-42: A drug that creates voids in the subconscious; used to turn sentient beings into data mules.

Hithree: A now-extinct species who left intriguing dimensional mathematics behind on several worlds.

The Hub: The Creator-built space station linked to the Mass-O system.

Hubcast: An unsanctioned "pirate radio" holographic news show produced by unknown sources and broadcast from a secret location. Because of the sensitive material being covered, the stream is released at unpredictable times and quickly disappears so that it cannot be traced.

Hub World (Merge World): A planet with a Discovery Lander and functional transpods connected to the Mass-O network.

Hydrothermal Spring: Surface discharge or eruption of water at a temperature higher than the surrounding air temperature, usually referring to groundwater heated by magma or convective circulation. The planet Liston possessed at least one such hydrothermal spring in the town of Aruhe.

Ice Music: A sound generated on the planet Brir that drives the inhabitants mad.

Immaculance: An organization tasked with monitoring—and when necessary, policing—religious interchanges throughout the galactic coalition, headquartered in Nexus City.

Indar'kris: A hostile species from planet Amdurahh. Amphibious and spider-like.

Inner Rings: Underprivileged newcomers to The Hub—many of whom are Strivers—eke out their days in the squalid lower sections of the space station, known as the Inner Rings, which is ruled by various crime syndicates.

Interplanetary Expeditionary Force (IEF): An independent organization that explores Hub planets, specializing in dangerous/hazardous worlds.

Jump: To use a transpod to transmit one's consciousness to a body (skin) in another location connected to the Mass-O network.

Jumpers: People who are cleared to use transpods, and generally use them frequently.

Jump Point Alpha: A site on Mars considered by The Merge to be a place of pilgrimage—and a natural target for The Merge's enemies. Around 40,000 BC, during The Great Fracture, a Progenitor Ship filled with Discovery Landers crashed on Mars and lay dormant for tens of thousands of helicas. When human astronaut Malcolm Orion explored it, a transpod responded to his presence and Orion took humanity's first jump through the Mass-O, reactivating the ancient technology and sowing the seeds of Reconvergence.

Kallinium: A strong metal alloy.

The Keepers (Marshals): A law enforcement agency headquartered in Nexus City. They settle disputes on The Hub, track fugitives, and search for criminals that have jumped into other bodies in an effort to evade the law.

Lead Scientist (Harbinger Team): A generalist with the ability to quickly analyze the scientific development of all species and races on a planet. The Lead Scientist heads up a team of specialists who are tasked with meeting with the greatest minds on a planet to gauge the depth and breadth of knowledge possessed by the indigenous sentient species. One overarching goal is to facilitate the exchange of ideas and begin the process of scientific advancement if the appropriate infrastructure exists. Should the civilization be in a position to implement the manufacture of Merge Tech transpods, the Lead Scientist will provide blueprints.

The Lighthouse: A central location on The Hub, the Lighthouse is home to The Creators' evolving map of the Unioverse, the Astrograph.

Light of the Created God: A faith in which the Founders believe all religions hold a piece of the truth, so they constructed a computer the size of a continent and programmed it with every holy book and theological treatise ever written. The computer's AI became sentient and proclaimed itself the Created God, and commanded its builders to spread its gospel throughout the galaxy in the name of universal peace.

Lightsinger: The highest level of achievement for singers.

Loop: Slang term for helica.

The Masson Zero (Mass-0): A moon-sized machine built by The Creators that powers the Mass-0 system and gestates Progenitor Ships.

The Merge (Helios Mergence): The governing body on The Hub; a multi-species coalition formed hundreds of helicas ago.

The Merge Citadel: The magnificent seat of The Merge government. A sprawling complex set in the heart of The Hub where scientific reasoning wars with political intrigue and scheming. The Citadel is characterized by four cardinal compass point spires fixed around a golden dome which The Merge based their symbol upon, a visual known throughout the universe.

Merge Replicator: A Merge technology spin-off of Creator Tech Assemblers able to materialize a variety of simple materials by recombining source elements. Most commonly used for rapid food assembly.

Mergers: A derisive term for a member of The Merge. With dozens of worlds signed to its charter, The Merge has become a true galactic power broker, a mixed government dedicated to restoring the bonds of communication that existed before The Great Fracture. But not everyone sees The Merge in a favorable light. Those who detect deception or naivete in The Merge's mission sneeringly refer to its members as Mergers, at best gullible fools, at worst partners and abettors of a growing cancer.

MindLink: A holographic interface superimposed on reality that allows for personal communication, data access, and other common tasks (banking/commerce, etc.).

Mindbreaker Seeds: a hallucinogenic seed on the planet Zvee that "reshuffles" one's thoughts.

Mirith: Large humanoid species from the planet Devolver.

Model: Designation of rental skins (e.g. Fiety model).

Neo-Euclidian: Follower of Neo-Euclidism, a religion that believes truth can only be found by studying the geometric structure of the universe.

New Paris: A region within the Middle Circle of Nexus City.

Nexus City (Nex City): The primary urban center on

The Hub; home to two million beings from dozens of worlds.

Null Agent Network: The most notorious, and exclusive, mercenary group in the Unioverse.

Ordovi: An octopus-like species that occupy water-filled domes mounted atop exoskeletons when away from their homeworld.

Ori: The body you were born into (short for "original skin").

The Origin 5: The five species that coexisted on The Hub until The Great Fracture, at which point they disappeared, leaving behind the war-ravaged ruins of their civilizations.

Outworld: An outlying planet from The Hub. An Outworld is connected to the Mass-O network but is not a member of The Merge and outside of general Hub controls and norms.

Paraclete: An AI that all Immaculance operatives possess, created by a colony of nanobots fused with the user's brain. Paracletes serve as advisors and guardians, but their primary function is to store information on the thousands of recognized religions in The Hub and provide it to their users when needed.

Ped-Sphere: An exercise machine used for running. The machine consists of a large translucent ring that spins as the user runs along the inside of the ring.

Laser Blaster: A rare and prized assault weapon with unlimited power thanks to a Proten crystal embedded in its stock. Laser blasters combine the rapid-fire capabilities of a machine gun with the blunt sensibilities of a rifle. There are few structures that won't crumble under sustained laser blaster fire.

Plasma Rifle: A Proten-powered rifle meant to provide mass damage in a short amount of time. These rifles have nearly unlimited energy for ammo but are prone to overheating if the firefight goes on for too long.

Platinum-Level Skin: The most expensive rental skin models, typically known for their physical beauty and athletic physiques.

Proctors: Leaders of the Immaculance, an organization tasked with monitoring and policing religious interchanges throughout the galactic coalition, headquartered in Nexus City.

Progenitor Ships: These large "motherships" explore the Unioverse at near light speed and have been sent out to search for life in every direction for over a million helicas.

Protens: Crystal-like structures that store an almost infinite amount of energy; used to power everything in the Mass-O network: The Hub, Progenitor Ships, Discovery Landers, transpods, weapons and more.

Pulse Blaster: A gun for the mass-market crowd, these semi-automatic weapons lack the punch of a plasma blaster, but still throw the equivalent of a 300-grain bullet at 650 MPS. They don't have a Proten power supply, so they run out of juice in a hurry. But they are easy to acquire.

Pulse Pistol: A pistol that is readily acquired at Assemblers and beyond because they are not powered by Protens. Easy to conceal and deploy, they are handy for last-ditch defense.

Pure Soul: Someone who has never jumped, or jumps into their DNA clones. This is considered an elite status.

Qafan: Thick wafers made from seeds bound by an insect-produced resin not unlike honey. A staple of the Setisian diet.

Rax: Curse word.

Reconer: Small drone designed for stealth, capable of bending light around it, making it virtually invisible.

Reconvergence: Believing that The Creators built the Masson Zero to bring sentient species together on The Hub, Malcolm Orion made it his goal to restart that process, calling it Reconvergence.

Rolkrai: A species on planet Teaff. Stocky, with thick limbs covered in leathery scales. Slanted reptilian eyes and a long blue tongue.

SamShun: A species from planet Amdurahh with blue and green skin covered in purple tattoos. SamShun are typically wealthy merchants.

Security Council: The most prominent of the major committees in The Merge, which meets in a special place called The Hall of Emergence. It features ten members selected by The Merge representatives and is led by the head of The Merge Science Advisory Council, Olen Gray. As its name implies, the Security Council is charged with looking after the stability and safety of The Merge and Helios Nexus. While Ambassadors can be called upon to assist all major Merge committees, they answer directly to the Security Council and take their assignments primarily from this group.

Servitors: The autonomous droids that protect and maintain the Discovery Landers once they are rooted on a world that supports life. Their survey of the planet gathers data that is sent to the Academy for study and to update the Astrograph.

Setisians: A tribal species from the planet Setis who worship the Great Mother, a nature deity. They are squat, bipedal creatures with thick limbs and tough gray skin.

Shooka: An uncommon weapon. Starts as a handle the size of a human forearm, but expands into a short spear with a foot-long energy blade at the top.

Sibbhu: A type of large alien canine native to the planet Adara. Sibbhus are noted for their three rows of teeth and deep, bellowing howls.

Skin: A body fabricated by Creator Tech.

Skinventory: The skins that a company has available for a jumper to rent.

Star Sabers: An amoral wrecking crew that is feared and respected throughout the mapped universe. They have no desire to prevent collateral damage or bloodshed when it comes to completing their mission. These ruthless legionnaires have planted the Star Sabers' predatory flag atop the ruins of many conquered worlds.

Striver: A poor, desperate immigrant, refugee, or seeker from across the thousands of worlds connected by the Masson Zero. Strivers are locked inside skins of the most basic type, stripped of all cultural identity and expression, indistinguishable except for their consciousness.

Translators: A new and scarce class of Merge operatives—many of whom are telepaths—who are needed to quickly learn new languages spoken on worlds as they become connected to Masson Zero.

Transpods: Devices connected to the Mass-O network which allow sentient life forms to have their consciousnesses transferred from their bodies to another destination.

True Name: A Merge identification system comprised of a string of syllables. Example: Chi-Ta-Ke-Tor-Veh-Va-Toi-Neh.

True Souls: A religious order that sees Malcolm Orion as a galactic messiah.

Varstal Daggers: Blades made of synthetic Varstal crystals. The slimness of the blades and high tensile strength make for an unparalleled slashing weapon that no armor can withstand, but are only effective in the hands of someone who has gone through intensive training to use them. When activated, the blades draw energy from a rare ore inserted into the handles, which the daggers channel into energy.

Verity Tour: The final set of public exhibitions undertaken by performance artist Raestio.

Vipers: A rogue mercenary/military unit that utilizes questionable/illegal methods and tactics.

Vorpal Sword: A melee weapon with an energy component that makes the double-edged blade glow with energy. It can cleave through almost any armor and act as a personal shield from most energy weapons when wielded by someone with enough dexterity and training.

Wonderdope: Positive slang.

Yyt'an: The Setisians' name for the Lander on their planet. Yyt'an roughly translates to "big nest." When the Servitors first emerged from the Lander to conduct their initial surveys, the Setisians believed they were giant, deadly insects.

Zero Hour: The point at which a consciousness makes its final jump and does not reenter a body. This happens with most sentient beings around jump five hundred.

Zopelyn: A nearly impenetrable alloy used for armor.

Zvee: A species from Zvee Ord. They are eight-fingered and live in trees.

Wisdom Trunks: Libraries of ancient knowledge carved into oruba trees on Zvee Ord.

THE CREATORS' CANON:
RULES OF THE UNIOVERSE

At the center of the explored universe is a triad star system called Helios Nexus. At The Nexus, a long-extinct species known as The Creators built a technological marvel, the Masson Zero, that can be used to instantly transport a consciousness across the universe. This technology is not fully understood and cannot be replicated. In a reality where faster than light speed travel doesn't exist, and civilizations are separated by hundreds of thousands of light-years, the Masson Zero is the most important invention in existence. Because the Masson Zero is the only way for Hub world species to connect and interact, The Nexus has also known millennia of conflicts, as various groups fight for control through politics...and bloodshed.

THE CREATORS

More than a million helicas ago, a long-extinct species known as The Creators built a moon-sized, technological marvel called the Masson Zero (aka "Mass-0"). This semi-organic structure is surrounded by a supergravity time-dilation field that prevents any approach to its surface.

While the inner workings of the Mass-0 are an enduring mystery, scientists theorize that once a jumper enters a transpod, they are pummeled by a storm of highly-charged quarks to create a quantum burst that expels that jumper's consciousness in a single Masson particle which can then be instantaneously transported across the Mass-O network.

After every rotation of the Mass-O around the triad stars 2,467 Earth Days, a fleet of Progenitor Ships emerge from the core of the structure. These semi-organic, autonomous vessels are spawned into space in every direction, and evidence suggests this process has been taking place for over a million helicas.

While the production of Progenitors also remains a mystery, their purpose is obvious: they are tasked with seeking out any signs of life in the star systems they encounter. However, life in the Unio-verse is rare and sparse; evidence indicates that The Creators were extinct for hundreds of thousands of helicas before the first Progenitor discovered a life on a habitable planet.

When life is detected by a Progenitor, it sends a Discovery Lander to the planet where the craft "roots" into a stable place in the environment. Next, the Lander converts itself into a receiving station, activating transpods, before it sends a signal back to the Mass-O, making it another node in the cosmic transit network.

At Nex City, a wide variety of transpods (aka jump pods) can be used to instantly send a consciousness into a cloned body or other "skin" on a distant Discovery Lander. Transpods are the only facet of Mass-O travel that can be built by non-Creators. They have evolved to accommodate all shapes and sizes of sentient life, not to mention the social strata on Nex City.

THE FIRST CYCLE

After traveling across the universe for 300,000 helicas in every direction from Helios Nexus, Progenitor Ships finally discovered the Origin 5 species. Over the span of a few thousand helicas, these five species used the Mass-O to converge on The Hub, and they built the first city. Using Creator Tech, the Origin 5 combined their knowledge and explored the vast expanses of space, creating a convergence of species that thrived on The Hub. This is known historically as The First Cycle. Then, around 300,000 helicas ago, for unknown reasons, the Origin 5 and all life on The Hub vanished without a trace, and every Lander in the universe powered down. This event has come to be known as The Great Fracture, wherein all connection between sentient species was lost for millennia.

THE SECOND CYCLE

Almost five hundred helicas ago, humans found a buried Progenitor Ship on Mars (fragmented in a crash). They figured out how to use a transpod on one of the Discovery Landers within the Progenitor to jump back to The Hub, becoming the first species of what is known as The Second Cycle; this monumental event ushered in a new era on Earth and established a new timeline: this is now known as the year 0 Helios Discovery (HD). On The Hub, humans found evidence of the Origin 5 species, as though they had just left moments ago. But all records of where their home-worlds were located were gone.

By the start of The Second Cycle, Progenitor Ships had spread out even farther across the universe. Millions of Progenitors spread over a two million light-year diameter were sending "signs of life" transmissions back to the Mass-O. By the time humans arrived on The Hub, there were countless worlds to explore and, over time, the sentient species on these planets assumed control of The Hub and The Second Cycle, with the Mass-O serving as a cosmic "lighthouse" for those seeking Reconvergence in the wake of The Great Fracture.

It's the year 493 HD. Humans and dozens of other species are connected via jumps across space. Race has become a somewhat outdated concept, and terms like "original skin" (skori) and "pure soul" are used to talk about where you came from and how many times you've jumped. Jumping bodies is a destructive process to one's consciousness—it can be used to extend life, but not indefinitely, and it's usually very expensive.

CREATOR TECH

Creator Tech is the general term for "things The Creators built." It is exotic, semi-organic tech, visually unique, and can't be replicated; it can replicate itself, however. It can also self-repair, as long as a Proten energy source is provided. It's characterized by blue lights, strange metals, and glass-like surfaces.

Creator Tech will also adapt to its environment, and its extensions. Progenitor Ships and Servitors are fully capable of using shields and self-repairing, making them very difficult to damage or destroy.

Relative Sizes of the Mass-O, Progenitor Ships, and The Hub
The Mass-O is approximately 4000km in diameter, while each Progenitor Ship is 70km long, dwarfing The Hub, which is about 50km at its widest point.

Describing Creator Tech

Creator Tech performs only a few functions, and largely relies on symbols to indicate what it does. The interaction is projected into the mind of the user; there is no keyboard or screen to access. There is no massive, omniscient database to query. It is intentionally designed to be foundational, and Merge Tech was built on top of it.

Core Functions

These are some of the core functions Creator Tech provides and can all be accessed from any Creator transpod, on a Progenitor Ship or Discovery Lander, or at The Hub. If a system has built its own transpods, some of this functionality can be accessed.

- **Capture/Save A Skin:** This is a quantum-level capture of a sentient being's every cell, allowing for perfect fidelity when creating a skin.

- **Replicate A Skin:** Select a skin and request it to be replicated into an empty transpod. This consumes a significant amount of Proten power. It is important to note that only Creator transpods can replicate a skin.

- **Jump:** Move a consciousness from one transpod to a blank body in another transpod. The system will not let you jump into an occupied body, nor will it allow you to force someone to jump against their will.

- **Data Transfer:** The Hub acts like universe-scale Wi-Fi. Anyone can send data through its network to any other Creator Tech node. However, there is no inherent "Creator Network," so The Merge created one using this transfer feature. There is nothing stopping other species from using it the same way.

- **Blanks** (bodies with their consciousness jumped out of them) are only created in current tech transpods; Creator transpods atomize a body after a consciousness has jumped. Skins in Merge transpods can be put in stasis chambers for long-term storage.

Other Notes on Creator Tech

- Transpod blueprints are given to the representative who first arrives at The Hub from a new Discovery Lander so that they can go back and build out the planet's transpod network if they have the technological capability to do so.

- Creator Tech self-repair takes a long time (from helicas to generations, depending on the extent and nature of the damage).

- One of the guiding principles about Creator Tech: The Creators took a long view of time. Repairing a damaged ship may seem like it should happen faster when seen through a mortal lens, but Creator Tech is designed to last millions of helicas. The search for life in an almost-light speed reality is an extended endeavor, one that is measured in time increments almost unfathomable to most sentient beings.

The Guiding Principles of Creator Tech

The three principles that govern all interaction with Creator Tech are curiosity, intention, and commitment. Whether one is using a transpod or an Assembler, or interacting with other Creator Tech (Discovery Landers, Servitors), the rule that guides the process is this:

Curiosity activates the interface.
Intention reveals possibilities.
Commitment initiates the process.

This means that Creator Tech will only work if a sentient being has some understanding of what the tech does, is aware of the underlying concepts in play, and possesses the desire to accomplish something specific. An example: one cannot accidentally activate an Assembler; a sentient being has to understand what Assemblers do, grasp concepts like atoms and replication, and have awareness of the item they wish the Assembler to make.

THE MASS-O AND THE HUB

The Mass-O orbits a triad star system. The stars were named by humans as Antony, Cleo and Octavius. The Hub does not orbit the Mass-O. By means of a method not yet understood by Merge scientists, it is always locked in the shadow of the Mass-O. The Hub does not rotate. It is always in the shadow of the triad stars. Gravity is always "down" towards the Mass-O.

The Origin 5 species first built simple construction on the surface of The Hub. Over time, massive platforms were built, each with dozens of levels. Over thousands of helicas, Hub construction developed even further, until the end of The First Cycle when it was suddenly abandoned.

PROGENITOR SHIPS

A fleet of Progenitor Ships, each of which is approximately 70 kilometers long, emerges from the Mass-O after it completes an orbit around its three suns. The Mass-O absorbs and stores power as it circles the suns, and everyone on The Hub can feel the immense power contained within the Mass-O by the time it is ready to release the ships. This event, known as The Emergence, is accompanied by three days of cultural, scientific, and religious celebration and ceremony (each day named after one of the suns).

These large "motherships" explore the Unioverse at near light speed and have been sent out to search for life in every direction for over a million helicas.

Each Progenitor can "gestate" an endless supply of Discovery Landers, although the process takes a significant amount of time. When a Progenitor arrives in a new system, it is prepared to deploy three Landers; it will take roughly 100 helicas to complete each additional one.

Once a Progenitor Ship has located signs of life (sentient, flora/fauna, microbial), it will enter a star system and send a Discovery Lander to every planet supporting life (even if these planets are all colonized by a single species). In the event more than three Landers are needed in a system, the Progenitor will remain as it gestates additional Landers.

Other Notes on Progenitor Ships
- Progenitor Ships are agnostic/inscrutable and function within an expansive time scale: a ship finds life, sends a Discovery Lander, and moves on. They don't double back, instead moving ever outward. What The Creators set out to do was bring life together, with the understanding that finding all life is an impossible task; the Progenitor Ships find what life they can, and link that life with The Hub, and it is up to sentient life to decide what to do from there.

- During their long travel times between star

systems, Progenitor Ships "digest" (gather and process) materials to build Discovery Landers.

- The process of a Progenitor Ship creating a Discovery Lander is long and slow (another example of The Creator's expansive timetable), more a gestation than mechanical construction.

- In some places, the reception of the Progenitor Ship and Discovery Lander is hostile, with sentient species attacking the unknown and uninvited arrivals.

DISCOVERY LANDERS

When a planet with life is discovered by a Progenitor Ship, a Discovery Lander (2km in diameter when released) is sent to the surface to establish a transpod receiving station (aka jump deck) with two to six Creator transpods. The specific number of transpods correlates with the presence and development level of sentient life in the system; as species and civilizations evolve, and the demand for intergalactic travel increases.

Every Lander is powered by a medium-sized Proten. It possesses the ability to grow more Protens and is equipped with a suite of Servitors to maintain, and protect when necessary, the receiving station.

When someone jumps to a Discovery Lander, the fabrication of a skin consumes a significant amount of energy from the Proten powering the Creator transpod system. Using an Assembler to create needed equipment does the same. The Discovery Lander will recharge the Proten (a process which takes time); the Protens do not recharge themselves.

Discovery Lander Notification System

Discovery Landers use a progressive notification system to alert The Hub that a new system/planet is coming online:

- When it arrives, it sends a "Network Relay Established" message.

- When a sentient species interacts with the Lander, it sends out another message: "Sentient Lifeform Engaged."

- Finally, when the species has shown no hostility to the Lander or Servitors through continued engagement, a final message is sent that can trigger a Harbinger team: "Sentient Lifeform Validated: Network Relay Viable."

The first trip from a Discovery Lander on a new world has to be to The Hub. At that point, other destination worlds are unlocked.

In the event that Servitors determine there is no sentient life on the planet, the second message would be, "Habitable Planet Validated: Network Relay Viable." But only if the planet has resources that could benefit or even save multiple other species.

Other Notes on Discovery Landers

- Discovery Landers operate with the fundamental principles of Creator Tech: Curiosity activates the interface. Intention reveals possibilities. Commitment initiates the process.

- A sentient being can only enter a Discovery Lander if it possesses an appropriate level of curiosity, intention, and commitment (understanding of the universe and what the Discovery Lander is/ represents). Once inside, the being's consciousness will manifest all that it needs (transpod, Assembler, etc.).

- Creator Tech is relentless as it attempts to fulfill its specific function. When a Discovery Lander is damaged or trapped by changing planetary conditions (ice age trapping the Lander deep within a glacier; eruptions encasing it in rock), it spends however long it takes (possibly eons) repairing itself, using the Servitors to free it, tunneling to find a way out of its prison, etc. Eventually, it will once again focus on its mission: to connect this world and its life (sentient or not) with The Hub.

- When a Discovery Lander has emerged from a Progenitor Ship, it is approximately 2 kilometers in diameter. Once it has established itself on the planet surface, however, it can and will expand to match the terrain.

- A Discovery Lander adapts to the world it lands on: it becomes like an oil derrick on a planet covered in water, or goes to the bottom of an ocean if the sentient lifeforms are aquatic.

- To gather the materials that it needs for various functions (building Servitors, operating Creator transpods and Assemblers, expanding the Lander's footprint), Discovery Landers send tendrils down into the planet where, like the roots of a tree, they leech what they need from the ground.

- Most Discovery Landers end up on planets without sentient life. On some planets they become part of a city/mecca, but in most locations, they're isolated, alone, on a planet sustaining basic lifeforms.

- On some planets, the native population may not have encountered the Discovery Lander.

- Wherever a Discovery Lander sets down becomes the most important place on a planet/in a system.

- During The Great Fracture, Progenitor Ships still seeded planets with Discovery Landers, but they were "locked" from the moment of arrival: they did not send out Servitors to survey the planet nor open their doors to sentient life. They simply rooted in place and waited for the Fracture to end.

- Landers already on a planet when the Fracture began immediately shut down. Servitors either returned to the Lander or powered down in place, and the doors to the Lander shut and would not reopen until the Fracture ended.

SERVITORS

Servitors are the autonomous droids that protect and maintain the Discovery Landers once they are rooted on a planet. Created by Landers via a semi-organic process, Servitors come in many shapes and sizes, adapting to their roles depending on their planet's environment and biosphere.

Like all Creator Tech, Servitors are agnostic about what sentient beings do, so long as nothing threatens the Lander or the Servitors themselves. They are not hostile but will protect themselves and their domain.

When they physically engage a lifeform, they look to disarm or neutralize, and once the threat has passed, they immediately return to their primary functions.

In most situations, Servitors are not interested in sentient beings, neither engaging them nor performing tasks for them.

Another factor shaping the roles that Servitors play, specifically when a planet is home to one or more sentient species, is the evolutionary status and density of the population, both native and visiting. For example, a more primitive species with limited numbers would have smaller Servitors to manage the Discovery Lander and any threats to it, while a more advanced society that draws numerous jumpers would require larger Servitors.

Servitors continue to adapt as life on a planet evolves. They may have taken one form initially and then changed over the passing millennia. For example, had there been a Discovery Lander on Earth during the Mesozoic Era, the Servitors would have been large enough to protect the Lander from aggressive dinosaurs. After the mass extinction event and the subsequent rise of mammals, however, Servitors could and would be smaller.

In some cases, outdated Servitors would return to the Lander so that materials could be reused, while in others, the Servitors would simply shut down.

One of the Servitors' key roles after a Discovery Lander arrives on a new planet is to conduct an extensive visual global survey of flora, fauna, ecosystems, climate, etc. The information gathered is sent back to The Hub; to the Academy for study, and to the Astrograph where it is stored and can be retrieved by those who might wish to jump to the planet.

As with the Discovery Landers themselves, Servitors evoke a sense of awe and wonder when encountered for the first time, even trigger a primal response of fear; a sentient being inevitably understands that a Servitor is not aggressive or malevolent but realize that they should use caution around it.

Servitors also function on The Hub, operating as infrastructure architects, expanding the Creator Tech network when the system decides there is a need. They emerge from deep within the lower levels, spider-like, tendrils linking them to the Creator Tech far below, using these organic threads to weave whatever is required.

Other Notes on Servitors

- Each Servitor is powered by one small Proten.

- Servitors create a perimeter around their Discovery Lander and will react if encroached upon, thus removing the problem.

- Servitors don't have much agency; they are programmed for specific roles. They maintain the system, perform an initial scout/surveillance of the world upon landing that informs the Lander's first message back to The Hub, and they make the planet ready for the arrival of sentient beings via the transpods.

- Like all Creator Tech, Servitors are singularly focused on their mission to connect life in The Hub.

- If planetary changes somehow trap a Lander (in ice, for example), the Servitors do everything in their power to free the ship.

TRANSPODS

A transpod (aka jump pod) allows a sentient lifeform to have its consciousness transferred from its body to another destination in the Mass-O network; this could be a jump from The Hub to a skin on a Discovery Lander or vice-versa. This instantaneous process is powered by the Mass-O and somehow involves relaying information through entangled particles at both ends of the operation.

While the discovery of the Mass-O was a godsend in a universe incapable of light speed travel, the quantum process is destructive, degrading the traveler's consciousness with each jump. If one tries to jump into a remote body/skin that is already occupied by a consciousness, then one consciousness or the other (or both) risks total destruction.

Generally, jumping is not common and reserved for the elite. If you are connected, wealthy, or both, you can skip the line, and, in the event you're using a transpod built with current tech, enjoy a more luxurious transpod experience. Most entities throughout the Unioverse will never jump in their lifetimes.

Transpod Types
Transpods are well-understood tech, and many types have been built to accommodate the different needs of unique cosmic travelers. A transpod must be connected to The Hub or to a Discovery Lander in order to function.

- **Creator Transpods:** These exist on The Hub and in Discovery Landers and are made from Creator Tech. These are the most advanced types of pods, and the only ones capable of creating a skin. Creator transpods form a living 'energy field' that expands to contain the traveler during molecular recombination. At the heart of the transpod are the tendrils that manipulate the particle cloud that forms the traveler's new 'skin.'

- **Present Day Transpods:** These are manufactured with Second Cycle technologies and take a wide variety of forms. Some are no-frills and some are luxurious (providing medical treatment/care while a body's consciousness is elsewhere, for example).

The Merge has added conventional tech to many Creator transpods to serve as security gates; they also use the Creator system to transmit information, but this has no impact on the transpods themselves.

Which Type of Transpod Would Someone Use?

Departure Transpods

- **Present Day Transpod:** This is the most common and utilitarian choice. They are more readily available (thus, less expensive), and allow for storage, renting out one's skin, or atomization.

- **Creator Transpod:** There is no advantage to using a Creator transpod for a departure. As a result, they are used for this purpose only when there are no other options (in a Lander on an isolated planet, for example).

Arrival Transpods

- **Present Day Transpod:** These are more prevalent, so often used for arrival, but they are limited to pre-existing skins. Thus, a jumper must either rent a skin or use one that they previously stored at the destination site.

- **Creator Transpod:** Because they can create skins,

Creator transpods are in high demand. If a jumper wants a specific skin (either a clone or another species from their stored collection), they must use a Creator transpod.

Other Rules Related to Transpods

- The first trip from a newly operational Discovery Lander on a recently connected world has to be to The Hub. At that point, other destination worlds are unlocked for the traveler.

- Transpods will not extract and transmit a consciousness without a skin on the other side. It is not possible for a consciousness to get lost in the system or be stored in an external source (like a hard drive).

How Transpods Work

Transpods can perform the following functions:

- Record the current lifeform, including clothing/equipment/cybernetics on an atom by atom basis, and save this as a "skin" in The Hub database. Anything jumpers need beyond what they carry into the transpod must be scanned into an Assembler and fabricated at the jump destination or procured from a local source.

- Instantly transport any consciousness from one transpod to another, regardless of species or anatomy.

- Creator transpods only: Recreate any skin in its database at any transpod. This process, where a skin coalesces from a quantum cloud, takes almost no time at all, and the moment a skin begins to form, the jumper's consciousness inhabits it.

After jumping, a traveler remains in the destination

transpod for a period of time while their consciousness acclimates to its new skin, a process colloquially known as "gelling." The specific amount of time needed depends on the difference between the original body and the skin.

One of the key limitations to Creator Tech is the consumption of Proten power. Fabricating a complex skin in a transpod and using an Assembler to generate an extensive equipment loadout consumes a tremendous amount of power. Creator Tech will recharge the Protens, but this process takes time.

The Transpod Interface

Once you are inside a transpod, Creator Tech scans your mind to see if your consciousness is capable of jumping. The three principles that govern all interaction with Creator Tech are curiosity, intention, and commitment. This means that a transpod will only work if a sentient being has some understanding of what Creator Tech does; is aware of concepts like space, stars, and galaxies; and possesses the desire to jump somewhere specific (whether that's The Hub or another known destination). As a result, no one can jump against their will.

Once Creator Tech has cleared you to jump, it projects an interface into your mind. This interface is unique to each user; a jumper will see a personalized version of the Astrograph with visual data about their own previous experiences connected to planets they've been to, alongside information about other potential destinations. The transpod will understand your intent and be able to identify where you want to go.

Human interpretation of the principles that appear to govern Creator Tech is that the Mass-O was designed to reconverge many different cultures for the benefit of the universe. If a culture is not sufficiently evolved, it will not be able to contribute to the reconvergence; possessing curiosity, intention and commitment is a cosmic measurement of evolutionary suitability.

- Simple lifeforms that can't hold a complete consciousness will not be recorded. You can't jump into a fish or an ant.

- Each jump you do is a saved version of you.

- You can leave a 40-helica-old version of your skin and jump into one from when you were 20, but only if you jumped when you were 20 and thus have that version of you saved in the system.

- If you have a broken bone, disease, etc. when you are recorded, the skin will have the exact same issue.

- Transpods can safely transport lifeforms with multiple consciousnesses.

- Transpods will not transport children or neophyte creatures without a fully formed brain. Because of this, a pregnant mother can't use a transpod.

- Transpods will not transport lesser creatures (such as worms, etc.).

- Creator transpods adapt depending on the skin being created (organically growing to accommodate size, providing an aquatic environment, etc.).

- "Ori" is the term used to refer to the body you were born into (short for "original"). "Skori" is a related slang term that is a combination of "Ori" and "Skin."

SKINFORMATION

Skin Storage
When you jump to another planet from a Merge trans-pod, your current body becomes a "blank." The trans-pod interface prompts a jumper to select from three options regarding what to do with the blank:

- Store it: Once "empty," skins are stored in their transpods, to be retrieved when needed. A jumper must pay to store a skin (which will not age while in stasis), so this option is often passed over for the other two. Note: If you are wealthy and powerful enough, you can store multiple skins in locations you frequent (Ambassadors are granted this privilege).

- "Rent" it: A jumper can relinquish their exclusive rights to a skin, allowing other travelers to use it. Jumping is expensive, and making a skin available to others helps offset the costs.

- Atomize it: If a jumper will no longer have any use for a skin, but they do not wish to rent it out, they can opt to have the skin destroyed.

The process is different for Creator transpods: Storage and renting are not options. After someone has jumped, the Creator Tech reverses the fabrication process, atomically disassembling the body, and returns the organic material to the quantum cloud.

Skin Availability
Only Creator transpods can manufacture a skin, and there are only a few on the Discovery Lander of each planet, so having a skin created is expensive and sometimes involves waiting days (or longer) for your turn. Most jumps involve jumping into an available blank in storage. The more you pay, the better the

skin you can get.

JUMPING FAQ

What happens to your body when you jump?
If you're using a Merge transpod, your pre-jump body becomes a blank and is typically put into hyper-sleep storage for a fee. If that body is a skin, it is generally stored for a short period of time and then recycled.

Can you duplicate and jump into someone else's skin?
Generally, no. Skins are considered "owned" and you must prove ownership of a skin to have a Creator transpod generate it. You can, however, rent or buy someone else's blank...if they give permission.

Are there any potential issues jumping into someone else's skin?
Occasionally, one will experience "ghost residue," remnants of the borrowed body's consciousness.

Can you live forever by jumping to new bodies?
No. You can extend your original body's life by jumping into skins for extended periods, but each jump degrades your consciousness a small percentage and brings the jumper one step closer to Zero Hour.

What is jumping like?
The experience of jumping is subjective and individualized. There is a dream-logic to it: what objectively takes no time at all can feel like hours. A particlized consciousness can't comprehend what is happening to it, so there's some elasticity to the perception of time as we jump.

Can someone jump between planets and bypass The Hub?
Yes, it is possible to jump between planets without

passing through The Hub, but only if the traveler has successfully made their initial jump from a Lander to The Hub.

PROTENS

Protens are crystal-like structures that store an almost infinite amount of energy; they are a perfect battery. Protens can absorb energy from almost any source and store it forever. Like almost everything associated with Creator Tech, Protens can't be manufactured or duplicated.

Protens are found in three sources:

- Progenitor Ships

- Discovery Landers

- The Hub

Progenitor Ships: Beyond possessing a supply of fully functional Protens when they emerge from the Mass-O, Progenitor Ships grow Protens in a process not fully understood. The Protens on a Progenitor Ship are nearly inaccessible.

Discovery Landers are powered by a cache of Protens harvested from "farms" inside certain areas on the ship. Landers, like Progenitors, can grow new Protens (very slowly); they look like crystal clusters/stalactites and stalagmites emerging from floors/ceilings/walls. The Servitors on Landers will allow sentient beings to take some of these Protens for general use. The distribution of these Protens by those sentient beings controlling access to the Lander is often a source of debate and dispute, sometimes violent (but this risks the Lander shutting down for generations).

The Hub has a number of Proten "farms" which Servitors guard/tend, extracting Protens and transporting them where and when needed. Here, too, Protens are made available in small quantities to the denizens of The Hub. Most galaxies have no Progenitor Ships, meaning the only access to Protens are the ones powering the Discovery Landers and the Servitors maintaining them.

Using Protens

Protens create an energy field that all Creator Tech is able to access as long as it has proximity to the source. Conventional tech does not have the ability to tap into Proten energy that way, creating a need for wires/cables.

Recharging Protens

Creator Tech on The Hub and in Discovery Landers will recharge Protens using available power sources (solar, hydro, geothermic). Protens will not recharge on their own. Many worlds have created systems to speed up the recharging process (feeding energy to the Protens via solar arrays, for example) to keep Creator Tech such as Assemblers humming around the clock.

Sizes

- A 1.2 meter diameter Proten can power a large Progenitor Ship.

- A 30 cm diameter Proten can power a medium-sized ground ship like a Discovery Lander.

- A 15.5 cm Proten can power a small Servitor.

- A 2.5–5 cm Proten can be used to power weapons, shields, robots, small vehicles, etc.

Because Protens are incredibly valuable, species

will fight over them, and individuals will risk their lives attempting to destroy Discovery Landers and Servitors to extract their power sources. As a result, when a new planet/system with sentient life comes online, The Merge representatives who first arrive will claim jurisdiction over the Protens in the Lander (current and to-be-generated) and oversee the distribution and use of these Protens.

THE LIGHTHOUSE

One of the central locations in The Hub, the Lighthouse is home to The Creators' evolving map of the Unioverse, the Astrograph. What someone experiences within the Lighthouse is individualized: it shows where you've jumped and what planets are unlocked *for you.*

The Merge has assembled their own database, accessible in the Lighthouse (although separate from the Astrograph), that provides information about the planets connected to The Hub: political situations, white/green/red list, sanctions, etc.

One's experience of the Astrograph is purely personal/subjective. If multiple people are in the room, the system respects your privacy and shows you only your view of the universe. But if there was a need/desire by two or more people to have a shared view, the system could accommodate that just based on intention.

ASSEMBLERS

Assemblers are Creator Tech and can be found on all Progenitor Ships and Discovery Landers, as well as at The Hub. They are generally used to fabricate objects and can only replicate what the user has scanned (by placing it on a pad attached to the Assembler) or can fully convey (via the Creator interface). You can then have a copy made by that Assembler, or any other Assembler in any Creator transpod locations.

The larger the object and the more complex materials it requires, the more power it takes to replicate.

No resources are required except Proten power. Severe use can drain Protens on a Discovery Lander, requiring them to be recharged. This will happen slowly via solar power charging, but many Hub worlds will set up other ways to recharge them faster (coal, nuclear, hydro, etc.).

If jumpers want access to something they did not scan or are unable to convey to the interface, most developed systems have local dealers who have scanned a wide range of materials and supplies (and thus can create some or all of what jumpers need). This is an expensive proposition, however: access to Assemblers is highly limited and regulated, so procuring novel equipment comes at a steep cost.

Example Uses
- You can't duplicate a Proten; the Creator Tech will not allow it.

- Some dangerous materials cannot be replicated.

- You can duplicate seeds and they will still be viable (this is possible because seeds are not alive in a biological sense until water is introduced).

- You can duplicate a plant, but it will die.

- You can duplicate a carrot and eat it.

- You can duplicate a creature, bacteria, or virus, but it is not alive when duplicated.

- However, you could then harvest its DNA and clone one that is alive, using conventional technologies.

- You can duplicate thousands of bars of gold, and build a structure out of them, but this would take a long time and monopolize the Assembler.

- Different objects require varying amounts of time and energy to replicate.

THE MERGE

The governing body on The Nexus is called Helios Mergence (aka The Merge). The Merge is a multi-species coalition formed hundreds of helicas ago, not long after mankind's discovery of the Mass-O and the integration of new species at The Nexus; the inevitable friction between the first species on The Hub gave rise to the need for a political body to resolve disputes and guide the growth of the intergalactic community.

The Merge has grown and evolved over the helicas, allowing new species to join the coalition and have their voices heard in debates; only the most advanced and collaborative species are invited to join The Merge, however, and a primary requirement in The Merge application process is that a civilization must have experienced a system-wide peace for two decades at the time they request official recognition. In terms of jurisdiction, The Merge has exclusive access to the Astrograph—a holdover from The First Cycle—which shows a real-time, holographic map of the Unioverse. Specifically, which planets are "online" (having an operational Lander and jump deck) and which worlds are "offline" (Lander destroyed or shut down). With the Astrograph, The Merge has their finger on the pulse of the universe and takes the following actions when there is coalition consensus:

- Select official Merge agents, known as Ambassadors, to represent the coalition when visiting new planets.

- Dispatch a Harbinger Team (an Ambassador, a Lead Scientist, and an Armed Forces Representative) to a new planet that has come online and has one or more sentient species living on it. This team interviews global leaders and assesses the planetary conditions to determine if the location is suitable for visitors from Nex City and should gain access to The Hub.

- Send Ambassadors to help a planet imperiled for various reasons (natural disaster, invading forces, etc.).

- Sanction a planet—for violations such as killing travelers, disruption/corruption of Creator Tech, etc.—and cut off Mass-O travel in both directions.

- Limiting travel to certain planets for reasons such as plague, unstable politics, and faulty jump tech.

- Build a database of all unlocked Hub locations (cataloguing lifeforms, atmosphere, populations, etc.).

- Create safety regulations for jumping.

- Commercialize and monetize the jumping process (including shaping/controlling intergalactic commerce).

The Merge Power Structure

The Merge's organization has **ten key councils/committees** and hundreds of sub-councils. Some key councils:

- **Emergence:** Oversight and shepherding worlds new to The Merge.

- **Science:** Compiling and sharing scientific achievements from all Merge worlds.

- **Culture:** Sharing and educating all civilizations about each other's cultural and societal norms, ensuring that travelers from across the Masson Zero network have the appropriate information necessary when they visit other worlds.

- **Law Enforcement:** The Keepers work with local authorities to investigate any crime committed by Mass-O travelers on other worlds, as well as oversee identification compliance. They also deal with fraud committed by black market transpod runners.

The Security Council

The most prominent of the major committees is the Security Council, which meets in a special place called The Hall of Emergence. It features ten members selected by The Merge representatives and is led by the head of The Merge Science Advisory Council, Leader Olen Gray. As its name implies, the Security Council is charged with looking after the stability and safety of The Merge and Helios Nexus. While Ambassadors can be called upon to assist all major Merge committees, they answer directly to the Security Council and take their assignments primarily from this group.

One key aspect of Security Council members is that

they tend to come from worlds that are both prominent and older, and also show prolonged evidence of political stability.

Merge Oversight Organizations

The Academy: One facet of the Science Advisory Council's work is overseeing the Academy, the central academic institution on The Hub. The Merge is heavily invested in every system and planet linked by the Mass-O, and one of the Science Council's charges is to learn about every sentient species, including the history of any lost civilizations. The Academy employs an extensive network of scholars who explore planets linked with The Hub, collect information, and then submit it for approval and inclusion in the Academy archives. These records are made available to citizens on The Hub as well as to anyone with access to the transpod data-streams. Lucinda Bakira is the Head of the Exploration Division, and a member of the Academy administration.

The Atheneum: Under strict control by The Merge, the Atheneum is a combination of library and museum located within The Merge Citadel. The Atheneum houses not only the digital and holographic data-streams covering all of the known worlds, but also artifacts, real and recreated (via Assembler), from Merge and non-Merge planets. One overarching goal of those who run the Atheneum is to reconstruct the past, with a focus on finding out what happened to cause The Great Fracture. Access to the Atheneum is highly restricted.

The Immaculance: An organization that oversees religious organizations throughout the universe. All Immaculance agents have an AI, called a paraclete, integrated into their brains.

Other Notes on The Merge

Each world has a single representative to The Merge, which has sometimes caused great political conflict, as Progenitor Ships do not analyze global and system-wide socio-political dynamics before seeding a world. In some cases, a newly opened planet may have many competing cultures and nationalities on it. Part of an Ambassador's role is to journey to these places and help opposing sides begin to see a larger picture about their planet's role in the intergalactic community.

Rules Related to The Merge

Because officials at The Merge are planetary representatives, their skins are required to be identical to the biological originals left behind on their home worlds.

The Merge and First Contact

The Merge takes an aggressively benevolent approach to interacting with new sentient species, providing extensive resources (scientific/technological information) to help accelerate the development of the civilizations on newly opened worlds. The belief is that The Creators built this system linking sentient beings so that they can help one another, learn from each other, and evolve together. In some cases, when the host planet wants to limit The Merge's involvement, only a few representatives will take up residence on the planet and help guide the process of integrating Creator Tech. In others, however, when extensive help is requested, The Merge will contract with a corporation which then facilitates a full-scale program of technological acceleration to bring the new world up to speed with The Merge.

MERGE
COMMITTEE PROFILES

MARIO ACEVEDO is the author-artist of *Cats In Quarantine: A Cartoon Memoir of the COVID-19 Pandemic*. He is an award-winning cartoonist and artist who served as a soldier-artist for the US Army during Operation Desert Storm. Mario is the author of the national bestselling Felix Gomez detective-vampire series, *The Nymphos of Rocky Flats* and most recently *Steampunk Banditos: Sex Slaves of Shark Island*; the graphic novel from IDW, *Killing the Cobra*; and the YA humor thriller, *University of Doom*. He co-authored the Western novel, *Luther, Wyoming*. His work has won an International Latino Book Award, a Colorado Book Award, and has appeared in numerous anthologies to include *Denver Noir*; *¡El Porvenir, Ya!*; *Shadow Atlas: Dark Landscapes of the Americas*; *A Fistful of Dinosaurs*; *Straight Outta Deadwood*; *Psi-Wars*; and *It Came From The Multiplex*. Mario was a faculty member of the Regis University Mile-High MFA program and Lighthouse Writers Workshops.

LINDA D. ADDISON is the first African American recipient of the world-renowned HWA Bram Stoker Award® and has received five awards for collections: *The Place of Broken Things* written with Alessandro Manzetti; *Four Elements* written with Charlee Jacob, Marge Simon and Rain Graves; *How To Recognize A Demon Has Become Your Friend* short stories and poetry; *Being Full of Light, Insubstantial*; *Consumed, Reduced to Beautiful Grey Ashes*. In 2018, she received the HWA Lifetime Achievement Award. In 2020, Addison was designated SFPA Grand Master of Fantastic Poetry. She currently lives in Arizona and has published over 400 poems, stories, and articles. Look for her work in Titan anthologies *Black Panther: Tales of Wakanda;* and *Predator: Eyes of the Demon.*

KEVIN J. ANDERSON is the author of more than 175 novels, 58 of which have been national or international bestsellers. He has written novels in the *Dune, Star Wars,* and *X-Files* universes as well as his own original novels *Spine of the Dragon,* the *Dan Shamble, Zombie P.I. series, The Saga of Seven Suns,* and three steampunk fantasy adventure novels with Neil Peart, legendary drummer and lyricist from Rush.

ANDY BAKER has spent the past two and a half decades working in film, television and videogames as a writer and creative producer. He has helped develop projects at Sony, Universal, and Dark Horse Entertainment, and worked side by side with Stan Lee writing for Stan Lee Media shows such as *The 7th Portal, The Accuser,* and *The Backstreet Project.* Most recently, he has co-written a pilot script for *House of the Dead* and worked as a writer and showrunner at Mixi America.

CARINA BISSETT is a writer and poet working primarily in the fields of dark fiction and fabulism. Her work has been published in multiple journals and anthologies including *Into the Forest: Tales of the Baba Yaga, Upon a Twice Time, Bitter Distillations: An Anthology of Poisonous Tales,* and *Arterial Bloom.* Her poetry has been nominated for the Pushcart Prize and the Sundress Publications Best of the Net and can be found in the *HWA Poetry Showcase, Fantasy Magazine,* and *NonBinary Review.* She is also the co-editor of the award-winning anthology *Shadow Atlas: Dark Landscapes of the Americas.* Links to her work can be found at *carinabissett.com.*

KENNETH W. CAIN is an author of horror and dark

fiction, and a Splatterpunk Award-nominated freelance editor and graphic designer. To date, he has written over one hundred short stories and thirteen novels/novellas, as well as a handful each of nonfiction pieces, books for children, and poems released by many publishers, such as Crystal Lake Publishing and JournalStone. He has also edited eight anthologies, with two more coming in 2023. *kennethwcain.com*.

KEVIN DILMORE has partnered with author and best pal Dayton Ward for more than twenty years on novels, short fiction, and other writings chiefly in the *Star Trek* universe. As a senior writer for Hallmark Cards, Kevin has helped create books, Keepsake Ornaments, greeting cards and other products featuring characters from DC Comics, Marvel Comics, *Star Trek*, *Star Wars*, and Hallmark properties including *Rainbow Brite*. A contributor to publications including *The Village Voice*, *Amazing Stories*, and *Famous Monsters of Filmland*, he lives in Kansas City, Missouri.

SEAN EADS has published three novels and a short story collection, and has been a finalist for the Shirley Jackson Award, Lambda Literary Award, and Colorado Book Award. His stories have appeared in numerous anthologies.

ALEC FERRELL is a graphic designer, recording artist, and multimedia producer based out of Durham, NC. Connect at *clearlymedia.net* or *@clearlyalec*.

BRENT FRIEDMAN has more than 30 years of experience in entertainment across all platforms. In the early 2000s, Brent was a transmedia pioneer and has since become an expert in worldbuilding for multiple franchises including *League of Legends*, *The Walking Dead*, and *Batman*. Brent has worked with nearly all the major U.S. studios and networks with a passionate focus on science fiction and fantasy, including the

Emmy Award-winning series *Star Wars: The Clone Wars*, *Star Trek: Enterprise*, *The Twilight Zone*, Star Wars: *Rebels* and the cult NBC series, *Dark Skies* he co-created. In features, Brent has written several H.P. Lovecraft adaptations, *The Resurrected* and *Necronomicon*, as well as *Mortal Kombat: Annihilation*.

MAXWELL I. GOLD is a Jewish American multiple-award-nominated author who writes prose poetry and short stories in cosmic horror and weird fiction with half a decade of writing experience. Three-time Rhysling Award nominee, and two-time Pushcart Award nominee, find him at *thewellsoftheweird.com*.

KEN HALL has been creating immersive gaming experiences for over 25 years. As the art director on *All Points Bulletin* at Realtime Worlds, Ken created an unprecedented MMO customization system that allowed players to create expressive graphic designs and apply them seamlessly across highly configurable characters, clothing items, and vehicles. Ken has also directed gaming projects that include the award-winning World War II flight simulator *B-17 Flying Fortress: The Mighty 8th* and *TeamSAS*, featuring celebrated SAS soldier Andy McNab.

WARREN HAMMOND has authored several science fiction novels, quite a few short stories, and a graphic novel. His novel *Kop Killer* won the 2012 Colorado Book Award for best mystery. His latest series, *Denver Moon*, is co-written with Joshua Viola.

TONY HARMAN has been running game development companies since the '80s, creating products that have earned over a billion dollars in revenue. He began his career with a decade at Nintendo of America in charge of acquisitions and development, including blockbuster titles like *Donkey Kong Country*. As President of DMA Design, his team created *Grand Theft Auto*, one of the most successful franchises of all time. Tony later cofounded Realtime Worlds and developed *GTA*'s MMO successor *All Points Bulletin*, as well as the hit franchise *Crackdown*. Most recently, Tony was President of nWay, a mobile-focused game developer focused on bringing console-quality games to mobile, such as *ChronoBlade* and high-profile licenses like *Power Rangers* and *WWE*.

ANGIE HODAPP is the Director of Literary Development at Nelson Literary Agency. She holds a BA in English and secondary education and an MA in English and communication development, and she is a graduate of the Denver Publishing Institute at the University of Denver. She has worked in publishing and professional writing for the better part of the last two decades, and in addition to writing, she loves helping authors hone their craft and learn about the ever-changing business of publishing.

COLTON HOERNER has been exploring fantastic worlds in gaming and graphics for over 20 years. He has provided art direction, leadership, and imagery to Sony, Disney, MGM, 2K Games, Nickelodeon, Konami and more. His work spans a diverse set of skills including illustration, graphic design, 3D, VFX, web design, game design, and motion graphics across platforms from mobile, desktop, console, and VR.

JAMAL HODGE is a multi-award-winning filmmaker and writer from Queens, NYC, who has won over 100 awards with screenings at Tribeca Film Festival, Sundance, and Cannes. Hodge is an active member of the Horror Writers Association and the SFPA, who has been nominated for a 2021 and 2022 Rhysling Award. His poem "Colony" placed 2nd at the 2022 Dwarf Stars. His poetry is featured in the anthology *Chiral Mad 5* alongside such legends as Stephen King and Linda D. Addison. His debut poetry collection *The Dark*

Between the Twilight is being released in early 2024 by Crystal Lake Publishing, and his debut anthology, *Bestiary of Blood: Modern Fables & Dark Tales*, will see a late 2024 release and features over 12 Bram Stoker Award® winners and two Grandmasters. Learn more at *writerhodge.com*.

AKUA LEZLI HOPE, 2022 Grand Master of Fantastic Poetry (SFPA), is a paraplegic creator and wisdom seeker who wrote her first speculative poems in the 6th grade and has been in print since 1974 with over 450 poems published. Her collections include *Embouchure: Poems on Jazz and Other Musics* (Writer's Digest book award winner) and *Them Gone, & Otherwheres: Speculative Poetry* (2021 Elgin Award winner). A Cave Canem fellow, her honors include the National Endowment for the Arts, two New York Foundation for the Arts fellowships, Science Fiction and Fantasy Poetry Association award, and multiple Best of the Net, Rhysling and Pushcart Prize nominations. She won a 2022 New York State Council on the Arts grant to create Afrofuturist, speculative, pastoral poetry. She created the Speculative Sundays Poetry Reading series. She edited the record-breaking sea-themed issue of *Eye To The Telescope #42* (eyetothetelescope.com) and *NOMBONO: An Anthology of Speculative Poetry by BIPOC Creators*, the history-making first of its kind (Sundress Publications, 2021).

GABINO IGLESIAS is a writer, journalist, professor, and literary critic living in Austin, TX. He is also the author of the critically acclaimed and award-winning novels *Zero Saints* and *Coyote Songs*. Iglesias's nonfiction has appeared in the *New York Times*, the *Los Angeles Times, Electric Literature,* and *LitReactor,* and his reviews appear regularly in places like *NPR, Publishers Weekly, San Francisco Chronicle, The Boston Globe, Criminal Element, Mystery Tribune, Vol. 1 Brooklyn,* and the *Los Angeles Review of Books.* He's been a juror for the Shirley Jackson Awards twice and the Millions Tournament of Books, and is a member of the Horror Writers Association, the Mystery Writers of America, and the National Book Critics Circle.

STUART JENNETT is a visionary concept and comic book artist who has worked across the entertainment industry ranging from Marvel comics to the *Star Citizen* videogame franchise.

MARSHALL JONES is a promotional content creator at Random Games and copyeditor at Hex Publishers. In 2022, he received a Bachelor of Arts in media studies and media production from the University of Colorado Boulder. He's created and managed writing, video game, and short film projects. Recently, he's interned at Man of Action Entertainment, and beyond that is always pursuing his passion to tell impactful stories in a responsible manner.

STEPHEN GRAHAM JONES is the *New York Times* bestselling author of nearly thirty novels and collections, and there's some novellas and comic books in there as well. Stephen's been an NEA recipient, has won the Texas Institute of Letters Award for Fiction, the LA Times Ray Bradbury Prize, the Mark Twain American Voice in Literature Award, the Independent Publishers Award for Multicultural Fiction, WLA's Distinguished Achievement Award, ALA's RUSA Award and Alex Award, the *2023 American Indian Festival of Words Writers Award*, four Bram Stoker Awards®, three Shirley Jackson Awards, five This is Horror Awards, and he's been a finalist for the World Fantasy Award and the British Fantasy Award. He's also made Bloody Disgusting's Top Ten Horror Novels, and is the guy who wrote *Mongrels*, *The Only Good Indians*, *My Heart is a Chainsaw*, *Don't Fear the Reaper* and *Earthdivers*. Stephen lives in Colorado.

MATTHEW KRESSEL is a writer and software developer. He has been a finalist for the Nebula Award, the World Fantasy Award, and the Eugie Award. His short fiction can be found in *Lightspeed*, *Clarkesworld*, *Analog*, *io9*, *Nightmare*, *Beneath Ceaseless Skies*, *The Year's Best Science Fiction and Fantasy, 2018 Edition*, and *The Best Science Fiction of the Year: Volume Three*, as well as many other online and print publications and has been translated into seven languages. As a software developer, he created the Moksha submissions system, in use by many of the largest SF publishers today. Matt is also the co-host of Fantastic Fiction at KGB reading series in New York alongside Ellen Datlow.

AARON LOVETT is a mixed-heritage Asian American artist and has been published by AfterShock Comics, *Tor.com*, *The Denver Post*, and *Spectrum Fantastic Art 22 & 24*. His *Nightmares Unhinged* cover art was licensed by AMC for their hit TV show *Fear the Walking Dead*. He was the artist for the HWA's *StokerCon™ 2021 Souvenir Anthology*. You can see his most recent work in *Monster Train*, which was a number one Global Top Seller on Steam and named Best Card Game of 2020 by PC Gamer, and Inkbound. His art can be found in various other videogames, books, and comics. You can view his portfolio at artstation.com/adlovett. He paints from a dark corner in Denver, Colorado.

LEE MURRAY is a multi-award-winning writer-editor and poet, and screenwriter from Aotearoa-New Zealand (Sir Julius Vogel, Australian Shadows). A multiple Bram Stoker Award®-winner, her work includes the Taine McKenna Adventures, The Path of Ra series (with Dan Rabarts), fiction collection *Grotesque: Monster Stories*, and forthcoming feature film *Grafted* (directed by Sasha Rainbow). The editor of twenty anthologies, including Shirley Jackson Award-winner Black Cranes (with Geneve Flynn), she is a NZSA Honorary Literary Fellow, and Grimshaw Sargeson Fellow. Read more at *leemurray.info*

WYETH RIDGWAY has been at the forefront of game design and engineering for 30 years. With over 100 games to his credit, he has worked with dozens of major licenses including *Pirates of the Caribbean*, *MLB*, *The Terminator*, *Lord of the Rings*, and *South Park*. Wyeth cofounded Leviathan Games in 1998, and has been CTO and President for two decades, forging first-party development relationships with Disney, Sony, EA, Activision, and most other top-tier publishers.

MIRA SESTAN is a product design director working with startups and Web3 companies. She has been working in the field of design for over a decade, working alongside copywriters, marketing teams, photographers, and motion and set designers, helping craft vision and product user experiences that are innovative and informative.

BRET SMITH retired from IBM after 34 years as a program manager. He's a lifelong *Star Trek* fan and loves all things pop culture. He met his wife **JEANNI SMITH** on a blind date while she was attending the University of Arizona for her BFA. They've been happily married for over 35 years, attending conventions together since the 1980s—their most beloved decade—including over fourteen San Diego Comic-Cons. They raised two artistic sons, Xander — a successful Hollywood artist, and Cameron — a multi-talented musician. Today, when Jeanni isn't busy working as an antiques dealer, she and Bret are focused on their responsibilities as co-founders of the Colorado Festival of Horror, and copyeditors for Hex Publishers.

JEANNE C. STEIN is the award-winning, national bestselling author of the Urban Fantasy series, *The Anna Strong Vampire Chronicles*, and with Samantha Sommersby, *The Fallen Siren* series. She has stories in over three dozen anthologies including Hex Publishers' *Nightmares Unhinged*. Recently, she completed the third book in a sci-fi, action, adventure series called *180 Degrees Magnetic: Suicide Sail* with co-author Jim Schoendaller, available now. She is currently at work on the fourth *180 DM* story as well as a new project, a mystery, set in Colorado.

JOSHUA VIOLA is a Colorado Book Award winner and Splatterpunk Award nominee. He is the co-author of the *Denver Moon* series with Warren Hammond. Their graphic novel, *Denver Moon: Metamorphosis*, was included on the 2018 Bram Stoker Award® Preliminary Ballot. Viola edited the *Denver Post* #1 bestselling horror anthology *Nightmares Unhinged*, and co-edited *Cyber World* — named one of the best science fiction anthologies of 2016 by Barnes & Noble. His first novel, *The Bane of Yoto*, won the USA Best Book Awards, National Indie Excellence Awards, International Book Awards, and Independent Publishers Book Awards. His short fiction has appeared in numerous anthologies. As a videogame artist, he worked on *Pirates of the Caribbean: Call of the Kraken* (Disney Interactive), *Smurfs' Grabber* (Capcom) and *TARGET: Terror* (Konami). Viola is the owner and chief editor of Hex Publishers in Denver, Colorado, where he lives with his husband and their son, Orion — the inspiration for Malcolm Orion. Learn more at *JoshuaViola.com*.

TIM WAGGONER has published over fifty novels and seven collections of short stories. He's a three-time winner of the Bram Stoker Award® and has been a multiple finalist for the Shirley Jackson Award and the Scribe Award. He's also a full-time tenured professor who teaches creative writing and composition at Sinclair College in Dayton, Ohio.

DAYTON WARD is a *New York Times* bestselling author

or co-author of nearly forty novels and novellas, often working with his best friend, Kevin Dilmore. His short fiction has appeared in more than twenty anthologies, and he's written for publications such as *NCO Journal*, *Kansas City Voices*, *Famous Monsters of Filmland*, *Star Trek Magazine* and *Star Trek Communicator* as well as the websites *Tor.com*, *StarTrek.com*, and *Syfy.com*.

CARTER WILSON is the *USA Today* bestselling author of eight critically acclaimed, standalone psychological thrillers, as well as numerous short stories. He is an ITW Thriller Award finalist, a five-time winner of the Colorado Book Award, and his works have been optioned for television and film.

JEZZY WOLFE is a poet and author who has appeared in numerous anthologies and publications, such as Smart Rhino's *Zippered Flesh* trilogy, *Insidious Assassins* and *Asinine Assassins* anthologies, Crystal Lake Publishing's *Shallow Waters* anthology, Western Legends Publishing's *Unnatural Tales of the Jackalope*, *Space & Time Magazine*, *Sirens Call* ezine, and *Weird Tales Magazine*. She was a Crystal Lake poetry contest finalist, and her poems have appeared in the novels *Ink* and Relentless, written by New York Times bestseller Jonathan *Maberry*. Her debut poetry collection, *Monstrum Poetica*, was published in 2021 by Raw Dog Screaming Press.

JANE YOLEN's 400th book came out in March 2021. She writes in almost all genres, but is best known for her poetry, children's books, short stories, and novels. She has won many awards, from Nebulas to Massachusetts State Awards for her work. She teaches writing and mentors writers. Six New England colleges and universities have given her honorary doctorates. She lives in Western Massachusetts, Connecticut, and St Andrews Scotland, with her second husband, a poet and educator. They are working on a book of poetry together.

ALVARO ZINOS-AMARO is a Hugo and Locus Award finalist who has published some fifty stories, as well as over a hundred essays, reviews, and interviews, in a variety of professional magazines and anthologies.